ALICE LECCESE POWERS

SPAIN IN MIND

Alice Leccese Powers is the editor of the
anthologies *Italy in Mind*, *Ireland in Mind*, *France
in Mind*, and *Tuscany in Mind*, and coeditor of
*The Brooklyn Reader: Thirty Writers Celebrate
America's Favorite Borough*. A freelance writer
and editor, she has been published in *The
Washington Post*, *The Baltimore Sun*, *Newsday*, and
many other newspapers and magazines. Ms.
Powers also teaches writing at the Corcoran
College of Art + Design. She lives in Washington, D.C.

Cuba in Mind, edited by Maria Finn Dominguez

France in Mind, edited by Alice Leccese Powers

India in Mind, edited by Pankaj Mishra

Ireland in Mind, edited by Alice Leccese Powers

Italy in Mind, edited by Alice Leccese Powers

Mexico in Mind, edited by Maria Finn

Paris in Mind, edited by Jennifer Lee

Tuscany in Mind, edited by Alice Leccese Powers

SPAIN IN MIND

SPAIN IN MIND

AN ANTHOLOGY

Edited and with an Introduction by

Alice Leccese Powers

Vintage Departures

VINTAGE BOOKS

A DIVISION OF RANDOM HOUSE, INC.

NEW YORK

 A VINTAGE DEPARTURES ORIGINAL, APRIL 2007

Copyright © 2007 by Alice Leccese Powers

All rights reserved. Published in the United States by
Vintage Books, a division of Random House, Inc., New York,
and in Canada by Random House of
Canada Limited, Toronto.

Vintage is a registered trademark and Vintage Departures
and colophon are trademarks of Random House, Inc.

Permissions can be found at the end of the book.

Library of Congress Cataloging-in-Publication Data
Spain in mind : an anthology / edited and with an introduction by Alice Leccese Powers.
p. cm.—(Vintage departures)
ISBN: 978-1-4000-7676-5
1. English literature.   2. Spain—Literary collections.   3. Spain—Description and travel.
4. American literature.   5. British—Spain.   6. Americans—Spain.
I. Powers, Alice Leccese.
PR1111.S57S73   2007
820.8'03246—dc22
2006037916

Author photograph © Brenna Powers
Book design by Jo Anne Metsch

www.vintagebooks.com

Printed in the United States of America
10 9 8 7 6 5 4 3 2 1

To my sister Maria Leccese Kotch

and my brother Michael Leccese . . .

and those who come after us

ACKNOWLEDGMENTS

With grateful acknowledgment to my editor Diana Secker Tes-dell and my agent Jane Dystel; to my colleagues and students at the Corcoran College of Art + Design; to Liz Reilly for sharing both her books and her knowledge about Spain; to my lifelong friends—those heroic New York City schoolteachers, John and Linda Napolillo; to Alice Gregal, Patti Macie, and Jim Cawley, Julie and Hugh Allen, Jon and Kem Sawyer, Jane Vandenburgh and Jack Shoemaker, Eileen O'Toole and Mike Dolan, Ann Greer, and, of course, Erich Parker and Marie Siegrist; to my family, especially my mother, Gaetana Leccese, and her relent-less inquisitiveness; Alison and Steve, Christina, and my travel-ing companions in Spain, Brenna and Brian. Muchas gracias.

CONTENTS

INTRODUCTION

Robert Penn Warren once said that he liked to write in a foreign country "where the language is not your own and you are forced into yourself in a special way." All the writers in this, my fifth volume in the "in Mind" series, are English or American and see themselves and Spain through Anglo-Saxon eyes. Travelers, exiles, occasionally soldiers, they filter the country through their own sensibility, advising other visitors, observing their hosts, and reveling in the celebrations and the sun. Each offers insight into a region, a ritual, or an event. *Spain in Mind* contains forty writers and forty different Spains.

As an anthologist, I must balance the portrait of a place. Not every writer in *Spain in Mind* appreciates the culture, commends the cuisine, or praises the people. Some behave boorishly, like castaways banished from their beloved homeland, comparing everything, unfavorably, to England or America. A few entries are shockingly insensitive to twenty-first-century political correctness. Like many expatriates, some authors live in Spain, but not among the Spanish. They stubbornly adhere to their own customs, refuse to learn the language, and demand special favor. In equal measure are the writers who are enchanted by the complexity of Spain and return again and again to try to solve its puzzle.

The writers in *Spain in Mind* form a web of connection, and their biographies read like a literary parlor game: the young writer John Affleck went to Pamplona in search of Hemingway; Hemingway knew Dos Passos and E. E. Cummings and visited Gerald Brenan at his cottage in Yegen; Edith Wharton, a lifelong friend of Henry James's, greatly admired the writing of Washington Irving, who stayed in the same Alhambra accommodations as Richard Ford.

Anthony Trollope (a distant relative of novelist Joanna Trollope's) fell in love with American adventuress Kate Field. Lucia Graves is the daughter of the poet Robert Graves. And James Michener, it seems, knew everybody.

Many of the authors traveled alone, unencumbered by family or friends. Richard Ford, one of Spain's first travel writers, noted, "A solitary wanderer is certainly the most unfettered as regards his notions and motions, *no tengo padre ni madre, ni perro que me ladre*. He who has neither father, mother, nor dog to bark at him can read the book of Spain, as it were, in his own room, dwelling on what he likes, and skipping what he does not." At the age of eighty-two, Mary Lee Settle drove her own rental car throughout the countryside and cultivated solitude like others cultivate friendship. She ate alone in her room recalling that on a similar trip thirty years before a waiter had put a little American flag on her table-for-one "to show that I was not a whore." "To be alone by choice is one of the great luxuries of the world," she wrote. "I went to Spain alone. I wanted to discover it, not have it pointed out to me by friends . . ." Three other women in this volume also traveled solo. The intrepid Kate Field spent ten days barging around the country in the late 1800s. Nothing if not opinionated, she wrote, "I don't propose to furnish information that will be of the slightest use to the most inexperienced traveller. All I shall relate is what stuck to me like burrs . . ." In the 1930s Kate O'Brien wrote so scathingly of the Franco regime that she was banned from the country. Rose Macaulay also took a motor trip, this time in the 1940s, when the roads were still pitted by shells from the civil war; her car was literally shaken loose. The sight of a woman driving was so unusual that her appearance always elicited the same response: "a long, shrill cat-call, reminiscent of a pig having its throat cut, usually wordless, but sometimes accompanied by 'Olé, Olé! Una señora que conduce!' For Spanish women do not drive . . . I saw not a single woman driving all the time I was in Spain." In a typically British gesture, Macaulay decided to forswear her hat, thinking that it made her less conspicuous.

Most travelers cannot resist comparing their host country to home. Byron thought that Spanish women were "in general very handsome," and they must have thought highly of him as well. He and a companion went to Spain and Portugal on the first leg of a two-year European tour in 1809. In a letter to his mother, he related that a female admirer gave him a three-foot lock of her hair as a remembrance and then noted that Seville has the most beautiful women in Spain, "the Cadiz belles being the Lancashire witches of their land." In the 1950s the great British travel writer H. V. Morton likened the Spanish nightly *paseo* to "St. James's Park in the eighteenth century, when the whole of London Society could have been seen strolling up and down, dressed for dinner." The indomitable Mrs. Favell Lee Mortimer, who wrote about other lands for children (although by all accounts she only traveled outside of England once), asked rhetorically, "What country do you love best? Your own country. I know you do." Henry James visited San Sebastián in the 1880s "grazing it so lightly as by a day's excursion from Biarritz" and found it "the Brighton of Spain."

Other writers thought Spain without compare. They willingly left their former lives and embraced the foreignness of a Spanish adventure. In 1919 Gerald Brenan moved to the remote village of Yegen in the Sierra Nevada, living on little more than his veteran's pension. George Orwell went to Spain to write about the civil war and ended up joining a communist brigade that was fighting Franco's Nationalists. No more moving portrait of the Spanish Civil War exists than Orwell's *Homage to Catalonia*. "It was an extraordinary life we were living—an extraordinary way to be at war, if you could call it war . . . Georges Kopp, on his periodical tours of inspection, was quite frank with us. 'This is not a war,' he used to say, 'it is a comic opera with an occasional death.'" Thirty years later, in the 1960s, James Michener looked around the small village of Badajoz and thought, "This can only be Spain."

And then there was Hemingway.

From youth to old age, he returned to Spain. Sepia photos show him sitting on the ground embracing the large horned head of a bull. He was there during the Spanish Civil War and then again—this time white-haired—in the front row of the corrida at Pamplona. With so much of Hemingway's work from which to choose, it was James Michener who pointed me to *The Dangerous Summer*, one of his last works. Commissioned by *Life Magazine*, Hemingway's report of a duel between two bullfighters was originally thought a failure—unreadable, unwieldy, and almost five times the word count that the magazine had requested. Yet, Michener wrote that it was the best narrative of the sport ever written. And it is magnificent—the bull's fate is sealed from the start, yet the essay reveals the majesty of his struggle. Hemingway was also battling his mental demons and physical infirmities—a fight he would lose to suicide only two years later.

Before Hemingway and other twentieth-century writers mythologized Spain, it was considered a mysterious and somewhat dangerous place. Grand Tourists descended on other parts of the Mediterranean, but geographic isolation, a peninsula separated from the Continent by the Pyrenees, kept Spain from becoming a whistle-stop on that well-worn tour. Edith Wharton's parents took her to Madrid when she was very young, shocking their friends, who thought it too perilous a place for a family. "I remember that the Spanish tour was still considered an arduous adventure, and to attempt it with a young child the merest folly. But my father had been reading Prescott and Washington Irving; the Alhambra was more of a novelty than the Colosseum . . . I brought back an incurable passion for the road."

Spain is still a cauldron of cultures. Celtic Galicia, north of Portugal, borders the Atlantic and boasts a fjordlike coastline and Irish-green countryside. Its traditional instrument is the bagpipe. On the Mediterranean coast, Catalonia, semiautonomous with its own language and traditions, has Barcelona at its heart. Artists like Dalí and Picasso sought refuge in the region's Costa Brava. The Basques of the north are also a culture and language apart, and their separatist movement aims to sever ties to Madrid. Their language, Euskera, is unrelated to any other, including Spanish. Southern Spain has the mark of the Moors on its architecture, cuisine, and soul. And in the center, holding together this unsteady alliance, is Madrid. Spain is not only different from north to south, east to west, but urban life is distinct from the countryside, where little has changed since Gerald Brenan noted that "the calendar of a South European village is made up by the seasonal work on the land and by the rites and festivals that correspond to it."

Add to Spain's geographical and political disparity a mélange of influences—Spanish, Arab, Jewish, and the new arrivals from South

America and Africa. The country is shifting so quickly that it is hard to comprehend that only forty years bridge the death of Franco and its entry into the European Union. At times, the stress of change seems so great that Spain might simply fracture.

And yet, there is an essence that remains—an exuberant spirit with an underpinning of melancholy noted by almost all the writers in *Spain in Mind*. A theatricality pervades life, both in the landscape and the customs. Jan Morris wrote that when you see Segovia, for example, rising above the fields "it feels like some slightly over-painted opera set—so theatrical that you almost expect it to revolve beneath your feet." Nowhere is this sense of drama more obvious than in the ornate rituals centered on the Catholic calendar. Brenan wrote that even in his small town of Yegen, the young people put on masks and organized a procession. "Afterwards people lit small fires on their rooftops and toasted popcorn, and in the evening there were dances." In Seville the elaborate Semana Santa celebrations have evolved into an ornate carnival described by Eric Newby. "Night and day . . . the great floats, all of them enormously heavy, embellished with silver, some decorated with flowers and bearing sumptuously dressed figures of the Virgin, costing thousands of pounds each year to decorate . . . had swayed through the streets . . . like great ships."

Both Newby and Brenan observe that the processions around Holy Week derive not from church doctrine, but from an "echo of pagan antiquity." Wrote Newby, "They are a direct continuation, thinly disguised, of the processions of images of gods and goddesses, carried on the shoulders of common men in the ancient world . . . for us, watching them take place, and at the same time reading accounts of similar processions in the ancient world, time was annihilated."

The Spanish like to put up a good front, what Italians call "bella figura." H. V. Morton wrote that a friend told him, "You must remember that every Spaniard is at heart a grandee, and his last economy would be in out-ward show . . . You may be as poor as a church mouse in Spain, but you must put up a show." And to put up a good show, one must have the right costume. Somehow matadors are able to project masculinity in short tight jackets, knee-high breeches, tights, and a black cape lined in red or pink. "Dress any Englishman in such garb and he will at once give you the idea of a hog in armour," wrote Anthony Trollope. "In the first place he will lack the proper spirit to carry it off, and in the next place the motion of his limbs will disgrace the ornaments they bear." Trollope concluded that the Spanish have a sense of style that the English simply lack. "If he is eating an onion, he eats it as an onion should be eaten."

Theatricality also suffuses daily life, especially in the *paseo*, a relic of the seventeenth century, when Madrid's aristocracy took the evening air along the Paseo del Prado. The Spanish still take to the streets long into the night. Young people, often without the privacy of their own apartments, couple against a building, avoiding the streetlight. Parents parade sleeping babies in elaborate strollers. Grandmothers stroll arm in arm. People shop, go to cafés and bars, meet neighbors. This public nightlife is intoxicating to Anglo-Saxons, although some travelers find Spain's famously late eating hours more disorienting than jet lag. In the 1920s the dictator Primo de Rivera tried to make the Spanish conform to the eating habits of other Europeans. But even a dictator could not enforce a civilized evening meal before ten. Typically lunch stretches until four. When most Americans are settling into bed and watching the late news, the Spanish are tucking into dinner. A night out typically ends when dawn comes up the next day. More than one American exchange student has crept into her Spanish family's home in the early hours of the morning—only to find that her "parents" are still out. Although there are reports of the decline of the midday siesta because of the pressures of modern life—commuting, two-working-parent households, a bustling economy—it is still difficult to find an open pharmacy in Madrid in the middle of the afternoon.

There's always something to celebrate in Spain, and the Spanish do it with abandon. Of course, there are the holidays around the Catholic calendar, and every town and province has a weeklong fiesta, but the Spanish also honor their regional cuisine. "It's not unusual for a town to have, say, a razor clam festival or a sardine festival or an *empanada* festival," wrote Calvin Trillin, who went to Spain in search of peppers. He found them, in abundance, in a pepper festival in Galicia: "For a week I watched myself living out pepper dreams. There we are eating *pimientos de Padrón* along with razor clams and Serrano ham in a *jamonería* (ham specialist) not far from the cathedral square in Santiago." In one notable meal I had in San Sebastián—a town filled with four-star restaurants—each course was served with military precision on huge square plates with ingredients artfully arranged like miniature actors in a tableau. It was so beautifully prepared and presented that I half expected the lights to dim between courses. At the end of the three-hour meal the chef came from the kitchen, his arms spread before him, and bowed from the waist. There seemed little else to do but applaud his director's turn. Even the most humble tapas bars have their own protocol, although it takes a while to figure out the etiquette of a place while you balance a glass of wine and three small plates on the edge of an upended wine cask shared with four strangers. In the Basque town of Orozco I stopped at one of two restaurants in town. Twenty tables were set for lunch and all were empty. I sat down only to have a waitress shoo me away. One o'clock "a punto," she said, not a minute before. Men stood at the bar waiting for lunch to begin. I was the only woman in the place. At exactly one everyone sat down. The waitress brought me a tiny piece of paper with four items written on it—two choices for a first course, two for an entrée, and one dessert. In half an hour thirty-nine men and one woman consumed three courses with wine. For seven euros, one of the best meals I had in Spain.

Food worship in Spain starts at the markets, and its cathedral might be La Boqueria in Barcelona. Rows of fruits, vegetables, fish, and slaughtered cows and sheep stretch for several city blocks. Calvin Trillin wrote of being overwhelmed in a similar market in Galicia: "I'm standing with something akin to a religious feeling in that lovely market, whose vaulted stone market sheds are actually called naves." For tourists accustomed to produce and meat being packaged in plastic, Spanish markets seem almost alarmingly direct. There is a cow's head, chickens hanging by their feet, the hooves of a sheep. Like the woman I saw selling her single basket of flipping fish at the tiny harbor in Cadaqués, there is little mediation in these transactions. The fish were caught, sold, and eaten in a single day.

The counterweight to exuberant Spain is a pervasive melancholy, a sonorous cello to the lyrical flute. History hangs heavy in a land in which domination of the world is four centuries past. In Toledo's great cathedral, "Valour for God and Spain" sounds like a hollow promise. The Moors were expelled in 1492 (and, in the same year, the Jews), yet their presence dominates southern Spain. Kate Field wrote, "Not to admire Moorish architecture is to be incapable of appreciation. Its sad, solemn beauty and exquisite taste made me think of minor keys."

So much in Spain is the appreciation of "minor keys." James Michener wrote, "When I heard the word Spain, I visualized not kings and priests, nor painters and hidalgos, nor Madrid and Sevilla, but the vast reaches of emptiness, lonely uplands occupied by the solitary shepherd, the hard land of Spain stretching off to interminable distances and populated by tough, weatherbeaten men with never a ruffle at their throats nor a caparisoned horse beneath them." Travel through Aragon and see land so desiccated that it could be mistaken for moonscape, a place that freezes in the winter and bakes in the summer. Even on the coast Rose Macaulay found "streets that run between the vanished houses, cypresses darkly and necropolistically stand, and fig trees sprawl stickily in the sun. The columns of arcaded porticoes and of temples rear broken stumps against sky and sea. You may wander through the city among ghosts of Greek traders, Iberian vendors, Roman gentlemen lounging outside their villas or gossiping in loud Roman voices in the agora, simple Visigoths knocking down heathen statues and drinking deeply the wines of the Ampurdán."

Spain is a traditional battleground: first between the Romans and the Visigoths, then the Visigoths and the Moors, then the Moors and the Christians (euphemistically called the "Reconquest"). It was occupied by Napoleon and suffered under two dictators in the twentieth century. And then there was the civil war. From 1936 to 1939 Spain was ravaged by the opposing armies of the Nationalists—supported by Hitler and Mussolini—and the Republicans, thousands of whom were executed in reprisals after the Nationalist victory under Franco. Artists and writers came to the defense of the Republicans, including English and Americans who fought in the International Brigades. Many are represented in *Spain in Mind*: W. H. Auden was an ambulance driver, John Dos Passos and Langston Hughes were journalists, and Ernest Hemingway delivered anti-Franco speeches and produced a documentary. George Orwell went to Spain as a writer and observer and became a soldier. He ended up wounded and in danger of imprisonment. The British consul spirited him out of Spain before he became one of thousands of partisans who disappeared.

Perhaps it is the unstable political climate that makes Spaniards ally themselves first with their families, then their towns, and finally their regions. Today a united Spain seems an uneasy confederation with a booming economy and an underclass with crushing unemployment. Northern Europeans have flooded Spain and built or bought holiday homes, creating a large expatriate community. Lucia Graves returned to her childhood home and found that "the new generations of rural Majorcans no longer work the land, but instead have become hotel managers, waiters or builders who speak to one another on mobile phones . . ." Chris Stewart bought a farm without running water, electricity, or an access road more than fifteen years ago. He and his wife, Ana, have made a life in the Alpujarra Mountains, recounted in his book *Driving Over Lemons.* "If you live abroad where there are other expatriates, you become a part of what is known as the Foreign Community . . . Being a part of a foreign community is a bit like being at school. Among other things seniority bestows respect . . . There seems to be a preponderance of eccentric women among the foreigners here. Some of them have husbands in tow, but they tend to be vapid creatures who fade into the background and are of little account."

The democratization of travel has brought tourists to Spain in huge numbers. Next to Italy, it is the most heavily traveled country in Europe. A hundred and fifty years ago Queen Maria Christina went to San Sebastián in Basque country to bathe in the waters of the Atlantic. The eponymous belle epoque Hotel Maria Christina once hosted the elite of Europe. Still grand, it is now a Westin and hosts American tour bus groups. Flamenco bars and corridas are filled with tourists looking for that authentic touch of Spain. The bullfight is possibly the most difficult sport for outsiders to comprehend. That famous nontraveling travel writer Favell Lee Mortimer wrote to her young readers, "And can women like to see such bloody sights? Yes, they do—and priests, who ought to show the people what is right, are pleased to view these wicked deeds . . . When the Prince of Wales visited Spain, he did not go to see a bull-fight." In the late nineteenth century Henry James watched a bullfight in San Sebastián and wrote, "A long list of bulls was sacrificed, each of whom had pretensions to originality . . . I thought the bull, in any case, a finer fellow than any of his tormentors, and I thought his tormentors finer fellows than the spectators."

The passion of the bullfight finds its physical manifestation in art—Velázquez, Goya, Picasso, Dalí—and architecture—especially in the architecture of Antoni Gaudí in Barcelona. Critic Robert Hughes said that Gaudí was more Catholic than the pope and more royalist than the king. A conservative Catholic, Gaudí envisioned a fanciful biomorphic cathedral. He was so invested in the project that he begged door-to-door for funds to complete it. His cathedral, the Sagrada Família, was the obsession of his last years and remains unfinished. Early in its construction Gaudí was run over by a tram, and no one knows exactly how he planned to complete it. Hughes says that the cathedral is "the most blatant mass of half-digested modernist clichés to be plunked on a notable building within living memory," and yet "it is to Barcelona what the Eiffel Tower is to Paris or the Harbour Bridge to Sydney: a completely irreplaceable logo." It may also be a metaphor for Spain itself, based in history, but with a rather uncertain blueprint for its future.

Modern Spain moves at warp speed. Building cranes are everywhere. The Guggenheim Museum in Bilbao revitalized that old port city, and nearly fifty major modern architectural projects are under way throughout the country, from a new curvilinear roof for Barcelona's Santa Caterina Market to a biomorphic terminal at the Barajas Airport in Madrid. Spanish cuisine is at the forefront of the food movement, and it might take months to get a reservation at Akelarre in San Sebastián. Women's groups are advocating the elimination of the siesta and the regularization of the workday to closer approximate the rest of the world. Last year, in a truly revolutionary measure, Spain outlawed smoking in restaurants.

Spain in Mind portrays both the layers of the past and the vivid present in a complex and sometimes contradictory picture. Kate Field wrote, "The conjunction of so much history, so much live art, and so much dead nature would set my brain on fire with conundrums." Lucia Graves, daughter of the poet Robert Graves, who was raised in Spain but lives now in England, wrote that when she returns to her childhood home, "there is at least one moment, either in the early morning, when all is quiet except for the sound of birds pecking at the fruit trees, or at night, when the moon lights up the olive trees across the valley, when suddenly the memory of what it felt like to be a child here flashes through me. Like an old song returning." Beneath the thrum of twenty-first-century Spain is Moorish Spain, Gothic Spain, Hemingway's Spain, Gaudí's Spain, Byron's Spain, Anthony Trollope's Spain, and my Spain.

SPAIN IN MIND

John Affleck

Writer John Affleck went to Pamplona to run with the bulls and search for Ernest Hemingway, a man obsessed with bullfighting in his life and in his writing. Hemingway never ran with the bulls, but he saw more than his share of bullfights. After his suicide in 1961, two tickets to the Pamplona arena were found in his desk. As a literary pilgrim, Affleck looked for Hemingway everywhere at the fiesta of San Fermín. Young men miming a bullfight reminded him of a mock corrida that ended tragically in Hemingway's short story "The Capital of the World." He found the bronze statue of "Papa" on the Avenida de Hemingway. And surveying the macho chaos of Pamplona, he recalled Hemingway's warning that it "was no place to take your wife."

Ultimately, Affleck concluded that Hemingway is not to be found in the courage of the matadors, but in the struggle of the bull, who can only wage a valiant, if futile, fight. Affleck wrote "Hemingway in Pamplona" for the *Literary Traveler*, a Web site that encourages travel to places that are part of the literary imagination. Cofounder Linda McGovern says, "Great literature, like great travel, is essentially about experience; one you read, the other you live, both reveal what is true."

HEMINGWAY IN PAMPLONA

I've fashioned a makeshift costume out of light khakis, a white T-shirt, and a wild west red bandanna. With me in the line at the bus station are young Spaniards, their uniforms exact: white trousers, white tunics, and the official San Fermín scarf, neatly tied in front and draped across the back. Inexplicably, I'm at the front of the line, a solitary American in questionable attire, and as such am duly ignored. They play at bullfighting, their index fingers as horns, and I can't help but think of Hemingway's short story, "The Capital of the

World," in which two young café waiters tie knives to a chair to simulate a bull, until one of them is fatally gored.

The bus leaves at eight in the evening. The trip from Barcelona to
Pamplona takes seven hours or so, and no one, including myself, gets
any sleep. Commandeered by these San Fermín pilgrims, it's a party
bus, and rules about smoking, drinking, drug use, eating, and disturb-
ing fellow passengers are happily disregarded. We arrive in the early
morning to find no battery of waiting loved ones, no old women
hawking accommodations. I follow the throng into the midnight
streets. Fireworks burst overhead, their exploding colors raining
down and painting the ubiquitous suits of white in dazzling, dancing
rainbows. I head for the bright lights and carnival sounds.

The carnival is a virtual bullfight. Young men snort and paw the
earth, making horns of their fingers and eyeing their adversary,
another youngster dangling a red scarf. The bull charges, the matador
pirouettes to the applause of onlookers. I watch from the outskirts,
drinking a beer and eating the Spanish version of a hot dog. Occasionally I catch an eye and join in the chant: "San Fermín! San Fermín!" A man ducks to lift me on his shoulders, and I am carried
above the crowd until he sets me down and charges a would-be matador. "San Fermín!" I say, and raise my hand in the sign of the bull:
index finger and pinkie extended as horns, the remaining three digits
pressed together to represent the snout.

As the sun starts to rise, the revelers start to fall. Wherever they
are, they simple crumble into slumber, until, by dawn, every patch of
grass is obscured in red and white. The cafés are filling, too; filling
with those who've sworn off sleep for the week and prime the adrenaline with triple espressos. The bulls are running soon, and they want
to be ready.

At the massive bull ring I shell out 800 pesetas for a seat in the *sol*.
Sombra costs nearly twice as much. The ticket admits me to see the
running of the bulls, then the bullfight later in the afternoon. Originally, the Fiesta de San Fermín was the first showing of the bulls, a
sort of pre-season event. Matadors, breeders, and aficionados like
Hemingway came to check out the latest in the venerable old blood-
lines, talk with the insiders, and spend a week thinking of nothing
but bulls. After Hemingway, San Fermín became the tourist draw it is

today, attracting over 40,000 people to the small city of Pamplona every year. I have the sense that the true aficionados now stay far away from the insanity that San Fermín has become.

Still, much has not changed. In his bullfighting memoir, *A Dangerous Summer*, Hemingway remarks, "Pamplona is no place to bring your wife." His reasons are the best description of those seven days.

The odds are all in favor of her getting ill, hurt or wounded or at least jostled and wine squirted all over her, or of losing her; maybe all three. It's a man's fiesta and women at it make trouble, never intentionally of course, but they nearly always make or have trouble. I wrote a book on this once. Of course if she can talk Spanish so she knows she is being joked with and not insulted, if she can drink wine all day and all night and dance with any group of strangers who invite her, if she does not mind things being spilled on her, if she adores continual noise and music and loves fireworks, especially those that fall close to her or burn her clothes, if she thinks it is sound and logical to see how close you can come to being killed by bulls for fun and for free, if she doesn't catch cold when she is rained on and appreciates dust, likes disorder and irregular meals and never needs to sleep and still keeps clean and neat without running water; then bring her. You'll probably lose her to a better man than you.

I've got a ticket because of Him, of course, because I've read that book, *The Sun Also Rises*, because I, too, have come from Paris, because almost more than the bulls I want to see Him, the great bronze Papa in front of the ring. Because I want to smell the dust and drink the wine and sleep in the streets he slept in. Because if Jesus watches over Rio, then Papa's got his eternal eye on Pamplona, at least for this week in June, and I want him to catch a glimpse of me.

Weighted with backpack and camera, I opt to watch. Hem never ran, but also sat in the stands, remarking on the bravery and stupidity of the kids, waiting for the real bullfight to begin. Hours early, the ring is already full. Chants echo from *sol* to *sombra*. San Fermín has no real schedule, but I check my watch, wondering at what time the bulls are unleashed, setting off the mad dash into the stadium. Where we wait, the cautious, the skeptical, the cowards.

It starts with a silence. Someone has heard the rumbling of a thousand feet. Inside the ring the din hushes, and soon we can all hear it: thunder that does not diminish, but grows stronger. Squeals of fear and delight. Cheers from those watching along the street. Then, like atoms in a chain reaction, those at the front of the chase burst into the ring, veering off in random directions and scampering over the walls to safety. Next comes the bulk of the mob, who race to the walls but choose to stay inside the ring, awaiting the bulls they have not yet seen. Finally come those who showed up early for the places closest to the starting gates, those who started the mad dash when they saw the eyes of the bulls flare as they burst from the cages. They are the adrenaline junkies, propelled forward by frantic leering glances over their shoulders, tossing insults at the hulking beasts. When they enter the stadium they simply turn, going toe to toe with the pursuers. Their game now is to steal the flowers from the horns.

Picadors are on hand to save such men from themselves. They ride horses and carry long spears, ready to distract any bull with too clear a bead. Gradually the full-sized bulls are led out of the ring, replaced by young bulls with short horns, perfect for playing matador. They have neither the wile nor the malevolence to do real harm. For more than an hour the ring is full with hundreds of youngsters, taking turns with the half dozen half-sized animals. Everyone is laughing, even the young men who have mistimed their evasions and are tossed effortlessly in the air.

The chaos gradually tapers off and assumes a sort of order. The bulls gather in the center of the ring, snorting and pawing the ground, while along the perimeter wait their tormentors. They pant and giggle. Occasionally a bull rushes, triggered by a flash of color or a sound, and the ragged line of red and white opens. The bulls have learned to turn away before ramming the wall, and they retreat back to the fold.

When the young bulls are finally led from the ring, I leave as well. I want to find Him. I circumnavigate the arena twice, then finally ask in my simple Spanish, *"Dónde está Hemingway?"*

"Hemingway?" responds my guide. He spreads his arms to indicate ubiquity. He points in every direction, labelling each as "Hemingway, Hemingway, Hemingway." He nods at me with narrowed eyes, as if to ask, "Do you understand?"

It's the street, I discover, as I consult my map. Avenida de Hemingway, one of Pamplona's main streets, runs past the arena. And at the end of the street, in the square at the main entrance, is my bronze, bearded Papa. His head, set atop an enormous slab of granite, strikes me as quite small, even meek, with eyes that still seem to be studying the scene. This was not the great Papa who could fill a bar with his bravado and his boasts; no, this was the writer still humbled by his craft, whose eyes never stopped searching for truth, who knew that in this world he was merely a reporter of what truth he could find.

Back inside the arena the real bullfight begins. There are no colors like it; the matador's costume, the streamers on the pics, even the blood, blaze in the July heat. I join the cries of "olé" at the good passes and cheer the courage of the matador and bull alike. It is a good bull, strong and hot-blooded, and in death receives much respect. The death of the bull is an inevitability in the ring; if the matador falls the picadors will come to his aid. I realize that it is the duty of the bull to accept that inevitability, and the duty of the matador to see that the bull is honored in death. While I am dazzled by the matador's magic, it is the doomed bull that enthralls me, for it has sensed its own demise. And I realize that in the ring Hemingway would not have donned the matador's costume and strutted with his cape, but that he would have bent his head and pawed the ground, smelling in the distance his own death, and that he would have charged it full-bore.

W. H. Auden

(1907–1973)

W. H. Auden was one of a brilliant circle of young men including Rex Warner, John Betjeman, Stephen Spender, Cecil Day-Lewis, and Louis MacNeice who went to Christ Church, Oxford, in the 1920s. Even among those luminaries, Auden was the brilliant young poet. He twice edited *Oxford Poetry*, and his first collection was printed by Spender in 1928. After university he joined Christopher Isherwood, a friend from secondary school, in Berlin (a time memorialized in Isherwood's *Goodby to Berlin*, 1939). He and Isherwood collaborated on several plays throughout the 1930s.

Early in his career Auden was an ardent socialist, and he joined the Spanish Civil War on the side of the Republicans as an ambulance driver. The result of this experience was his masterful poem "Spain 1937," an examination of the war and a call to action. Auden lauds the Republican struggle against the Fascists and urges others to join the cause. Before the Second World War, he and Isherwood emigrated to New York; Auden became a United States citizen in 1946.

When Auden left England, he abandoned his left-wing political beliefs and became interested in Christianity, an increasingly important part of his verse. In the 1940s he met his lifelong companion, Chester Kallman (their life together is celebrated in Auden's memoir *About the House*, 1967). As his politics became more conservative, Auden reexamined his earlier work and expunged "Spain 1937" from many of the later volumes of his collected poems. Auden died in Austria in 1973.

SPAIN 1937

Yesterday all the past. The language of size
Spreading to China along the trade-routes; the diffusion

Of the counting-frame and the cromlech;
Yesterday the shadow-reckoning in the sunny climates.

Yesterday the assessment of insurance by cards,
The divination of water; yesterday the invention
    Of cart-wheels and clicks, the taming of
Horses; yesterday the bustling world of the navigators.

Yesterday the abolition of fairies and giants;
The fortress like a motionless eagle eyeing the valley,
    The chapel built in the forest;
Yesterday the carving of angels and of frightening gargoyles.

The trial of heretics among the columns of stone;
Yesterday the theological feuds in the taverns
    And the miraculous cure at the fountain;
Yesterday the Sabbath of Witches. But today the struggle.

Yesterday the installation of dynamos and turbines;
The construction of railways in the colonial desert;
    Yesterday the classic lecture
On the origin of Mankind. But today the struggle.

Yesterday the belief in the absolute value of Greek;
The fall of the curtain upon the death of a hero;
    Yesterday the prayer to the sunset,
And the adoration of madmen. But today the struggle.

As the poet whispers, startled among the pines
Or, where the loose waterfall sings, compact, or upright
    On the crag by the leaning tower:
"O my vision. O send me the luck of the sailor."

And the investigator peers through his instruments
At the inhuman provinces, the virile bacillus
    Or enormous Jupiter finished:
"But the lives of my friends. I inquire, I inquire."

And the poor in their fireless lodgings dropping the sheets
Of the evening paper: "Our day is our loss. O show us
              History the operator, the
Organiser, Time the refreshing river."

And the nations combine each cry, invoking the life
That shapes the individual belly and orders
              The private nocturnal terror:
"Did you not found once the city state of the sponge,

"Raise the vast military empires of the shark
And the tiger, establish the robin's plucky canton?
              Intervene. O descend as a dove or
A furious papa or a mild engineer: but descend."

And the life, if it answers at all, replies from the heart
And the eyes and the lungs, from the shops and squares of
       the city:
              "O no, I am not the Mover,
Not today, not to you. To you I'm the

"Yes-man, the bar-companion, the easily-duped:
I am whatever you do; I am your vow to be
              Good, your humorous story;
I am your business voice; I am your marriage.

"What's your proposal? To build the Just City? I will.
I agree. Or is it the suicide pact, the romantic
              Death? Very well, I accept, for
I am your choice, your decision: yes, I am Spain."

Many have heard it on remote peninsulas,
On sleepy plains, in the aberrant fishermen's islands,
              In the corrupt heart of the city;
Have heard and migrated like gulls or the seeds of a flower.

They clung like burrs to the long expresses that lurch
Through the unjust lands, through the night, through the
      alpine tunnel;
                  They floated over the oceans;
They walked the passes: they came to present their lives.

On that arid square, that fragment nipped off from hot
Africa, soldered so crudely to inventive Europe,
                  On that tableland scored by rivers,
Our fever's menacing shapes are precise and alive.

Tomorrow, perhaps, the future: the research on fatigue
And the movements of packers; the gradual exploring of
      all the
                  Octaves of radiation;
Tomorrow the enlarging of consciousness by diet
      and breathing.

Tomorrow the rediscovery of romantic love;
The photographing of ravens; all the fun under
                  Liberty's masterful shadow;
Tomorrow the hour of the pageant-master and the musician.

Tomorrow, for the young, the poets exploding like bombs,
The walks by the lake, the winter of perfect communion;
                  Tomorrow the bicycle races
Through the suburbs on summer evenings: but today
      the struggle.

Today the inevitable increase in the chances of death;
The conscious acceptance of guilt in the fact of murder;
                  Today the expending of powers
On the flat ephemeral pamphlet and the boring meeting.

Today the makeshift consolations; the shared cigarette;
The cards in the candle-lit barn and the scraping concert,

The masculine jokes; today the
Fumbled and unsatisfactory embrace before hurting.

The stars are dead; the animals will not look:
We are left alone with our day, and the time is short and
                    History to the defeated
May say Alas but cannot help or pardon.

Gerald Brenan

(1894–1987)

Like many young veterans after World War I, Gerald Brenan was disillusioned and dispirited. He was raised in England, South Africa, and India and served with the British army on the western front, earning the Military Cross. As soon as he was discharged, he took his total fortune of less than 200 pounds and moved to Spain, where he hoped to find a more relaxed and economical life. After traveling to several places, he settled on Andalusia in the region of La Alpujarra—specifically the village of Yegen.

Brenan was a curiosity in Yegen. He had a simple house and furnishings and employed a local woman to cook and clean. And he brought his entire library from England—two thousand books—which arrived on a wagon from Almería. Brenan was quickly drawn into the politics of village life. "Like most villages of the Sierra Nevada, Yegen was composed of two barrios or quarters, built at a short distance from one another. The *barrio de arriba* or upper quarter, which was the one in which I lived, began just below the road and ended at the church. Here there was a level space some two or three acres in extent . . . and immediately below it the *barrio de abajo*, or lower quarter began. The extraordinarily strong feelings of attachment which Spaniards have to their native place showed themselves even in the case of these *barrios*, for although there was no difference in their social composition, there was a decided feeling of rivalry between them." In his memoir *South from Granada* (1957), from which this excerpt is taken, Brenan recounts his early years in Yegen.

As isolated as he was, Brenan had many visitors, including Leonard and Virginia Woolf, Lytton Strachey, and Ernest Hemingway. He recalled that when the Woolfs visited, he and Virginia argued about literature; she "defended Scott, Thackeray and Conrad against my attacks, disagreed with my high opinion of *Ulysses* . . . and listened humbly to my criticisms of her own novels."

Brenan wrote many books about Spain, including *The Spanish Labyrinth* and *History of Spanish Literature*. He died in Spain. A plaque was fixed to his old house in Yegen that read, "In this house lived the British Hispanist Gerald Brenan who universalized the name Yegen and the customs and traditions of La Alpujarra."

From SOUTH FROM GRANADA

THE VILLAGE CALENDAR

The calendar of a South European village is made up by the seasonal work on the land and by the rites and festivals that correspond to it. In my village this calendar was a particularly full one because, since the winters were relatively mild and water for irrigation abundant, a great variety of crops was grown. The year began with olive picking and, as this was mainly a woman's task, the olive groves were invaded by gay parties of matrons and girls, wearing white head-handkerchiefs and brightly coloured dresses and accompanied by younger children. The girls climbed the trees, and if any man approached too close there would be screams and a scuttle to descend, because none of them wore drawers. The olives were collected in striped rugs laid out on the ground, then tipped into panniers and carried off to an oil mill. Here a donkey, revolving in semi-darkness in the low confined space, pulled a cone-shaped stone that crushed the olives and released a stream of oil into the vats.

While the women were busy in this way the men were pruning the vines and fruit trees, after which came the planting of the onions and garlic (the two principal cash crops) and the hoeing of the corn. Then early in May the cutting of the barley and soon after the wheat began on the coast. Gradually it spread up the mountain-side, reaching our village in July (every three hundred feet of altitude makes a difference of four days), but on the high mountain farms not starting before September. The crop was cut with a short curved sickle. The reaper seized in his left hand a bunch of stalks and severed them with his right a little below the ear. They were then collected in panniers and carried off on donkey-back to the threshing-floor. If there was a moon the barley would be reaped and collected by night, since, if it gets too dry, the grain falls out.

In August, when all the corn has been cut, came the *parva*, as it was called here, or threshing. This was the culminating moment of the year, the true harvest. The unthreshed corn, or *mies*, was spread out on the circular paved threshing-floors that were dotted about on the mountain-side, generally on some rocky bluff which would catch the wind. Two mules were harnessed to the *tabla*, a small plank of wood armed with iron or quartzite teeth, and a man balancing on it held the reins. Another man stood by and brandished a long whip, and the mules cantered round and round. As soon as they were tired another pair took their place. All day long these circuses revolved on the mountain-side, the drivers leaning back mutely on their reins like charioteers, the mules' coats glistening with sweat and the man with the whip breaking into an occasional shout. Then, as darkness fell, preparations for the winnowing would begin. A group of men and women would assemble on the threshing-floor, a lantern would be lit, someone would strum on a guitar. Unexpectedly a voice would rise into the night, would hang for a few seconds in the air, and then fade back into the silence again. From the poplar trees close by the trill of a nightingale answered it.

And now the wind had begun to blow. At first it came in little puffs, then it died down, then it came on again. Whenever it seemed strong enough, one or two men would take their long wooden forks of ash or *almez* (the lotus or nettle tree) and begin tossing up the ears. This went on at intervals all night. The wind blew most steadily towards sunrise, and often I would come out of my room, where I had sat up reading, and climb the slope to watch the work going on. The great trough of mountains below would fill, as from a tank of water, with rippling light, the shadows would turn violet, then lavender, would become thin and float away, while, as I approached the threshing-floor, I would see the chaff streaming out like a white cloak in the breeze and the heavy grain falling, as the gold coins fell on Danaë, on to the heap below. Then without clouds or veils the sun's disc appeared above the Sierra de Gádor and began to mount rapidly. The sleeping figures rose and stretched themselves: the men took a pull at their wine-skins, the women packed their baskets of provisions and returned home. Within half an hour they would be out again at the streamside washing clothes.

Late spring and early summer were the busiest seasons. The beans, whose flowers scented the air at Easter, had to be picked and the potatoes planted. At the same time, tomatoes, pimentoes, egg-plants, french beans, melons, watermelons had to be sown. Then came the cutting of the wheat and a quick ploughing and replanting with Indian corn, the collection of lentils, chick peas, and vetches, followed by the great celebration of the *parva*. Almost at once the grapes, which were grown on the trellises and irrigated, were picked and trodden in the wine vats, and all the other fruits of the autumn garnered. Tomatoes, pimentoes, and figs were spread out on mats on the rooftops and dried, chestnuts were brought in, onions, garlic, and potatoes dug up and either sold or stored. The husking of the maize or Indian corn had a ritual. A group of young men and girls would sit in a circle in the *azotea*, or open attic, with a jug of wine and a plate of cakes or roasted chestnuts beside them, and whenever a girl turned up a cob that had red grains she would strike all the young men lightly on the forehead with her knife: when it was a young man who turned one up, he would embrace in turn all the girls. By "embracing" was meant putting one's arm round someone's shoulder and patting them. It never meant kissing. This was such a serious operation that some very proper girls would not allow their young men to kiss them before they were married.

My village was almost self-supporting. The poorer families ate nothing that was not grown in the parish, except fresh fish (which was brought up on mule-back from the coast in a night's journey) and dried cod. Cotton materials, earthenware, ironmongery, and cheap trinkets reached us from the towns, but the villagers wove and dyed their own woollen fabrics, their blankets of cotton-rag, and their silk handkerchiefs and bedcovers. In other words, the economy of an Alpujarran village had scarcely changed since medieval times. And the instruments of husbandry were of an even greater antiquity. Our plough was closely modelled on the Roman plough, while a slightly different form with an upright handle, which was in use on the coast and through the greater part of Andalusia, was the same as that shown on Greek vases. No doubt this was the primitive plough of the whole Mediterranean region. Equally ancient was the threshing board or sled—both Amos and Isaiah allude to it—and as for our sickle, it was identical in form with those found in Bronze Age tombs near Almería. Yet our system of agriculture must not be written off as backward. Towards 1930 a few petrol-driven winnowing machines were introduced and found useful, but so perfectly suited were the other implements to the local conditions that I doubt whether it would be possible to improve on them. Since at this time I was reading Virgil and working my way through the twelve volumes of Frazer's *Golden Bough* and the Old Testament, I got a special pleasure from these archaic survivals.

Spring was, as in most countries, the best season. It began on the coast in February or March, and then spread like a stain of green up the mountain-side, reaching the village in April. The fig leaves and the mulberry leaves opened, the wheat and the barley shot up a little more every night, the sticky poplar buds unwrapped and displayed their thin, silky sails. The swallows arrived and began to build their nests, and before long one heard the cuckoo and the nightingale. Above the village the whole mountain was breaking into life. Those families who had plots of land there moved up to their *cortijos*— rough stone-built cabins built under the chestnut trees—and the making of cheeses began. Shouts, songs, brays of asses, cockcrows, bleating of sheep and goats resounded everywhere.

Far up the Mecina valley, two or three hours' walk away, there was a scattered ilex wood—all that remained of the *monte* or oak forest that had once covered the slope above the chestnut zone. A little beyond this Don Fadrique had his farm, with about seventy head of cattle, a flock of goats, and a few sheep. I used sometimes to go there on the excuse of botanizing; columbines, gentians, saxifrages, scillas lined the stream, and one could bathe in the icy snow water. Here lived Juan el Mudo, so called because his father had been dumb, a tall athletic man who was married to the buxom Araceli, Doña Lucía's last maid, running the farm on a sharecropper's lease and maintaining through his wife's influence an intimate feudal relationship with his master. Most of the land was pasture, but they sowed some rye and reaped it at the end of August. Don Fadrique kept a room here for himself, and when I wished for a change from village life I used to go and stay in it. I then discovered that there is nothing like a spell of monotony and deprivation from books for renewing the faculties. By day the solitude and emptiness of the mountain valley ate into my mind: I searched for flowers, I found a dipper's nest under a water-fall, I watched the falcons and eagles that circled overhead, and then I came back in the evening to sit by the log fire with the silent Juan, the gentle, bearded Felipe, clad in rags, and a couple of wild, speech-less shepherd boys. When after a few days of this I returned to the village, I felt that I was entering a metropolis.

These shepherd boys, or rather goat-herds, deserve some descrip-tion. They were often strikingly good-looking, with long snaky locks of hair falling over their necks, and olive complexions, but they had grown up in the isolation of the mountain farms or watching their flocks of goats in the *secanos*, and so had almost lost the power of speech. When spoken to they answered in a sing-song voice that was difficult to understand and loud enough to carry from one hill-top to another. Listening to them, it seemed to me as though in all Mediter-ranean lands there was one common speech for goat-herds and that a youth from the Spanish sierras would be able to make himself under-stood in the mountains of Sicily or Albania. On the rare occasions when they came down to the village they were shy and hid themselves away, but sooner or later, since their beauty made them attractive to the girls, they would find themselves married. Then their purgatory began, for their wives were invariably unfaithful to them. If they were tough, they beat them, but more often they were gentle, defenceless creatures, and then, as if in self-excuse, they developed their powers of speech and became good conversationalists. Such was Felipe, whose wife Victoriana had a dozen lovers, among them her employer. He had a face like Christ, a character as weak as water, and was the only person in that remote *cortijo* one could converse with.

Some of his stories were about wolves. He maintained that if one met a single wolf and looked it steadily in the face it would run away, but that if there were two of them there was nothing for it but to wave a stick and shout and hope for the best. To shoot at them with a sling provoked them. However, he had not been brave enough to test his theory, for on the only occasion when he had seen a wolf he had scrambled up a live-oak, in case, as he remarked, there might be another in the offing. The wolf had then slunk away. Lately, however, there had not been any wolves. The cutting of the *monte* had discouraged them, and none had been seen for some years. The last one had jumped over the wall of the corral in the middle of the night and eaten the sheep-dog but left the flock alone. Today, however, they are back again. The police regulation forbidding anyone to carry firearms has given them a free ticket, and last year (1953) two of them came down to the very edge of the village and broke into a sheepfold, killing every one of the sheep.

The agricultural events of the year were celebrated, as I have said, with appropriate rituals. The first of these was the carnival. The young people dressed up, put on masks, and organized a procession. Among the various Moors, giants, and other figures of fancy who walked or were carried past, there was always a litter in which two young men, one of them dressed as a girl, pretended to make love to one another with obscene words and gestures. This seemed to me to bear out Frazer's view that the carnival is derived from the Roman Saturnalia. Afterwards people lit small fires on their rooftops and toasted popcorn, and in the evening there were dances. The last day was celebrated by a torchlight procession in which a stuffed fox-skin (or failing this a rabbit-skin) was carried in triumph round the village and buried in front of the church, with mock religious ceremonies and a sermon. This rite presumably represented the burial of the old year.

The Easter ceremonies had a peculiar vividness. From the morning of Palm Sunday a silence fell on the village and lasted till the end of the week. During this time no one shouted or sang, and the sound of the pestle and mortar, that gay prelude to every Andalusian meal, ceased to be heard. Then on the night of Holy Thursday the figure of the Crucified Christ was borne in slow procession with torches and candles as far as the stone calvary that stands among the olive trees a little below the village. At every halt a low, sad *copla* was sung. On the following evening there was a yet more lugubrious procession, when his dead body was carried in silence in a glass coffin to the same place and then brought back to the church to be interred. That night a group of old women bearing esparto torches would walk, as in a *via crucis*, round the outside of the church, moaning and singing *saetas* (not in that *flamenco* or debased gipsy style that is the fashion for *saetas* today, but in the purer *cante andaluz* of Granada), while within the building the candles of the *capilla ardiente* burned round the tomb. Then at ten o'clock on Saturday morning, as the priest was saying mass, the Gloria bell was rung as a sign that the Resurrection had taken place, and the holy water for the year was blessed. People carried back glasses of it from the church to sprinkle on their houses to keep away the evil spirits.

The fast was now ended, but the final scene of the drama had yet to be played. At daybreak on Easter Sunday the young men got the church key from the sacristan, took out the figure of the Risen Christ, and carried it to the square at the lower end of the village. He was represented as a young man in a green dress and, as if to associate him with Adonis and Osiris and all the other man-gods who had died in order that the corn might spring again and the sap rise yet once more in the stems, he was crowned with leaves; a bunch of flowers was placed in his right hand and a sheaf of barley in his left. He was set up on a platform in the humble square with its low unplastered houses, and the villagers—especially the poorer families—collected round with cries of *Viva, viva el Señor*. Then at nine o'clock the priest opened the doors of the church. The alcalde and all the principal persons of the village were waiting and when the Virgin was carried out in her green, star-spangled dress they fell into line behind her and formed a procession. This was the dramatic moment of the Easter ceremonies, which even the simplest of the shepherd boys understood, for the Virgin had found the grave open and missed her son, and was sallying out to seek for him. With slow steps, in complete silence, the procession moved down the uneven street, the stiff green-robed figure swaying from side to side till it came to the entrance to the square. The little enclosure was filled with people. Every window was crammed with women's faces, and the low rooftops were lined by men who made a long ragged fringe as of cranes or storks against the sky. As soon as the figure of the Virgin arrived in front of that of Christ, she curtsied to him three times: the priest stepped forward to sprinkle him with holy water and incense him, and she was brought up tottering to the edge of the platform on which he stood. Then, when she was only a couple of feet away, his arms, which moved on strings, were raised in a jerky movement to touch her shoulders. This was the signal for the silence to break. The drummer, a tall, lank youth who stood in a corner of the square, raised his hands above his head, and with contorted face brought them down on his drum. Every voice shouted *Viva la Purísima, Viva el Señor*, trumpets blew, boys beat on sheets of tin, and the men on the rooftops let off rockets and fired their shot-guns. To reload them through the muzzle took much waving of arms and ramrods, and their sudden, nervous gestures carried one out of Europe into Africa.

And now the procession, bearing both the reeling Mother and her Son, had re-formed and was returning at the same snail's pace to the church. The drum beat, the trumpets blew, the women broke out into singing. It was not a litany they sang but one of those four-lined verses known as *coplas*, of which everyone knew by heart a large number. The boys' voices, high and piercing, rose above all the others. More rockets hissed into the sky, more guns were let off, till at length among loud huzzas the procession, bearing the two solemn marionette-like figures, re-entered the church.

That afternoon the youth of the village collected round the swings. The young men had spent the previous night erecting them in the streets in front of their girls' houses. They were different from English children's swings, for, instead of a seat, a plank was suspended lengthwise from two ropes and a man and a girl took their places at each end of it. Every evening for a fortnight or more, the swinging went on to the accompaniment of a special swinging song and only people of marriageable age were allowed to take part, because this was a rite to make the crops, which had just been renewed by the death and resurrection of the God, put on strength and grow.

The next festival came on St. Mark's day, which falls on the twenty-fifth of April. For the Spanish peasant St. Mark is not the author of the Synoptic Gospels, fountain-head with Q of the narratives of St. Matthew and St. Luke and the subject of many learned works by Tübingen professors, but the patron saint of bulls and of all grazing animals. It is on his day, therefore, that they are brought to be blessed. A procession was formed behind his wooden image, everyone leading his cow or goat or mule or donkey, each with a bunch of flowers tied to its horn or ear, and the shepherds and goatherds driving their herds in front of them. In this manner the whole animal population was brought through the narrow streets to the church square, where the priest, turning round, blessed and incensed them. As soon as this had been done, small bracelet-shaped rolls of bread known as *roscos* were distributed, one for each person and animal. They were the gift of a confraternity whose members drew lots each year as to which of them was to provide the flour and make them. After being blessed by the priest, they were hung on the horns of the cows and goats and over the ears of the donkeys and the procession resumed its march through the lower *barrio*. Other *roscos* were handed round to friends and relatives, to whom they were believed to bring luck, and at the end of the day each of the animals was given a piece. In our village, with its steep, crooked streets, no sight was more picturesque or pagan-seeming than this procession of many sorts of animals, decorated with flowers and led by their owners—old men, women, and children.

May Day had no place in our calendar, but on the third of May fell the day of the Cross—*la Cruz de Mayo*. This is a great occasion in many parts of Spain, when the children set up little crosses in the streets, decorate them with flowers, and waylay passers-by for pennies, but in our village we spent it in killing the Devil. Parties of young people set off for the fields, ate and drank under the olive trees, and thus fortified went in search of the Universal Enemy. They found him in the form of a tall plant of wood spurge, which has the reputation of being poisonous to animals, and having selected their specimen they tore it up by the roots, tied a rope to it, and dragged it round the country and through the streets with shouts of triumph. When they had grown tired of this, they attached it firmly to a tree and left it. Meanwhile the houses would be decorated with branches and flowers, homespun silk hangings would be taken out of the chests in which they were stored, and an altar set up in the principal room with a wooden cross on it. In the evening there would be dancing and drinking in front of it. The Day of the Cross was, of course, a substitute devised by the Church to take the place of May Day, with its pagan associations. Originally the ceremony celebrated the death and resurrection of the tree spirit, just as Easter celebrated that of the corn.

The next occasion observed by the village was Midsummer Day.

On the evening before it, the young men decorated the doorways of their girls with branches and sang serenades, and early on the following morning the girls would go to the spring, dip their faces and hands in the water, and sing songs. In the afternoon they put on their gayest kerchiefs and went in a body with the young men to eat the wild cherries that grew high up on the mountain-side. Then came the feast of the Assumption, in August, when they made up parties to eat figs in the *secanos*, and in September the birthday of the Virgin sent them again to the fields to eat melons.

All these festivals that I have described were associated with the growth of plants and trees, the collection of fruits, and the fertility of cattle. A Christian veneer had been given them, but they were much older than Christianity. Easter alone superimposed on the vegetation ritual a deeper significance, for the drama that was played out then was a sign that not only the corn but man too would rise again. On that week Christ and the Virgin transcended Adonis and Demeter. But our other rites were pagan and, since the essence of paganism is gaiety, they mostly ended in eating and drinking and in excursions to the fields which were in fact courting parties. So little tolerance did the village show for sad things that, while All Saints was made the occasion for a dance with much drinking of wine and toasting of chestnuts, All Souls, the feast of the dead, was passed over, except that a *candil* or oil-lamp was kept lit all night for every deceased member of the family. No visits were made to the cemetery, as in other parts of Spain, no wreaths deposited on tombs. The living village alone was real, and the dead were not long remembered.

The last festival of the year was Christmas. Everyone went to the *misa del gallo*, or midnight mass, and then stayed quietly at home. It was the solstice. The only special feature was the appearance of that disagreeable noise-making instrument, the *zambomba*. This consists of a piece of rabbit-skin or goat-skin drawn tightly across the mouth of a broken flowerpot or drainpipe: a stick is inserted through the skin and, after the hand has been wetted, is pushed up and down, so that it gives out a half-squeaking, half-moaning sound. The sexual significance is obvious, and no doubt it was originally intended as a magical rite to give strength to the declining sun. In Yegen it was chiefly the young men who performed upon it and, when girls were present, they did so with a conscious gusto, and among much tittering and laughter. In the towns it has now sunk to being a children's toy.

In Cádiar and in some villages, however, Christmas was celebrated in the old style, by dances that took place after dark on the roofs of the houses. Fires were lit, parties of young men and girls toasted chestnuts and played on the *zambomba* and then danced holding hands in a circle and singing. These dances were known as the *remelinos* or *remolinos*—that is, whirling dances. On the Feast of the Purification of the Virgin on 2 February, they held them again and ate *rosetas* or popcorn, and this continued every fine night till Carnival. Once upon a time these dances had been held at Yegen too, but they had been given up because it was said that they damaged the roofs.

The weeks around Christmas were always fine and sunny. The violets were in flower on the banks, and a little white plant like candytuft. The usual windless calm prevailed. Then the women went out to the olive groves to pick the last crop of the year, and before long the cold winds and rain that marked our two months' winter began. In the streets below my house the ivy came into flower, and every time I went out in the sunshine I smelt it.

George Gordon, Lord Byron

(1 7 8 8 – 1 8 2 4)

Byron's fame as a poet has almost been eclipsed by his reputation as a lover of both men and women. His parents separated before his birth, and his mother raised him in Scotland until 1798, when the death of his great-uncle made him the sixth Baron Byron. By the time he went to Cambridge University at the age of seventeen, he had already been seduced by his nurse. He had affairs with choirboys, his half sister, a cousin, his best friend's sister-in-law, and a married countess. When he was in Venice he claimed to have had 200 affairs with 200 different women in 200 nights.

Byron did not feel comfortable in England. He once said that "the only virtue they honor in England is hypocrisy." In 1809 he set out on his first long tour outside the country. He and his friend from Cambridge, John Cam Hobhouse, traveled through Spain, Portugal, and Turkey for two years. Byron's letters are extremely vivid, and it is clear that the Mediterranean experience changed his life. He returned to England, wrote his most famous poem, "Childe Harold's Pilgrimage" (1812), married—disastrously—and separated. The English public turned against Byron for his profligate ways, and he left forever in 1816.

Byron settled first in Geneva with Percy Bysshe Shelley, his wife, Mary, and Mary's half sister, Claire Clairmont. Claire became Byron's mistress, bore his child—and was abandoned by him. Byron moved on to Italy and his most endur-ing relationship, with the Countess Guiccioli, married to a man several times her age. While in Italy he worked for Italian independence, but was eventually bored with the countess, her country, and the cause. In 1821 he embraced Greek lib-eration and armed a brig to join the fight. Byron died in 1824 of a chill caught in an open boat. His heart was buried in Greece and his body returned to England. Westminister Abbey refused to bury it, and he was interred in Newstead Abbey. On hearing of his death, Alfred Lord Tennyson, then fourteen, said that when Byron died "the whole world seemed darkened to me."

This letter was written by Byron to his mother in 1809. The reader can spec-ulate if Byron was as virtuous as his letter implies. The three-foot strand of hair given to him by Donna Josepha is preserved in the relics of his publisher, John Murray.

LORD BYRON: LETTER TO HIS MOTHER

[TO MRS. CATHERINE GORDON BYRON]

Gibraltar
August 11th. 1809

Dear Mother,—I have been so much occupied since my departure from England that till I could address you a little at length, I have forborn writing altogether.—As I have now passed through Portugal & a considerable part of Spain, & have leisure at this place I shall endeavor to give you a short detail of my movements.—We sailed from Falmouth on the 2d. of July, reached Lisbon after a very favourable passage of four days and a half, and took up our abode for a time in that city.—It has been often described without being worthy of description, for, except the view from the Tagus which is beautiful, and some fine churches & convents it contains little but filthy streets & more filthy inhabitants.—To make amends for this the village of Cintra about fifteen miles from the capitol is perhaps in every respect the most delightful in Europe, it contains beauties of every description natural & artificial, Palaces and gardens rising in the midst of rocks, cataracts, and precipices, convents on stupendous heights a distant view of the sea and the Tagus, and besides (though that is a secondary consideration) is remarkable as the scene of Sir H[ew] D[alrymple]'s convention.—It unites in itself all the wildness of the Western Highlands with the verdure of the South of France. Near this place about 10 miles to the right is the palace of Mafra the boast of Portugal, as it might be of any country, in point of magnificence without elegance, there is a convent annexed, the monks who possess large revenues are courteous enough, & understand Latin, so that we had a long conversation, they have a large Library & asked [me?] if the *English* had *any books* in their country.— I sent my baggage & part of the servants by sea to Gibraltar, and travelled on horseback from Aldea Gallega (the first stage from Lisbon which is only accessible by water) to Seville (one of the most famous cities in Spain where the Government called the Junta is now held) the distance to Seville is nearly four hundred miles & to Cádiz about 90 further towards the Coast.—I had orders from the Government & every possible accommodation on the road, as an English nobleman in an English uniform is a very respectable personage in Spain at present. The horses are remarkably good, and the roads (I assure you upon my honour for you will hardly believe it) very far superior to the best British roads, without the smallest toll or turnpike, you will suppose this when I rode post to Seville in four days, through this parching country in the midst of summer, without fatigue or annoyance.—Seville is a beautiful town, though the streets are narrow they are clean, we lodged in the house of two Spanish unmarried ladies, who possess *six* houses in Seville, and gave me a curious specimen of Spanish manners.—They are women of character, and the eldest a fine woman, the youngest pretty but not so good a figure as Donna Josepha, the freedom of women which is general here astonished me not a little, and in the course of further observation I find that reserve is not the characteristic of the Spanish belles, who are in general very handsome, with large black eyes, and very fine forms.—The eldest honoured your *unworthy* son with a very particular attention, embracing him with great tenderness at parting (I was there but 3 days) after cutting off a lock of his hair, & presenting him with one of her own about three feet in length, which I send, and beg you will retain till my return—Her last words were "Adio tu hermoso! me gusto mucho" "Adieu, you pretty fellow you please me much."—She offered a share of her apartment which my *virtue* induced me to decline, she laughed and said I had some English "Amante" (lover), and added that she was going to be married to an officer in the Spanish army.—I left Seville and rode on to Cádiz! through a beautiful country, at Xeres where the Sherry we drink is made I met a great merchant a Mr. Gordon of Scotland, who was extremely polite and favoured me with the Inspection of his vaults & cellars, so that I quaffed at the Fountain head.—Cádiz, sweet Cádiz! is the most delightful town I ever beheld, very different from our English cities in every respect except cleanliness (and it is as clean as London) but still beautiful and full of the finest women in Spain, the

Cádiz belles being the Lancashire witches of their land.—Just as I was introduced and began to like the grandees I was forced to leave it for this cursed place, but before I return to England I will visit it again.—The night before I left it, I sat in the box at the opera with Admiral Cordova's family, he is the commander whom Ld. St. Vincent defeated in 1797, and has an aged wife and a fine daughter.— Signorita Cordova the girl is very pretty in the Spanish style, in my opinion by no means inferior to the English in charms, and certainly superior in fascination.—Long black hair, dark languishing eyes, *clear* olive complexions, and forms more graceful in motion than can be conceived by an Englishman used to the drowsy listless air of his countrywomen, added to the most becoming dress & at the same time the most decent in the world, render a Spanish beauty irresistible. I beg leave to observe that Intrigue here is the business of life, when a woman marries she throws off all restraint, but I believe their conduct is chaste enough before.—If you make a proposal which in England would bring a box on the ear from the meekest of virgins, to a Spanish girl, she thanks you for the honour you intend her, and replies "wait till I am married, & I shall be too happy."— This is literally & strictly true.—Miss C[ordova] & her little brother understood a little French, and after regretting my ignorance of the Spanish she proposed to become my preceptress in that language; I could only reply by a low bow, and express my regret that I quitted Cádiz too soon to permit me to make the progress which would doubtless attend my studies under so charming a directress; I was standing at the back of the box which resembles our opera boxes (the theatre is large and finely decorated, the music admirable) in the manner which Englishmen generally adopt for fear of incommoding the ladies in front, when this fair Spaniard dispossessed an old woman (an aunt or a duenna) of her chair and commanded me to be seated next to herself, at a tolerable distance from her mamma.—At the close of the performance I withdrew and was lounging with a party of men in the passage, when "en passant" the Lady turned round and called me, & I had the honour of attending her to the Admiral's mansion.—I have an invitation on my return to Cádiz which I shall accept, if I repass through the country on my way from Asia.—I have met Sir John Carr Knight errant at Seville & Cádiz, he is a pleasant man.—I like the Spaniards much, you have heard of the battle near Madrid, & in England they will call it a victory, a pretty victory! two hundred officers and 5,000 men killed all English, and the French in as great force as ever.—I should have joined the army but we have no time to lose before we get up the Mediterranean & Archipelago,—I am going over to Africa tomorrow, it is only six miles from this Fortress.—My next stage is Cagliari in Sardinia where I shall be presented to his S[ardinian] Majesty, I have a most superb uniform as a court dress, indispensable in travelling.—

Billy Collins

(1 9 4 1 –)

Former poet laureate Billy Collins is often greeted by audiences of the sort usually reserved for rock stars. Hundreds of people turn up to hear him read poetry that Collins himself says is "suburban, it's domestic, it's middle class and it's sort of unashamedly that." One critic wrote, "In his poems, we're constantly recognizing bits and pieces of our lives, uncanny insights gleaned from passing thoughts and articulated with luminous compassion."

Collins was born in New York City and classically educated by Jesuits. He has been an academic for most of his life and still teaches English at Lehrman College at the City University of New York. His work has been featured in *Poetry*, *American Scholar*, *Harper's*, and *The Paris Review*, and his collections include *Nine Horses* (2002) and *The Art of Drowning* (1995). When he was appointed Poet Laureate in 2001, he brought the sensibilities of an educator to the job. "One of my ambitions as poet laureate was to bring high school students a quick exposure to very contemporary poetry. I don't think they hear those voices in the classroom."

In this poem, "Candle Hat," Collins imagines the painter Goya wearing a hat of his own invention, one with candles stuck into the brim so that his work would be illuminated after dark. Central to the verse is not Goya's fame, nor the allusions to the work of other painters like Cézanne, Van Gogh, and Rembrandt, but the lovely image of Goya and his wife laughing at their private joke. That domestic image is pure Billy Collins.

CANDLE HAT

In most self-portraits it is the face that dominates:
Cézanne is a pair of eyes swimming in brushstrokes,
Van Gogh stares out of a halo of swirling darkness,

Rembrandt looks relieved as if he were taking a breather
from painting The Blinding of Sampson.

But in this one Goya stands well back from the mirror
and is seen posed in the clutter of his studio
addressing a canvas tilted back on a tall easel.

He appears to be smiling out at us as if he knew
we would be amused by the extraordinary hat on his head
which is fitted around the brim with candle holders,
a device that allowed him to work into the night.

You can only wonder what it would be like
to be wearing such a chandelier on your head
as if you were a walking dining room or concert hall.

But once you see this hat there is no need to read
any biography of Goya or to memorize his dates.

To understand Goya you only have to imagine him
lighting the candles one by one, then placing
the hat on his head, ready for a night of work.

Imagine him surprising his wife with his new invention,
the laughing like a birthday cake when she saw the glow.

Imagine him flickering through the rooms of his house
with all the shadows flying across the walls.

Imagine a lost traveler knocking on his door
one dark night in the hill country of Spain.
"Come in," he would say, "I was just painting myself,"
as he stood in the doorway holding up the wand of a brush,
illuminated in the blaze of his famous candle hat.

E. E. Cummings

(1894–1962)

Edward Estlin Cummings considered himself as much a visual artist as a poet. Usually he painted during the day and wrote at night. Cummings's creativity was encouraged by his liberal and indulgent parents. Raised in Cambridge, Massachusetts, he graduated from Harvard, where he delivered a challenging commencement address on modernism in the arts. He and his fellow student and friend John Dos Passos worked on a school newspaper, *The Harvard Monthly*, together.

World War I interrupted Cummings's postcollege explorations, and he went to France as a volunteer for the ambulance corps. It was his first exposure to Paris, a city with which he would have a lifelong love affair. After the war he returned to France and joined many American writers and artists in the Bohemian life. When he returned to New York in 1924, he found himself famous; his old classmate John Dos Passos had found a publisher for his two books of poetry: *The Enormous Room* and *Tulips and Chimneys* (both published in 1923). Cummings returned to Europe to work as a writer and artist for *Vanity Fair* and during his travels in the 1920s and 1930s met one of his artistic idols, Pablo Picasso. Politically left-wing, Cummings went to Russia in 1931 and detailed his experiences in his travel book *Eimi* (1933).

Cummings was always more popular with the public than the critics. Despite what appeared to be an avant-garde style, his poems were actually quite simple, direct, and lyrical. He was influenced by modernists like Gertrude Stein, Ezra Pound, and Amy Lowell, but much of his poetry has a recognizable sonnet structure of fourteen lines. Its most revolutionary element is the lack of punctuation or capitalization. Although Cummings's name is often written in lowercase, it was not his doing. A publisher liked the lowercase form on a cover design and the conceit stuck. However, Cummings himself always wrote his signature with capital letters.

PICASSO

Picasso
you give us things
which
bulge: grunting lungs pumped full of sharp thick mind

you make us shrill
presents always
shut in the sumptuous screech of
simplicity

(out of the
black unbunged
Something gushes vaguely a squeak of planes
or

between squeals of
Nothing grabbed with circular shrieking tightness
solid screams whispers.)
Lumberman of the Distinct

your brain's
axe only chops hugest inherent
Trees of Ego, from
whose living and biggest

bodies lopped
of every
prettiness

you hew form truly

John Dos Passos

(1896–1970)

Novelist, reporter, and artist, John Dos Passos arrived in Spain right after his graduation from Harvard. For three months he studied art, architecture, and literature. His trip was interrupted by the death of his father, a famous corporate attorney. Dos Passos returned to Europe in 1917 and, along with Hemingway and E. E. Cummings, joined the ambulance corps, serving in France and Italy. After the war, he returned to Spain, this time for eight months. Spain fueled Dos Passos's writing, and he produced essays, travel writing, and poetry, including a series called "Winter in Castile" (of which the first four of twenty-seven poems are reproduced here), published in his book *Pushcart at the Curb* (1922).

Dos Passos returned to the United States in the 1920s and became known for both his experimental writing (often compared to the cinematic style of a newsreel) and his political activism. He campaigned against the death sentences of Sacco and Vanzetti and spent several months in Russia studying communism. His political involvement did not slow his literary production: in the 1930s his major work, a trilogy (*The 42nd Parallel*, 1930; *1919*, 1932; and *The Big Money*, 1936), known collectively as *U.S.A.*, was published. But Dos Passos's politics were changing.

In 1933 he signed a contract to write a book about Spain, and he took a short trip there, curtailed by a bout of rheumatic fever. He wrote to his editor, "Things in Spain are not as interesting as I'd thought." Despite his misgivings, he joined his old friend Hemingway during the civil war (Hemingway called him "Dos"). Finally, he revealed his growing conservatism and what he felt were the shortcomings of the left in a series of articles. He lost many friends and readers. Although he continued writing until his death, Dos Passos never regained the popularity of his youth. The publication of John Dos Passos's work by the Library of America renewed interest in one of the least-remembered writers of the Lost Generation of the 1920s.

From PUSHCART AT THE CURB

WINTER IN CASTILE

The promiscuous wind wafts idly from the quays
A smell of ships and curious woods and casks
And a sweetness from the gorse on the flowerstand
And brushes with his cool careless cheek the cheeks
Of those on the street; mine, an old gnarled man's,
The powdered cheeks of the girl who with faded eyes
Stands in the shadow; a sailor's scarred brown cheeks,
And a little child's, who walks along whispering
To her sufficient self.
      O promiscuous wind.
           Bordeaux

I
A long grey street with balconies.
Above the gingercolored grocer's shop
trail pink geraniums
and further up a striped mattress
hangs from a window
and the little wooden cage
of a goldfinch.

Four blind men wabble down the street
with careful steps on the rounded cobbles
scraping with violin and flute
the interment of a tune.

People gather:
women with market-baskets
stuffed with green vegetables,
men with blankets on their shoulders
and brown sunwrinkled faces.

Pipe the flutes, squeak the violins;
four blind men in a row
at the interment of a tune . . .
But on the plate
coppers clink
round brown pennies
a merry music at the funeral,
penny swigs of wine
penny gulps of gin
peanuts and hot roast potatoes
red disks of sausage
trip steaming in the corner shop . . .

And overhead
the sympathetic finch
chirps and trills
approval.
                    Calle de Toledo, Madrid

II
A boy with rolled up shirtsleeves
turns the handle.
Grind, grind.
The black sphere whirls
above a charcoal fire.
Grind, grind.
The boy sweats and grits his teeth and turns
while a man blows up the coals.
Grind, grind.
Thicker comes the blue curling smoke,
the moka-scented smoke
heavy with early morning
and the awakening city
with click-clack click-clack on the cobblestones
and the young winter sunshine
advancing inquisitively

across the black and white tiles of my bedroom floor.
Grind, grind.

Grind, grind.
The coffee is done.
The boy rubs his arms and yawns,
and the sphere and the furnace are trundled away
to be set up at another café.

A poor devil
whose dirty ashen white body shows through his rags
sniffs sensually
with dilated nostrils
the heavy coffee-fragrant smoke,
and turns to sleep again
in the feeble sunlight of the greystone steps.

                              Calle Espoz y Mina

III
Women are selling tuberoses in the square,
and sombre-tinted wreaths
stiffly twined and crinkly
for this is the day of the dead.

Women are selling tuberoses in the square.
Their velvet odor fills the street
somehow stills the tramp of feet;
for this is the day of the dead.

Their presence is heavy about us
like the velvet black scent of the flowers:
incense of pompous interments,
patter of monastic feet,
drone of masses drowsily said
for the thronging dead.

Women are selling tuberoses in the square
to cover the tombs of the envious dead
and shroud them again in the lethean scent
lest the dead should remember.

                    Difuntos; Madrid

IV

Above the scuffling footsteps of crowds
the clang of trams
the shouts of newsboys
the stridence of wheels,
very calm,
floats the sudden trill of a pipe
three silvery upward notes
wistfully quavering,
notes a Thessalian shepherd might have blown
to call his sheep
in the emerald shade
of Tempe,
notes that might have waked the mad women sleeping
among pinecones in the hills
and stung them to headlong joy
of the presence of their mad Iacchos,
notes like the glint of sun
making jaunty the dark waves of Tempe.

In the street an old man is passing
wrapped in a dun brown mantle
blowing with bearded lips on a shining panpipe
while he trundles before him
a grindstone.

The scissors grinder.

                    Calle Espoz y Mina

Lawrence Ferlinghetti

(1919–   )

Lawrence Ferlinghetti may be America's most popular poet, with over one million copies of his best-known work, *A Coney Island of the Mind* (1958), in print. Well into his eighties, Ferlinghetti still runs City Lights Bookstore in San Francisco, which he started over fifty years ago with Peter Martin. It was at City Lights that many of the Beat poets, including Allen Ginsberg, read their work. Ferlinghetti also published many of his friends in the now-famous Pocket Poet Series. Now only Ferlinghetti is left—still writing and still riding his bicycle to the bookstore every day.

Ferlinghetti was born in Yonkers, New York, but was sent to France to live with relatives shortly after his birth. He did not return to the United States until he was five. After fighting in Europe in World War II and graduate work at the Sorbonne, Ferlinghetti settled in San Francisco, a city with which he is inextricably linked. His poetry is characterized by the free-flowing style and political bent of the Beats, but his travel verses are also romantic and lyrical. The following poem, "Seated in the Courtyard in the Alhambra," is from *A Far Rockaway of the Heart* (1997).

In a recent interview Ferlinghetti was asked how he would like to be remembered. "I really can't worry about my reputation. It's a waste of time." He added that an agent had been after him for years to write an autobiography, "but I don't have time to look backward."

From A FAR ROCKAWAY OF THE HEART

#76

In the gardens of the Alhambra
           I stole a small orange and ate it
The pulp dry and bitter

and the juice
(acrid as an arab driven from his land)
made a desert of my mouth
and shriveled up my tongue
in the Sultan's last revenge

And I fell upon the ground
in a deep swoon

Deep as the *duende*
in a gypsy's keening

Kate Field

(1838–1896)

Born to a well-to-do St. Louis family, Mary Katherine Keemle Field tried acting, singing, lecturing, and playwriting before settling on journalism. "Oh, if I were a man!" she said. "There is not an ambition, a desire, a feeling, a thought, an impulse, an instinct that I am not obliged to crush. And why? Because I am a woman, and a woman must content herself with indoor life, with sewing and babies." However, Field was not content with indoor life and became one of the best-known American journalists of the nineteenth century. In 1890 she founded *Kate Field's Washington*, a weekly of sixteen pages that sold for two dollars a year.

Field wrote about women's causes and founded the Cooperative Dress Association in the early 1880s, which not only hired women, but offered reasonable and "more healthful" clothing for women. Perhaps Field's most successful venture was her travel writing, and the public loved her dispatches, recounting her adventures as a woman traveling solo. She wrote that she went to Spain by accident, having missed her stop in Biarritz. "I was frightened and am not ashamed of the confession. Night had set in, a storm of wind and rain spread a wild gloom over a country of which I had no knowledge, and there was no return train until very late . . . I saw an admirable opportunity for brigands and all the other horrors told in story-books that I hardly enjoyed the novelty of the dramatic situation." Despite being warned about Spain by her fellow travelers and without a passport ("I had no need of a passport. I was a woman. It was satisfactory to be assured of my sex."), Field acquires a servant and guide whom she calls "the Blinker." Kate Field and the Blinker's adventures in Spain were published as *Ten Days in Spain* (1875), from which this is excerpted.

From TEN DAYS IN SPAIN

A Child of the Escorial.—Spain's Eighth Wonder of the World.
—The Tagus.—Toledo's Streets and only Hotel.—Mental Dyspepsia.
—Frozen Music.—The Toledan Cathedral and Alcazar.—A Carlist.

I might have had two comfortable days at Madrid for the study of
Velasquez and Murillo, had not public opinion been too much for
me. When Castelar asked whether I were going to Andalusia, where
he was born, and I answered, "No," he said I would see nothing of
Spain. I knew it; but, not having visited Spain to become acquainted
with the country, I bore up under the President's astonished gaze.
Seville was far away, comparatively, and I could defy criticism con-
cerning it; but when the Escorial and Toledo were mentioned, my
courage oozed out at the pores. Both were too near Madrid to be
ignored, and I "did" them on successive days. First came the Escorial—built by Herrera, "architect of *ennui*"—the eighth wonder of
the world according to Spanish criticism; the monstrous conception
of that tyrant, monk, and hypochondriac, Philip II, according to my
own. I am not Murray. I don't propose to furnish information that
will be of the slightest use to the most inexperienced traveller. All I
shall relate is what stuck to me like burrs after the guide had poured
the entire Escorial into my aching ears. And he was an excellent
guide, mark you. He had a conscience. His father had been a guide
before him. He was, as it were, a child of the Escorial, and felt that
the eyes of the Bourbons were upon him. He made shoes in the dull
season, but all seasons were dull nowadays, he said, and it was very
hard to provide for his family. He didn't know how the war would
end, for his part. He was quite tired of commotion. He would like an
intelligent government that educated the people. Whatever happened, he should submit. That which most concerned him was the
welfare of his wife and children.

I did my utmost to excite the guide, but I might as well have
attempted to make the Escorial dance. There was a repose about him
that would have done credit to the remains of Philip II. Perpetual
contact with dead kings seemed to have wrought a spell upon him.

On his brow I read "All is vanity." His gait illustrated the dignity of Spain. In his conversation there was such submission to fate as is sometimes visible in very much married men and women. Artemus Ward's best joke could not have undermined his gravity.

"Tell me," I said, "are all the inhabitants of this place as serious as you?"

"There are but a few hundred, Señora. We are all more or less connected with the Escorial. Our lives are quiet. We are poor. What is there to laugh at? We behave ourselves. The jail is always empty. In other parts of Spain, men stab one another. Here the knife is unknown. The only instance of crime I remember is recent. Two small and valuable paintings were stolen, and, as their custodian could not account for their disappearance, he has been imprisoned, but not here. He was sent to Madrid. When people want bread, Señora, they cannot think of much else."

Was it not my turn to be serious?

Five long hours I wandered over the great, yellow, barren, gloomy building, resting only on the finely carved bench in the church choir, where Philip II used to sit.

"He sat here," said the guide, "because a secret door communicates with it. He could come and go without being observed, and so he kept the monks on the alert, I assure you. They treated themselves tenderly, nevertheless. The seats, you perceive, turn down. This is in order to afford standing-room when their occupants rise; but those monks did not like being on their feet. You remark the shelves arranged above the seats? On them the monks sat while appearing to stand up. Ah, ah! this is very shrewd, very ingenious." And the guide almost smiled. It was such an attempt at a smile as becomes funerals.

The guide was a good Catholic, but he entertained very little regard for priests. In this, however, he is not peculiar. "Our religion is one thing, our clergy quite another," assert all the Latin Catholics I know. "We don't wish to become Protestants. All we desire is that our church shall mind its legitimate business, and not interfere with temporal affairs."

A granite gridiron, covering a regular parallelogram of 200 metres, containing 1,010 outside windows, consuming twenty-one years in construction, costing unknown millions of francs, arising in the midst of an arid, mountainous wilderness—for what? To celebrate the miserable pride and bigotry of a bad king. Thank Heaven, even Spain can never repeat the enormous, hideous burlesque of the Escorial. Apart from harboring a few paintings and a library of rare books, art gains nothing by it; and the time is not far distant when Madrid will claim both books and canvas. On the ground-floor of one wing can still be seen half a dozen old masters, one of which, a Rubens, so delighted the present Emperor of Brazil that he offered to build a fine hospital in exchange for it; but the government did not dare to entertain the proposition. In the dark corner of an obscure room I was shown an unframed portrait of Isabella Segunda. "We put her here, Señora, to have her out of harm's way; otherwise she would be cut to pieces." In a neighboring gallery stood a clever wooden statue of St. Michael overcoming the Devil. "That has a history," said the guide. "It is the work of a very talented female sculptor. St. Michael's face is her own. Handsome, was she not? Satan's face is her husband's. Her lover was the king whose portrait hangs opposite, and the eyes of which are fixed upon St. Michael. If you write, Señora, behold good material!"

Of course I visited the dark den once inhabited by Philip II. Of course I sat on the two chairs dedicated to his gout—Summer and Winter. Both were as hard as the monarch's heart; and then, by the aid of a tallow candle, I descended to the octagonal crypt where repose the mortal remains of twenty-six Spanish kings and queens. Cold, cold, almost as cold as the dead, I read the names of Charles V, Philip II, and Philip IV. I saw five empty shelves, and I predicted that not more than one would ever be occupied. "You'll have little more royalty to stow away," I said to the guide.

"I do not say you are wrong, Señora, but who can tell? You've no idea what a people we are! Anything may happen to-morrow."

"Mañana." There it was again.

The Royal Gridiron has many corners. I do believe I went into every one of them. Church and palace were "done" religiously, and when, dragging one slow leg after the other, I finally reached the station, in default of chairs I dropped into a wheelbarrow and asked to be let alone.

"It is well, Señora," remarked the guide; "you have walked twenty miles."

"It is not the walking, Mr. Guide, it is the miles I have stood up. How many are they?"

Strangely enough the guide could not tell me. The Blinker attempted to make a remark, but, as usual, threw no light upon the subject; and, when the Madrid train arrived, only an hour late, I crawled into a compartment, feeling as though I had supported the dome of the Escorial ever since its existence.

"Long life to you, Señora. I hope I have given you satisfaction," exclaimed the guide. Satisfaction! He had given me such an amount that I ached from head to foot. I knew so much as to hope never to know anything again. Fortunately "cramming" escapes into thin air, otherwise sight-seers would blow themselves up in a manner calculated to terrify high-pressure steamboats.

Being quite alive the next morning, the Blinker and I started at six o'clock for Toledo. The amount of effort required to leave my bed, and, as usual, go without breakfast, drew so largely on my moral courage that I felt another such call would kill me. In flying to evils that you know not of there is the bliss of ignorance, but in deliberately embracing slow torture there is not even the satisfaction of novelty. Between travelling on a snail's back and a Spanish railroad there is little choice, saving in matter of accommodation. The road to Toledo is no better than that of the North, while the scenery is infinitely worse. Flat and uncultivated, the country seemed branded with a curse, and not until we arrived at Aranjuez, half-way between Madrid and Toledo, did life begin to assert itself. Having no curiosity to inspect the "Spanish Fontainebleau," where once stood a temple of Jupiter—Ara Jovis, hence Aranjuez—I accepted it on faith, contenting myself with glimpses of that "mighty river," the Tagus, 375 miles long, yet so inhospitable as to receive few towns upon its banks and to welcome no commerce upon its waters. No sensation could be extracted from it. Mud is mud, though called Tagus, and if I must gaze upon rivers of it, give me my own, my native Mississippi.

At noon I saw a city set on a hill. We stopped. It was Toledo. Leaving the cars at a ragged station and running the gantlet of beggars—there were twenty beggars to three passengers, giving us six beggars and two thirds of a beggar apiece—we took refuge in a remarkable vehicle, courteously called an omnibus, the only public conveyance known to Toledo. Passenger No. 3 hobnobbed with the Blinker, and exhibited a curiosity regarding our movements that would have brought a blush to even a Yankee cheek. The driver, a man of immense stature, scowled at us for not being more numerous, and, with a round oath and much snapping of his long whip, started his four mules up the hill. Why Spanish mules should wear bells, and why they should require so much beating, I don't know, but they certainly get a deal of both. Every saint in the calendar was called upon by the driver to witness the ingratitude, the obstinacy, the total depravity, of those animated mules, that I thought were exerting themselves to pieces. Through clouds of dust we whirled over the bridge of Alcantara, thrown across the deep-set, winding Tagus, up a second steep hill, in and out of the narrowest, queerest, quaintest, most impossible streets, under an archway, and then we found ourselves at the Fonda de Lino, the only hotel the guide-books dare to mention.

"First I want something to eat, and then I want the guide Cabezas," said I to the proprietor, on descending from the noble omnibus.

"You can't have Cabezas," replied the ever-important Blinker, "because he is dead."

"How do you know?"

"Because he was buried shortly after my last visit to Toledo."

"Who says I'm dead? I'm nothing of the sort. I'm as alive as he, Señora." And up hobbled a withered old man, who was no other than Cabezas himself.

It is not pleasant to be told you are dead and buried before you have stopped breathing. Cabezas looked cross, but the Blinker received him with a pitying smile, as if to say, "I accept your apology for being alive, but don't do it again, my old fellow. You ought to be dead, you know. Be sure you are so before I return."

Though alive and hobbling, Cabezas, who knows every nail and stone of Toledo, could not accompany me in my tour of the tortuous old town, "because you see, Señora, there are two guides and very little to do. You are the first foreigner we have had for a month. We divide the work. I went last, so the other guide, who is good, must go with you."

Colonel John Hay, in his charming "Castilian Days," the atmosphere of which is as clear and bright as Castile itself, advises travellers to ignore guides at Toledo; nevertheless, if Colonel Hay had but a few hours to devote to many centuries, I think he would hire the fastest possible engine to rush through them. Who can saunter with one eye on a watch and the other on a railroad?

If the Fonda de Lino be a specimen of Toledan housekeeping, I am not surprised that the number of inhabitants has been reduced from 200,000 to 17,000. The marvel is that anybody can be prevailed upon to remain over night, or, remaining, does not die before morning. The longer I live the more amazed I become at the quantities of people in existence. Ushered into the eating-room, I sat before a table at which several Spaniards were devouring knives and pork. Not being able to digest either, I ordered beefsteak, and tea, whereupon the Spaniards nudged one another and said, "English!" When the steak came I shuddered. It was very thin, very stringy, very young, had been fried, and was flavored with vinegar. The bread was sour, and the tea! well, it was that pink kind of tea, found only in Italy and Spain, which tastes like some unknown medicine and excites a mild form of nausea as it goes down. Pounds would not make it strong enough to come up again.

Thus fortified, I began my pilgrimage. Guidebooks state that it requires a year to become acquainted with Toledo. More exacting still, M. Villa Amil declares that after studying its treasures nine months you know nothing about them. This is encouraging to a traveller on the wing, particularly after being presented with a monograph entitled *Toledo en la mano*, in two volumes of 1,550 pages. After this "handful" I gave up trying to know anything about Toledo. All I can say is that I was introduced to the town with much ceremony, and have an indefinite idea of its features, which are such a mixture of Goth, Moor, Jew, and Christian that, at the end of six hours, I suffered from as acute an indigestion as though I had swallowed an architectural mince-pie. If I lived in Toledo I should go mad. The conjunction of so much history, so much live art, and so much dead nature would set my brain on fire with conundrums. There is nothing more tragic than living among great things and little people. The very air is heavy with hopeless age, and stifles with every breath. I

never felt so thankful for America as while walking through those
narrow Toledan streets, every stone of which could tell tales of
bloodshed and violence. The wildest Western settlement, populated
with the most discouraging stumps, became in my eyes a far more tolerable home. Meditation belongs to the past, aspiration to the future.
There is more hope in a pioneer's log-cabin than in all Toledo's monuments, and, platitude or no platitude, I must ask, What is life worth
without hope? Time, that has reduced the "city of the Visigoths"
from great riches to pauperism, may bring about a still more wondrous revolution, but Time's wheel turns slowly in dead latitudes.
Before this change takes place, all Europe will be republican, Spain's
deserts will become oases, and the United States will be governed by
its best and honestest brains. After—the millennium!

Touching both sides of the streets with my hands, I was first taken
to a beautiful Moorish house, now the residence of a banker. "Look,"
said the guide, and as I entered the great door I saw a modern carriage. "It is the only carriage in town, Señora, and when the banker's
family drive they go round and round the square." As the square is
very small and exceedingly crowded, this dissipation in horse-flesh
must be excessive. However, the satisfaction of doing what nobody
else can afford may compensate for unparalleled monotony.

Not to admire Moorish architecture is to be incapable of appreciation. Its sad, solemn beauty and exquisite taste made me think of
minor keys, and how truly Madame de Stael had called architecture
"frozen music." Chopin's dreamiest nocturnes and reveries came
into my head, and then harmony would be disturbed by contact with
great Gothic pillars or portals. Thus it happened that all through the
town my nerves were shocked by discords—Goth and Jew rudely
jostling the Moor, who alone preserved the dignity of repose, as if
conscious of superior art. Through sight my ear was charmed one
moment to be tortured the next, and I quickly found another reason
for preferring the backwoods to Toledo. What musician can endure
false notes? Thus tortured, I sympathized with Gautier and Irving in
their lamentations over the downfall of the Moors. "For my part,"
says the Frenchman, "I've always regretted that the Moors did not
remain masters of Spain, which has only lost by their expulsion."
"They deserved this beautiful country," writes the American. "They

won it bravely; they enjoyed it generously and kindly. . . . I am at times almost ready to join in sentiment with a worthy friend and countryman of mine, whom I met in Malaga, who swears the Moors are the only people that ever deserved the country, and prays to heaven they may come over from Africa and conquer it again." Who knows but they may? Stranger things have happened; and why do the Moors jealously cherish the keys belonging to their old homes, if it be not with the hope of some time turning them in the rusty locks?

The queer turns, the sharp corners (now rounded) in the streets, were for what? For fighting. Ah, well, the world is not perfect, but, in spite of architecture and sculpture, I don't think it has retrograded. From ruin to ruin, from beggar to beggar, from church to church, we passed into the cathedral, two hundred and fifty years in building, costing the architect, Pedro Perez, fifty years of his life. What modern architect would give his existence to one work? Nothing but the patience of genius can so dedicate itself. Though very noble, there is much that is theatrical about the interior of the building. As in most Spanish cathedrals, the choir, being in the centre, destroys the grandeur of the *coup-d'oeil*. The severe simplicity of the Cologne cathedral is infinitely more impressive, but I dared not say so, for Toledo is as dependent upon its cathedral as the play of "Hamlet" is upon the melancholy Dane.

Obstructive though it be, the choir is a marvel of ingenuity in itself, the three rows of wooden stalls carved by Philippe de Bourgogne et de Berruguete being marvels of ingenuity. The art—Gothic bordering upon the Renaissance—cannot be called sacred, unless monkeys pursuing their own tails, and the strangest of unknown animals in the most ludicrous of poses, exhale a religious atmosphere; but, as carving, it is irreproachable. While I sat in the archbishop's stall the custodian showed me a great gash on his head, received two years before, from two men, who felled him to the floor, bound him, and then robbed the church of jewels. They were afterwards arrested, recognized, and imprisoned.

"Ever since the blow I've been deaf," said the custodian.

"Yes; and when those rascals come out of prison they will kill you," rejoined my guide. "Better to have made no struggle and given no alarm. Your hearing will go from bad to worse."

The good-natured custodian shrugged his shoulders, and seemed content to have done his duty. How many victims to virtue are? Would the sacristan allow us to see the *custodia* of gilded silver with a "*richesse inouie*" of ornament, inlaid with diamonds and emeralds, costing three generations of artists a century's labor, the Virgin's mantle containing eighty-five thousand pearls?

"No," replied the sacristan, looking very hard at me. "A woman tried to steal some of the jewels recently."

I did not feel crushed by the imputation, because I knew a valuable *douceur* was what the sacristan wanted. I would not allow the Blinker to give it, and so I was a thief in disguise. How that sacristan scowled when we walked away, and how I wanted to devote those useless jewels to redeeming Toledo from dirt and ignorance!

In his "Handful" of Toledo, M. Parros devotes 745 pages to the cathedral. Do you think then that I dare touch an inexhaustible subject? I will not even mention the Virgin Mary's appearance to St. Ildefonso, nor speak of a Toledan masterpiece, the Puerta del Sol, but will ask you to gaze at a unique scene from the top of the long-unfinished Alcazar, which stands on the highest point of the town. Toledo lay sleeping at my feet, and the lazy Tagus wound around it like a horseshoe. Thankful that sight-seeing was off my mind and legs—six hours had all three been tramping—I gave myself up to the quiet delight of breathing the soft, pure air that fanned us. It was a fine picture—Toledo with its quaint, gray towers, turrets, and cathedral dome, and the naked russet hills that lost their look of poverty and desolation in their reflected glow of rich, warm sunshine.

"Is Toledo healthy?" I asked the guide.

"Not very, Señora. We have fevers because we have no drainage, and the river is very low and poisonous in summer. No one dares drink it."

Politically Toledo is the Faubourg St. Germain of Castile. Its brains, like its monuments, are in ruins, and cling to the past, the dearest souvenir of which is Carlism. Still seeking my Republican, I thought he might be found in an intelligent guide, but the guide shook his head.

"No, Señora, I am a Carlist. Have you remarked the deep gash on my face? That is a trophy of which I am proud. I got it fighting for the

Carlists. And there are other wounds about my person. Now I'm too old to fight. One of our principal citizens raised a company of two hundred volunteers about ten days ago and went off to join Don Carlos. They didn't all leave at once, you know. The deed was accomplished gradually, and the men wore their ordinary clothes. But before starting the Carlists did us great service. The country about here had been infested with brigands. The Carlists planned an expedition and captured twenty-seven of them. Now we take long breaths. There are Carlists in disguise among the mountains here, acting as spies upon the government and upon brigands. Republicans will tell you that Carlists are bandits, but don't you believe it, Señora. They are gentlemen. We've a fine lot of Republicans in Toledo. They threaten to destroy the town. What did they do a month ago but attempt to burn down our glorious cathedral! Think of that! But our best people heard of the plot, and frustrated it by surrounding the cathedral before the arrival of the incendiaries. They can't do that sort of thing, you know. We won't endure it."

"But surely these men are not Republicans like Castelar. They do not support the government."

"No; they are Intransigentes. The government Republicans behave very well; only we don't like them. We want our King."

The setting sun warned us of the approaching train, and we sauntered back to the omnibus, taking *en route* an old curiosity-shop. There were Toledo blades made in Sheffield that I refused to buy, notwithstanding the Maid of Saragossa wrought upon the handles. I contented myself with bearing off a noble Moorish nail, and then learned how an appreciative Frenchman had recently bought several hundred of these unique nails with which to stud the great doors of his new Parisian hotel. Toledo is a paradise of *bric-à-brac*. When I make my fortune writing for newspapers, I shall follow the Frenchman's example, and hitting the right nail on the head, ask for Moor!

How I enjoyed that return trip to Madrid! We were only three hours behind time, and the dinner-party I was to have joined at nine o'clock did coldly furnish forth a midnight supper-table, at which the guests were as conversational as blinking owls.

Richard Ford

(1796–1858)

Almost every travel writer in Spain during the last two centuries references the work of Richard Ford, author of one of that country's first guidebooks. He not only advised his fellow Englishmen about their trips, but produced five hundred drawings and watercolors to accompany his notebooks. Ford was an accidental tourist—he and his wife, Harriet, moved to Seville in 1831, hoping that the warmer climate would improve Harriet's fragile health. They moved into buildings adjacent to the then-dilapidated Alhambra, the same quarters that had been occupied by Washington Irving a few years before. Several times during their tenure Ford set out alone to explore the Peninsula, including visits to Madrid, Salamanca, and Santiago de Compostela. He later wrote that these arduous solitary expeditions were "the equivalent to serving in a campaign."

But it was not until he left Spain that Ford considered turning his notebooks into a travel guide. Twelve years after his departure, John Murray published *A Handbook for Travellers in Spain* (1846), one of their travel series. Ford's work in two volumes totaling 1,064 pages was encyclopedic. *Handbook* cost thirty shillings, a high price at the time, and sold 1,800 copies in its first year. Buoyed by the success of the *Handbook*, Murray commissioned *Gatherings from Spain*, a shorter, less formal book based on material excised from the *Handbook*. Ford suggested to his publisher that the new volume be "plums from the handbook" prepared with "much more yeast in the dough & the cake prepared more in the puffpaste style than the rich plum." In his preface to *Gatherings from Spain*, Ford said that his new book was, in part, a response to female travelers for whom the *Handbook*'s form was too large and the text too small.

In *Gatherings from Spain* (1846), Richard Ford proves an entertaining traveling companion. He advises about geography, cuisine, fashion, customs, and medicine, and devotes an entire chapter to sherry. "The sound principles in Spain sight-seeing are few and simple," he wrote, "but if observed, they will generally prove successful; first, persevere; never be put back, never take an answer if it be in the negative, never lose temper or courteous manners . . ." In this excerpt Ford advises on the rewards and rigors of traveling in Spain on horseback.

From GATHERINGS FROM SPAIN

A man in a public carriage ceases to be a private individual: he is merged into the fare, and becomes a number according to his place; he is booked like a parcel, and is delivered by the guard. How free, how lord and master of himself, does the same dependent gentleman mount his eager barb, who by his neighing and pawing exhibits his joyful impatience to be off too! How fresh and sweet the free breath of heaven, after the frousty atmosphere of a full inside of foreigners, who, from the narcotic effects of tobacco, forget the existence of soap, water, and clean linen! Travelling on horseback, so unusual a gratification to English men, is the ancient, primitive, and once universal mode of travelling in Europe, as it still is in the East; mankind, however, soon gets accustomed to a changed state of locomotion, and forgets how recent is its introduction. Fynes Moryson gave much the same advice two centuries ago to travellers in England, as must be now suggested to those who in Spain desert the coach-beaten highways for the delightful bye-ways, and thus explore the rarely visited, but not the least interesting portions of the Peninsula. It has been our good fortune to perform many of these expeditions on horseback, both alone and in company; and on one occasion to have made the pilgrimage from Seville to Santiago, through Estremadura and Gallicia, returning by the Asturias, Biscay, León, and the Castiles; thus riding nearly two thousand miles on the same horse, and only accompanied by one Andalucian servant, who had never before gone out of his native province. The same tour was afterwards performed by two friends with two servants; nor did they or ourselves ever meet with any real impediments or difficulties, scarcely indeed sufficient of either to give the flavour of adventure or the dignity of danger, to the undertaking. It has also been our lot to make an extended tour of many months, accompanied by an English lady, through Granada, Murcia, Valencia, Catalonia, and Aragon, to say nothing of repeated excursions through every nook and corner of Andalucía. The result of all this experience, combined with that of many friends, who have *ridden over* the Peninsula, enables us to recommend this method to the young, healthy, and adventurous, as by far the most agreeable plan of proceeding; and, indeed, as we have said, as regards two-thirds of the Peninsula, the only practicable course.

The leading royal roads which connect the capital with the principal seaports are, indeed, excellent; but they are generally drawn in a straight line, whereby many of the most ancient cities are thus left out, and these, together with sites of battles and historical incident, ruins and remains of antiquity, and scenes of the greatest natural beauty, are accessible with difficulty, and in many cases only on horseback. Spain abounds with wide tracts which are perfectly unknown to the Geographical Society. Here, indeed, is fresh ground open to all who aspire in these threadbare days to book something new; here is scenery enough to fill a dozen portfolios, and subject enough for a score of quartos. How many flowers pine unbotanized, how many rocks harden ungeologized; what views are dying to be sketched; what bears and deer to be stalked; what trout to be caught and eaten; what valleys expand their bosoms, longing to embrace their visitor; what virgin beauties hitherto unseen await the happy member of the Travellers' Club, who in ten days can exchange the bore of eternal Pall Mall for these untrodden sites; and then what an accession of dignity in thus discovering a terra incognita, and rivalling Mr. Mungo Park! Nor is a guide wanting, since our good friend John Murray, the grand monaque of Handbooks, has proclaimed from Albemarle Street, *Il n'y a plus de Pyrénées.*

As the wide extent of country which intervenes between the radii of the great roads is most indifferently provided with public means of inter-communication; as there is little traffic, and no demand for modern conveyances—even mules and horses are not always to be procured, and we have always found it best to set out on these distant excursions with our own beasts: the comfort and certainty of this precaution have been corroborated beyond any doubt by frequent comparisons with the discomforts undergone by other persons, who trusted to chance accommodations and means of locomotion in ill-provided districts and out-of-the-way excursions: indeed, as a general rule, the traveller will do well to carry with him everything with which from habit he feels that he cannot dispense. The chief object will be to combine in as small a space as possible the greatest quantity of portable comfort, taking care to select the really essential; for there is no worse mistake than lumbering oneself with things that are never wanted. This mode of travelling has not been much detailed by the generality of authors, who have rarely gone much out of the beaten track, or undertaken a long-continued riding tour, and they have been rather inclined to overstate the dangers and difficulties of a plan which they have never tried. At the same time this plan is not to be recommended to fine ladies nor to delicate gentlemen, nor to those who have had a touch of rheumatism, or who tremble at the shadows which coming gout casts before it.

Those who have endurance and curiosity enough to face a tour in Sicily, may readily set out for Spain; rails and post-horses certainly get quicker over the country; but the pleasure of the remembrance and the benefits derived by travel are commonly in an inverse ratio to the ease and rapidity with which the journey is performed. In addition to the accurate knowledge which is thus acquired of the country (for there is no map like this mode of surveying), and an acquaintance with a considerable, and by no means the worst portion of its population, a riding expedition to a civilian is almost equivalent to serving a campaign. It imparts a new life, which is adopted on the spot, and which soon appears quite natural, from being in perfect harmony and fitness with everything around, however strange to all previous habits and notions; it takes the conceit out of a man for the rest of his life—it makes him bear and forbear. It is a capital practical school of moral discipline, just as the hardiest mariners are nurtured in the roughest seas. Then and there will be learnt golden rules of patience, perseverance, good temper, and good fellowship: the individual man must come out, for better or worse. On these occasions, where wealth and rank are stripped of the aids and appurtenances of conventional superiority, a man will draw more on his own resources, moral and physical, than on any letter of credit, his wit will be sharpened by invention-suggesting necessity.

Then and there, when up, about, and abroad, will be shaken off dull sloth; action—Demosthenic action—will be the watchword. The traveller will blot out from his dictionary the fatal Spanish phrase of procrastination *by-and-by*, a street which leads to the house of *never*, for *por la calle de después, se va a la casa de nunca*. Reduced to shift for himself, he will see the evil of waste—the folly of improvidence and want of order. He will whistle to the winds the paltry excuse of idleness, the Spanish *no se puede*, it is impossible. He will soon learn, by grappling with difficulties, how surely they are overcome—how soft as silk becomes the nettle when it is sternly grasped, which would sting the tender-handed touch—how powerful a principle of realising the object proposed, is the moral conviction that we can and will accomplish it. He will never be scared by shadows thin as air, for when one door shuts another opens, and he who pushes on arrives. And after all, a dash of hardship may be endured by those accustomed to loll in easy britzskas, if only for the sake of novelty; what a new relish is given to the palled appetite by a little unknown privation!—hunger being, as Cervantes says, the best of sauces, which, as it never is wanting to the poor, is the reason why eating is their huge delight.

Again, these sorts of independent expeditions are equally conducive to health of body: after the first few days of the new fatigue are got over, the frame becomes of iron, *hecho de bronze*, and the rider, a centaur not fabulous. The living in the pure air, the sustaining excitement of novelty, exercise, and constant occupation, are all sweetened by the willing heart, which renders even labour itself a pleasure; a new and vigorous life is infused into every bone and muscle; early to bed and early to rise, if it does not make all brains wise, at least invigorates the gastric juices, makes a man forget that he has a liver, that storehouse of mortal misery—bile, blue pill, and blue devils. This health is one of the secrets of the amazing charm which seems inherent to this mode of travelling, in spite of all the apparent hardships with which it is surrounded in the abstract. Oh! the delight of this gipsy, Bedouin, nomad life, seasoned with unfettered liberty! We pitch our tent wherever we please, and there we make our home—far from letters "requiring an immediate answer," and distant dining-outs, visits, ladies' maids, band-boxes, butlers, bores, and button-holders.

Escaping from the meshes of the west end of London, we are transported into a new world; every day the out-of-door panorama is varied; now the heart is cheered and the countenance made glad by gazing on plains overflowing with milk and honey, or laughing with oil and wine, where the orange and citron bask in the glorious sunbeams, the palm without the desert, the sugar-cane without the slave. Anon we are lost amid the silence of cloud-capped glaciers, where rock and granite are tost about like the fragments of a broken world, by the wild magnificence of Nature, who, careless of mortal admiration, lavishes with proud indifference her fairest charms where most unseen, her grandest forms where most inaccessible. Every day and everywhere we are unconsciously funding a stock of treasures and pleasures of memory, to be hived in our bosoms like the honey of the bee, to cheer and sweeten our after-life, when we settle down like wine-dregs in our cask, which, delightful even as in the reality, wax stronger as we grow in years, and feel that these feats of our youth, like sweet youth itself, can never be our portion again. Of one thing the reader may be assured—that dear will be to him, as is now to us, the remembrance of those wild and weary rides through tawny Spain, where hardship was forgotten ere undergone: those sweet-aired hills—those rocky crags and torrents—those fresh valleys which communicated their own freshness to the heart—that keen relish for hard fare, gained and seasoned by hunger sauce, which Ude did not invent—those sound slumbers on harder couch, earned by fatigue, the downiest of pillows—the braced nerves—the spirits light, elastic, and joyous—that freedom from care—that health of body and soul which ever rewards a closer communication with Nature—and the shuffling off of the frets and factitious wants of the thick-pent artificial city.

Whatever be the number of the party, and however they travel, whether on wheels or horseback, admitting even that a pleasant friend *pro vehiculo est*, that is, is better than a post-chaise, yet no one should ever dream of making a pedestrian tour in Spain. It seldom answers anywhere, as the walker arrives at the object of his promenade tired and hungry, just at the moment when he ought to be the freshest and most up to intellectual pleasures. The deipnosophist Arthenaeus long ago discovered that there was no love for the sublime and beautiful in an empty stomach, aesthetics yield then to gastronomics, and there is no prospect in the world so fine as that of a dinner and a nap, or *siesta* afterwards. The pedestrian in Spain, where

fleshly comforts are rare, will soon understand why, in the real jour-
nals of our Peninsular soldiers, so little attention is paid to those
objects which most attract the well-provided traveller. In cases of
bodily hardship, the employment of the mental faculties is narrowed
into the care of supplying mere physical wants, rather than expanded
into searching for those of a contemplative or intellectual gratification; the footsore and way-worn require, according to

> The unexempt condition
> By which all mortal frailty must subsist,
> Refreshment after toil, ease after pain.

Walking is the manner by which beasts travel, who have therefore
four legs; those bipeds who follow the example of the brute animals
will soon find that they will be reduced to their level in more particu-
lars than they imagined or bargained for. Again, as no Spaniard ever
walks for pleasure, and none ever perform a journey on foot except
trampers and beggars, it is never supposed possible that any one else
should do so except from compulsion. Pedestrians therefore are
either ill-received, or become objects of universal suspicion; for a
Spanish authority, judging of others by himself, always takes the worst
view of the stranger, whom he considers as guilty until he proves
himself innocent.

Before the pleasures of a riding tour through Spain are mentioned,
a few observations on the choice of companions may be made.

Those who travel in public conveyance or with muleteers are seldom likely to be left alone. It is the horseman who strikes into out-
of-the-way, unfrequented districts, who will feel the want of that
important item—a travelling companion, on which, as in choosing a
wife, it is easy enough to give advice. The patient must, however,
administer to himself, and the selection will depend, of course, much
on the taste and idiosyncrasy of each individual; those unfortunate
persons who are accustomed to have everything their own way, or
those, happy ones, who are never less alone than when alone, and
who possess the alchymy of finding resources and amusements in
themselves, may perhaps find that plan to the best; at all events, no
company is better than bad company: *más vale ir solo, que mal acom-*

pañado. A solitary wanderer is certainly the most unfettered as regards his notions and motions, *no tengo padre ni madre, ni perro que me ladre.* He who has neither father, mother, nor dog to bark at him can read the book of Spain, as it were, in his own room, dwelling on what he likes, and skipping what he does not, as with a red Murray.

Every coin has, however, its reverse, and every rose its thorn. Notwithstanding these and other obvious advantages, and the tendency that occupation and even hardships have to drive away imaginary evils, this freedom will be purchased by occasional moments of depression; a dreary, forsaken feeling will steal over the most cheerful mind. It is not good for man to be alone; and this social necessity never comes home stronger to the warm heart than during a long-continued solitary ride through the rarely visited districts of the Peninsula. The sentiment is in perfect harmony with the abstract feeling which is inspired by the present condition of unhappy Spain, fallen from her high estate, and blotted almost from the map of Europe. Silent, sad, and lonely is her face, on which the stranger will too often gaze; her hedgeless, treeless tracts of corn-field, bounded only by the low horizon; her uninhabited, uncultivated plains, abandoned to the wild flower and the bee, and which are rendered still more melancholy by ruined castle, or village, which stand out bleaching skeletons of a former vitality. The dreariness of this abomination of desolation is increased by the singular absence of singing birds, and the presence of the vulture, the eagle, and lonely birds of prey. The wanderer, far from home and friends, feels doubly a stranger in this strange land, where no smile greets his coming, no tear is shed at his going—where his memory passes away, like that of a guest who tarrieth but a day—where nothing of human life is seen, where its existence only is inferred by the rude wooden cross or stone-piled cairn, which marks the unconsecrated grave of some traveller who has been waylaid there alone, murdered, and sent to his account with all his imperfections on his head.

However confidently we have relied on past experience that such would not be our fate, yet these sorts of Spanish milestones marked with *memento mori*, are awkward evidences that the thing is not altogether impossible. It makes a single gentleman, whose life is not insured, not only trust to Santiago, but keep his powder dry, and look every now and then if his percussion cap fits. On these occasions the falling in with any of the nomad half-Bedouin natives is a sort of godsend; their society is quite different from that of a regular companion, for better or worse until death us do part, as it is casual, and may be taken up or dropped at convenience. The habits of all Spaniards when on the road are remarkably gregarious; a common fear acts as a cement, while the more they are in number the merrier. It is hail! well met, fellow-traveller! and the being glad to see each other is an excellent introduction. The sight of passengers bound our way is like speaking a strange sail on the Atlantic, *Hola Camara!* Ship a-hoy. This predisposition tends to make all travellers write so much and so handsomely of the lower classes of Spaniards, not indeed more than they deserve, for they are a fine, noble race. Something of this arises, because on such occasions all parties meet on an equality; and this levelling effect, perhaps unperceived, induces many a foreigner, however proud and reserved at home, to unbend, and that unaffectedly. He treats these accidental acquaintances quite differently from the manner in which he would venture to treat the lower orders of his own country, who, probably, if conciliated by the same condescension of manner, would appear in a more amiable light, although they are inferior to the Spaniard in his Oriental goodness of manner, his perfect tact, his putting himself and others into their proper place, without either self-degradation or vulgar assumption of social equality or superior physical powers.

A long solitary ride is hardly to be recommended; it is not fair to friends who have been left anxious behind, nor is it prudent to expose oneself, without help, to the common accidents to which a horse and his rider are always liable. Those who have a friend with whom they feel they can venture to go in double harness, had better do so. It is a severe test, and the trial becomes greater in proportion as hardships abound and accommodations are scanty—causes which sour the milk of human kindness, and prove indifferent restorers of stomach or temper. It is on these occasions, on a large journey and in a small *venta*, that a man finds out what his friend really is made of. While in the more serious necessities of danger, sickness, and need— a friend is one indeed, and the one thing wanting, with whom we share our last morsel and cup gladly. The salt of good fellowship, if it cannot work miracles as to quantity, converts the small loaf into a respectable abstract feed, by the zest and satisfaction with which it flavours it.

Nothing, moreover, cements friendships for the future like having made one of these conjoint rambles, provided it did not end in a quarrel. The mere fact of having travelled *at all* in Spain has a peculiarity which is denied to the more hackneyed countries of Europe. When we are introduced to a person who has visited these spell-casting sites, we feel as if we knew him already. There is a sort of freemasonry in having done something in common, which is not in common with the world at large. Those who are about to qualify themselves for this exclusive quality will do well not to let the party exceed five in number, three masters and two servants; two masters with two servants are perhaps more likely to be better accommodated; a third person, however, is often of use in trying journeys, as an *arbiter elegantiarum et rixarum*, a referee and arbitrator; for in the best regulated teams it must happen that some one will occasionally start, gib, or bolt, when the majority being against him brings the offender to his proper senses. Four eyes, again, see better than two, *más ven cuatro ojos que dos*.

By attending to a few simple rules, a tour of some months' duration, and over thousands of miles, may be performed on one and the same horse, who with his rider will at the end of the journey be neither sick nor sorry, but in such capital condition as to be ready to start again. We presume that the time will be chosen when the days are long and Nature has thrown aside her wintry garb. Fine weather is the joy of the wayfarer's soul, and nothing can be more different than the aspect of Spanish villages in good or in bad weather; as in the East, during wintry rains they are the acmes of mud and misery, but let the sun shine out, and all is gilded. It is the smile which lights up the habitually sad expression of a Spanish woman's face. The blessed beam cheers poverty itself, and by its stimulating, exhilarating action on the system of man, enables him to buffet against the moral evils to which countries the most favoured by climate seem, as if it were from compensation, to be more exposed than those where the skies are dull, and the winds bleak and cold.

As in our cavalry regiments, where real service is required, a perfect animal is preferred, a rider should choose a mare rather than a gelding; the use of entire horses is, however, so general in Spain, that one of such had better be selected than a mare. The day's journey will vary according to circumstances from twenty-five to forty miles. The start should be made before daybreak, and the horse well fed at least an hour before the journey is commenced, during which Spaniards, if they can, go to church, for they say that no time is ever lost on a journey by feeding horses and men and hearing masses, *misa y cebada no estorban jornada.*

The hours of starting, of course, depend on the distance and the district. The sooner the better, as all who wish to cheat the devil must get up very early. *Quien al demonio quiere engañar, muy temprano levantarse ha.* It is a great thing for the traveller to reach his night quarters as soon as he can, for the first comers are the best served: borrow therefore an hour of the morning rather than from the night; and that hour, if you lose it at starting, you will never overtake in the day. Again, in the summer it is both agreeable and profitable to be under way and off at least an hour or two before sunrise, as the heat soon gets insupportable, and the stranger is exposed to the *tabardillo*, the coup de soleil, which, even in a smaller degree, occasions more ill health in Spain than is generally imagined, and especially by the English, who brave it either from ignorance or foolhardiness. The head should be well protected with a silk handkerchief, tied after a turban fashion, which all the natives do; in addition to which we always lined the inside of our hats with thickly doubled brown paper. In Andalucía, during summer, the muleteers travel by night, and rest during the day-heat, which, however, is not a satisfactory method, except for those who wish to see nothing. We have never adopted it. The early mornings and cool afternoons and evenings are infinitely preferable; while to the artist the glorious sunrises and sunsets, and the marking of mountains, and definition of forms from the long shadows, are magnificent beyond all conception. In these almost tropical countries, when the sun is high, the effect of shadow is lost, and everything looks flat and unpicturesque.

The journey should be divided into two portions, and the longest should be accomplished the first: the pace should average about five miles per hour, it being an object not to keep the animal unnecessarily on his legs: he may be trotted gently, and even up easy hills, but should always be walked down them; nay, if led, so much the better, which benefits both horse and rider. It is surprising how a steady, continued slow pace gets over the ground: *Chi va piano, va sano, é lontano*, says the Italian; *paso a paso va lejos*, step by step goes far, responds the Castilian. The end of the journey each day is settled before starting, and there the traveller is sure to arrive with the evening. Spaniards never fidget themselves to get quickly to places where nobody is expecting them: nor is there any good to be got in trying to hurry man or beast in Spain; you might as well think of hurrying the Court of Chancery. The animals should be rested, if possible, every fourth day, and not used during halts in towns, unless they exceed three days' sojourn.

On arriving at every halting-place, look first at the feet, and pick out any pebbles or dirt, and examine the nails and shoes carefully, to see that nothing is loose; let this inspection become a habit; do not wash the feet too soon, as the sudden chill sometimes produces fever in them: when they are cool, clean them and grease the hoof well; after that you may wash as much as you please. The best thing, however, is to feed your horse at once, before thinking of his toilet; the march will have given an appetite, while the fatigue requires immediate restoration. If a horse is to be worried with cleaning, etc., he often loses heart and gets off his feed: he may be rubbed down when he has done eating, and his bed should be made up as for night, the stable darkened, and the animal left quite quiet, and the longer the better: feed him well again an hour before starting for the afternoon stage, and treat him on coming in exactly as you did in the morning. The food must be regulated by the work: when that is severe, give corn with both hands, and stint the hay and other lumber: what you want is to concentrate support by quality, not quantity. The Spaniard will tell you that one mouthful of beef is worth ten of potatoes. If your horse is an English one, it must be remembered that eight pounds' weight of barley is equal to ten of oats, as containing less husk and more mucilage or starch, which our horse-dealers know when they want to *make up* a horse; overfeeding a horse in the hot climate of Spain, like overfeeding his rider, renders both liable to fevers and sudden inflammatory attacks, which are much more prevalent in Gibraltar than elsewhere in Spain, because our countrymen will go on exactly as if they were at home.

At all events, feed your horse well with *something or other*, or your Spanish squire will rain proverbs on you, like Sancho Panza; the belly must be filled with hay or straw, for it in reality carries the feet, *O paja o heno el vientre lleno—tripas llevan a pies*, and so forth. The Spaniards when on a journey allow their horses to drink copiously at every stream, saying that there is no juice like that of flints; and indeed they set the example, for they are all down on their bellies at every brook, swilling water, according to the proverb, like an ox, and wine when they can get it, like a king. If therefore you are riding a Spanish horse which has been accustomed to this continual tippling, let him drink, otherwise he will be fevered. If the horse has been treated in the English fashion, give him his water only after his meals, otherwise he will break out into weakening sweats. Should the animal ever arrive distressed, a tepid gruel, made with oatmeal or even flour, will comfort him much. At nightfall stop the feet with wet tow, or with horse dung, for that of cows will seldom be had in Spain, where goats furnish milk, and Dutchmen butter.

Let the feet be constantly attended to; the horse having twice as many as his rider, requires double attention, and of what use to a traveller is a quadruped that has not a leg to go upon? This is well known to those commercial gentlemen, who are the only persons now-a-days in England who make riding journeys. It is the shoe that makes or mars the horse, and no wise man, in Spain or out, who has got a four-footed hobby, or three half-crowns, should delay sending to Longman's for that admirable "Miles on the Horse's Foot." "Every knight errant," says Don Quixote, "ought to be able to shoe his own *Rosinante* himself." *Rosin* is pure Arabic for a hackney—at least he should know how this calceolation ought to be done. As a general rule, always take your quadruped to the forge, where the shoes can be fitted to his feet, not the feet to ready-made shoes; and if you value the comfort, the extension of life and service of your steed—*fasten the fore shoes with five nails at most in the outside, and with two only in the inside, and those near the toe*, do not in mercy fix by nails all round an unyielding rim of dead iron, to an expanding living hoof; remember also always to take with you a spare set of shoes, with nails and a hammer—for the want of a nail the shoe was lost; for the want of a shoe the rider was lost. In many parts of Spain, where there are no fine modern roads, you might almost do without any shoes at all, as the ancients did, and is done in parts of Mexico; but no unprotected hoof can stand the constant wear and tear, the filing of a macadamized highway.

The horse will probably be soon in such condition as to want no more physic than his rider; a lump, however, of rock-salt, and a bit of chalk put at night into his manger, answers the same purposes as Epsoms and soda do to the master. You should wash out the long tail and mane, which is the glory of a Spanish horse, as fine hair is to a woman, with soda and water; the alkali combining with the animal grease forms a most searching detergent. A grand remedy for most of the accidents to which horses are liable on a journey, such as kicks, cuts, strains, etc., is a constant formentation with hot water, which should be done under the immediate superintendence of the master, or it will be either done insufficiently, or not done at all; hot water, according to the groom genus, having been created principally as a recipient of something stronger. A crupper and breast-plate are almost indispensable, from the steep ascents and descents in the mountains. The *mosquero*, the fly-flapper, is a great comfort to the horse, as, being in perpetual motion, and hanging between his eyes, it keeps off the flies; the head-stall, or night halter, never should be removed from the bridle, but be rolled up during the day, and fastened along the side of the cheek. The long tail is also rolled up when the ways are miry, just as those of our blue jackets and horse-guards used to be.

Lucia Graves

(1943 –   )

Born in England, raised in Majorca, and educated in Switzerland and at Oxford, Lucia Graves has made a career of bridging the cultures of her birth and her adopted country. She spoke English at home (her father was Robert Graves and her mother, his second wife Beryl Hodge), Spanish at school, and Catalan with her village friends. "Spanish became associated in my mind with the return to my home . . . It became the language of a lively life under the sun, of happy childhood memories and of holiday time—it held in its sounds and images a whole series of feelings for which I found no parallel in English."

Robert Graves and Beryl Hodge arrived in Majorca after World War II. They took residence in the same house that Graves had inhabited with his lover Laura Riding. (Graves and Riding fled the Spanish Civil War in 1936 and then parted. Beryl had been the wife of Graves's former collaborator Alan Hodge. Graves and Beryl Hodge married in 1950.) Lucia and her siblings were raised in a Bohemian home, although they were educated in the rigid public schools of Franco's Spain. Her memoir, *A Woman Unknown: Voices from a Spanish Life* (2000), from which this is excerpted, recounts her sense of not belonging to the British culture of her parents or accepting the Catholic doctrine of Spain. "I found myself creating an imaginary land where I spent much of my time," she wrote. In her twenties Graves married a Spaniard—a union that was crushed under the unyielding sexism of traditional Catalan society. Lucia Graves, translator and novelist, now lives in London.

From A WOMAN UNKNOWN

WATER-FAIRIES AND ALTARS

If I close my eyes, I can almost feel the soft warmth of the winter sun on the nape of my neck, and hear the sheep bells and the occasional shouts of the shepherd somewhere up in the olive groves above our house, and the long silences between his shouts—back in the quiet days of my early childhood. I find it easy to enter that uncluttered memory chamber.

As the months and the years went by, and I turned six and seven and eight, I began to appreciate the rhythm and cycles of rural life, the tastes and smells that went with each season, and the way things worked in the village. Outside the confines of my English home, where copies of the airmail *Times* in their light blue wrappers were vague reminders of the comfortable land of my grandparents, there was nothing to distract my thoughts from my natural surroundings and I became immersed in a primitive way of life that flowed predictably from one event to the next, like the water that flowed from the fountains, like the water that ran down the torrent to the sea.

It was a genuinely rural society, almost untouched by twentieth-century modernisation or even the industrial revolution; where carts were much more common than cars, cooking was done on charcoal fires, and women still fetched water from the fountain for their daily needs, unless they had their own well in which to collect the rainwater that fell off the roof. Nor was there any electricity in the village—unless you called electricity a dim orange glow produced by a privately owned generator, with not enough voltage for any domestic appliances; irons were heated over the charcoal fires, and those who had iceboxes cooled them with the large blocks of ice that arrived in the bus at half past three in the afternoon, wrapped in sackcloth. When we had an Aga imported from England and installed in our house in the late fifties, it was considered such a novelty that people would drop by during their Sunday-afternoon stroll just to have a look at it. But by then things were already beginning to change, and soon the tourist boom would take all the young workers away from the olive groves and the fruit orchards to work in the new hotels that lined the sandy shores on the other side of the island. The rugged land, which had for centuries been a source of production, would soon become a landscape to be consumed by tourists—to feed the mind and not the body; and the efforts of men and women, once dedicated to its cultivation, would be channelled into providing new services for the viewers.

In the late forties, when I was growing up in the mountain village, the link between man and nature—man's control over the elements— was far more apparent than it is today. It was a way of life that, with hindsight, risks being classed as picturesque or quaint, but at the time was not like that at all, especially for the village people themselves. The forties were difficult years for them, with few comforts in the home and little to buy in the village shop: a few sausages hanging from the ceiling, a few tins of sardines, a sack of potatoes, another of dried broad beans . . . The country was still suffering the aftereffects of the Civil War, with rationing and a rampant black market. Women would take the bus down to the capital with bottles of olive oil hidden under their skirts and come back with packets of rice or sugar. The Spartan living conditions matched the toughness of the land, the dark clothes of the women, their seriousness and reserve. They matched the sullen expressions of the men whom I sometimes saw playing cards and dominoes in a cloud of smoke at the café.

At weddings and christenings and village feasts, after a few glasses of sweet wine, men and women abandoned their normally serious expressions to laugh and tell loud jokes. But there was one person who never laughed, a young woman who lived in the farmhouse just above the main road, on the way out of the village towards our home. She must have been mentally handicapped. I used to see her standing outside the front door, or sitting on a chair, with a piece of bread in her hand, watching people go by. She had a protruding purplish lower lip and short straight hair parted at the side and held back with a hairgrip. In any village gathering, or in church, she stood next to her good-looking mother, too shy to speak or even look up.

By this time I had completely forgotten the Devonshire geography that had formed my visual world until the age of three. The pleasing lines of dark hedges on soft green fields, the rambling roses, the fairy-tale banks of the river Dart with its wild flowers and bushes, all those images had been blotted out of my mind by the stark shapes and colours of my new Mediterranean home. Here a wide valley rolled down from the steep mountainside as far as the sea-cliffs, with rows and rows of terraces held up by dry-stone walls—the only way in which the reddish-brown earth could be retained and give nourishment to olive, almond and carob trees. The sun rose from behind the mountains and set in the sea, and the valley changed colour during the day as sun and clouds journeyed across it. Frequent changes of weather meant that nothing ever looked the same for very long: the olive trees turned dark green with black trunks after rainfall, or silvery grey in the wind, and the mountains could disappear altogether in a sudden mist.

In the middle of the valley, which was like a large bowl with one side broken off where it met the sea, a village of pale brown stone houses clustered round a small hill, with the church of St. John the Baptist and the graveyard on its summit, and the town hall at its foot. Our house was situated a little beyond the village, facing the southern rim of the bowl, behind which lived Blanca and Antonio in their house on the coast. Here and there, on the sides of the basin that surrounded the village, were large farmhouses called *possessions*, each with at least one very tall palm tree to mark its location and remind one of its prestige—and of the presence of water. Most of the land surrounding the village belonged to these farmhouses, whose owners, the *senyors*, generally lived in Palma, whereas the *amo*, with his wife the *madona*, ran the house and the property.

On the eve of St. Anthony, 16 January, bonfires were lit at night in various parts of the village—a Christian adoption of an old pagan ritual to celebrate the New Year. But the most exciting bonfires were on Good Friday, when they were lit in the *possessions*, and from the village all one could see were the bright orange flames licking the dark semicircle of mountains. The farmhouse situated furthest to the right, which had a view of the church door, would wait to catch sight of the silent candlelit procession leaving the church after Mass, and would then light its bonfire; the next farmhouse, on seeing the flames of the first bonfire, would light up too, and so each farmhouse would light its pile of wood and brambles until the full semi-

circle was completed. I was fascinated that people could communicate through distant signs; that they could make fires speak to one
another, sending messages of fraternity from one powerful house to
the next and at the same time showing off their wealth through the
size and brightness of the flames. But, above all, that they could
communicate to the villagers, who were slowly walking down the hill
towards the town hall and up again on the other side, that the farmhouses were the ancient guardians of the mountain and were there to
protect them. Is this power to communicate another reason why we
say "tongues of fire"?

Fire could also be destructive and frightening. One summer afternoon, when trees and bushes were parched after months of dry
weather, I was in the village with my friends when a fire began to
spread in some terraces above the village. The smoke was dense,
forming clouds that hung over the mountainside, spreading a strange
heat and the smell of burnt leaves. People were gathering quickly,
running to the scene with empty buckets which they filled with water
in the fountain by the road. In minutes, a human chain was formed
all the way up a path towards the fire, and I have a clear recollection
of the buckets being passed from one person to the next, up the
chain. Some men were shouting, giving orders, and we children hud-
dled together, at a safe distance, comforted by the authority they projected.

There were also tame fires in the mountains, useful fires: the fires
of the charcoal-burners who spent weeks at a time in the oakwoods
high above the village, sleeping alone under the stars, tending their
pyres like priests of some mysterious oracle. But no flames came out
of those large round piles of wood because they were covered by
earth, to give the wood a slow combustion and allow it to turn into
firm black charcoal. I once went up the mountain with a young girl
from the village to take provisions to her father who was up there
burning wood. I remember that as we walked up the winding path
the ground was covered with small dry oak leaves and we had to take
care not to slip on them. Then we came to a flat clearing and saw the
charcoal-burner sitting alone on a rock, looking tired and unshaven.
In the middle of the open space was the round pile of wood with a
thin streak of blue smoke rising from it, and in a shady corner I saw

an old blanket and some tin plates, and an earthenware water-pitcher. The dark man took the pitcher and offered us a drink of the cool water which, he said, came from a nearby spring. I had heard about the *dones d'aigo*, the water-women who lived in the springs, and wondered whether he had seen them, flitting around the wood at night, but was too shy to ask.

At different levels of the mountainside, underground water, channelled through man-made tunnels, flowed out into the basins of stone fountains placed like shrines at the dark mouths, with fern and moss and ivy growing profusely around them. And beneath the smooth dark ripples lived the *dones d'aigo*, the water-women, fairies who came out only at night, like bats, to roam the woods. In ancient times they had lived in broad daylight, filling the woods with mysterious powers, giving speech to birds, trees, water and wind, carpeting their groves with wild flowers. But the arrival of the True Cross had condemned them to darkness: they had vanished, like the thick grey mist that sometimes sweeps through the trees in the early morning. The earth had swallowed the *dones d'aigo*, but it is said that they created marvellous palaces underground, with lakes and waterfalls, with spacious halls where they sat sadly in the shadows and wove watery garments for their flights into the upper world. Each one guarded a mountain spring, each was the living spirit of its water: the Fresh Spring, the Profuse Spring, the Spring of Lies (called this because if you drank from it you might start telling lies); their glassy currents ran down to the public washing places in the town, where women scrubbed their clothes on the grey stone slabs and dipped them into the running waters of the basin; or formed new fountains in the town, or were channelled into large reservoirs belonging to the mountain farmhouses and from there sent downhill to other farmlands and groves.

For although the farms owned olive groves, and flocks of sheep, and olive presses, their most treasured possession was the water from these springs, without which the fruit trees and vegetables could not grow. Some *possessions* had their own springs, others owned rights that gave them perpetual use of the water on certain days of the week, when they would accumulate it in the reservoirs for irrigation. These water rights were often a source of trouble: they could cause rifts between good neighbours, feuds between families who had been

close for generations; they led to spiteful remarks in the café made by
men wearing berets and brown corduroy trousers, and to silent looks
between women at each other across the street. But for us children,
water was always a source of joy. On summer evenings it flowed
down the narrow cement canal set about four feet from the ground
above the main road and it was fun to dip our fingers into it and
watch little bits of twigs and leaves pushing their way along, getting
stuck, loosening, continuing their journey down to the big farmhouse
on the way to the cove, with its rows of orange trees and tomato
plants.

When we were thirsty on the way up from the beach, we would
sometimes stop there to ask for water. Or if we were playing in the
village we would walk into one of the open *entrades* shouting, "*Ave
Maria!*" and out would come the lady of the house, drying her hands
on her grey apron, and saying in a kind voice reserved for children,
"What do you want, children?"

"*Mos dóna un poc d'aigo, madona?* Can we have some water?" we
answered. The word *aigo* (pronounced eye-go), "water" in Majorcan,
seemed to me a perfect word, a word that I still associate with summer thirst and the cool mineral taste of pure spring water or rainwater, and with the *madona*'s words as we drank: "Don't drink so fast,
it will do you harm!"

It was my world, and I understood it; I could see how things
worked, how the lives of the village people blended in with the
mountain, the farmland and the sea. It wrapped itself neatly round
the kernel of my home—so different from the homes of my village
friends—where my father worked in a room filled with books, or was
out in the garden picking tangerines or digging up weeds; where my
mother sometimes sat and read by the fireplace with a cat on her lap,
or was busy cooking in the kitchen, or else was out in the garden
watering the lettuces or picking flowers to put in a pretty vase on the
dining-room table; where at night my parents would listen to the
BBC on our large wooden radio, while my brothers and I cut out
illustrations from English or American magazines—coloured pictures of a faraway land of telephones, red sports cars and electric
washing machines that did not seem quite real to us—and then
pasted them with care into our scrap books.

Real life for me was what went on outside the green wooden gates of our home. Once a week a sheep was slaughtered by the village butcher and once a year—for St. Martin's, in October—most families killed a pig to make sausages for the months to come. My mother never allowed us to see the actual slaughtering, but I remember hearing the frantic squeals of the pigs once or twice, and thinking they were never going to stop. Later in the day, we sometimes went to the house where the *matança* was taking place. By then the pig's throat had been cut, its blood collected in a pot, its meat cut and classified, its entrails carefully washed and dried. The women of the family sat round a table, outdoors, mixing spices and meats in large yellow bowls, their hands red and shiny from paprika and animal fat, while the men, who had done the slaughtering and the butchering, turned the handle of a large grinding machine, or carried platefuls of finished sausages into the house. There was a smell of meat and blood and spices, and an exhilarating atmosphere of pagan feast.

Many other events made up the village calendar. Almonds were husked and cracked in September for making Christmas *torrons*; olives were picked in November for pickling while they were still green, and pressed for oil in December when black and juicy; spinach and cabbages were grown in backyards, refuse was fed to the chickens or to the mules and their droppings in turn fed to the earth. The fisherman's wife came up to the village in the mornings when there was enough fish to sell. She stood outside the town hall blowing a conch that was heard up and down the streets, because those were days before mechanical noises had invaded their homes, before televisions and telephones closed houses upon themselves, when people's ears were alert to every sound and could tell what was happening around them. The fisherman's wife was thin and wiry and rather bad-tempered and had given up changing her mourning clothes in the months between the death of one distant relative and another; her dark figure, her tanned, sinewy arms, made the red and blue fish all the more colourful as they gaped and stared at death in the old wicker basket.

School started in late September, when those long summers finally came to an end and the dark carob beans had been collected into sacks that were stacked against the pale stone walls of the terraces;

when our bathing clothes had been put away in a chest with the beach towels, hardened and faded by sun and salt; when the fisherman came up from his seaside hut to live in his village home.

The school was run by three or four Franciscan nuns. The girls' class was known as *costura*, which literally means "needlework," and in fact we did little else there, as far as I remember, except pray and learn the catechism. It was halfway up the steep hill that leads to the church, the last building in a row of houses, with three very tall steps of worn grey stone leading up to the entrance, where we pulled a thin dangling chain and heard a faraway tinkle, followed by a shuffle of feet and the sound of the door clicking open. Before letting us in, the nun would look down the hill to see if anyone else was coming up to school and take a quick look at the world outside. My younger brother Juan would be taken off to the boys' room on the right and I went into the room on the left. A tiny patio at the back of the building—no more than three square yards, as I realised when I revisited the school some thirty years later—was our playground, divided in two by a piece of string. On one side, the girls played, on the other the boys. At the end of the patio a few steps led up to the *excusat*, a hole in the ground with sackcloth for a door and bits of cut-up newspaper or brown wrapping paper hanging on a hook on the wall. One for the girls, one for the boys. We girls skipped and played hopscotch. The boys played marbles or leapfrog, or else rushed around kicking each other and shouting.

In one of my mother's photograph albums there is a black and white snapshot of me and Catalina, the baker's daughter, whom Blanca remembered seeing at the christening party. She is wearing a tight-fitting coat with a neat row of buttons on either side of the front panel, puffed sleeves and a large round collar. Her hair is tied in tight bunches high above her ears, with large white bows (of course, they may have been pink, like the sugared almonds). I have my arm round her shoulder and we are both laughing. Catalina and I sat next to each other in the girls' classroom, learning our times tables and filling our exercise books with rows of *mi mamá me ama* ("my mummy loves me") and *la pipa de papá* ("Daddy's pipe"). The nuns lost their temper very easily, if you got a stitch wrong or a word wrong when reciting the ten commandments, and especially if you swore by mistake—even saying "*Punyeta!*" which was a very satisfying word to use when you were annoyed, and meant no more than "Bother!"—so there was always some girl standing or kneeling with her face to the wall, arms stretched out, being punished for something she had done. But nobody seemed to care; there was no real anger in the nuns, and I recall no unhappiness, even when kneeling on the cold floor. Sometimes they took us on excursions into the pinewoods by the sea, and as a great treat would tell us stories about the Majorcan St. Catalina Thomàs, who was born in the neighbouring village of Valldemossa, and had even spent a few months of her life living with an aunt in our village before she became a nun. St. Catalina, known affectionately as *Sor* Thomaseta, was given a very hard time by the devil, who played lots of dirty tricks on her to tempt her and lead her astray. She used to take meals to her father, who worked in the olive groves in the hills above her house, and as she walked up the rocky path the devil would suddenly appear and trip her up, spilling all the food on the ground. Once he even pushed her over a high cliff not far from Blanca's house, on the road to Palma, but two angels came flying down with a blanket and saved her from falling.

Catalina and I used to sing a song about her namesake. Translated, it went something like this:

> Sister Thomaseta, where are you?
> You'd better hide somewhere fast
> 'Cause the devil's looking for you
> and will throw you down a shaft!

In the classroom they encouraged us to take example from the Virgin Mary and Baby Jesus. They were so sincere in their belief that I was soon drawn by their enthusiasm and came top of the class in religion. The Virgin Mary became my idol, so beautiful, so pure, so perfect! The statue in the church, with her sky-blue mantle, her long wavy blond hair, her sweet smile, her neat hands and feet, elated me. It was as if I was being lifted up into the starred ceiling of her niche, as if I was one of the cherubs surrounding her. Those lovely soft cheeks, those eyes looking ecstatically up at Heaven as I looked ecstatically at her. She was above languages, you could speak to her in

Latin, Majorcan, Spanish, English—she understood them all, because when you prayed your words changed to some other concept of communication, they became pure emotion. Perhaps, I thought, I could become a saint when I died, and sit close to her in Heaven. Catalina had given me a small metal image of the Virgin Mary, and I made little altars for her on the olive terraces above our house, or in some quiet corner of our garden, in secret crevices that I would tend with care; I gathered tiny blue flowers that grew like weeds by the roadside, petals of geraniums and roses and daisies, and formed a patterned tapestry all around her. One day I went down the garden to the place where I kept the little figure and found it had gone. To this day I wonder what happened to it, for I did not dare tell my parents or my brothers about my loss. I knew I could not bring my Catholic devotion into my English world. The nearest we ever got to religious practice at home was singing "O Come All Ye Faithful" round the Christmas tree, first in Latin, then in English; and I remember how my father, when it came to "born the King of Angels," always raised his voice and sang "born the King of Israel!"

At that time, however, there was little difference in my mind between the Virgin Mary and the *dones d'aigo*, between the angels who rescued St. Catalina or the fairies from my storybooks; they were all part of the world of fantasy that children create for themselves at an early age, while the line between reality and fiction is still nebulous. Sometimes these fantasy figures could cross the line into the real world of the mountain village and hide among the olive trees or in caves by the sea. But the countryside, however beautiful, was not an enchanted countryside for me: it was real, and often harsh, even if it was full of things to fire a child's imagination, like the golden oil that came out of the bitter black olives, or the smell of the orange blossom when the trees had been irrigated, or the crystal-clear water flowing down the open canals.

Today, those canals have been replaced by plastic underground pipes, and consumption of water has increased so disproportionately as a result of the tourist industry—because of demands for swimming pools, showers, washing machines, luscious gardens and golf courses—that every summer there is a shortage. Water is still the subject of many heated discussions, but the feuds have moved from the café table to the lawyer's desk, while water lorries race around the island trying to meet the demands of holiday-makers from the north of Europe who have never needed to be careful with the precious liquid. So much else has changed: many of the old village houses have been sold to foreigners to be used as holiday homes, and many new houses have been built; the new generations of rural Majorcans no longer work the land, but instead have become hotel managers, waiters or builders who speak to one another on mobile phones; the Franciscan nuns have left the village, and our *costura* is now a private residence; there are no more charcoal-burners; the fisherman's wife is long dead. Yet every time I go back to the mountain village to visit my mother and my brothers, who still live there, there is at least one moment, either in the early morning, when all is quiet except for the sound of birds pecking at the fruit trees, or at night, when the moon lights up the olive trees across the valley, when suddenly the memory of what it felt like to be a child here flashes through me. Like an old song returning.

Robert Graves

(1895–1985)

British poet Robert Graves lived much of his life in Deya, Majorca, with an assortment of wives, mistresses, "muses," and children. He was born in Wimbledon,
attended Oxford, and at nineteen enlisted at the outbreak of World War I. During his service he developed an intense friendship with the poet Siegfried Sassoon and through Sassoon met Wilfred Owen. He was wounded so severely
during the war that his parents were notified of his death. The war was a trans-
formative experience for him, as it was for many men of his generation. After the
war Graves married Nancy Nicholson, but in 1926 he began an affair with the
American poet Laura Riding, a relationship that sundered his marriage. He and
Riding decamped from England to live in Majorca.

Life with Riding was tempestuous, but intellectually stimulating. They formed
their own press under the name Seizin Press and edited the literary journal *Epi-
logue*. Graves wrote a memoir, *Goodbye to All That* (1929), about his war years
and *I, Claudius* (1934), his popular historical novel. War once again interrupted
Graves's life and he and Riding left Majorca. Their personal life began to unravel
and they parted in 1939.

After World War II Graves returned to his home in Majorca, this time with a
new love, Beryl Hodge, the wife of his former collaborator Alan Hodge. They
married in 1950 and lived with their children in the same house that Graves had
with Riding. He continued to write prolifically, eventually producing 140 books—
poetry, novels, and literary criticism. Although he had an enduring second marriage, Graves continued affairs with "muses," young women who inspired him.
Except for a five-year period in the early 1960s when he was a professor at
Oxford, Graves lived in Spain for the rest of his life.

Graves considered himself primarily a poet. He wrote, "Since the age of fifteen poetry has been my ruling passion and I have never intentionally undertaken any task or formed any relationship that seemed inconsistent with poetic
principles; which has sometimes won me the reputation of an eccentric." This
selection is from *Collected Poems* (1958).

From COLLECTED POEMS

SIROCCO AT DEYA

How most unnatural-seeming, yet how proper;
The sea like a cat with fur rubbed the wrong way,
As the sirocco with its furnace flavour
Dashes at full tilt around the village
["From every-which-a-way, hot as a two-buck pistol"]
Stripping green olives from the blown-back boughs,
Scorching the roses, blinding the eyes with sand;
While slanderous tongues in the small cafés
And in the tightly-shuttered granite houses
Clack defamation, incite and invite
Knives to consummate their near-murders . . .
Look up, a great grey cloud broods nonchalant
On the mountain-top nine hundred feet above us,
Motionless and turgid, blotting out the sun,
And from it sneers a supercilious Devil:
"Mere local wind: no messenger of mine!"

Ernest Hemingway

(1898–1961)

No American writer is more identified with Spain than Ernest Hemingway. During his first visit in 1923, he saw his first bullfight in Pamplona. Hemingway was captivated and often returned to it in his writing. The running of the bulls was part of his second novel, *The Sun Also Rises* (1926); in 1932 he wrote *Death in the Afternoon*, a nonfiction account of the sport that remains the seminal work on the subject.

In the 1930s Hemingway was drawn to the mythic struggle of the Spanish Civil War. Unlike George Orwell, he did not enlist, but covered it as a journalist. Hemingway supported the Loyalists against the Fascists, delivered anti-Franco speeches, and even helped produce the documentary *Spanish Earth*. In Madrid Hemingway met the woman who would become his third wife, Martha Gelhorn, an intrepid war correspondent and, in part, the model for Maria in his novel about the civil war, *For Whom the Bell Tolls* (1940).

Near the end of his life Hemingway returned to Spain to write a nonfiction account, commissioned by *Life* magazine, of a one-on-one contest between two matadors, brothers-in-law, Luis Miguel Dominguín and Antonio Ordóñez. Throughout the summer of 1959 the bullfighters dueled as the writer followed them through the corridas of Spain. Hemingway, then sixty, showed the effects of a lifetime of heavy drinking and symptoms of the mental illness that would lead to his suicide in 1961. According to James Michener, who wrote the introduction to *The Dangerous Summer* (1960), from which this is excerpted, "It was unwise to have attempted this return to his youth." Instead of the 10,000 words that *Life* requested, Hemingway produced 120,000. His friend A. E. Hotchner tried to cut the manuscript to a manageable size, but not enough to please the readers of *Life*. They complained that the published articles were long and made unnecessary digressions. The editors considered their experiment a failure.

In perspective, *The Dangerous Summer* is not only an account of an epic competition between two bullfighters, but of an aging author facing his mortality. Michener wrote, "Hemingway's description of the historic Málaga corrida of 14 August 1959 in Chapter 11 is one of the most evocative and exact summaries of a corrida ever penned. It is a masterpiece." And it is reproduced here.

From THE DANGEROUS SUMMER

It was one of the very greatest bullfights I have ever seen; Luis Miguel and Antonio both came to it as the most serious thing in their lives. Luis Miguel had gone through his grave wound in Valencia and the wound, and how lucky it turned out, had given him back his confidence that Antonio's unbelievably perfect work and his lionlike rush and courage had impaired. Antonio's being gored in Palma de Mallorca had proven that he was not invulnerable and it was lucky for Luis Miguel that he had not seen Antonio's work with the last bull of the fight at Valencia. I cannot truly think that he would have wanted any more of him if he had. Luis Miguel did not need the money although he loved money and what it bought very much. More than anything it was important to him to believe he was the greatest matador alive. He no longer was but he was the second greatest and on this day he was very great indeed.

Antonio came to fight with all the confidence he had in Valencia. What had happened in Mallorca meant nothing to him. He had made a small mistake that he did not wish to discuss with me and he would not make it again. He had been sure for a long time that he was a better matador than Luis Miguel. He had proved it last in Valencia and he could not wait to prove it again on this day.

The bulls were from the ranch of Juan Pedro Domecq and none of them looked different except the first. There were two though that could have been difficult for any other matadors but Luis Miguel and Antonio. Luis Miguel was pale and gaunt and tired-looking when he took his first bull. The bull was dangerous and chopping both ways with his horns. Luis Miguel dominated him with tired grace. It was not a bull he could be brilliant with but he handled him with intelligence and skill and made what passes the condition of the bull would permit. When he killed him he went in solidly but the sword slid in sideways and the point showed out through the hide behind the bull's shoulders. A banderillero pulled the sword out with a swing of his cape and Luis Miguel killed the bull with the descabello on his first attempt. Watching from the fence I was worried about how Miguel looked and I hoped he was sound with the sword again. This one had been an accident but it made me worry.

Another thing that worried me was the many photographers and motion picture men present who had no previous bull ring experience. Any movement while the matador is working the bull that the bull can see may distract him and make him charge, thus breaking the matador's control of him with the cloth without his knowing why it has happened. Everybody in the callejón knows this and is careful at all times to keep their heads below the fence level when moving and to remain absolutely still whenever the bull is facing them. A conscienceless or criminal bullfighter leaning against the fence inside the ring could attract the bull's attention by an involuntary-looking flick of the cape and launch him on another fighter who was preparing to go in to kill.

Antonio's first bull came out and he took him with the cape as though he were inventing bullfighting and it was going to be absolutely perfect from the start. It was how he fought all summer. That day in Málaga he surpassed himself again and he made poetry of movement with the hunting, seeking, pressing mass of the bull. Then, with the muleta, he sculptured his passes gently and slowly making the whole long faena a poem. He killed him with a single estocada going in perfectly and the point of entry of the sword an inch and a half down from the top of the death notch. They gave him both ears and the crowd asked for the tail.

Luis Miguel's second bull came out trotting and I thought what bad luck he has now that it has turned. It was hard to make the bull stand still long enough to charge the horses, and the pics he took did not steady him. I felt worse and worse for Miguel who was taking it without complaint. He could not run to put in banderillas but he directed exactly how he wanted them placed. They steadied the bull down a little.

Luis Miguel took him with slow, two-handed, low passes and began his education with the muleta. He stopped his trotting tendency and held him so he would charge from one place and then fol-

low the cloth at the rhythm that he created for the bull. He passed
him high and under the cloth and then he commenced to work him
with low, soft, swinging naturales with the sword in his right hand
slanted out from his hip.

Tall, straight and unsmiling, unmoving from the terrain where he
had elected to work the bull, Luis Miguel adjusted the muleta to the
normal level of the bull's eyes so that he would not cramp his neck
and commenced to swing him around him in the sort of naturales
that Joselito would have signed. He finished off with a beautiful pase
de pecho, the left-handed pass that brought the bull's horns past his
chest and let the folds of the muleta sweep down the bull's body
from his horns to his tail. He squared the bull up, furled the muleta
on its stick, sighted high up and went in perfectly with all he had. It
was the third bull of the fight to be killed by a single sword thrust.
Miguel had fought him beautifully and had to make him in order to
fight him. He had the sword back now and all his confidence with it.
He came in with a deprecating smile and took the two ears and the
tail modestly and circled the ring with them. I noticed that Miguel
was favoring his right foot a little where his first bull had stepped on
him but he was not concealing it. I knew his right leg hurt him and he
did not feel completely solid with it. He was being wonderful and I
never admired him more.

I did not think Antonio could be better with the cape than he had
been in his first bull. But he was. As I watched him from the fence I
tried to think how he could do it and do it always and make it so
beautiful and moving. It was the closeness and the slowness that
carved the figure and made each pass seem permanent. But it was the
complete naturalness and the classic simplicity as he watched the
death go by him as though he were overseeing it and helping it and
making it his partner all in one ascending rhythm that made it so
moving.

With the muleta, this time, he started out with the four great low
passes he used with the right knee and leg extended on the sand to
take command of the bull. Each pass was a model in execution but it
was not cold work. It was done so close that the horns passed at mil-
limeters from his thighs or his chest at every pass. There was no leaning against the bull's body after the horn had gone by. There were no

tricks and every pass was a long pause in the breathing of the people
who watched the man and the bull. I was never afraid for Antonio
with the cape and I did not have any worry in all this wonderful faena
although each pass was the most truly difficult and dangerous for a
man to make in bullfighting. The bull was good, much better than
Miguel's had been. Antonio was happy with him and he made a perfect, beautiful and deeply moving faena. He did not let it go on too
long and he went in perfectly to kill his friend with a single estocada.

Four bulls were now dead from one sword thrust each and the fight
had been one long crescendo. They gave Antonio both ears, the tail
and cut a lower leg with hoof attached. He circled the ring as happy
and unpreoccupied as though we were at the pool. The crowd wanted
him to take one more ovation and he asked Luis Miguel and Don Juan
Pedro Domecq, who had bred the bulls, to go out with him.

It was up to Luis Miguel now. He took his bull on both knees with
a large cambiada letting the bull almost reach him with the horn
before he swung him clear with the cape. This bull was good and Luis
Miguel made the most of him. He was well pic-ed and Luis Miguel
had the banderillas put in rapidly. At the fence I thought he looked
very tired but he was paying no attention to his physical condition,
absolutely avoiding any limping and was fighting with the same passion as though he were a hungry boy beginning his career.

With the muleta he had the bull placed a little out from the fence
and jamming his back against the planks and sitting on the estribo, the
strip of wood that runs around the inner side of the barrera to give
the fighters a toe-up to vault it, he passed the bull five times past his
outstretched right arm that signalled the bull's way with the outspread
red cloth. The bull went by each time with a whoosh of heavy breath
and with a clatter of banderillas, his hooves heavy on the sand, his
horn passing close to Miguel's arms. It looked suicidal but with a good
bull that charged straight it was only a fairly dangerous trick.

After this Miguel took him out into the ring and commenced to do
classic passes with his left hand. He looked tired but confident and
he was working well. He made two series of eight naturales in beautiful style and then on a right-hand pass with the bull coming at him
from the rear the bull had him. From where I was leaning on the
fence the horn seemed to go into his body and the bull tossed him a

good six feet or more into the air. His arms and legs were spread wide, the sword and muleta were thrown clear and he fell on his head. The bull stepped on him trying to get the horn into him and missed him twice. Everybody was in with their capes spread and this time it was his brother Pepé, who had vaulted the barrera, who dragged Miguel free.

He was up in an instant. The horn had not gone in but had passed between his legs to toss him and there was no wound.

Miguel paid no attention to what the bull had done to him and waving everyone away went on with his faena. He repeated the pass on which the bull had caught him and then repeated it again as though to teach both himself and the bull a lesson. He went on to make other passes mathematically close and correct, giving no importance to anything the bull had done to him. He made the passes more emotional and a little trickier. The public liked them better. But he fought cleanly and well and did none of the telephone tricks. Then he killed well, slamming in as though he had never had any trouble with the sword in his life. They gave him everything as they had to Antonio and he deserved it. When he had made his tour of the ring, and it was impossible to dissimulate his limp now that the leg had stiffened, he called Antonio out to salute the crowd with him in the center of the ring. The President ordered the bull to be given a tour of the ring too.

Five bulls were dead from five sword thrusts when the final bull came out and the noise from the crowd was silenced when Antonio moved way into him with the cape and commenced the long, slow magic passes. The crowd was shouting now on each pass.

The bull seemed to come out limping a little from under the pic although it was well placed. I think he hurt one forefoot slightly pushing against the pic while he was trying to get at the horse through the heavy protector. This lameness cleared up, or loosened up at least, when Ferrer and Joni placed the banderillas but when Antonio took the bull with the muleta he was still a little uncertain in his charges and had a tendency to brake with his front hooves instead of charging clearly through.

Leaning on the planks of the fence I watched Antonio work this out. He took the short charge from close to the bull and then lengthened it suavely. He got the bull moving with the slow movement of his muleta and, holding him in the cloth, extended his charges almost imperceptibly until he was finally charging the scarlet serge cloth from a good distance and passing well. None of this showed to the crowd. They only saw an animal that was hesitant and reluctant to charge change into an animal that charged perfectly and seemed exceedingly brave. They did not know that if Antonio had simply worked in front of the bull's face and tried to show them that the bull would not pass, as most matadors do, the bull never would have passed and the matador would have had to do half-passes or chops. Instead he taught him to charge well and to pass him completely with the horns. He taught him to do the truly dangerous thing and then controlled it and prolonged it with the magic control of his arm and wrist until he was making the same beautiful sculptured passes with this bull that he had made with the two others that were easy for him to work with. Nothing of this showed and after he had done all the great passes with this bull and made them with the same purity of line and emotion of their closeness and their ordered danger the public thought he had merely drawn another great and noble animal.

He made a perfect, emotional faena with this bull, holding him controlled in the long, slow passes in any one of which, if he had hurried or been even a shade abrupt, the bull would have broken in his charge and left the cloth to gore him. This way of fighting is the most dangerous in the world and on this last bull he gave an entire course in how to do it.

There was only one thing for him left to do. He had to kill absolutely perfectly; taking no advantage to himself; not dropping the point of entry of the sword just a touch, or a bare suggestion to one side, where it would still pass but have less risk of hitting bone. So when he furled the muleta and sighted with the sword, he aimed for the very high top of the notch between the shoulder blades and drove in over the horn, his left hand low and guiding with the cloth. He and the bull formed one solid mass and when he came out over the horn the bull had the long steel death in him to the hilt and the aorta was severed. Antonio watched him go down in a foot-gripping, staggering, rolling crash and the second mano a mano was over.

There was still the hysteria of the crowd, the ears, the tail, the hoof, the tour of the ring by the bull, the triumphal trip of both matadors and the chief herdsman of Domecq who had brought the bulls from ranch to ring, now carried on the shoulders of the crowd to the Miramar Hotel. There were the postmortems, the empty, purged feeling after a great fight, the things we said to each other, the dinner that night at La Consula, and in the morning early we were off in a chartered plane to repeat it all, with luck, at the Bayonne ring in France. The statistics had gone ahead by telegram and radio; ten ears, four tails, two hooves. But these meant nothing. What was important was that the two brothers-in-law had fought an almost perfect bull-fight that had been unmarred by any tricks by the men or shady maneuvers by the managers or promoters.

Langston Hughes

(1902–1967)

Influenced by the rhythms of jazz and the themes of the blues, poet Langston Hughes was one of the most important writers of the Harlem Renaissance. Born in Joplin, Missouri, he had a rootless childhood, living at times with his mother and her second husband, his father, or his grandmother. After graduating from high school in Cleveland (where his stepfather worked in the steel mills), Hughes went to Columbia University in New York. He only lasted a year, abandoning his studies in favor of the allure of music in nearby Harlem. He set out to see the world and worked as a bouncer in Paris, a steward on a freighter bound for West Africa, and a busboy in a Washington, D.C., hotel. The poet Vachel Lindsay was eating at the hotel dining room one evening and Hughes slipped three poems beside his dinner plate. Lindsay read several at one of his poetry readings and Hughes, "the busboy poet," was discovered.

By the mid-1930s Langston Hughes was one of the leading voices of the Harlem Renaissance. He supported himself through his writing, both poetry and novels, and teaching. In 1937 he went to Spain, visiting troops on the Republican side of the civil war as a correspondent for the *Baltimore Afro-American*. He attended bullfights, became friends with Ernest Hemingway, and wrote "Letter from Spain" (1937) and "Postcard from Spain." Both are in dialect (to which some black soldiers objected) and adopt the voice of a black volunteer in the Lincoln Battalion. Hughes grapples with the racial implications of the Spanish Civil War, including the capture of one of Franco's Moorish troops "as dark as me."

In an essay, "Negroes in Spain," Hughes wrote, "I've met wide-awake Negroes from various part of the world—New York, our Middle West, the French West Indies, Cuba, Africa . . . all of them here because they know that if Fascism creeps across Spain, across Europe, and then across the world, there will be no more place for intelligent young Negroes at all."

LETTER FROM SPAIN

ADDRESSED TO ALABAMA

> Lincoln Battalion,
> International Brigades,
> November Something, 1937.

Dear Brother at home:

We captured a wounded Moor today.
He was just as dark as me.
I said, Boy, what you been doin' here
Fightin' against the free?

He answered something in a language
I couldn't understand.
But somebody told me he was sayin'
They nabbed him in his land

And made him join the fascist army
And come across to Spain.
And he said he had a feelin'
He'd never get back home again.

He said he had a feelin'
This whole thing wasn't right.
He said he didn't know
The folks he had to fight.

And as he lay there dying
In a village we had taken,
I looked across to Africa
And seed foundations shakin'.

Cause if a free Spain wins this war,
The colonies, too, are free—

Then something wonderful'll happen
To them Moors as dark as me.

I said, I guess that's why old England
And I reckon Italy, too,
Is afraid to let a workers' Spain
Be too good to me and you—

Cause they got slaves in Africa—
And they don't want 'em to be free.
Listen, Moorish prisoner, hell!
Here, shake hands with me!

I knelt down there beside him,
And I took his hand—
But the wounded Moor was dyin'
And he didn't understand.

> Salud,
> Johnny

POSTCARD FROM SPAIN

ADDRESSED TO ALABAMA

> Lincoln–Washington Battalion,
> April, 1938

Dear Folks at home:

I went out this mornin'
Old shells was a-fallin'
Whistlin' and a-fallin'
When I went out this mornin'.

I'm way over here
A long ways from home,
Over here in Spanish country
But I don't feel alone.

Folks over here don't treat me
Like white folks used to do.
When I was home they treated me
Just like they treatin' you.

I don't think things'll ever
Be like that again:
I done met up with folks
Who'll fight for me now
Like I'm fightin' now for Spain.

                        Salud,
                            Johnny

Robert Hughes

(1 9 3 8 –   )

Robert Hughes, once *Time* magazine's chief art critic and now a contributor, is opinionated and passionate—and one of his passions is the city of Barcelona. Hughes has written two books about the city, the encyclopedic *Barcelona* (1992) and the impressionistic *Barcelona the Great Enchantress* (2004), from which this is excerpted. Hughes, a native Australian, has lived in Europe and the United States since 1964, and Barcelona is a place that he considers a second—or third—home. Hughes went to Barcelona for the first time in 1966. "I hardly knew a word of Spanish let alone Catalan but I went there for the oblique reason that I was fanatically keen on George Orwell and wanted to see the place to which he had paid his homage—the one city in Europe in which that insular Englishman felt moved to write with his wholehearted affection."

The last decade has been difficult for Hughes. In 1997 he suffered a nervous breakdown. His book about Australia, *The Fatal Shore* (1987), was updated into the documentary *Beyond the Fatal Shore*, and in 1999, while filming the documentary, he had a near fatal car accident; the ensuing legal difficulties have exiled him from Australia. He and his second wife divorced and his thirty-three-year-old son, a sculptor, committed suicide.

And yet Hughes still wields a muscular punch. His verbal jabs are legendary. On Francis Bacon: "Some art is wallpaper. Bacon's is flypaper." On Julian Schnabel: "Schnabel's work is to painting what Stallone's is to acting." Hughes's knowledge of Barcelona is expansive, encompassing literature, architecture, art, history, and gastronomy. He makes an erudite guide to the enchanted city. In this passage he writes of Spain's most famous architect, Antoni Gaudí.

From BARCELONA THE GREAT ENCHANTRESS

The most famous architect—indeed, for many people today, especially foreign visitors, the single most famous human being—that
Barcelona ever produced was killed by a streetcar one June day in
1926, as he toddled across Gran Via near the corner of Carrer Bailen.
Evidently he was lost in thought and fairly deaf, so that he neither saw
the No. 30 tram bearing down on him nor heard the passersby shouting their warnings. He was an old codger in a rusty black suit. His
pockets were empty (except, by one account, for some orange peel),
he carried neither identification nor money, and he was taken at first
for one of the thousands of seedy old pensioners with whom the
city abounded. Only later, as he lay dying in the public hospital, was
it found that he was the seventy-four-year-old Antoni Gaudí, architect of the unfinished temple of the Sagrada Família and a dozen
other smaller (but, many believe, better) buildings in and just outside
his city.

The Sagrada Família, or, to give its full name, the Templo de la
Sagrada Família (Expiatory Temple of the Holy Family), is beyond
rival the best-known structure in Catalunya. It is to Barcelona what
the Eiffel Tower is to Paris or the Harbour Bridge to Sydney: a completely irreplaceable logo. Being unfinished, it is also much misunder-
stood, starting with the fact that so many of the millions of tourists
who visit it every year imagine that it is a "cathedral." But Barcelona
had already had a perfectly fine cathedral since feudal times. The
Sagrada Família was intended to be what its name says: a "temple,"
where Catalans (and, Gaudí hoped, eventually the whole Catholic
world) would converge to do penance for the sins of "modernity,"
sins which had so horribly and mortally offended Christ, his Virgin
Mother, and—presumably when he wasn't busy carpentering—
Christ's stepfather, St. Joseph. Viewed in the context of Church history, this made sense, admittedly of a somewhat lugubrious kind.
In the last third of the nineteenth century, the Catholic Church felt
it was under siege from all those forces of atheism, scientism, dis-
obedience, and doubt, which its hierarchy rolled together into the
portmanteau word, modernism. Because of this, massive rearguard

actions were fought by Rome. There was Pope Pius IX's "Syllabus of Errors," launched against the threat of a growing liberalism and listing just about every conceivable advanced or critical idea about sin, belief, and duty as a loathsome heresy, to be punished in hellfire. Extreme dogmas were promulgated, such as that of papal infallibility. It is probably true to say that between 1830 and the death of the ultraconservative Pope Pius IX in 1878, the Catholic Church became more ferocious in its perception of heretical threat than it had been since the time of the Crusades. It could no longer burn the actual bodies of sinners, but it certainly could and did cut them off from the body of the Church and participation in the Sacraments, and threaten them with eternal punishment in the afterlife. And Gaudí, to whom a penitential relationship with an implacable God was the very core of religious belief, was just the architect to convey this in stone. What the Church wanted was a new Counter-Reformation, based on an extreme ratcheting-up of cultic devotion to Jesus, Mary, and the saints. Gaudí conceived his temple as a means to that end. It would be an ecstatically repressive building that would help atone for the "excesses" of democracy: Not only was Gaudí more Catholic than the pope, he was more royalist than the king, not that he thought the king was worth much compared to the pope. Anyone so misdirected as to imagine that radicalism in art is in some necessary way connected to radicalism in politics, and that its purpose is to make men happy, might think about Gaudí and be corrected. "Everyone has to suffer," he once told a disciple. "The only ones who don't suffer are the dead. He who wants an end to suffering wants to die."

Gaudí was born in 1852 in Reus, a fair-size provincial town in the Baix Camp (lower plains) of Tarragona. He came from an artisan family of metalsmiths who had married into the families of other smiths, for generations back. Their workshop near Reus was known as the Mas de la Caldera, or "caldronmaker's house."

The country around Tarragona, when Gaudí was a boy, had changed little since it was parceled out to Roman settlers nearly two millennia before. Gaudí developed a passionate curiosity about its plants, animals, and geology. Nature, he said later, was the "Great Book, always open, that we should force ourselves to read." Everything structural or ornamental was already prefigured in natural form, in limestone grottoes, a beetle's shining wing case, or the twisty corrugations of an ancient olive trunk.

Gaudí never ceased to draw on, and from, nature. Each paving block of Passeig de Gràcia features a starfish and an octopus, originally designed for the Casa Batlló. Turtles and tortoises support the columns of the Nativity facade of the Sagrada Família, which also has thirty different species of stone plants copied from the vegetation of Catalunya and the Holy Land. Mushrooms become domes, or columns with capitals. The columns of the Güell Crypt are a grove of brick trunks, sending out branches—the ribbed vaults—that lace into one another.

Gaudí knew and never forgot country building in stone, clay, and timber—materials (he said, with a sovereign disregard for the leisure hours of common folk, which he expected them to sacrifice willingly for the greater glory of God and perhaps of Gaudí, too) that "can be gathered by the peasants themselves in their spare time between their labors." Thus the rough stone walls of terraces in the Baix Camp became the "rustic" colonnades of the Güell Park. In the latter years of his life, while making the figures for the Nativity facade of the Sagrada Família, he made literal transcriptions from nature by chloroforming birds and even a donkey so as to cast them in plaster. Sometimes this effigy-making was of a rather more gruesome kind: Since nobody, and certainly not the bristly and childless patriarch Gaudí, could induce a live baby to be still, when he needed infants for his scene of the "Slaughter of the Innocents" on the Nativity facade he got permission from the nuns in the old Hospital de la Sant Creu to cast the corpses of stillborn babies in plaster. There exists an old photo of one of Gaudí's studios, looking like a charnel house or perhaps the dreadful ogre's cave of Polyphemus in *The Odyssey*, with plaster limbs and bodies hanging on every wall.

But what mattered most to Gaudí was twofold. First, the forms and structural principles that could be deduced from inanimate matter, such as plants. And second, his own artisan background.

This ancestry mattered immensely to the architect. He thought of himself, not as a theoretician, but as a man of his hands. He said, no doubt truthfully, that he learned about complex curvatures and membrane structures by watching his father beat iron and copper sheets, making up the forms without drawing them first, producing the miracle of volume and enclosure from the banality of flatness. It is a fact that tells you almost all you need to know about why Gaudí was not a "modern" architect, in the Mies-Gropius-Le Corbusier sense of "modernity." Unlike such people, unlike even his Catalan contemporaries Domènech i Montaner and Puig i Cadafalch, he thought in terms of manual not conceptual space. Others were ruled by the grid; Gaudí didn't give beans for it. His mature work cannot even be imagined adequately from flat drawings. Its surfaces twist and wiggle. The space flares, solemnly inflates, then collapses again. Gaudí did not like to draw; drawing did not preserve enough information about the complex volumes and hollows he carried in his head. He much preferred to make models, from wood, paper, clay, or cut turnips.

Gaudí's instinctive preference for the haptic over the conceptual worked against him when he entered the school of architecture, housed in the Llotja in Barcelona, where he would study from 1873 to 1877. Because abstractions bored him and he did not think easily in terms of orthographic projection (T-square architecture: plan, elevation, section), he did poorly as a student—not the first time that a genius at school has seemed not to be one. His teachers were far more interested in transmitting the basics of Greco-Roman planning and ornament than in teaching what most interested Gaudí, rural vernacular building ("architecture without architects") and Catalan medievalism. Both fused, or so he came to believe, in a unique sensibility which was nationalist at root and could only be expressed in Catalunya. "Our strength and superiority lies in the balance of feeling and logic," he wrote, "whereas the Nordic races become obsessive and smother feeling. And those of the South, blinded by the excess of color, abandon reason and produce monsters." This, though untrue, reveals not only Gaudí's regionalist mind-set but also, in its last five words, his acquaintance with Goya's "Caprichos."

One medieval complex in particular fired Gaudí's imagination as a teenager, and that of his close friend Eduardo Toda i Güell. It was the monastery of Santa Maria del Poblet, in the Baix Camp of Tarragona, within easy reach of Reus. This once mighty Cistercian foundation had begun in the mid-twelfth century and had benefited greatly from the church building boom that also transformed Barcelona itself in the fourteenth, during the reign of Peter the Ceremonious. Beginning with this monarch, all the kings of Aragon and Catalunya had been buried there. Hence, it was the national pantheon and its import, both historic and patriotic, was immense. As architecture it was the grandest Cistercian building in Catalunya, strong, severe, and plain. Its chapter house, nine vaulted square bays carried on four central columns, ranked with Santa Maria del Mar and the Saló de Tinell as one of the supreme formal utterances of early Catalan Gothic.

But when Gaudí and Toda were boys, Poblet was a ruin and they conceived the mad, devout notion of restoring it to at least a memory, an eloquent vestige of its former glories. To them it was an arch-symbol of Catholic supremacy and Catalan identity, and the liberals had ruined it in the name of freedom and rights. "What is this freedom?" young Toda demanded in an angry verse, if it meant

> to rip up the tomb-slabs
> and violate the sepulchres of heroes
> and sow terror and death everywhere . . .
> and smash monuments to rubble . . .
> if this is freedom, a curse on it!

Thus in Gaudí's mind, religious conservatism—the more extreme, the nobler—fused with the retention of Catalan identity. The Mendizábal Laws, having forced the Church to sell its property, had condemned Poblet to desertion and decay. Gaudí obviously could not undertake its restoration on his own. Patrons must be found. And he had to have his own career as an architect. In the end, no private person offered to pay for the renewal of Poblet, but Gaudí did find a patron for his own work—the sort of patron artists dream of, one who shares all their creative obsessions and does not question their cost. He was Eusebi Güell i Bacigalupi, industrialist, rising politician, and quintessential grandee of the Catalan establishment.

Gaudí's first projects for Güell were a palace in Barcelona and a *finca*, a country estate, up the hill from Barcelona toward the medieval convent of Pedralbes. Of the Finca Güell, only the main gate and its flanking lodges were done to Gaudí's design. But the gate (1884) is an amazing work, a huge guardian dragon in wrought iron, illustrating a poem by the laureate of Catalan religious verse, Jacint Verdaguer.

The palace, which stands on Carrer Nou de la Rambla, is entirely Gaudí's. With it, his maturity as an artist really begins, and it is the first of his buildings to justify his posthumous fame. It was his showpiece and he took infinite pains over its design, doing at least three complete versions of its facade before settling on the final one. Everything from the parabolic entrance to the wooden louvers that sheathe the tribune on its rear facade in a curved membrane like the scales of an armadillo bears the mark of an insatiable inventiveness.

It is also intensely theatrical, which adapts it well to its present-day function as the library of the Institut del Teatre, the Theatrical Archive of Barcelona. This first emerges in the basement, where Güell stabled his horses and kept his carriages. Its rugged vaults spring from squat, fat, brick columns whose capitals are funguslike pads of cooked earth: a cavelike, Wagnerian crypt.

From the start, Gaudí and Güell shared a taste for morbid penitential rhetoric. It would be refined and developed as time passed. Sometimes it produced a gloomy mélange. But at other times, when brought under strict control, the result was a masterpiece, as in the columns and capitals that support the screens of the miradors in Palau Güell. Cut and polished from the metallic gray limestone of Garraf, a quarry that belonged to the Güell enterprises, they look as radically new as Brancusi's sculpture (which Gaudí, of course, had never seen). Their fairing and subtle concavities, their utter purity of line, seem to owe nothing to other sources, though they were possibly inspired by the thirteenth-century capitals in the refectory of Poblet.

The other unique aspect of Palau Güell is its roof: It is truly a masterpiece, a beautiful acropolis of chimneys and ventilators, dominated by a central spire which contains the high slender dome of the main salon.

There are twenty chimneys, all roughly similar in shape: an obelisk or cone mounted on a shaft, which sits on a base, the whole sheathed in fragments of tile or glass. This kind of tilework is ancient and predates Gaudí, although many foreigners wrongly suppose that he invented it. It is known as *trencadis*, *trencar* being the Catalan verb "to break." It originated with the Arabs in Spain but Gaudí was the first architect to revive it. It can cover curved surfaces, and it's cheap, too, because the material can be scrap. Gaudí was fascinated by how the mosaic fragmentation of trencadis, its shifts of color and pattern, could play against the solidity of architectural form, dissolving its stability. It is at least plausible that trencadis lies at the root of cubism, because the young Picasso, living just down the Carrer Nou de la Rambla from Palau Güell, would have seen its chimneys any day of the week. They are a prelude to the trencadis-covered serpentine benches in the Parc Güell, which Gaudí and his brilliant but lesser known colleague Josep Marià Jujol created as part of a large (but financially unsuccessful) housing project on Mont Pelat above Barcelona.

As an enlightened capitalist, Güell knew it was in his interest to reduce friction between workers and management. He thought this could be done by paternalism, avoiding the hard-fisted control that had caused riots, strikes, and machine breaking in other Barcelonan firms. So he decided to set up a self-contained *colonia*, or industrial village, for making cotton goods, velvet, and corduroy, south of Barcelona on the banks of the Llobregat River. Its workers would be isolated from the temptations of the big city. They could live, work, and pray together under the eye of the benign boss. All their needs would be taken care of. The Colonia Güell, as it was known, would have its own clinic and infirmary, its library, even a football club. Of course it would also have a church, which Gaudí would design.

Gaudí started thinking about the church in 1898 and the first stone was laid in 1908. When Eusebi Güell died ten years after that, the crypt was still unfinished and the church's walls above ground were scarcely underway. A few of Gaudí's surviving sketches show a monster edifice with parabolic spires that would have looked quite out of place in the Catalan countryside, though one can well imagine Gaudí replying that medieval cathedrals would have looked incongruous in the flat acres of northern France at first. But though it is only a fragment of a dream, the crypt of the Colonia Güell's church is one of Gaudí's masterworks, a building that looks wildly and arbitrarily expressive until one grasps the logic of construction that removes it from the domain of mere fantasy and creates one of Europe's greatest architectural spaces.

He did this upside down, with string and little bags of bird shot. Drawing out the ground plan of the crypt, he hung a string from each point where a column would meet the floor. Next he joined the hanging strings with cross-strips to simulate arches, beams, and vaults, attaching to each string a tiny bag of bird shot, its weight carefully scaled at so many milligrams per pellet to mimic the compressive load at each point. None of the strings in these complicated cat's cradles hung vertically. All the stresses in them were pure tension—the only way that string, which has zero resistance to bending, "knows" how to hang.

Gaudí then photographed the string model from all angles (seventy-two photographs, representing the rotation of the model five degrees at a time, totaling 360 degrees or one complete turn)—*and turned the photos upside down.*

Tension became compression and these "funicular" models (string models, in plain English, from the Latin *funis*, a cord) gave Gaudí a visual basis for making advanced and painstaking transferences. He could design forms without structural steel reinforcement that traditional masons could build in a brick-stone technology, which had not changed since the fourteenth century, when the wide shallow choir arch of Santa Maria del Pi was built. Gaudí wanted to imagine a kind of space that was both new and deeply archaic. The columns that support the roof of the crypt are hexagonal "pipes" of basalt, brought from a quarry in northern Catalunya and set in lead instead of mortar. (This gives the joints an imperceptible but sufficient flexibility under stress, whereas mortar would crumble.) They lean in a way that recalls ancient forms of shelter: the cave, the ledge, the hollow trunk. One of Gaudí's contemporaries, a friend of Josep Pla named Rafael Puget, called Gaudí "not an architect of houses but an architect of grottoes; not an architect of temples, but an architect of forests." It seemed so in the 1920s and still does today, and if you feel the crypt of the Colonia Güell is the great prototype of the far later, computer-designed structures by Frank Gehry, you are certainly right.

Josep Jujol's finest collaboration with Gaudí, apart from the Parc Güell, was done for another textile mogul: Josep Batlló i Casanovas. The Casa Batlló, on Passeig de Gràcia, was not done from scratch. It was a drastic conversion (1904–1906) of an existing apartment building from the late 1870s. By the time Gaudí was through with it, little survived of the original except the floor levels, and not all of those either. Jujol and Gaudí produced a new facade, an undulant sheet of mosaic wrapping around the windows (whose framing columns resemble bones)—a five-story crust of shifting, aqueous color which resembles nothing so much as one of Claude Monet's "Nymphéas," those enormous, shimmering paintings of light on water. It is one of the most exquisite sights in Spain, this jewel-box fantasy of a street wall surmounted by a roof made of what seem to be giant ceramic scales— which they are. The facade of Casa Batlló was meant to be read as an homage to Sant Jordi, patron of Barcelona. The scales belong to the dragon he killed, as does the serpentine hump in the roof. The white balconies, pierced with holes for eye sockets, are the skulls of the hor-rid reptile's victims. The half-round tower set in the facade ends in a form like a garlic bulb (Catalans, one should remember, can never get enough garlic) surmounted by a cross. This is St. George's lance, and its tip is inscribed with the holy and efficacious names of Jesus, Mary, and Joseph.

When it was finished in 1906 the Casa Batlló became the wonder of Passeig de Gràcia, and this distinction invited competition. It came from the other side of the street, a few blocks uphill, where one of Battló's friends, a property developer named Pere Milà i Camps, com-missioned a new building from Gaudí. The Casa Milà, as it was called, was designed from the ground up, not adapted from an existing build-ing. Its owner gave the architect a free hand. (By then it was clearly pointless *not* to give Gaudí complete design autonomy; without it, he would not consider a commission.)

He produced a sea cliff with caves in it for people. Its forged iron balconies are based on kelp and coral incrustation. Though La Pedrera ("the stone quarry," as Casa Milà was soon christened) looks formidably solid, with its massive projections and overhangs like the eye sockets of a Cyclopean head, it is much less so than it looks. The mighty folds and trunks of stone are actually more like stage grot-toes. Despite its dramatic plasticity the stone is a skin and not, like true masonry, self-supporting.

Thus the Casa Milà becomes a kind of hermaphroditic fortress: on one hand, its maternal aspect—soft swelling, shelter, undulation;

on the other the bizarre and contradictory "guardians" on the roof, invisible from the street. These are intensely masculine, so much so that George Lucas's costume designers based the figures of Darth Vader and the Death Star's guards on them—air-breathing and smoke-bearing totems, helmeted centurions which serve as chimneys and ventilators for the apartments below.

Singular though it is, La Pedrera fell short of Gaudí's original idea, a fact in which we are entitled to rejoice. Discussing Gaudí's taste, an acquaintance of his once remarked, was like talking about the "taste" of whales, something enormous, remote, and, in the end, meaningless. In some areas, like painting, he seems to have had no taste at all: The most beautiful color effects on Gaudían buildings usually turn out to be the work of Jujol, and the paintings Gaudí favored were usually repulsive in their gloomy, saccharine piety.

The same was true of his use of sculpture. It seems almost beyond understanding that a man who created some of the most marvelous three-dimensional forms of his time—for no other words will do for the chimneys of Palau Güell or the unfinished roof of Casa Milà— could have wanted to add to his work the sort of vulgarities Gaudí sometimes had in mind. A striking example was the sculptural allegory of the holy rosary (Rosario being the name of Milà's wife) that he planned to put on top of the Casa Milà as its crowning feature, culminating in a figure of the Virgin Mary flanked by the archangels Gabriel and Michael, forty feet high and in bronze—the Virgin as colossus. The artist Gaudí wanted to do it was Carles Mani i Roig, whose vulgarity was as depressing as his piety was unassailable. The piety, it seems, counted most for Gaudí; in this respect the ugly sculptures being put on the Sagrada Família by its present anti-genius, Josep Subirachs, are desolatingly true to the Gaudían spirit. Mani i Roig would have turned La Pedrera into little more than a convoluted base for a huge, and hugely bad, sculpture. Perhaps its origins in Gaudí's imagination lay in another banal dominatrix of the skyline, the Statue of Liberty in New York Harbor.

That this did not happen was one of the few good results that can be attributed to the frenzy of church burning and street violence known as the Setmana Trágica or Tragic Week, which broke out in Barcelona in 1909 and came close to devastating the city. It was sparked by workers' resentment over a Spanish colonial war, which quickly devolved into a frenzy of anticlerical violence. This, a worse repeat of the Burning of the Convents in 1835, resulted in the destruction of some eighty churches, convents, and religious schools. Any building that declared itself to be Catholic was a potential target of popular wrath, and Milà sensibly figured that an apartment block with a giant Virgin Mary on its roof was unlikely to escape intact. So the commission, mercifully, never went ahead.

By now Gaudí had only one job left, the Sagrada Família. He had to raise the money for it; more or less alone, he had to keep its momentum going without any secure employer (one has to remember that the thing was not and never had been an official Church project). It was the obsession of his last years. In the wake of the Tragic Week it also became Barcelona's chief symbol of rebirth and transcendence for Gaudí's friend, the poet Joan Maragall:

> Like a giant flower, a temple blossoms,
> amazing to be born here
> amid such a coarse and wicked people
> who laugh at it, blaspheme, brawl, vent their scorn
> against everything human and divine.
> Yet among misery, madness and smoke
> the temple (so precious!) rises and flourishes,
> waiting for the faithful who must come.

The Expiatory Temple of the Holy Family represented faith and obedience in purest form. At least, it was meant to. And so, by transference, did Gaudí, whom the Tragic Week turned into a legendary figure in his lifetime, a walking emblem of penitence and devotion.

Lay associations had sprung up like mushrooms in Europe, and particularly in Spain, to propagate the cult of obedience to the infallible pope, Pius IX, who had infallibly defined his own infallibility as a dogma, binding on all the faithful under pain of mortal sin, and therefore, of condemnation to hell.

The chief of these associations in Catalunya called itself the Josephines. They first met at Montserrat, the holy mountain of the Black Virgin, in 1866. They chose a reactionary quartet as honorary patrons, Pius IX, the future king Alfonso XIII, Queen María Cristina, and a soon-to-be-beatified Catalan priest named Antoni Claret. The actual, or managing, leader of the Josephines was a bookseller and amateur flutist named Josep Bocabella i Verdaguer (no relation to the great Catalan poet). Bocabella, it seems, knew very little about architecture. At first the expiatory temple was assigned to a pious mediocrity named Villar, who did Gothic Revival designs. But Villar resigned the next year, 1883, and in 1884 the Josephines found another architect: Antoni Gaudí. Why he was selected remains something of a mystery. He had built very little, and none of his major works, at that time, existed. There is a persistent story, probably too good to be true, that Gaudí got the job because he had such clear, ice blue eyes. One of Bocabella's religious visions had been that the Sagrada Família would be designed by a true Aryan, a man with blue eyes.

Whatever the case, Gaudí had a completely free hand from the moment the Josephines hired him. But no architect can live on the proceeds of a single building, unless he is designing something like the Getty Center, which the Sagrada Família was not. Especially this is so if the building is a church sponsored by a near-penniless organization. Hence the aura of saintly poverty in which Gaudí's name is still enveloped. In the latter years of his life, the old man used literally to beg for funds, knocking on the doors of the wealthy in Sarrià and along the Passeig de Gràcia. No doubt the sight of his close-cropped white poll and shabby black suit struck fear into the bones of families of the city. *"Fets aquest sacrifici,"* he would demand. "Make this sacrifice." "Oh no, Señor Gaudí," the target would protest, fishing out a couple of duros, "Really it's no sacrifice at all, believe me." "Then *make* it a sacrifice," the implacable old man would insist. "Sometimes a gift is not a sacrifice. Sometimes it is nothing but vanity. Be sure."

Washington Irving

(1783–1859)

Washington Irving is identified with two places: the bucolic Hudson River Valley of New York and Spain. Best known for his short stories "The Legend of Sleepy Hollow" and "Rip Van Winkle," which are set in Tarrytown, New York, Irving was the youngest of eleven children born to a wealthy merchant family. He practiced law briefly before turning to journalism and gained fame by writing sketches authored by the fictitious Dietrich Knickerbocker, a Dutch American scholar. From 1815 to 1832 Irving lived in Europe and specialized in writing about Spain, including the volumes *Conquest of Granada* (1920), *The Companions of Columbus* (1931), and *The Alhambra* (1932, from which this excerpt is taken).

Irving returned to the United States acclaimed as America's first international author. He toured the country relentlessly promoting his books. A trip to the western states resulted in his book *A Tour of the Prairies* (1835), in which he suggests a reverse Grand Tour. "We send our youth abroad to grow luxurious and effeminate in Europe; it appears to me that a previous tour on the prairies would be more likely to produce that manliness, simplicity, and self-dependence, most in union with our political institutions." Despite his own advice, Irving returned to Europe as U.S. ambassador to Spain from 1842 to 1845.

In the last years of his life Irving resided at Sunnyside, his home in Tarrytown. He retired, but never stopped writing and completed a five-volume biography of Washington shortly before his death.

From THE ALHAMBRA

PUBLIC FÊTES OF GRANADA

My devoted squire and whilom ragged cicerone Mateo Ximenes, had a poor-devil passion for fêtes and holidays, and was never so eloquent as when detailing the civil and religious festivals of Granada.

During the preparations for the annual Catholic fête of Corpus Christi, he was in a state of incessant transition between the Alhambra and the subjacent city, bringing me daily accounts of the magnificent arrangements that were in progress, and endeavoring, but in vain, to lure me down from my cool and airy retreat to witness them. At length, on the eve of the eventful day I yielded to his solicitations and descended from the regal halls of the Alhambra under his escort, as did of yore the adventure-seeking Haroun Alraschid, under that of his Grand Vizier Giaffar. Though it was yet scarce sunset, the city gates were already thronged with the picturesque villagers of the mountains, and the brown peasantry of the Vega. Granada has ever been the rallying place of a great mountainous region, studded with towns and villages. Hither, during the Moorish domination, the chivalry of this region repaired, to join in the splendid and semi-warlike fêtes of the Vivarrambla, and hither the elite of its population still resort to join in the pompous ceremonies of the church. Indeed, many of the mountaineers from the Alpuxarras and the Sierra de Ronda, who now bow to the cross as zealous Catholics, bear the stamp of their Moorish origin, and are indubitable descendants of the fickle subjects of Boabdil.

Under the guidance of Mateo, I made my way through streets already teeming with a holiday population, to the square of the Vivarrambla, that great place for tilts and tourneys, so often sung in the Moorish ballads of love and chivalry. A gallery or arcade of wood had been erected along the sides of the square, for the grand religious procession of the following day. This was brilliantly illuminated for the evening as a promenade; and bands of music were stationed on balconies on each of the four façades of the square. All the fashion and beauty of Granada, all of its population of either sex that had good looks or fine clothes to display, thronged this arcade, promenading round and round the Vivarrambla. Here, too, were the *Majos* and *Majas*, the rural beaux and belles, with fine forms, flashing eyes, and gay Andalusian costumes; some of them from Ronda itself, that stronghold of the mountains, famous for contrabandistas, bullfighters, and beautiful women.

While this gay but motley throng kept up a constant circulation in the gallery, the centre of the square was occupied by the peasantry from the surrounding country; who made no pretensions to display, but came for simple, hearty enjoyment. The whole square was covered with them; forming separate groups of families and neighborhoods, like gipsy encampments, some were listening to the traditional ballad drawled out to the tinkling of the guitar; some were engaged in gay conversation; some were dancing to the click of the castanet. As I threaded my way through this teeming region with Mateo at my heels, I passed occasionally some rustic party, seated on the ground, making a merry though frugal repast. If they caught my eyes as I loitered by, they almost invariably invited me to partake of their simple fare. This hospitable usage, inherited from their Moslem invaders, and originating in the tent of the Arab, is universal throughout the land, and observed by the poorest Spaniard.

As the night advanced the gayety gradually died away in the arcades; the bands of music ceased to play, and the brilliant crowd dispersed to their homes. The centre of the square still remained well peopled and Mateo assured me that the greater part of the peasantry, men, women, and children, would pass the night there, sleeping on the bare earth beneath the open canopy of heaven. Indeed a summer night requires no shelter in this favored climate; and a bed is a superfluity, which many of the hardy peasantry of Spain never enjoy, and which some of them affect to despise. The common Spaniard wraps himself in his brown cloak, stretches himself on his manta or mulecloth, and sleeps soundly, luxuriously accommodated if he can have a saddle for a pillow. In a little while the words of Mateo were made good; the peasant multitude nestled down on the ground to their night's repose, and by midnight, the scene on the Vivarrambla resembled the bivouac of an army.

The next morning, accompanied by Mateo, I revisited the square at sunrise. It was still strewed with groups of sleepers; some were reposing from the dance and revel of the evening; others, who had left their villages after work on the preceding day, having trudged on foot the greater part of the night, were taking a sound sleep to freshen themselves for the festivities of the day. Numbers from the mountains, and the remote villages of the plain, who had set out in

the night, continued to arrive with their wives and children. All were
in high spirits; greeting each other and exchanging jokes and pleas-
antries. The gay tumult thickened as the day advanced. Now came
pouring in at the city gates, and parading through the streets, the deputations from the various villages, destined to swell the grand procession. These village deputations were headed by their priests, bearing
their respective crosses and banners, and images of the blessed Virgin and of patron saints; all which were matters of great rivalship
and jealousy among the peasantry. It was like the chivalrous gatherings of ancient days, when each town and village sent its chiefs, and
warriors, and standards to defend the capital or grace its festivities.

At length all these various detachments congregated into one
grand pageant, which slowly paraded round the Vivarrambla, and
through the principal streets, where every window and balcony was
hung with tapestry. In this procession were all the religious orders,
the civil and military authorities, and the chief people of the parishes
and villages: every church and convent had contributed its banners,
its images, its relics, and poured forth its wealth for the occasion. In
the centre of the procession walked the archbishop, under a damask
canopy, and surrounded by inferior dignitaries and their dependants.
The whole moved to the swell and cadence of numerous bands of
music, and, passing through the midst of a countless yet silent multitude, proceeded onward to the cathedral.

I could not but be struck with the changes of times and customs,
as I saw this monkish pageant passing through the Vivarrambla, the
ancient seat of Moslem pomp and chivalry. The contrast was indeed
forced upon the mind by the decorations of the square. The whole
front of the wooden gallery erected for the procession, extending
several hundred feet, was faced with canvas, on which some humble
though patriotic artist had painted, by contract, a series of the principal scenes and exploits of the conquest, as regarded in chronicle
and romance. It is thus the romantic legends of Granada mingle
themselves with every thing, and are kept fresh in the public mind.

As we wended our way back to the Alhambra, Mateo was in high
glee and garrulous vein. "Ah, Señor," exclaimed he, "there is no place
in all the world like Granada for grand ceremonies (*funciones grandes*),

a man need spend nothing on pleasure here, it is all furnished him gratis. Pero, el día de la Toma! Ah, Señor! el día de la Toma! But the day of the Taking! ah, Señor, the day of the Taking"—that was the great day which crowned Mateo's notions of perfect felicity. The Día de la Toma, I found, was the anniversary of the capture or taking possession of Granada, by the army of Ferdinand and Isabella.

On that day, according to Mateo, the whole city is abandoned to revelry. The great alarm bell on the watchtower of the Alhambra (*la Torre de la vela*), sends forth its clanging peals from morn till night; the sound pervades the whole Vega, and echoes along the mountains, summoning the peasantry from far and near to the festivities of the metropolis. "Happy the damsel," says Mateo, "who can get a chance to ring that bell; it is a charm to insure a husband within the year."

Throughout the day the Alhambra is thrown open to the public. Its halls and courts, where the Moorish monarchs once held sway, resound with the guitar and castanet, and gay groups, in the fanciful dresses of Andalusia, perform their traditional dances inherited from the Moors.

A grand procession, emblematic of the taking possession of the city, moves through the principal streets. The banner of Ferdinand and Isabella, that precious relic of the Conquest, is brought forth from its depository, and borne in triumph by the Alferez mayor, or grand standard-bearer. The portable camp-altar, carried about with the sovereigns in all their campaigns, is transported into the chapel royal of the cathedral, and placed before their sepulchre, where their effigies lie in monumental marble. High mass is then performed in memory of the Conquest; and at a certain part of the ceremony the Alferez mayor puts on his hat, and waves the standard above the tomb of the conquerors.

A more whimsical memorial of the Conquest is exhibited in the evening at the theatre. A popular drama is performed, entitled *Ave Maria*, turning on a famous achievement of Hernando del Pulgar, surnamed "el de las Hazañas" (he of the exploits), a madcap warrior, the favorite hero of the populace of Granada. During the time of the siege, the young Moorish and Spanish cavaliers vied with each other in extravagant bravadoes. On one occasion this Hernando del

Pulgar, at the head of a handful of followers, made a dash into Granada in the dead of the night, nailed the inscription of "Ave Maria" with his dagger to the gate of the principal mosque, a token of having consecrated it to the Virgin, and effected his retreat in safety.

While the Moorish cavaliers admired this daring exploit, they felt bound to resent it. On the following day, therefore, Tarfe, one of the stoutest among them, paraded in front of the Christian army, dragging the tablet bearing the sacred inscription "Ave Maria," at his horse's tail. The cause of the Virgin was eagerly vindicated by Garcilaso de la Vega, who slew the Moor in single combat, and elevated the tablet in devotion and triumph at the end of his lance.

The drama founded on this exploit is prodigiously popular with the common people. Although it has been acted time out of mind, it never fails to draw crowds, who become completely lost in the delusions of the scene. When their favorite Pulgar strides about with many a mouthy speech, in the very midst of the Moorish capital, he is cheered with enthusiastic bravos; and when he nails the tablet to the door of the mosque, the theatre absolutely shakes with the thunders of applause. On the other hand, the unlucky actors who figure in the part of the Moors, have to bear the brunt of popular indignation; which at times equals that of the Hero of Lamanche, at the puppet-show of Gines de Passamonte; for, when the infidel Tarfe plucks down the tablet to tie it to his horse's tail, some of the audience rise in fury, and are ready to jump upon the stage to revenge this insult to the Virgin.

By the way, the actual lineal descendant of Hernando del Pulgar, was the Marquis de Salar. As the legitimate representative of that madcap hero, and in commemoration and reward of this hero's exploit, above mentioned, he inherited the right to enter the cathedral on certain occasions, on horseback; to sit within the choir, and to put on his hat at the elevation of the host, though these privileges were often and obstinately contested by the clergy. I met him occasionally in society; he was young, of agreeable appearance and manners, with bright black eyes, in which appeared to lurk some of the fire of his ancestors. Among the paintings in the Vivarrambla, on the fête of Corpus Christi, were some depicting, in vivid style, the exploits of the family hero. An old gray-headed servant of the Pulgars shed tears on beholding them, and hurried home to inform the marquis. The eager zeal and enthusiasm of the old domestic only provoked a light laugh from his young master; whereupon, turning to the brother of the marquis, with that freedom allowed in Spain to old family servants, "Come Señor," cried he, "you are more considerate than your brother; come and see your ancestor in all his glory!"

In emulation of this great *Día de la Toma* of Granada, almost every village and petty town of the mountains has its own anniversary, commemorating, with rustic pomp and uncouth ceremonial, its deliverance from the Moorish yoke. On these occasions, according to Mateo, a kind of resurrection takes place of ancient armor and weapons; great two-handed swords, ponderous arquebuses with matchlocks, and other warlike relics, treasured up from generation to generation, since the time of the Conquest; and happy the community that possesses some old piece of ordnance, peradventure one of the identical lombards used by the conquerors; it is kept thundering along the mountains all day long, provided the community can afford sufficient expenditure of powder.

In the course of the day, a kind of warlike drama is enacted. Some of the populace parade the streets, fitted out with the old armor, as champions of the faith. Others appear dressed up as Moorish warriors. A tent is pitched in the public square, inclosing an altar with an image of the Virgin. The Christian warriors approach to perform their devotions; the infidels surround the tent to prevent their entrance; a mock fight ensues; the combatants sometimes forget that they are merely playing a part, and dry blows of grievous weight are apt to be exchanged. The contest, however, invariably terminates in favor of the good cause. The Moors are defeated and taken prisoners. The image of the Virgin, rescued from thraldom, is elevated in triumph; a grand procession succeeds, in which the conquerors figure with great applause and vainglory; while their captives are led in chains, to the evident delight and edification of the spectators.

These celebrations are heavy drains on the treasuries of these petty communities, and have sometimes to be suspended for want of funds; but, when times grow better, or sufficient money has been hoarded for the purpose, they are resumed with new zeal and prodigality.

Mateo informed me that he had occasionally assisted at these fêtes and taken a part in the combats; but always on the side of the true faith; "*porque Señor,*" added the ragged descendant of the cardinal Ximenes, tapping his breast with something of an air, "*porque Señor, soy Christiano viejo.*"

Henry James

(1843–1916)

Although best known for his novels, including *The Europeans* (1878), *Daisy Miller* (1879), and *Portrait of a Lady* (1881), Henry James was also an accomplished travel writer. James began traveling as an infant when his parents took him and their other young children to Europe for four years. Convinced that his children (including William James, who would become a theologian and philosopher) would get a superior education abroad, Henry James Sr. moved his family between New York and the Continent for most of their upbringing. Predictably, his son's writing often dealt with the clash between European tradition and American sensibilities.

In 1875 James decided to live abroad and settled in Paris, where he arranged to write a column for the *New York Tribune* about his experiences. His tenure was short, as he delivered thoughtful impressions of European life, including an early, unfavorable review of the early French impressionists; his editor wanted more about Paris gossip, so James resigned. Free of his obligations to the *Tribune*, James set out to travel to the south of France and briefly crossed the border at Biarritz and entered Spain. Although his foray into San Sebastián was brief, as was his report of his experience, his writing contains wonderfully pithy observations that are typical James. Of a bullfight he wrote, "I thought the bull, in any case, a finer fellow than any of his tormentors."

James loved to travel and late in life became fast friends with another expatriate writer, Edith Wharton. They motored together through the Continent, Wharton at the wheel. Based in London for four decades, James was shocked that he had to register as an "alien" with the British police because of sedition laws enacted during World War I. In a show of solidarity with the cause of his adopted home, he became a British citizen at the age of seventy-two. He died less than a year later in London, a few weeks before King George V gave him the Order of Merit. Although buried in the family plot in Cambridge, Massachusetts, Henry James is memorialized in the Poet's Corner of Westminster Abbey.

The excerpt included here is from James's *From Normandy to the Pyrenees*, which was originally published as an article in *The Galaxy* (1877). It has since been reprinted in booklet form for modern readers.

From COLLECTED TRAVEL WRITINGS

FROM NORMANDY TO THE PYRENEES

The best thing at Biarritz is your opportunity for driving over into Spain. Coming speedily to a consciousness of this fact, I found a charm in sitting in a landau and rolling away to San Sebastián behind a coachman in a high glazed hat with long streamers, a jacket of scarlet and silver and a pair of yellow breeches and jack-boots. If it has been the desire of one's heart and the dream of one's life to visit the land of Cervantes, even grazing it so lightly as by a day's excursion from Biarritz is a matter to encourage visions. Everything helping—the admirable scenery, the charming day, the operatic coachman, the smooth-rolling carriage—I am afraid I became more visionary than it is decent to tell of. You move toward the magnificent undulations of the Pyrenees, as if you were going to plunge straight into them; but in reality you travel beneath them and beside them, pass between their expiring spurs and the sea. It is on proceeding beyond San Sebastián that you seriously attack them. But they are already extremely vivid—none the less so that in this region they abound in suggestions of the recent Carlist war. Their far-away peaks and ridges are crowned with lonely Spanish watch-towers, and their lower slopes are dotted with demolished dwellings. It was hereabouts that the fighting was most constant. But the healing powers of nature are as remarkable as the destructive powers of man, and the rich September landscape appeared already to have forgotten the injuries of yesterday. Everything seemed to me a small foretaste of Spain; I discovered an unreasonable amount of local colour. I discovered it at Saint-Jean-de-Luz, the last French town, in a great brown church, filled with galleries and boxes, like a play-house—the altar and choir, indeed, looked very much like a proscenium; at Bohébie, on the Bidassoa, the small yellow stream which divides France from Spain, and which at this point offers to view the celebrated Isle of Pheas-

ants, a little bushy strip of earth adorned with a decayed commemo-
rative monument, on which, in the seventeenth century, the affairs of
Louis XIV and the Iberian monarch were discussed in ornamental
conference; at Fuentarabia (glorious name), a mouldering relic of
Spanish stateliness; at Hendaye, at Irún, at Rentería, and finally at San
Sebastián. At all of these wayside towns the houses show marks of
Alphonsist bullets (the region was strongly Carlist); but to be riddled
and battered seems to carry out the meaning of the pompous old
escutcheons carven above the doorways, some of them covering
almost half the house. It struck me, in fact, that the narrower and
shabbier was the poor little dusky dwelling, the grander and more
elaborate was this noble advertisement. But it represented knightly
prowess, and pitiless time had taken up the challenge. I found it a luxury to ramble through the narrow single street of Irún and Rentería,
between the strange-coloured houses, the striped awnings, the universal balconies and the heraldic doorways.

San Sebastián is a lively watering-place, and is set down in the
guide-books as the Biarritz or the Brighton of Spain. It has of course
a new quarter in the provincial-elegant style (fresh stucco cafés, barber-
shops, and apartments to let), looking out upon a planted promenade
and a charming bay, locked in fortified heights, with a narrow portal
to the ocean. I walked about for two or three hours and devoted
most of my attention to the old quarter, the town proper, which has
a great frowning gate upon the harbour, through which you look
along a vista of gaudy house-fronts, balconies, awnings, surmounted
by a narrow strip of sky. Here the local colour was richer, the manners more naïf. Here too was a church with a flamboyant Jesuit façade
and an interior redolent of Spanish Catholicism. There was a life-
sized effigy of the Virgin perched upon a table beside the great altar
(she appeared to have been walking abroad in a procession), which I
looked at with extreme interest. She seemed to me a heroine, a solid
Spanish person, as perfect a reality as Don Quixote or Saint Theresa.
She was dressed in an extraordinary splendour of laces, brocades and
jewels, her coiffure and complexion were of the finest, and she evidently would answer to her name if you should speak to her. Muster-
ing up the stateliest title I could think of, I addressed her as Doña
María of the Holy Office; whereupon she looked round the great

dusky, perfumed church, to see whether we were alone, and then she dropped her fringed eyelids and held out her hand to be kissed. She was the sentiment of Spanish Catholicism; gloomy, yet bedizened, emotional as a woman, and mechanical as a doll. After a moment I grew afraid of her, and went slinking away. After this, I didn't really recover my spirits until I had the satisfaction of hearing myself addressed as "Caballero." I was hailed with this epithet by a ragged infant, with sickly eyes and a cigarette in his lips, who invited me to cast a copper into the sea, that he might dive for it; and even with these limitations, the sensation seemed worth the cost of my excursion. It appeared kinder, to my gratitude, to make the infant dive upon the pavement.

A few days later I went back to San Sebastián, to be present at a bull-fight; but I suppose my right to descant upon this entertainment should be measured less by the gratification it afforded me than by the question whether there is room in literature for another chapter on this subject. I incline to think there is not; the national pastime of Spain is the best-described thing in the world. Besides, there are other reasons for not describing it. It is extremely disgusting, and one should not describe disgusting things—except (according to the new school) in novels, where they have not really occurred, and are invented on purpose. Description apart, one has taken a certain sort of pleasure in the bull-fight, and yet how is one to state gracefully that one has taken pleasure in a disgusting thing? It is a hard case. If you record your pleasure, you seem to exaggerate it and to calumniate your delicacy; and if you record nothing but your displeasure, you feel as if you were wanting in suppleness. Thus much I can say, at any rate, that as there had been no bull-fights in that part of the country during the Carlist war, the native dilettanti (and every man, woman, and child of them comes under this denomination) returned to their precious pastime with peculiar zest. The spectacle, therefore, had an unusual splendour. Under these circumstances it is highly effective. The weather was beautiful; the near mountains peeped over the top of the vast open arena, as if they too were curious; weary of disembowelled horses and posturing *espadas*, the spectator (in the boxes) might turn away and look through an unglazed window at the empty town and the cloud-shadowed sea. But few of the native spectators availed themselves of this privilege. Beside me sat a blooming matron, in a white lace mantilla, with three very juvenile daughters; and if these ladies sometimes yawned they never shuddered. For myself, I confess that if I sometimes shuddered I never yawned. A long list of bulls was sacrificed, each of whom had pretensions to originality. The *banderilleros*, in their silk stockings and embroidered satin costumes, skipped about with a great deal of attitude; the *espada* folded his arms within six inches of the bull's nose and stared him out of countenance; yet I thought the bull, in any case, a finer fellow than any of his tormentors, and I thought his tormentors finer fellows than the spectators. In truth, we were all, for the time, rather sorry fellows together. A bull-fight will, to a certain extent, bear looking at, but it will not bear thinking of. There was a more innocent effect in what I saw afterward, when we all came away, in the late afternoon, as the shadows were at their longest: the bright-coloured southern crowd, spreading itself over the grass, and the women, with mantillas and fans, and the Andalusian gait, strolling up and down before the mountains and the sea.

1876

Peter Kerr

(1940–   )

Provence has Peter Mayle, Tuscany has Frances Mayes, and Majorca has Peter Kerr. Like Mayle and Mayes, Kerr left his home (in his case, Scotland) for a slower, Mediterranean life. Raised in rural East Lothian in Scotland, Kerr was nineteen when he set out for Germany with his seven-piece Dixieland band. After that two-month engagement, he joined the Clyde Valley Stompers, a Scottish jazz band that recorded for George Martin, the Beatles' producer. Through the 1960s Kerr produced records himself, including a bagpipe version of "Amazing Grace" that sold 13 million copies.

Tired of the music industry, Kerr and his family returned to Scotland and took up farming, specializing in growing barley and raising beef. By the mid-1980s he was ready for another change. Nothing in his previous life prepared Kerr for growing oranges in Majorca. Anyone familiar with the Mayle/Mayes genre can predict what happens to the Kerrs: they jump into an impulsive heart-over-head purchase, are buffaloed by locals, battle the elements (including a freakish snow-storm), and ultimately triumph—or not.

The most successful enterprise that resulted from Peter Kerr's Majorcan idyll was his writing career, including two bestsellers, *Snowball Oranges* (2000, from which this excerpt is taken) and its sequel, *Mañana, Mañana* (2002). In the con-clusion of *Snowball Oranges*, he wrote rhapsodically, "We were beginning to realize that the passage of time through the unhurried serenity of Majorcan country life was something to be marked by the slowly changing face of nature, not by the hands of a clock or the pages of a calendar." After three years in Majorca, Peter Kerr and his family returned to farming in Scotland.

From SNOWBALL ORANGES

"I know that there are no hens on your farm any more, because Francisca Ferrer strangled them all for the pot the day before you arrived." The old peasant woman smiled, handing me a basket of large brown eggs. "Feel—some of them are still warm," she said, taking my hand and shoving it into the basket. *"Muy frescos, estos huevos, no?"*

They certainly were fresh—good old-fashioned fresh, with little, downy feathers stuck to the shells on smudges of hen droppings, just like the eggs I used to collect in my granny's henhouse when I was a kid. Suddenly, it made me realize how our more "progressive" ways had made us accustomed to buying sanitized, supermarket eggs, all squeaky clean and officially graded in their boring little plastic boxes. Hell, I thought, there could be millions of kids these days who really believe that hens actually lay their eggs in six-packs.

I must have gone slightly dewey-eyed at the sight of those "real" eggs.

"You do not like the eggs, *señor?*" asked the puzzled old woman.

"Oh, *sí, sí,*" I assured her. "The droppings just reminded me of my granny for a moment."

She scratched her gray head and muttered a string of unintelligible oaths, ending, I was sure, in *loco extranjero*—a common enough term in Majorca, meaning "crazy foreigner."

Hastily thanking her for her kindness, I said that I hoped that I hadn't appeared ungrateful. It was difficult for me to explain in Spanish the feeling of nostalgia which her basket of honest, dung-dotted eggs had provoked, but I tried.

She laid a work-worn hand on mine, stopping me in mid-stammer. *"Tranquilo, señor*—do not worry. Spanish is not my native tongue either, and when I am forced to speak it, I must also search for the correct words. In the old days, we Majorcans spoke only *mallorquín*, so now, if I have to converse in the tongue of the *españoles*, it is necessary for me to speak very slowly . . . just like you . . . like *un extranjero*, no?" Her eyes twinkled like little black pearls, and her face creased into a wide, open-mouthed smile, revealing five sparkling white teeth—two up, three down. It was one of those instantly infectious smiles, one of those visual tickles that defy resistance, and seeing my grinning reaction, the old woman clasped her hands together and chuckled quietly for a moment or two, her expression darkening into a scowl as she reverted to mumbling yet another stream of abuse to herself—this time about eggs, the Civil War and soldiers, I guessed, and the *profesión inmoral* of the *madres* of those thieving *españoles*.

I started to introduce myself.

"I know, I know," she interrupted. "Francisca Ferrer—*La Condesa*, the Countess, we call her—has told me all about you. *Com estàs?* I am Maria Bauzá, your neighbor in the next farm to the north. And I must thank you, *señor*, for the land which you have bought here separates my *finca* at last from that of *La Condesa* Ferrer—*gracias a Dios*."

She had now made it fairly plain that she had precious little time for Francisca Ferrer (not to mention the *españoles*), but tempted as I was to ask why, I judged it best to contain my curiosity for the present, my prime objective as a newcomer to the valley—and a *loco extranjero* to boot—being to establish friendly terms with *all* of our neighbors . . . if at all possible.

We were standing under the sweeping, upward-curved outer branches of a sprawling fig tree near the stone wall that separated our two farms. Señora Bauzá's stooped, frail-looking frame was clad entirely in black, as is the custom of the older Majorcan countrywomen, and I hadn't even been aware of her standing there in the shade as I walked through the orchard—the first of many times I would notice how the island's old *campesinos* merge so naturally into their tree-speckled landscape. In truth, if old Maria hadn't greeted me with a cheery "*Buenos!*" I would have passed right by without even knowing she was there.

It had only just turned nine o'clock on a beautifully calm winter's morning, and the warmth of the early sun was already dispersing the gossamer-thin veil of mist that had been rising from the fields, still wet from the previous day's melted snow. My head was filled with the musty smell of the damp earth and the sharp, exotic fragrance of citrus blended with faint hints of juniper and wood smoke from the surrounding hillsides. A trace of wispy cloud hung over the table-top summit of *Ses Penyes* mountain, the rounded, rocky mass blocking the high northern end of the valley and sheltering the lower reaches from the worst of the cold blast which can hurtle down from northern Europe in winter, picking up speed and fury disguised as the Mistral as it funnels southward through the Rhône valley in France, before howling unobstructed over the Mediterranean Sea to vent its final wrath on the Balearic Islands.

But the *Tramuntana* had blown itself out during the night, and a placid silence had returned to the valley, broken only by the distant barking of a dog on one of the high mountain *fincas*. Most of those remote farms are impossible to see from the valley below, the only sign of their existence being the thin straggles of white smoke from their chimneys drifting up through the densely wooded upper slopes on clear winter days.

"Very few people live up there any more," said old Maria, following my gaze to the high ridges. "But in the old days . . . well, there are little hidden valleys in the mountains up there where the soil was walled into terraces many centuries ago—they say by the Moors when they ruled this island. And families used to scratch a living from those narrow *bancales*, growing whatever they could. *Sí*, and in the woods, they would rear a few pigs—little, black Majorcan *porcs*. Ah, those *porcs* . . . what a taste, and all because of the acorns and things. The pigs had to find their food by rooting among the trees, you understand. Pigs and forests go well together, no? *Sí*, the forest floor feeds the pigs, and the pigs keep the forest floor clean. *Un sistema perfecto, eh? Sí, sí*—no forest fires in the old days . . ."

I started to ask how they got water up to those mountain farms before the days of tanker trucks, but her train of thought was not to be diverted.

"You need a pig, *señor*. Everyone with a fruit farm needs a pig . . . maybe two. Depends on how much fallen fruit you have. You need to make use of everything on these farms, and pigs are good for that. Hens too. You need new hens now that *La Condesa* has wrung the necks of the old ones. Yugh!"

She shook her head rapidly and shuddered, as if she had just tasted something foul. Francisca Ferrer was definitely not the flavor of the month.

I thanked her for her useful advice and assured her that I would see to buying a pig and some hens once we had settled in. But I was more urgently concerned about our two hundred or more trees of oranges that were almost ready to pick. Perhaps she could suggest a merchant who might buy the fruit from me?

"How did they get the water up there? *Hombre*, they did not . . . they could not," she shrugged, reverting to my penultimate question with no sign of a mental gear-change. "When it rained, all the roof water ran into an underground tank—*un aljibe*, just like the one at your house, no? *Sí*, and not many mountain farms have wells like down here in the valley, so the winter rain in the *aljibes* had to last most of them all summer long." She rubbed her forefinger and thumb together. "Water is gold to the Majorcan farmer, eh, and many feuds have been fought over wells and their precious *agua*. You will learn soon enough, *señor*. Ah *sí*, you will learn. *Agua, agua, agua* . . ."

She nodded sagely and shuddered again, prompting me to wonder if the Señoras Bauzá and Ferrer were adversaries in a water war. The words Ferrer and *agua* certainly seemed to have the same nauseating effect on the old woman.

"Tomàs Ferrer told me that the well on this farm is one of the best in the valley, so we're lucky. Of course, the Ferrers still have sole use of the well at weekends. That was the deal when we bought the place, but my lawyer did assure me that this sort of arrangement is quite common here when part of a farm is sold and part is retained by the seller. It seems a fair enough system . . . if both parties play the game. You must be very trusting and co-operative people, you Majorcans, eh?" I quipped.

Old Maria glanced quickly at the orange trees. "Just ask Jaume, my son-in-law, about selling your fruit," she advised, picking up again on my penultimate topic. "He helps me to work my *finca*, you see. I cannot lift the fruit crates any more—not like I could in the old days." She looked down and tapped the fingers of her left hand in turn. "*Sí*, I am . . . um, eighty-two, you know, so Jaume deals with selling the fruit. But I still look after the money, though. I am not too old for that." She beamed her five-tooth smile again. "*Hombre*, I will never be too old for that. *Nunca jamás!*" Laughing quietly to herself, she turned to leave. "*Adéu, señor*. My regards to your wife . . . and I hope you enjoy the eggs."

The old woman hobbled off through a colonnade of lemon trees, paused, half-turned toward me, and shouted out in a shrill treble which could have been heard throughout the whole valley, "AND DO NOT TALK TO ME ABOUT SHARING WATER WELLS WITH NEIGHBORS!" She winked impishly, then added in a loud whisper, "You will learn soon enough, *señor*. You will learn."

Hell's bells, I really did have a lot to learn, I thought to myself while I trudged back through the fields to the house. God, look at all those bloody fruit trees . . . I still had to find out how to feed them, prune them, spray them, irrigate them, and the only ones I could even identify yet were the ones with oranges and lemons hanging from them. Still, at least old Maria Bauzá had given me a bit of a lead regarding the selling of the fruit. That was good . . . but now there was this tricky water-sharing business, and pigs, and hens, and all the weeds growing under the trees . . . and I didn't even have a tractor yet, and . . .

"Have you had a shower this morning?" Ellie called from the bathroom window as I emerged from a little grove of almond trees in front of the house.

"No, not yet—but I didn't think you'd be able to smell me from that distance."

"Never mind that. There's a problem with the shower. No hot water."

The boiler was situated in a dark corner of the *almacén*, a large room used for sorting and storing the fruit, which took up more than half of the ground floor of the house, and by the time I arrived on site, Ellie was already there, banging the gas cylinder on the floor and tugging at its rubber connecting pipe.

"Right," she said, "there's gas in the bottle, and it's joined up to the boiler okay. The pilot light's still on, so that's all right. But wait a minute. Hmmm, there's a smell of gas, isn't there? Yes, it's a job for a plumber."

There was nothing left for me to say, except a rather futile, "Yeah, and if you ask me, that old boiler looks a bit small for the size of the house, anyway . . ."

* 　 * 　 *

Juan the plumber was no ordinary plumber, but a plumber *and* an electrician. His tiny front shop in the Andratx market place was an Aladdin's cave of mini-chandeliers, wall lights, electric irons, toasters, radiators, electric fans—even a couple of fridges, a washing machine, and a microwave oven. The shop was tended by Juan's wife, a petite, happy-faced girl who looked no older than a teenager herself, yet she had three tiny tots pulling at her skirts behind the counter, and we could hear the sound of at least one more baby crying in the back room.

"My husband is very busy," she told us.

"Not busy enough, it seems," murmured Ellie, looking over the counter at her swarm of under-fives.

"Nevertheless, he will be at your house to fix your water boiler tonight at eight o'clock. We live not far from you, so he can come by before he comes home for dinner."

"So much for the so-called *Mañana* Syndrome," I remarked as we left the shop. "That's what I call service."

The trucks that delivered the butane gas bottles were too long to turn at our gate, so Francisca Ferrer had told us to leave our empty canisters (with the refill money underneath) at the end of the lane on Wednesdays, although—in emergencies—we could also get a full canister on Mondays and Fridays by driving around the streets of Andratx until we came across one of the trucks making its town deliveries. This being a Monday, we had put the empty canister from the stove into the car, and by timing our truck search to start promptly at ten A.M., we guessed that we had a fair chance of hitting the jackpot immediately by heading straight for the main square, the Plaza de España. And there, as expected, was the *butano* man, relaxing over his mid-morning coffee and *coñac* with a few local worthies outside the Bar Nuevo, his orange-colored *camión* fully loaded and completely abandoned, half mounted on the pavement at the corner of the square.

"*Perdón,*" I said, when at length he had decided that it was about time to saunter back to his truck, smoke streaming from the fat, stubby cigar, which wobbled between his lips like a broken brown banana in a face-shaped strawberry blancmange. "*Perdón*, but I'd like to buy a bottle of gas, *por favor.*"

He heaved a full canister from the truck and replaced it with my empty one. I handed him some notes, and he wedged his lit cigar into the neck of my full canister while he fumbled for change in the pockets of his overalls. I closed my eyes and waited for the bang, but the only explosion was a crepitous chuckle from the *butano* man.

"Isn't that a bit dangerous—smoking when you're working with gas bottles?" I asked edgily.

"Dangerous?" He handed me my change and raised his shoulders. "*Coño*, if someone crashes into me on the road—and there are always plenty of *lunáticos* driving around on this island—this *camión* will go up like an atom bomb, and me with it. I live on borrowed time, *amigo*, so I enjoy myself while I am still alive . . . I smoke." He retrieved his cigar and climbed into the truck.

"While you're there, why not buy two full canisters," Ellie shouted from the car. "We could do with a spare."

"*No es posible, señora,*" the *butano* man called back, shaking his head with one eye closed against the rising smoke from his cigar, now stuffed safely back in his face. In order to buy a second full *botella*, he explained, we either had to give him a second empty *botella* or show him a certificate from the *butano* office verifying that we were entitled to buy another full *botella*. An empty *botella* or an official *certificado*—and that was that. "I am sorry, *amigos*. *Es el sistema.*" He raised his shoulders again, revved up the engine, and rumbled off, leaving puffs of cigar and diesel smoke drifting up over the square.

"Why the blazes do we need a piece of paper to allow us to buy a spare bottle of gas?" I fumed. "Why can't they just charge a deposit on the bloody thing like they do at home?"

"Like the man said—it's the system. There must be a kind of logic in there somewhere," Ellie concluded, "but we won't get to the bottom of it standing here. Let's go to the *butano* office."

"We would like *un certificado* to allow us to buy *una botella de butano*. We have no empty *botella*, so we need *un certificado, sí*?" I droned parrot-fashion to the disinterested *butano* clerk. A coach roared past on the busy road outside.

"Qué? Un certificado?" The clerk frowned as if I had just informed him that his wife had given birth to sextuplets, every one a spitting image of the Pope. *"Por qué? No comprendo."* Another heavy vehicle thundered past.

Suddenly my inadequate Spanish seemed totally useless. I didn't really understand why I had to ask for a certificate anyway, and every stilted attempt I made to elucidate was being drowned out by the din of passing traffic. I was sorely tempted to employ the old Brit-abroad tactic of bawling loudly and slowly at the clerk in English, but I instinctively knew that this would be pointless. This guy could see that I was sweating blood, and the bastard was enjoying every minute of it. I struggled on in Spanish.

After several more abortive attempts to explain what we wanted, I was about to suggest to Ellie that the simplest solution would be to go all-electric, when the clerk pulled a self-satisfied smirk and announced in English that he couldn't issue the certificate we wanted unless we presented him with a receipt for the new appliance for which the extra gas canister was required.

"But we don't *need* another gas appliance," Ellie objected, her normally inexhaustible patience rapidly running out, "just a spare bottle. I mean, all this certificate, appliance, receipt business—it's just plain crazy!"

The clerk leaned back in his chair, crossed his feet on his desk, and declared smugly, "Maybe crazy, *señora*, but the receep system, she works good. And nobody never steal no empties in Spain."

"That may well change today, mate," I mumbled, taking Ellie by the arm and leading her to the door before she could clobber the clerk with her already-cocked handbag.

She was still in a rage when we got back to the house.

"Connect the new canister," she barked, "and I'll fix something for lunch with old Maria's eggs. I'll pretend it's that damned clerk's brains I'm scrambling!"

I snapped the stove's hose connection to the top of the full cylinder, then tried to turn on one of the gas rings. The knob came away in my hand.

"What the hell's next, Ellie? Now the bloody stove's falling apart!"

"Don't over-dramatize. Just turn it on with a wrench or something. Improvise."

I duly grabbed the knobless spindle with a pair of pliers, and gave it a twist. The hiss and smell affirmed that the gas was getting through all right, but solving that problem had merely created another. I couldn't turn the gas off again. The spindle was now firmly stuck in the "On" position, and no amount of wrenching or swearing would budge it. In desperation, I gave the spindle a hefty thump with the pliers, thus producing problem number three—the spindle disappeared with a clatter inside the stove, and the gas continued to pour out.

"We're really in trouble now," I spluttered, staggering back from the stove. "RUN!"

"Use your noggin, for God's sake. Disconnect the canister before you either gas us or blow up the house!" She clashed the eggs back in the fridge and slammed the door shut. "Okay, Red Adair [the daredevil master of extinguishing oil rig fires]—yesterday we had a stove but no gas—now we've got gas but no stove. Any more bright ideas?"

The Bay of Palma had never looked more glorious. We drove down off the *autopista* from Andratx to be greeted by the midday sun, a golden ball suspended against a curtain of sapphire blue, shining down on the aquamarine expanse of the Mediterranean Sea and its glittering sequins of reflected light. The recent wash of melted snow left the landscape refreshed and renewed, the green wooded hills around the beige, circular bulk of Bellver Castle on our left mirrored the clear sunlight with an emerald glow, and offered up subtle scents of pine and myrtle to blend with the sea's salty tang in an invigorating cocktail of balmy winter air.

We passed the escalating terraces of Palma's most chic hotels and restaurants, which boast (and charge sweetly for) unrivaled views of the bay from densely urbanized slopes where once only sheep and goats grazed peacefully in millennial groves of olive and almond. We continued on along the Paseo Maritimo, a spectacular sweep of palm-lined highway that hugs the curve of the bay on a broad garland of land reclaimed from the sea. It serves not only as a vital artery for the transportation demands of mass tourism, but also as an elegant avenue. Native Palmesanos and visitors alike stroll or linger for refreshment at a promenade café overlooking Palma harbor, once both a haven for marauding corsairs and the home port of honest sailing ships that plied the island's trade on the world's oceans.

I stopped at the traffic light, taking time to look out at the old quayside. Fishermen were drying and mending their nets in the sun, while a few nearby tourists sat sipping drinks beneath the tall date palms, gazing up at the city's historic landmarks protruding above the now redundant impregnability of the old sea walls; the ancient windmills of Es Jonquet, now transformed into trendy bars and nightclubs; the handsome mansions of rich merchants of a bygone maritime era, their stately homes now sub-divided into apartments of great style for today's successful traders in tourism; and finally, the awe-inspiring magnificence of Palma's mighty cathedral, La Seo—the honey-gold limestone of its twin spires and pinnacled rows of flying buttresses glowing with a rosy hue in the winter sunlight, and manifesting the eternal domination of the church over the city and the sea.

The light changed to green, and in the couple of seconds it took me to engage first gear and release the clutch, a dozen car horns blared impatiently behind us.

"*TURISTAS!*" yelled a taxi driver, bouncing the palm of his hand off his forehead and glaring at me as he roared past in a mad dash to gain pole position at the next set of lights. I still hadn't mastered the racetrack technique the car-bound must exercise in Palma lest the native drivers leave you feeling about as welcome as a pork pie salesman in Tel Aviv.

The urban racers nose-to-tailed it past us (on both sides), mandatory cigarettes dangling from their heavily mustachioed lips, left hands draped out of side windows, and horns honking at the merest suspicion that the driver in front has eased his foot off the gas pedal by even a fraction of an inch. The presence of any eye-catching female driver only added to the chaos, considerably increasing the risk of a multiple pile-up, as the lady was targeted for torrid ogling from all sides—some particularly lascivious males lurching halfway out of their drivers' windows to look back and eye her car up and down as if it were an extension of her own body . . . and all the while searing along flat-out, glued to the car ahead.

Armed with the stove's instruction manual, we were heading in the general direction of the agent's showroom in Palma's busiest shopping district.

Wheeling left off the Paseo, we charged along three abreast past the lush gardens of the old Moorish Almudaina Palace, where cool fountains played amid sub-tropical arbors and whispered their soothing song to a line of weary-headed horses, standing on three legs and hitched to open-topped carriages in which drivers sprawled and dozed, awaiting the rare winter fare from an occasional passing group of sightseers.

Without warning, the avenue funneled into a narrow lane beneath the arcaded canopy of plane trees flanking the broad boulevard of the Borne, the bumper car derby grinding to an impatient, single-file crawl past the lavishly dressed windows of up-market shops selling high-fashion clothes, luxury leatherware, and expensive watches and jewelery below magnificent, sculpted stone façades of grand and ornately balconied Spanish elegance.

"The stove shop is up that street on the left, just ahead," Ellie said. "Keep your eyes peeled for a parking space."

"You'll be lucky. There's no left turn, and anyway, there's about as much chance of finding a parking place around here as there is of Pere Pau's restaurant being included in the Michelin Guide."

Picking up speed and lanes as the street fanned into the Plaza Rei Joan Carles I, we were swept along again in the free-for-all stampede, veering right at the Bar Bosch, where the pavement tables were crowded as ever, with rubber-necked tourists in shorts and flip-flops, dapper businessmen sitting cross-legged in cashmere suits and Carrera shades, and see-and-be-seen students eyeing up the talent as long as is humanly possible before actually buying a drink.

"Say good-bye to the stove shop," I grumped. "We'll be stuck in this traffic jam for the rest of the day, and God knows where we'll end up."

"Look!" Ellie shrieked. "There's an underground parking lot right there. And there's a green *libre* sign, so there must be a space. Go for it!"

She gripped the sides of her seat as I swung the car to the right, nipping in between two buses and almost colliding with a carload of nuns who were also signaling to enter the parking lot. It was one of those fifty-fifty situations, and back in Britain I surely would have shown good manners by deferring to the ladies, but this was Spain. I had just been subjected to a scrotum-tightening initiation into their driving methods, and besides, I was only a *loco extranjero*.

"Bugger it!" I snarled. "When in Rome!" Swerving brazenly in front of the nuns, I barely beat them to the ticket barrier.

"Peter! That was awful," gasped Ellie, aghast. "I'm absolutely mortified. Those poor nuns. Your 'When in Rome' attitude is right out of order when it comes to being unchivalrous to women in Spain—especially nuns."

"So it's all right to letch after women like the randy Spanish drivers, but nicking their parking space is right out, is that what you're saying?"

"Something like that, and I'm completely ashamed. That wasn't nice, and if nuns weren't above such things, they'd be giving you a good tongue lashing. Lucky for you they're gentle ladies of the cloth."

"Maybe, but a tongue lashing from a nun is still a cheap price to pay for a parking space in this area. I got in first—fair and square. The nuns can look after themselves."

"Ah, *buenos días*. And how may I be of service to your honors?" smarmed the salesman, gliding over the showroom floor, patent leather pumps peeping from under his circa-1970 flares. A pudgy little man with unnatural black hair slicked down over his skull like a greased bombazine swimming cap, a Zapata mustache trimmed slightly higher at the left to focus attention to a gold eye-tooth bared in a permanent one-sided sneer, he had the appearance of a swarthy Peter Lorre gigolo with Bell's palsy, and looked as though he might have been more at home tangoing the night away in some dingy, downtown dancehall than hawking fridges and stoves in a swank, uptown department store.

I handed him the stove manual, pointing my finger at an illustration of the control panel. "*Roto* . . . the knob, the spindle . . . all *roto* . . . all broken."

The sneer evened into a full-faced grin, his chameleon eyes sparkling in commission-anticipating delight. Our particular stove was obsolete, he elatedly informed us. The manufacturer had gone bust years ago. No spare parts were available, of course, and in its present condition, the stove was positively dangerous—*muy peligroso . . . una bomba!*

Sashaying over to the display area, he begged to advise our honors that the only solution would be to scrap the old stove forthwith, and buy a new one . . . and in this showroom, we had the good fortune of being able to choose from the most comprehensive array in Majorca.

Five minutes later, we were many hundred dollars lighter and the proud (if somewhat stunned) owners of a sturdy, wide-bodied model with a special compartment alongside the oven in which to conceal the gas canister. *Muy importante*, that.

A wise choice—a stove well suited to the traditional farmhouse kitchen, confirmed the salesman, handing Ellie the guarantee and receipt. "*Muy importante*, the receipt . . . to enable your honors to purchase the new *botella de butano* for the special compartment. *Muy importante*, the receipt," he stressed.

Didn't we know it! And bidding farewell to *muchas pesetas* right out of the blue put me in no mood for the sight that greeted us back in the underground parking lot either.

"I don't bloody well believe it," I wailed when my eyes grew accustomed to the gloom. "We've got a flat!"

Ellie stood humming quietly to herself while I rummaged angrily in the trunk for the spare wheel.

"Now, where's the hole to slide the jack into?" I was down on my knees now, peering under the car, fumbling in the darkness, and getting absolutely nowhere.

Then Ellie opened the car door. "There you are. That's turned on the interior light. Maybe that'll help."

"Ah, that's better. There!" I pushed the jack firmly home. "Now we're getting somewhere. Good idea that, Ellie."

I quickly pulled my head out from under the car, only to hit it a resounding whack on the underside of the open door. The pain was excruciating. "Why the bloody hell is that still open?" I yelled, lashing out a sideways kick at the flat tire, which I missed, and battering my cat-lacerated shin against the corner of the bumper.

"Jesus Christ!" I howled in agony. "JESUS H. CHRIST!"

Right on cue, the nun-mobile materialized from the shadows, and slipped slowly past en route to the exit. I could just make out the serene, satisfied expressions on the sisters' faces as they looked down at me sitting pathetically on the concrete floor nursing my head and leg.

"They couldn't have. They wouldn't have," I thought aloud.

An elderly nun smiled out of the rear window of their car, and made a mid-digital gesture that only the most devoutly gullible could have mistaken for the sign of benediction.

"They could have, and they most certainly should have," Ellie opined dryly. "But as I said before, I'm sure those ladies are above such things. Our flat is more likely a case of divine retribution."

I remained less convinced.

Back at the *butano* office, we presented our new receipt to the clerk who then made out the much-valued *certificado* with a told-you-so smirk.

"There you go, *señores*. Like I say, the receep system, she is very, very good, no? Now you gonna have two gas *botellas* for only one stove. *Olé!*"

We conceded defeat silently and went home.

Despite my misplaced faith in the improbable, Juan the plumber (like plumbers everywhere) eventually turned up three days later. Our increasingly frantic calls to his wife were met with all the stock excuses—a burst pipe here, a choked drain there, and every job an absolute emergency that had to be attended to *inmediatamente*. Why, she hadn't seen him home before midnight for almost a week.

"*Es un desastre!*" Juan declared, looking extremely fresh and bright-eyed for such an over-worked and under-slept young man. "Your water boiler is useless. It is leaking gas. *Es una bomba!*"

So now we had another potential bomb disguised as one of Señora Ferrer's modern conveniences. Bloody marvelous! First the stove, now this. I felt myself going all light-walleted again.

He knew this boiler well, Juan informed us. It had been dangerous for ages, but Ferrer was too mean to replace it. It had always been too small to provide hot water for a house this size, anyway. He pointed to the little porcelain tub underneath it. That was all the boiler had been designed to heat water for—one sink!

"Yes, I thought it was a bit too small as well," I agreed feebly, realizing that young Juan must have regarded us as typical, starry-eyed foreign idiots—an easy mark for a houseful of rubbish sold by a pair of crafty locals.

"And by the way, how is your *electricidad*?" inquired Juan, donning his electrician's hat and squinting suspiciously at the ancient fuse box on the wall. Hadn't we had any problems yet?

"Well, now that you mention it, the fuses sometimes blow if we try to use the electric kettle and the toaster at the same time," I admitted, feeling increasingly stupid.

Juan shook his head and shrugged a slow Spanish shrug. "*Hombre, es un catástrofe.* You have *problemas . . . problemas grandes*." What this house needed was a complete electrical overhaul, he announced, looking me squarely in the eye. It was a miracle that there hadn't already been an electrical fire or a gas explosion . . . or both. We would need a much bigger fuse box, *un interruptor moderno*, to comply with regulations, and much of the wiring would have to be replaced with the correct gauge. The present stuff was only heavy enough for a few lights. "*Hombre—un catástrofe potencial!*" Then there was the problem of the water boiler. We should forget about silly little contraptions run off a gas canister. Get an electric boiler—a good big one—much cleaner and safer. Keep the gas bottle as a spare. Always handy, a spare *botella de gas*, no?

Tell me about it. If only he had known what a wild gas chase we had already been on to get just one spare canister, and now we were going to have two!

"Um, could you have a look at the washing machine while you're here?" Ellie asked timidly, dreading the inevitable reply. "It . . . well, it doesn't seem to spin very well."

"Washing machine? *Señora*, I must tell you honestly . . ." Juan paused and ambled over to the vintage *lavadora*. "This can of bolts has been useless for years. The fast-spin function broke down nearly ten years ago, and old Ferrer would not spend the money to have it fixed. His wife has done the washing in their Palma apartment ever since. This heap of junk should have been thrown out long ago. *Basura!*" He gave the base of the machine a gentle kick, there was a metallic rattle in its bowels—then the door fell off. Juan did his best to conceal a smile by stroking the end of his nose with his thumb. "*Lo siento, señores.* I am sorry."

Ellie and I looked at each other and started to laugh—rueful, shoulder-shaking giggles of pathos at first, then loud, almost hysterical laughter, tear-wiping, thigh-slapping, leg-crossing laughter. It was as obvious as a dog's balls that we had been well and truly taken for a couple of mugs by the Ferrers, and laughter was the best medicine. *Hombre*, it was the only medicine!

Juan moved over to the door, toying nervously with the handle, and probably thinking that the old house was now occupied by a pair of foreign nutcases. He was ready to leave—quickly, if necessary.

"Don't worry, Juan," I said, struggling to regain my composure. "It's just our way of relieving the, um . . . *problemas*." I gave him a reassuring nudge. "Know what I mean?"

I was quite sure from the look of confused mistrust on his face that he most certainly did not know what I meant, so I prudently got back to the business in hand. "Okay, Juan, you make a list of all the things that need to be done, work out an estimate of the cost, and we can pick it up from your shop tomorrow. If the price is right . . ." I placed a hand on his shoulder, and he drew away as if he had been touched by a live cable. "If the price is right, and if you can promise a quick job, you'll have a deal. Okay, Juan?"

"Okay, *señor . . . muy bien*, okay," he stammered, fumbling for the door handle. "*Mañana . . .* okay."

The door swung open and he was gone.

"We scared the living daylights out of the poor chap," said Ellie, still dabbing her eyes. "He'll never set foot in this house again."

"Don't you believe it. We're talking about a sizeable contract here. He'll be keen to get the work, even if he does think we're escapees from an asylum for *locos extranjeros*. You'll see."

This time, my hunch was right, and Juan proved the internationalism of plumber-profit-motivation. His estimate was ready for us at his shop the next day, and though (true to the trait of his trade) his price was roughly double what we expected, we were desperate, so we told him the job was his—but only if he could start *inmediatamente*.

"*Inmediatamente, señores!* I will pick up a new boiler and install it today. It will be temporary, of course, until the new *interruptor* and wiring are in, but it will give you abundant hot water—*inmediatamente!*"

While Juan was still high with the elation of having secured our contract, Ellie grabbed her chance to squeeze a bargain price out of him for the new washing machine on display in his shop.

"*Sí, una lavadora excelente, señora. Una máquina fabulosa!*" Juan enthused, tapping the base of the gleaming new washing machine lightly with his foot. "Good for relieving the, uh ... *problemas*, no?" He looked at us apprehensively, gave me a dig in the ribs with his elbow, and let out a peal of forced, nervous laughter.

We joined in obligingly, no doubt confirming in the plumber's confused mind that we were a couple of perverted weirdos who got their jollies by watching someone sinking the boot into washing machines.

Having decided, perhaps, that it was best not to cross such oddballs, Juan stuck to his word, and by that same evening we had copious quantities of steaming hot water bubbling through the pipes of a shiny white electric boiler of grand proportions. After days of taking birdbaths with kettle-heated water in the washbasin, we reveled in this rediscovered luxury—Ellie in the upstairs bath and I in the downstairs shower. The rafters fairly rang with singing and splashing. And yes, I told myself, the old house *did* have a happy atmosphere after all.

Ah, the magic of hot water, and oh, how easily it lulls the bathing human into a false sense of well-being and goodwill. But for the moment, we only knew that life had taken a definite turn for the better. Even the lumpy old bed seemed more comfortable when we snuggled under the covers that night, feeling all pink and cozy and clean.

"Incidentally, Ellie," I said, switching off the bedside light, "I picked up the tire from the garage today, and there hadn't been a puncture after all. All they had to do was reinflate it."

"Mm-hmm . . ."

"Even if, as you thought, it *was* heavenly justice that was done in that underground parking lot, it seems to have been administered by an earthly hand."

But Ellie was already asleep.

Barbara Kingsolver

(1 9 5 5 –   )

Growing up in rural Kentucky, Barbara Kingsolver was a born storyteller, although it never occurred to her that she would—or could—be a professional writer. "I used to beg my mother to let me tell her a bedtime story," she said. Kingsolver kept a journal from the age of eight and wrote stories and essays, but her writing role models were "old, dead men from England. It was inconceivable that I might grow up to be one of those myself . . ." In college in Indiana she majored in biology and ecology, and her novels are infused with a knowledge and love of the natural sciences. Although Kingsolver lost the inflections of her native Kentucky ("I lost my accent . . . People made terrible fun of me for the way I used to talk, so I gave it up and slowly became something else"), her roots run deep in Appalachia.

Best known for her novels *The Bean Trees* (1988), *Animal Dreams* (1990), *Pigs in Heaven* (1993), and *The Poisonwood Bible* (1998), Kingsolver is committed to social justice and says that novels can educate "but first have to entertain— that's the contract with the reader: you give me ten hours and I'll give you a reason to turn every page . . . I want the people I grew up with—who may not often read anything but the Sears catalogue—to read my books."

After college Kingsolver lived in France and Greece, and in addition to her novels, she writes an occasional travel article, including "Where the Map Stopped," which first appeared in the *New York Times* in 1992. She, her husband, Steven Hopp, and their two daughters now divide their time between Tucson, Arizona, and a farm in southern Appalachia.

WHERE THE MAP STOPPED

The Canary Islands weren't named for birds, but for dogs. Pliny the Elder wrote of "Canaria, so called from the multitude of dogs [canes] of great size." In Pliny's day this crooked archipelago, flung west from the coast of Morocco, was the most westerly place imaginable; the map of the world ended here. For 14 centuries navigators used that map to stop in and visit: Arabs, Portuguese and eventually the Spanish, and still it remained Meridian Zero, the jumping-off place. When Columbus gathered the force to head west and enlarge the map, it was from La Gomera, in the Canaries, that he sailed.

The other six islands have airports now; Tenerife and Gran Canaria are reasonable tourist destinations for Europeans in a hurry. But the traveler who wishes to approach or escape La Gomera takes the sea road, as Columbus did. I am such a traveler, in no particular hurry on a bright Saturday. I've been told dolphins like to gambol in the waves in these waters, and that sighting them brings good luck. The sun on the pointed waves is hard as chipped flint but I stare anyway, waiting for a revelation.

The ferry leaves from Tenerife, whose southern coast is a bleached, unimaginative skyline of tourist hotels. For reasons difficult to fathom or appreciate, the brown hills dropping away behind the port display giant white letters spelling out "HOLLYWOOD." An hour and a half ahead of us lies the tiny island of La Gomera, where the hills don't speak English yet.

Among urban Canarians La Gomera has a reputation for backwardness, and Gomerans are sometimes likened to the people known as Guanches—the tall, blue-eyed, goat-herding aboriginals whom the Spaniards found and extinguished here in the 15th century. Throughout the Canaries the Guanches herded goats, made crude, appealing pottery and followed the lifestyle known as neolithic, living out their days without the benefit of metal. They were primarily farmers, not fishers; anthropologists insist these people had no boats. On La Gomera they used a language that wasn't spoken but *whistled*, to span the distances across steep gorges. I've been told that this language, called silbo, still persists in some corners of La Gomera, as do pottery making and farming with the muscle of human and ox. If I see dolphins in the channel, I'll believe the rest of the story.

The blue cliffs of La Gomera seem close enough to Tenerife to reach by means of a strong backstroke. It's hard to imagine living on islands this small, in plain view of other land, and never being stirred to go to sea. Suddenly the dolphins appear, slick and dark, rolling like finned inner tubes in the Atlantic.

San Sebastián de la Gomera is the port from which Columbus set sail for the New World. Elsewhere on earth the quincentennial anniversary of that voyage is raising a lot of fuss, but it looks quiet here. Fishing boats sit like sleeping gulls in the harbor, rolling in the ferry's wake. A store in port sells T-shirts with the ambiguous message: "Aquí partió Colón"—"Columbus Departed from Here." So did everyone else, apparently. San Sebastián's narrow streets are empty save for the long shadows of fig trees and a few morning shoppers. We drive steeply uphill to the parador overlooking the harbor.

The paradors are Spain's nationally run hotels, usually expensive and generally fine; the reputation of the Parador Conde de La Gomera sets it apart even from other paradors. It is an old, elegant replica of an estate that stood here in Columbus's time. The immense front door leads to a cool interior of cut-stone archways and dark, carved woodwork and bright courtyards where potted ferns grow head-high, brushing the door frames. The hallways open everywhere onto hidden sitting areas dappled with light, each one arranged like a perfect photograph. The rooms have tall beds with carved wooden posts. Our balcony overlooks the tops of palms and tamarinds leaning perilously over the edge of the cliff, and far below, the harbor. From a rocking chair on the balcony I watch the ferry that brought me here, now chugging back toward the land of white high-rises. The day is bright white and blue. The quiet rattle of wind in the palm fronds invites napping.

In my sleep I hear a conversation of birds. I wake up and still hear it: the birds in the garden are asking each other questions. I look down through the trees. A gardener with bristling white hair thrusts a finger into his mouth and makes a warbling, musical whistle. In a minute, an answer comes back. The silbo.

Walk down to investigate. The gardens are as deep and edible as Eden: guavas, figs, avocados, a banana tree bent with its burden of fruit. Another tree bears what looks like a watermelon-sized avocado. I find the gardener I saw from the balcony and ask him about the giant avocado, not so much for information as to nurture my fantasy that he will answer me in silbo. He explains (in Spanish, disappointingly) that the tree comes from Cuba, where they use the impressive fruit as a musical instrument. I ask him to tell me its name in silbo. His mouth turns down in a squelched smile, and he stands long enough for me to hear dragonflies clicking in the palm trees over our heads. Finally he says, "She doesn't have a name in silbo. She's not from here." He walks off toward the guava trees. A parrot in a wrought-iron cage behind me mutters Spanish words in a monotone; I whistle at him but he, too, holds me in his beady glare and clams up.

At breakfast there are rosebuds on the tables and a sideboard laden with fresh bread and jars of a sweet something called "miel de palma"—palm honey. I'm suspicious. It takes both bees and flowers to make honey, and a palm has nothing that would interest a bee. I mention this to the cook, who concedes that it's not honey, but syrup, boiled down from the sap of palms just the way New Englanders make syrup from maple sap. I'm still suspicious: palm trees are something of a botanical oddity, in some ways more closely related to grass than to a maple tree and just about as difficult to tap in the ordinary way. To get the sap, you'd have to decapitate a mature tree. The cook allows that it's true, in the old days miel de palma was a delicacy fatal to the trees. North Africans developed a gentler palm-tapping technique and introduced it to La Gomera in this century. He says I should go see the palm groves.

My companion and I are reluctant to leave this elegant paradise, as Columbus surely was—Gomerans maintain that he delayed his voyage for months, having grown comfortable in the arms of the widow of the first Count of La Gomera, Beatriz de Bobadilla. But there are worlds to be discovered. We drive up into the highlands of whitewashed villages, vineyards and deep-cut valleys that ring with the music of wild canaries (ancestors of their yellower, domestic cousins). The whole island is a deeply eroded volcanic rock, just 11 miles across and flat-topped, with six gorges radiating from the center like the spokes of a wheel. Farms and villages lie within the gorges, and the road does not go anywhere as the crow flies. Often we round a corner to face a stunning view of cliffs and sea and, in the background, the neighboring island of Tenerife. From here it shows off the pointed silhouette of its great volcano, Pico de Teide, snow-clad from November to April, the highest mountain on soil claimed by Spain.

The rugged farmland brings to mind my grandfather's tales of farming the hills of Kentucky: planting potatoes in plots so steep, he said, you could lop off the ends of the rows and let the potatoes roll into a basket. Growing here are mostly grapevines on narrow, stone-banked terraces that rise one after another in steep green stairways from coastline to clouds. Hawks wheel in the air currents rising from the gorges. Birds of prey are a sign of a healthy ecosystem, a good omen for La Gomera, as surely as the dolphins are. For the moment, this island supports a small population, low-intensity agriculture and a relatively low tide of tourism.

At the bottom of the gorge sits the Hotel Tecina, out of sight and unimaginable from here: a microcosm of hibiscus and swim-up bars, tennis lessons, a chrome-and-glass elevator down to the beach. This and the Parador, the island's two principal hotels, have as much in common as Don Quixote and Madonna. The valley of the Hotel Tecina is an up-and-coming tourist area; in its interest, there is talk of finally carving an airport into La Gomera. The day it happens will be bad luck for the hawks.

The island's green heart is the Garajonay National Park, a central plateau of ancient laurel forest. On an otherwise dry island, the lush vegetation here drinks from a mantle of perpetual fog. At some point between the dinosaur days and the dawn of humankind, forests like this covered the whole Mediterranean basin; now they have receded to a few green dots on the map in the Madeira and Canary Islands. An ecologist friend of mine who studies the laurel forest has warned me to watch out for sleek, black rats in the tree-tops. At certain seasons the laurels accumulate in their leaves a pow-erful toxin the rats crave, against their own and the trees' best interests. The local park ranger confirms this—his advice is to watch for gnawed twigs in the path, then look up to spot the little drug addicts. (The colorful Spanish word for drug addiction is "toxico-manía.") Eventually, he says, the rats get so drunk they fall and lie trembling on their backs.

We hike into the forest, which seems enchanted. The laurels are old twisted things with moss beards on their trunks and ferns at their feet. Green sunlight falls in pools on the forest floor. I feel drugged myself. I watch the path closely, where I see tiny orchids and fallen leaves but no toxicomaniac rats.

When we break out of the cloud layer we're in treeless highlands, on Alto de Garajonay. The peak is named for the legendary lovers Gara and Jonay, Guanche equivalents of Romeo and Juliet, who killed themselves on this mountaintop. The wind whistles over the peak's stone lid, and in the brightness we can see the islands of El Hierro and La Palma to the west, Tenerife nearby and dominant to the east and behind it, hazily, Gran Canaria; beyond that lies a long bank of clouds signifying the coast of West Africa. We are that close. The easternmost Canary Island is only 65 miles from the Saharan sands of mainland Africa. Canary Islanders are citizens of Spain, but geography asserts itself from time to time, as a reminder that this land will always be Africa's: the trade winds get interrupted by strong gusts from the east that bring hot dust and sometimes even torpid, wind-buffeted locusts. Canarians call this dismal weather the Kalima. They like to suggest that its meteorological cause is camel racing in the Sahara.

Today, above the clouds, the air is as clear as glass. We descend from the peak and drive west to a clearing in the forest called La Laguna Grande. In a country restaurant we're served watercress soup and the country staple, "wrinkled potatoes," served with a spicy cilantro sauce. The soup is thickened with gofio, the ubiquitous, strong-tasting roasted flour that Canarian housewives buy in 10-kilo bags. The local wine has personality. So does the waiter. I tell him we've heard rumors of a village where they make pottery the way the Guanches did. "Go to Chipude," he says. "That's not where they make it. The town where they make it doesn't have a name, but you can see it from Chipude."

We follow his advice, and at Chipude they wave us down the road to a place not marked on any map, but whose residents insist *does* have a name: Cercado. I spot a group of white-aproned women sitting in an open doorway, surrounded by red clay vessels. One woman wears a beaten straw hat and holds a sphere of clay against herself, carving it with a knife. She is not making coils or, technically speaking, building the pot; she is sculpturing it, Guanche fashion. When she tilts up her straw hat, her gold earring glints, and I see that her eyes are Guanche blue. I ask her where the clay comes from and she points with her knife: "that barranco"—the gorge at the end of the village. Another woman paints a dried pot with reddish clay slip; mud from that other barranco, she points. After it dries again, she rubs its surface smooth with a beach rock. Finally, an old woman with the demeanor of a laurel tree polishes the finished pot to the deep, shiny luster of cherry wood. Her polishing stick is the worn-down plastic handle of a toothbrush. "What did the Guanches use?" I ask, and she gives me a silent smile like the gardener's and the parrot's.

The youngest of the women, a teenager named Yaiza, carries a load of finished pots to the kiln. We walk together through the village, past two girls sitting on the roadside stringing red chilies, down a precarious goat path into the grassy gorge. The kiln is a mud hut with a tin roof and a fire inside. Yaiza adjusts pots on the scorching tin roof, explaining that each one must spend half a day there upside down, half a day right side up, and *then* it's ready to go into the fire, where it stays another day. If the weather is right, it comes out without breaking. After this amount of art and labor, each pot sells for about $13. I tell Yaiza she could charge 10 times that much. She laughs. I ask her if she has ever left La Gomera and she laughs again, as if the idea were ludicrous. I ask her if a lot of people know how to make this pottery, and she replies, "Oh sure. Fourteen or fifteen." All belong to two or three families, all in this village. We return to the pottery house, and I buy a pair of clay bowls. I pack them into my car with care, feeling that they belong on an endangered species list.

We leave the forest for the dry, windy side of the island, a terrain with the feeling of North Africa. Date palms wave like bouquets of feathers. These are the trees tapped for miel de palma, and I can see that it doesn't kill the tree but it doesn't do it any good, either. The new leaves that spring up after tapping are dwarfed and off kilter. In the gorge below we look down on groves of palms with bad haircuts.

The Playa de Alojera, at the base of the gorge, is a deserted beach on the island's western margin. If this is not the end of the map, you can surely see it from here. The shoreline is windy, rocky and wild. In tide pools, fish and crabs scuttle in their claustrophobic soup, waiting to be rescued by the next high tide. On the black sand beach I find shells so beautiful I pocket them with the feeling I've stolen something, but there are no witnesses. In this village of maybe two dozen white houses and half a dozen streets, nothing moves, not even a cat, and I feel spooked. We creep tentatively into one of the empty houses and sit on its terrace to watch the sun go huge and round, then drown itself, leaving a mournful red streak on the face of the sea.

We weren't alone, it turns out; back at our car, a brightly dressed pair of German hippies ask for a ride to the nearest food. They've rented an apartment here, from a proprietor who promised peace and quiet but neglected to say how *much* peace and quiet. These two seem unfazed, and it occurs to me that people pay fortunes to find this much emptiness. At length we come to a village with lights burning in the windows, where we leave them, and make our slow way back through the cloud forest. Winding into the fog, it's impossible to keep the word "ghost" out of mind: long fingers of mist reach down to touch the windshield, looking exactly like special effects.

In the morning, the air is changed. The garden of the Parador is quiet, and the sky is stifled with pale haze: they're racing camels in the Sahara.

The Kalima deepens its hold as we board the ferry and head back toward an invisible destination. The white-block hotels of southern Tenerife and even the giant cone of Pico de Teide are mirages in white. As we leave the port of San Sebastián the haze closes down behind us, suspending our ship on a blank sea between lost worlds. If there are dolphins here now, they are only someone's dream of good luck.

Rose Macaulay

(1881–1958)

In the late 1940s novelist Rose Macaulay set out to travel the coast of Spain. Like Mary Lee Settle fifty years later, she went alone and drove her car herself. Franco's Spain was far different from the modern country that Settle encountered. Macaulay maneuvered over roads still pitted from civil war shells; fuel was in short supply. She was such a curiosity as an Englishwoman that whenever she stopped children swarmed over the running boards of her car. She wrote that a foreigner was "a quaint baboon, an ape, an owl," and she decided that she would be less conspicuous if she forswore her hat. In her whole journey she only encountered one other Englishman.

In her introduction to *Fabled Shore* (1949), from which this excerpt is taken, Macaulay describes her preparation for the trip: "I had with me Baedeker, who told me everything that occurred to the railways on which he traveled . . . the Blue Guides; it is interesting to note how they and Baedeker occasionally show their independence of each other . . . I had too the inimitable Murray, the first edition, by the learned and irate Richard Ford . . ." and half a dozen other volumes by male authors both in English and Spanish. She finally concludes, "What I mainly found peculiar was the extreme interest that many of them displayed in the personal appearance of the female Spaniards, who always seem to me to be among the less interesting objects in any landscape . . . This is, no doubt, my personal limitation of taste which finds buildings and landscapes more aesthetically pleasing than the animal creation."

Daughter of a Cambridge classics professor, Rose Macaulay was a social satirist, novelist, and journalist. Her more than a dozen novels (the best known, *The Towers of Trebizond*, 1956) were well received for their intelligence and humor. Macaulay was also known for the company she kept, and she counted Rupert Brooke, E. M. Forster, and Elizabeth Bowen as friends. Shortly before her death in 1958, she was named a Dame Commander of the British Empire.

From FABLED SHORE

CATALONIAN SHORE

Leaving the Catalan mountains of Roussillon for those of the Ampurdán, one knows that it is already Spain. The small dark frontier guards in olive-green uniforms and shiny black cocked hats are of another century; they have grace and beauty rather than apprehension; they pore over passports with interest and absorption and apparent surprise at what they find there. "British Subject" . . . is that, they inquire, a name? Perhaps they find the handwriting of British passport officials obscure. It takes time; but they are pleasant and friendly, and when they have digested the passport and driving licence, and, with interest, searched the car, they wish one good fortune and a happy visit to Spain, which they hope one will enjoy, and one is away.

The road, the old Roman road from Gaul to Tarragona, sweeps up from Port Bou in wild and noble curves, lying like a curled snake along the barren mountain flanks of the Alta Ampurdán, climbing dizzily up, darting steeply down into gorges and ravines, above deep rocky inlets where blue water thrusts into rock-bound coves, and small bays of sand where it whispers and croons in its tideless stir. Points and capes jut boldly through thin blue air above a deep cobalt sea; rocky islets lie offshore; the road dips down to the little bay of Culera, where once throve a little fishing port, where now is an almost abandoned village, pounded to pieces by the bombarding naval guns of the civil war, which ranged down the Catalan coast with their capricious thunder. Here, in a quiet valley behind the quiet village of San Miguel de Culera, moulder more ancient ruins, those of a great Benedictine convent, one of those great monasteries to which Ampurdán gave its feudal allegiance through the Middle Ages. There is a cloister left, some broken arches, a few columns and capitals, three Romanesque apses; they and the church are twelfth century, built on the ruins of an older, probably Visigothic, convent and church: they have an air of having been there from the earliest Christian times, brooding, remote, fallen, but still dominating those bare, pine-clad hills where little vines sprout like cabbages out of the stony mountain sides.

The first beach of any size is that of Garbet, shut between two points and much frequented by Catalan *veraneantes*. Cross the Punta de Gates, and there is another wide bay with the road running close above it. On this July day it was very smooth, iridescent, turquoise with bands of cobalt and indigo further out; it is a most lovely bay, or rather a series of tiny bays. These Catalan bays, with the blue and green boats drawn up at the sea's edge and the brown nets spread out on the hot sands to dry, while bare-legged women sit and mend them, have a grace and beauty far more pictorial than the fishing beaches of Provence, or even those of Liguria; they suggest an antiquity still more remote, a tradition more unbroken. So did boats and nets lie, so did Iberian fishermen wade and lounge, Iberian fisherwomen cobble and gossip on the hot sands, before the Greeks sailed down this coast from Phocæa five-and-twenty centuries ago.

The road, bending inland, runs into the old town of Llansá (the Roman Deciana). Llansá is charming. High above its plaza stands its fine Romanesque church, San Vicente, partly destroyed, like so many Catalan churches, by the anarchists in 1936. Two kilometres from the town is the little port, Puerto de Llansá, a crescent of sandy beach full of fishing boats (sardines are the main haul), shut at its southern tip by a rocky island and a castle, so that the little bay is smooth and sheltered like a lake. On the beach just above the nets and boats is a small white inn with green shutters, the Miramar, with tables and benches on the sand outside it. Here I spent the night; from it, on that hot July evening, I bathed in the smooth curve of sea, that lapped about me as cool and warm as silk, while stars came out, and the great rock jutted into still water against a rose-flushed west. Afterwards I dined at one of the little tables on the sandy verandah, among the local fishermen and a few Catalan visitors. The *patrón* and his family were charming. They had seen, it seemed, few British passports; anyhow, they and their acquaintances who were dining there pored over mine with absorbed interest. They sat and gossiped and drank coffee at the little tables till long after midnight; *vieja costumbre española*, shared to the full by Catalans. It includes, naturally, late morning rising; my inn got stirring about half-past eight, and I got my coffee about half-past nine, after an exquisite early bathe in the still, limpid, opal, waveless sea, to which I stepped carefully down the sands between the drying nets. At ten I took the road winding above silver-blue coves and rocky shores round the deeply indented bay that holds Puerto de Selva in its southern crook. Vines, olives, figs, cactus and aloes filled the hot morning with their aromatic breath. Puerto de Selva is, to my mind, almost the most attractive little port of all the Costa Brava. Sheltered by the crook of the point behind it, and by the great jut of the Cadaqués peninsula that pushes out, vine-leaf shaped, north of the Gulf of Rosas, the little port lies on one side of the inner curve of a horse-shoe, facing west to the opposite shore and hauling in nets full of sardines. Above it on both sides of the bay tower great bare mountains, their faint evanescent colours shifting with each turn of light and shadow, so that they are here opal, there transparent indigo, there again faint rust; it is like the shifting colours on a dove's breast. The houses round the port are gaily and freshly painted white, their doors and shutters a vivid blue and green; they wear balconies with tubs of geranium, blue convolvulus and plump-leaved sprawling shrubs. Some people prefer and would restore the less gaudy rust, moss and ochre colours, with which the town camouflaged itself against bombardment during the civil war, producing an effect of melting into its mountain background; and indeed this must have been very lovely. But so also is the vivid white and blue that dazzles on the luminous air. The camouflage, it seems, was not very effective, for Puerto de Selva suffered much damage from bombs. Like so many Catalan villages, it was bombed by one side and had its church destroyed by the other, thus getting the worst of two worlds. The interior of the church has been rebuilt: over the altar is the legend "Radix salva. Erecta in ruinis A.D. 1944. Salva Porta."

Two miles inland from the port is the still more ancient village of Selva de Dalt. The woods which gave village and port their name have long since been destroyed; now only little vines scramble over the lower slopes of the great hill flanks. Selva was hot, tiny, and smelt of figs. Its little lanes were blocked with donkeys and great loads of grass, and trailed off into hill paths. One of these led up the mountain on whose top towers the great ruined Benedictine abbey of San

Pere de Roda. A car, they told me, could get up the mountain to within two kilometres of the monastery, and one would finish the climb on foot. A donkey, said Murray, would make it in an hour and a half. I dare say it would; but I had no donkey; it was very hot, and very steep; I renounced the enterprise and turned my back on Selva.

But the shadow of this mighty ruin haunted me, and haunts me still. I should have seen it. Instead, I read all about it in books by Catalans—how it was one of the major Benedictine foundations, which wielded feudal power over the country for miles round, sheltering the villages of Selva and Llansá and encouraging the fishing in the ports because the monks loved fish. The monastery was abandoned in 1798; the monks wearied of their lonely life on the mountains, and came down to the cheerful plains, nearer the fish, moving finally to Besalú. The deserted abbey was sacked and plundered of its doors, windows, pillars and stones; it fell into ruin, long before the dissolution of the monasteries put it into the hands of the State. To-day it broods in sombre Romanesque magnificence, a pile of broken walls, Byzantine arches, square towers, solitary on the bare mountain, looking down over Ampurdán and the sea. Not even Poblet or Ripoll is a more tremendous relic of the monastic grandeur that dominated eastern Spain during the *Edad Media*.

From Selva a rough road jolts inland across the vine-leaf promontory to Cadaqués. The coast, which has here at present no road (it is said that there is to be one), is indented by one lovely small bay after another, only accessible by foot; coves, caves, beaches and points, rocky islets, little harbours, none so well sheltered as Puerto de Selva, except Port Lligat, which is shut round by an island and is smooth and still, like a lake; among its three or four fishermen's cottages the square white house of Salvador Dalí stands out. Lligat has a fascination not incongruous with Dalí, and not quite of this earth.

The first port to be reached by the road from Selva is Cadaqués; a very pleasant and beautiful place, with its wide open plaza on the sea, shaded by mimosas and planes, the white town with deep blue doors and windows, the long curve of beach with the coloured fishing boats drawn up, the magnificent church standing high and sheer on the top of a pile of houses and narrow streets. Cadaqués is an historic port; in its bay the French, through the Count of Foix, met the

Catalan admiral, Roger of Laurier, to negotiate peace after the French invasion of 1285. Barbarossa's squadrons took and sacked the town when they raged down that coast in 1543. Cadaqués has always been exposed to the people of the sea, as well as to storms, strong currents and winds that have made the lives of its fishermen hard. It is remote; until the making of the roads from Selva and from Rosas, it lay isolated in its bay at the tip of this easternmost spur of the Pyrenees. It is said to be still archaic, behind the times, in spite of the recent incursions of *veraneantes*. Archaic or not, it is a lovely place, white and clear and curved like a crescent moon. They fish for pearl in the bay. The church, Santa Maria (undamaged both by republicans and rebels), has a fine Romanesque-looking exterior, but inside is dated 1662, and is a gorgeous riot of baroque. It was in the porch of this church that I first read the placards which, all over Spain, warn señoras and señoritas what they must wear in church. "Señora! Señorita! You present yourself without stockings? In a short dress? With short sleeves? You go into church? Stop! Stop! If you go thus into church, you will be turned out. If you go thus indecorously to confession, you will not be given absolution. If you have the audacity to approach the Blessed Sacrament, you will be refused in the presence of all."

Apart from the sex unfairness of this (for it seems that señores may wear what they like), what strikes one is the profound difference of attitude between the Roman and the Anglican Churches, the one making church-going an occasion, a mystery, to be approached *en grande tenue*, in especial clothes, the other easy, casual, laissez-faire, go-as-you-please, come-as-you-are, come in your working and playing clothes, bare headed, bare armed, bare legged, just as you happen to be. (Vain hope, for how seldom do we come at all!) To surround religious devotion with pomp and ceremony, awe, stockings, voluminous ceremonial clothes, has much to be said for it, though the stocking requirement must keep many women from church; in these fishing ports stockings are seldom seen; the women mending nets on the beach and marketing in the town never wear them; they may keep a pair for church, but to go home and put them on when the bell clangs for a service must be difficult. On the other hand, those who do go to church thus decorously attired, thus set apart from their secular workaday selves, must, I suppose, feel very blest and spiritually prepared. As, no doubt, church-goers in Victorian England used to feel, processing churchward on Sunday mornings in top-hats and Sunday frocks. The Anglicans, who have dropped so much, have dropped all that; "come as you are, my dear people," is now the vicar's vain and coaxing plea. What English vicar would dare to placard his church door with "Ladies! Stop! Stop! Change your clothes or you will be turned away!" The same difference in attitude lies, I think, behind the so careful guarding of Spanish churches, so that between one and four, when caretakers and sacristans are having their midday meal and their siesta, you will find every church and cathedral locked against visitors; very disappointing for those who are passing through in the afternoon and cannot wait. In England, cathedrals and churches stand casually and negligently open to all comers all day until dark; you may wander about them, stockingless, in midafternoon. The difference may, in part, be due to fear of the ancient Spanish tradition of ecclesioclasm, which has done in the past such irretrievable hurt to churches. But there is, I think, also a difference in attitude; the Holy Mysteries, the Heavenly Sanctuary, too hallowed for unguarded approach, as against come-and-go-as-you-please.

From outside the Cadaqués church one looks down a sheer precipice of a wall over the moon-like port and pale-blue bay set with fantastic rocks. A flight of steps takes one down into narrow streets, clean and steep, and so into the broad, delicious plaza, which was this afternoon bathed in soft and luminous brightness; it seemed a serene and happy place. At one side is the curve of sea; at the other restaurants and café tables. A waiter came and talked to me in charming American; he had, he said, waited for ten years in New York (and I remembered reading that many Cadaqués men emigrate to America, because life in Cadaqués is hard). "They live very good there," said the waiter, on a wistful note. "Sure thing, they live very good." But it seems to the casual visitor that life in Cadaqués too might be good; the place has an exquisite tranquillity, dignity and grace.

Leaving it reluctantly, I took the coast road for Rosas. It is a good road, winding up and down great olive-grown and rocky mountains, whose rust-coloured slopes sweep down to blue bays. I believe these mountains are the Sierra of Rosas, the eastern end of the Pyrenees.

Above the olive zone they tower, barren and noble, in the magnificent uselessness of uncultivated mountain lands.

The road dips down to the sea at the lovely little bay of Montjoi.
From here one may—indeed one must—walk to Cape Norfeu, and
get, on a clear day, one of the most glorious views of the Costa
Brava—all down the Gulf of Rosas as far as the Medas islands and
Cape Bagur, and inland across the Ampurdán to the high Pyrenees.

Leaving Montjoi, the road sweeps round the bay of La Pelisa and
curls north-west, dropping down from the heights into Rosas Bay,
between bamboo groves where the cicadas ziz and churr without
stop in the July heat, making the sound of a thousand saws. A great
azure gulf opens at one's feet; the Gulf of Rosas; one slides down
into the port, along a road where boats are building, smelling of tar
and sweet timber; and here is the long bay beneath the mountains,
where the Greeks (having lost their southern Spanish marts to the
Carthaginians) anchored and traded two thousand five hundred years
ago, and, at the gulf's southerly end, made their settlement of Emporion. The gulf was sheltered—"portus effuse jacet nullisque flabris
æquor est obnoxium," wrote Avienus. Yet not so sheltered as all that,
for the day I was there a little breeze was ruffling the sea.

There is, it seems, no certain proof that the town now Rosas was
founded by the Greeks. The Greek settlement of Rhodus (probably
an offshoot from Emporion) may have been not on the site of the
present town, but near it, and now buried beneath the silting sands.
Traces have been found. "Here too," says Strabo, "is Rhodus, a small
town belonging to the Emporitans. . . ." And Scymnus, writing in the
fifth century B.C., says that Rhodus was founded by the Massiliots
after Emporion. But just where in the gulf it was, both they and
other writers leave tantalizingly vague.

Rosas does not emerge much into history until the Middle Ages,
when it was part of the domains of the Counts of Ampurias, who
kept the Ampurdán in such a continuous bustle, and may well have
disturbed and buried ancient sites beneath the weight of the fortifi-
cations and castles that they threw up all round Castellón de
Ampurias. Under these so militant and enemy-conscious counts,
Rosas was a naval port, anchoring the squadrons that guarded the
trade of Castellón and the river Muga, to which came merchants

from far Mediterranean and Adriatic ports. Rosas lay under the dominion and shadow of the great Benedictine convent of Santa Maria, which, greatly ichthyophagous like all monasteries, encouraged the fishing industry all up the coast to Cape Creus. The city encircled a walled and fortified abbey citadel, of which remains are still to be seen. Suchet blew it up in 1814. Fish and coral brought the town prosperity, and revived it after its many assaults and destructions, for through centuries it was a centre of the storms that always raged over Ampurdán both from within and without. A tough and adventurous seafaring population was reared in this dangerous city; often in recent centuries they have fared, like my Cadaqués waiter, out of their own exquisite sea across the wild dark wastes of the Atlantic to try new lands. Some, like him, have returned, to talk American to tourists in the plaza, or to sail their fishing boats about their blue and jade and silver bay, and to lounge on the sea wall beneath the trees, as I did now, looking down the long bay that the sinking sun turned to a great rose, looking at the white, west-facing town delicately flushed, and across the bay to the opposite coast, where Castellón de Ampurias rises on its hill among the shadow-blue plains of Ampurdán. Rosas is lovely, though it has not the remote outpost charm of Cadaqués. I drove along the short coast road to the point where the lighthouse stands, and beyond it to the point of Poncella (view, as Baedeker would say; and a view indeed it is). On the hill-side above the faro is the ruined castle of La Trinitat, smashed up in 1808 by the French. I began to climb up to it, but was stopped by a sentry; probably it bristles with guns that foreigners may not see. I returned to the town, and took the road to Castellón de Ampurias, five miles west.

Once the capital of Ampurdán and the residence of the counts, Castellón stands on the river Muga, under three miles from the sea, surrounded by reservoirs and marshes. It stands on a hill; a fine mediæval walled city, with a fourteenth-century church, castle, moat and bridge. The church—or rather cathedral—is magnificent; a tall square-pinnacled tower, arcaded in three tiers, with fine buttresses and gargoyles, a broad nave of seven bays, west door sculptured with alabaster apostles, rich retablo and high altar. It is one of the most pleasing Gothic churches I saw in Catalonia. Close to it (I think

joined on) is the castle, with its moat and its steep fortress walls brilliant all the way up with flowers and green plants. The streets are fascinating; you come at unexpected corners on some broken arch that
may once have been part of a cloister, or of some chapel of ease; in
them fig trees grow and goats graze. Coming to Castellón from the
shore where the Greeks trafficked and made their settlements, from
that golden shore, classical, Mediterranean, pagan, urbane, is to step
into feudalism, into the rough, turbulent life of Gothic barbarism,
where wild counts and dominating abbots and their retainers fought
one another and defended their cities from assault. Everything seems
built for defence or for prayer; and even the churches are forts. There
is nothing Greek about these walled and castled cities.

I had to get on to Figueras, five miles further, where there would
be petrol and oil (both scarce in the country north of Barcelona).
Figueras, the capital of Ampurdán, and, after the fall of Barcelona in
the last months of the civil war, for a short time capital of Republican Spain, is noisy and crowded, its narrow streets a maze, through
which I and my car were guided to an hotel by a kind youth who was
studying English and collected stamps; for both these hobbies he
found me profitable, though, for all I understood of what he said, he
might as well have talked Catalan. He collected and introduced to me
his instructress in English, a smiling little spectacled lady who conversed with me in the street, but seemed to understand the remarks
she made to me better than those I made to her; with me it was the
other way round. She said, "You make long stay in Figueras?" I said,
one night only. She said, "You will be a week staying, yes." I said one
night. She said, "Yes, one week. You like Figueras." I said it was beautiful. She said, apologetically, that she could not quite understand my
English, which was not, was it, of London. She said some more, in
the English of Figueras, and we parted with mutual compliments
and friendship. I like the people of Figueras. But not the church
clock, which made the night unquiet by resonantly striking every
quarter. Wakeful and fretful, I began to understand the Spanish passion for church-burning. But, in the case of Figueras, I was mistaken.
I saw the church in the morning; a fine fifteenth-century building
which had been destroyed by the church-burners and was being very
beautifully rebuilt; the new part included the bell tower which so

sonorously disturbed the night; the old one, I was told, had not struck the night hours. Perhaps sleepless nights in Figueras had been planned as a form of reparation for sacrilege, and I thought it served Figueras right.

Some of the old church remained; part of the nave, the base of the tower, the sculptured figures over the west door. San Pedro must have been a magnificent church. I was shown over the ruins and over the new building by an intelligent priest; he gave me a booklet about its history, which related also much of the history of the town. Figueras was the Roman Juncaria, and stood on a Roman military road; it was destroyed by Saracens in the early Middle Ages, and rebuilt, further from the road, a plain and humble town which the inhabitants called Tapioles; in the course of time it became Ficerias, Figariæ, Figueras. To-day the ancient name is only preserved in one district, called Tapis. Tradition says that St. Paul (so busy in Spain) visited Juncaria, landing at Emporion, and preached the Christian religion there with immense success, which produced later several martyr saints. The Saracens destroyed Figueras and its first (probably Visigothic) church; after the reconquest it was rebuilt, with the help of the San Pere de Roda Benedictines. This Romanesque church was burnt down, with the whole town, by an incendiary count of Ampurias. With its indefatigable powers of recuperation, Figueras built itself and its church up again, the latter in the purest Catalan Gothic of the fifteenth century; austere and tremendous, its severity lightened by its graceful *campanario*. There were later disasters and attacks, and the *campanario* was scarred by French bullets; but the church remained standing for nearly five hundred years, its longest period yet. Then, on July 21, 1936, the Figuerenses began to set fire to churches; "surgió la chispa necrosificadora, el espíritu satánico de destrucción y de ruina . . ." the mob broke into the parish church during Mass, seized benches and chairs, and set them ablaze. What a conflagration! Flames leaped to the roof. "The faithful, livid with fear, retired into a corner of the church, believing their last hour to have come," but they were allowed to go without molestation. The flames consumed nearly everything; what they left was looted or destroyed.

Mysterious madness which ever and anon attacks the Spanish, driving them to these strange pyrrhic frenzies! It seems the reverse side of religious devotion: in Anglican England we have little of either; in consequence our churches and cathedrals remain standing, though somewhat sparsely filled. It was odd to picture the cheerful Figuerenses at their fiery work, seeing them so peaceably and gaily employed in their broad market square on this July morning eleven years later. Indeed, this morning market was a lovely sight—a brilliant orchard of gay fruits piled on stalls—oranges, peaches, apricots, greengages, melons, tomatoes; and behind each stall a smiling buxom woman selling, before it other smiling buxom women buying; had they, I wondered, eleven years ago tossed pictures and images on the bonfire in San Pedro as now they tossed oranges and apricots into straw bags, and with the same zest? From all accounts, yes.

Meanwhile, the new San Pedro goes up apace, and will be beautiful. If it lasts another five hundred years, it will be lucky. The ancient castle of San Fernando, north-east of the town, was blown up in 1939, a last explosion of the Republicans when Franco's army marched in. Figueras is a pleasant capital; it has broad ramblas and narrow streets, and is difficult to find one's way out of. It had no petrol. They told me at the garages that petrol north of Barcelona was chancey; one might find some pump which had just got its quota, or one might not. La Escala, they said, might have some. They spoke as embittered men: the Ampurdán, one gathered, was being starved of petrol to feed Barcelona, which drank it with gluttonous profusion.

My mind was now set on Ampurias; I hurried out of Figueras, with my basket full of fruit and pots bought in the market. It was another hot and shining day. My way to La Escala and the coast ran through fifteen miles of level country, along a jolting road, past little ochre-coloured mediæval villages and farms, across the river Fluvia, and so through Vilademat to the little port of Escala, at the southern end of the Gulf of Rosas, whence a short road goes through woods to Ampurias. I arrived in La Escala in a propitious hour: petrol had just arrived, and there was a queue of camions at the pump in the street leading down to the shore, and a busy woman working it. (Most petrol pumps in northern Spain, as in France, are worked by women; further south, not; in the south women are not, I think, supposed to meddle with anything to do with motoring; they stick to donkeys.) The little port was crowded with beautiful fishing boats, great and small; I think it was a holiday, for it was gay with music and coloured paper festoons. Fantastically shaped rocks jutted up about the sea. Señor Pla says Escala is the chief fishing centre of the Costa Brava, and that the fishermen have a hard life, for the port faces north, and in winter gets the tramontana and the icy winds from Canigou and Provence. This, says he, has made the *escalanes* a rather sad, pessimistic people. Fortunately it was not winter when I was there; on that July morning La Escala was blue and exquisite, though its rock-strewn bay was ruffled by a breeze. The town did not look sad and grey, as my book said, though it does lack the brilliant white-wash and paint of many of the harbour towns. At nights the fishing boats go out with lights, the whole Gulf sparkles as with fireflies, and is very exquisite. Tiny coves of rock and sand surround the town to north and south; that morning they were pale jade and aquamarine, the waves lapping against jagged rocks.

The short road to Ampurias crosses a bridge just outside La Escala and runs through a sandy pine-wood. The ruins lie above the road, back from a bay of delightful sand and jutting rocks, the bay where Gnaeus Cornelius Scipio landed with his squadron to fight the Carthaginians, "at a place in Iberia called Emporium," says Polybius. "Starting from this town, he made descents upon the coast, landing and besieging those who refused to submit to him along the seaboard as far as the Iber . . ."

The Emporium where Scipio landed in 211 B.C. was already over three centuries old as a Greek settlement, and illimitably older as an Iberian village. Somewhere about 550 B.C. Phocæan sailors and traders from Marseilles, cut off from the southern coast by the iron curtain of the Carthaginian conquest, made here, in the shelter of this Gulf of Rosas, and close to a small native town, a trading settlement. They settled first on what was then an island, where the almost ruined little mediæval village of San Martí now stands, guarding that buried town of Paleopolis, and a temple of the Ephesian Artemis which must have stood there. This first settlement is still unexcavated. The second, Neapolis, made a few years later, on the other side of the little harbour and buried from sight for many centuries, only yielding up occasional treasures to casual searchers, was first systematically excavated by the Barcelona archæological society forty years ago; interrupted by the civil war, the work is now again in progress. Neapolis has been revealed, layer below layer, each period identifiable by its fragments of pottery and sculpture and its coins, from the Visigothic town superimposed on it by the barbarian invaders, through the Roman city of splendid and ornate buildings, market places, temples and rich villas, the Hellenistic city that preceded and merged with the Roman, the Attic town of the fifth century, down to the earliest levels, the level of the sixth-century Massiliotes who founded the settlement and of the Iberian town joined to it; of those earliest towns there is little to show now. Neapolis was, when Strabo described it in the first century A.D., a double city, divided by a wall. . . .

> because formerly the city had for neighbours some of the Indicetans, who, though they maintained a government of their own, wished for the sake of security to have a common wall of circumvallation with the Greeks, with the enclosure in two parts, for it has been divided by a wall through the centre; but in the course of time the two peoples united under the same constitution, which was a mixture of barbarian and Greek laws.

Livy's account is more detailed.

> Even at that time [195 B.C., when Cato landed there with army and fleet] Emporiæ consisted of two towns separated by a wall. One was inhabited by Greeks from Phocæa (whence came the Massilienses also) the other by the Spaniards: but the Greek town, being entirely open to the sea, had only a small extent of wall, while the Spaniards, who were further back from the sea, had a wall three miles round. A third class of inhabitants, Roman colonists, was added by the deified Cæsar . . . and at present all are fused in one mass, the Spaniards first, and later the Greeks, having been received into Roman citizenship. One who saw them at that time would wonder what secured the safety of the Greeks, with the open sea on one side and the Spaniards, so fierce and warlike a people, their neighbours on the other. Discipline was their protector against their weakness. . . . The part of the wall

which faced the interior they kept strongly fortified, with only a single
gate, and at this one of the magistrates was posted as a continuous
guard. At night a third of the citizens kept vigil on the walls. No
Spaniard was admitted to the city, nor did the Greeks themselves leave
the city without good cause. Towards the sea the gates were open to
all. Through the gate which led to the Spanish town they never passed
except in large bodies, usually the third which had kept the watch on
the wall the night before. The cause of going out of the town was this:
the Spaniards, who had no experience with the sea, enjoyed transact-
ing business with them, and wanted both to buy the foreign merchan-
dise which they brought in their ships, and to dispose of the products
of their own farms. The desire of the benefits of this interchange
caused the Spanish city to be open to the Greeks.

The remains of the walls, huge and massive, with their single gate,
are of the fifth century B.C. By then, Emporion had Greek works of
art, Attic vases, the famous statue of Asklepios and other Athenian
objects. Emporitans grew richer and more cultivated; by the fourth
century, the Hellenistic age, their town was enlarged and beautified, a
long, crowded rectangle of crossing streets and open squares, villas
with mosaic floors, tombs, temples, statues. There was the temple of
Juniper Serapis, surrounded by a spacious colonnade, the door giving
on the sea. There was a stoa, or market place, with shops within the
pillared ambulatory without, where buyers and sellers walked, chaf-
fering and bartering in Greek, Iberian, Latin, all the dialects of the
Middle Sea. And through the city the winds from this sea, and the
sound of it, murmured always.

The Romans came; Emporion wisely allied itself with Rome, as a
defence against Carthage. Romans colonized the Hellenistic town,
making a city behind it far larger, richer, finer, than Emporion itself.
There were beautiful houses, grand temples, rich mosaic floors, cis-
terns, plumbing, baths. The name was now Emporiæ, for there were
three cities, the Roman, the Greek, the Iberian. Recent excavations of
the Roman town have discovered its great wall, built by Cæsar, on the
base of an older wall of the cyclopean type. There have also been
exposed a gymnasium, and a large elliptical amphitheatre. Emporion
under the Romans had advanced far from the early cramped Greek

town. In the third century Frankish pirates attacked the coast and destroyed Neapolis; its inhabitants abandoned it, and settled in the Roman city, which was presently Christianized; there was a basilica, and a Christian burial ground. Then, in Rome's decadence, arrived the barbarians, and the Visigothic town superimposed itself on Emporion. It became the seat of a bishopric.

Then, by the ninth century, Ampurias disappears from history; it has been conjectured that it was sacked and destroyed by the Norman pirates who raged up and down the coast, though some historians blame the Saracens. Villanueva, in his *Viaje Literario a las Iglesias de España*, quotes a record from the archives of the monastery of Santa Maria de Roda—"The pagans came and sacked the whole town, and the pirates laid waste the territory; its inhabitants and peasants were in large numbers taken captive, and many others, abandoning their farms during that time because of the oppressions of the wicked pirates, emigrated elsewhere."

A common story all down that perilous coast. Ampurias was apparently abandoned; and, after some attempts by its counts to revive it, they retired inland to Castellón de Ampurias, and the sea town gradually sank deeper beneath the silting sands, and was forgotten, to wait a thousand years for its unburial. The guidebooks of a century ago, such as Ford's, count Emporion a complete loss, but for the "miserable ruined fishing hamlet" on the hill close by; all that the Baedeker of 1901 says is that the name of Castellón de Ampurias "recalls Emporion, an ancient Greek colony on the Gulf of Rosas." Later English guidebooks only give Ampurias a few lines.

Ampurias to-day is a place inexpressibly moving in its beauty and desolation. Along the intricate criss-cross of the streets that run between the vanished houses, cypresses darkly and necropolistically stand, and fig trees sprawl stickily in the sun. The columns of arcaded porticoes and of temples rear broken stumps against sky and sea. You may wander through the city among ghosts of Greek traders, Iberian vendors, Roman gentlemen lounging outside their villas or gossiping in loud Roman voices in the agora, simple Visigoths knocking down heathen statues and drinking deeply of the wines of Ampurdán.

Across a sandy stretch of land to the north the tumbled, ruinous little pile of San Martí climbs its rocky hill; beneath it sleeps forgotten the old, the original Paleopolis. In front of Ampurias the sea whispers and creams; its tang breathes about the ghostly city like a song. Before Herodotus wrote, Greeks lived and traded here; before Rome was a republic, this little Greek mart was doing business on the shores of the gulf that sheltered merchant ships beneath this great spur of the eastern Pyrenees. Now, along the massive wall above the sea road, red oleanders sprawl. A model of the Asklepios statue presides serenely over that broken desert of little streets. In the western corner, close to the Roman city, on the site of a ruined convent, stands the little museum, where some of the Ampurias finds can be seen—mosaics and vases, pottery of all the periods, fragments, some most lovely. Most of the important things are in the Barcelona archæological museum, and some at Gerona; but this little branch of it has kept some valuable finds, and also some interesting and pleasing model reconstructions of buildings. It is an unpretentious, rather charming little place.

From Ampurias one goes a few hundred yards along the sea road to San Martí, the walled hamlet on the hill that was once an island. It is the quietest mediæval hamlet imaginable; but for one gay-tiled villa, the houses, inhabited by a few peasants and animals, seem all tumbling or tumbled into ruin. Its square-towered church crowns the steep streets. Why the village is in such dilapidation, and how long it has been so, I was not able to discover. I wandered about its empty, stony streets, and spoke with a few people outside a tumbling house; a peasant was driving a donkey cart piled with grass up the street; by the gate there was an ancient well. The counts of Ampurias used long ago to frequent this fortified town on its hill; but they retired inland to the safer fortress of Castellón, and San Martí was abandoned to peasants and pirates.

I ate my lunch in the pine woods below the high, steep walls, then went back to Ampurias to spend the afternoon among its whispering centuries of ghosts. Leaving it at last, I drove back along the wood road to La Escala. From there a new road, made during the civil war, runs south for a few kilometres down the rocky coast of coves and

capes as far as El Milá. But to explore these coves properly one needs
a boat. The gnarled grey rocks jut out into a cobalt and azure sea
with, in profile, the mute ferocity of couching beasts, sheltering
between them here and there white coves of sand, above some of
which a few cottages sprawl, and in and out of which fishing boats
slip. A stormy sea among these fantastic wild-cat rocks must be an
affair of sound, foam and fury; that July afternoon the Mediterranean was a suave and cooing murmuration of blue doves. But my
road turned from it inland towards Gerona.

It was a bad road. As a road there was nothing to be said for it,
except that it ran through good scenery and passed fine mediæval
towns. It was rough and jolting, like so many of the roads that lead to
important cities in Spain, roads that shook my car continually to
pieces. The pot-holes on the Gerona road were perhaps caused by
Roman chariots thundering along them from the coast; or perhaps
the Romans had found them thus and made them worse. No doubt
they cursed. Then 'twas the Roman, now 'tis I. It was also, no doubt,
the rough and turbulent counts of Ampurias, who, throughout the
Middle Ages, thundered about Ampurdán, making such disturbances
as they threw up castles and palaces and forts, and attacked anything
they met which did not submit to them. The bishops of Gerona
(often the cousins or uncles of the count) may also have done their
share.

Anyhow, and whosesoever fault it was, the road from La Escala to
Gerona, via Belcaire and up the Ter valley, is execrable. My front
bumper was jerked off, beginning a long series of such decadences.
Throughout the nearly four thousand miles of road that I covered in
the peninsula, I learnt that cars are not so firmly held together as one
had hoped. One piece after another is liable to drop from them; there
is a sudden intimidating clatter, and it will be either a bumper or an
exhaust pipe or (more perilously, for I was once all but over the edge
of a very steep mountain precipice) the steering axle, that, still
attached at one end, has broken its bolts at the other and is clattering
with a noise of machine guns along the road. If these objects, which
I detested, but which were, it seemed, essential to my car's structure,
action, and well being, could be fastened on again with straps, I fastened them on with straps, until I reached the next garage. If they

could not (like the steering axle) be fastened on with straps, or otherwise replaced by amateur effort, I left the car on the road and walked or got a lift to the next garage, to bring back mechanics with the necessary tools. It was not always quite easy to explain to the mechanics what the necessary tools would be. I had a Spanish motoring phrase book with me, but it said few of the things that I wished to say. It said, "Have you a really trustworthy man on whom I can rely to clean my car?" and, "My car has fallen into a ditch. Do me the favour to send an ox (two oxen) to extricate it," and (more vaguely and pessimistically), "My car has discomposed itself. I have left it in charge of a peasant —— kilometres from here." (Fortunately I never acquired this peasant, since my car locks.) Once arrived at a garage, even without one's car, one can explain what has gone wrong by indicating similar appliances on other cars and remarking "Esto no marcha," "This part does not go," or "This thing has fallen off." Spaniards are very helpful, kind and intelligent about cars. If they see a woman changing a wheel on the road, they leap from their camions or their cars and offer help; it is, I suppose, one side of their intense and apparently universal astonishment that a woman should be driving a car at all. All over Spain, except in the more sophisticated cities, my driving by was greeted with the same cry—a long, shrill cat-call, reminiscent of a pig having its throat cut, usually wordless, but sometimes accompanied by "Olé, Olé! Una señora que conduce!" For Spanish women do not drive cars. I was told this many times, and indeed, observation confirmed it; I saw not a single woman driving all the time I was in Spain. Why not, I sometimes asked. "It is not the custom here. Spanish ladies live very quietly." One man, more analytic, explained, "You see, we Spanish do not live in this century at all, nor in the last, but several hundred years back. We hear that in England women do the things men do, but in Spain it has never been the custom." This is not true: the peasant women work in the fields and drive donkey carts everywhere; what he meant was señoras. And, apparently, so few foreign señoras are seen driving that they are still regarded as prodigies and portents, much like a man suckling a baby. This, together with the intense Spanish interest in people, and particularly in women, makes it impossible for a woman-driven car to be allowed to pass without comment, as a harmless foreign oddity, as we more sophisticated, live-and-let-live English let foreigners and their strange habits go by without turning the head. In Spain, all heads are turned; and there is a disconcerting outcry. If any student of national psychology can analyse and explain this ancient Spanish custom (one gathers from all travellers that it is ancient) it would be an interesting investigation. The demonstrations sound mainly astonished and derisive; some times rather inimical; always excited and inquisitive. Strange ambivalence of the Spanish! If their curiosity is sometimes partly hostile, their helpfulness to foreigners in difficulty, and their flattering compliments to females (even elderly females such as myself) are delightful and admirable; we can never rival or repay them.

But on the Gerona road that evening I needed no help; I tied on my bumper to a headlamp and proceeded to jolt and bound along.

I came to Belcaire, three miles along this vile road: a fine fortified town where the counts of Ampurias had built themselves an imposing palace or castle; its ruined walls and towers magnificently crown the little city—the old Roman Bedenga. Both in Roman and feudal times Belcaire was full of stir; the counts made it a constant resort, as they galloped so destructively about Ampurdán. All those noisy Frankish aristocrats, who supplied members of their families for every place, lay or clerical, that would give them feudal powers over the natives of Spain—one pictures these Catalans like stormtroopers, or Black-and-tans, rushing about the Spanish Marches fortifying mountains, plains and cities, fighting Moors, Norman pirates, and one another, massacring Jews, marching north to give battle to the Franks of Provence or Toulouse, never tranquil, always tough, strong and devout. Their Romanesque churches were superb, even before the year 1000, even while the *terror milenario*, the knowledge that no building could outlive the Day of Judgment, kept architecture simple and austere. This danger point safely passed, Romanesque flowered into its full Catalan beauty. And their castles, both before and after *l'an mil*, were noble and grand, as we see them in ruin to-day, for castles were what they understood and did well; "necesse est edificare castela . . ." the lords of the Spanish Marches always knew that, and in time their castled land came, by the Franks beyond the Pyrenees, to be called Catalonia for that reason. It was the Frankish counts who set the tradition of the small Catalan walled town as we see it still today—high, ochre-brown citadels, many of the houses arcaded and terraced (perhaps from the brief Moorish influence?), tiled roof climbing above tiled roof to the solid, fortress-like church that crowns the pile, with its heavy nave and apse and square tower— embattled churches, with belfries like watch towers to observe and clang the warning news of approaching foes. All have a family look as to colour and shape; all are beautiful; all look mediæval, though of which century one could not say without nearer inspection. Many have castles. Belcaire is such a citadel; so are Ulla, Verges, and the other towns that ennoble (this has to be the word) the valley of the Ter, and, indeed, most of Catalonia. To follow a road that runs through them is to travel through the dark turmoil of history, through what Gautier called "cette obscure tourmente qu'est le haut moyen âge."

I reached Gerona before dark. The approach to it is startlingly beautiful; it stands high above the river Oñar where it joins the Ter; its houses seem to climb precipitously, river-washed, up the steep slope of the hill. It is brown in colour, narrow-streeted, mediæval. The Gothic cathedral dominates it with stupendous splendour, standing at the top of a long and lovely seventeenth-century flight of golden stone steps. Except the long avenue and steps at Guadix, I know of no more beautiful approach to any cathedral or church; it beats Tarragona, because there is more space in front of it, and the baroque curve of the flight is lovelier. I believe that the effect of the outside of Gerona cathedral is not too well thought of architecturally, the nave being too large and too bare; but I admired it. Inside, the tremendous span of the single-vaulted nave is magnificent; its effect is heightened by the sombre darkness that nearly all Catalan churches affect, and to enter which from the dazzling radiance of the Spanish sunshine is like groping one's way from a burning shore into a deep cool cave.

Gerona, the Roman Gerunda, had a church and a bishopric from the first years of Spanish Christendom. One of the earliest bishops was Narcissus, Gerona's tutelar saint. Tradition gives the foundation of the present church to Charlemagne, in 786, when Gerona was taken for a brief time by the Franks from the Moors. When the Moors got it back again they used it for a mosque, letting the Christians worship in what is now the lovely fourteenth-century collegiate church of San Felíu (but what it was then is obscure). The cathedral was rebuilt in the early eleventh century when the Christians finally captured the city, rebuilt again and added to through the fourteenth, fifteenth and sixteenth. Guillermo Boffiy's famous nave, the widest in Christendom, was designed in the fifteenth century. Its spacious breadth makes a remarkable effect of tranquil strength and lack of fuss. That it was a great engineering feat is proved by its unshaken resistance to the storms and shocks of battle which have raged down the centuries round Gerona, a city with at least five-and-twenty sieges in its history.

There are interesting things in the cathedral (which I saw next morning)—a fourteenth-century retablo, covered with enamel and silver plate, a shafted wood and silver baldacchino, a few good tombs. To the north-west are the Romanesque twelfth-century cloisters, with very charmingly sculptured capitals, like the Elne cloisters in style. One is reminded again of the unity of Catalan culture on both sides of the Pyrenees. As beautiful is the Romanesque cloister of San Pedro de Galligans, the tenth or eleventh-century Benedictine chapel built against the city walls. The cloisters are of the same date and style as those of the cathedral. They now house a museum. In San Felíu's chancel walls there are some beautiful Roman bas-reliefs.

Apart from churches and museums, there are things to see all about Gerona, and I spent an agreeable day seeing them. It is a fascinating city; the crowded streets and houses, girdled by their ancient walls, rising above the running river (unlike most Spanish rivers in summer, it did run), and above these the steep fortressed hill to guard the town. No wonder every one has always tried to take Gerona. To the Romans, it was rather a place of strategic importance and a loyal city than a pleasure resort such as Tarragona; but they resided in it a good deal. The Moors fought for it again and again; under the Franks, it was head of a countship; ecclesiastically, it clung tenaciously to power, and fought that of the counts with grim determination. The present bishops of Gerona must look back with some wistfulness to the grand feudal state kept by their mediæval predecessors, their wealth and wide lands, their trains of slaves and concubines, their noble libraries, their great monasteries (though the abbots often gave trouble), the dues they extorted from their vassals, even the wars of envy and fear waged against them by the counts of Barcelona and the kings of Aragon, who pursued, as a rule, a policy definitely anti-clerical. The lives of bishops in Ampurdán now, alas! move on more restricted lines.

Andrew Marvell

(1621–1678)

Andrew Marvell's poem "On the Victory Obtained by Blake over the Spaniards" celebrates the defeat of a Spanish fleet by the British in the Anglo–Spanish War. In the 1600s the two countries dueled for supremacy over the seas; both had magnificent, well-equipped navies. While "On the Victory" appears to be nationalistic chest-thumping verse, the poem was actually something of a job application.

Marvell was a rather mysterious English poet. His biography is full of gaps, and at one point in his early twenties biographers cannot account for six years of his life. Some speculate that he was a spy; others that he was a tutor. He resurfaced during the English Civil Wars, although what part he played and to whom he was loyal is a question. Marvell's most famous poem, "To His Coy Mistress," was published around 1650 while he was the tutor to the daughter of a former parliamentarian. Although thought to be a Royalist, he needed Oliver Cromwell's help to get work. His poem "On the Victory" may have been a ploy to get Cromwell's attention.

And apparently it worked. Cromwell appointed Marvell to the post of Latin secretary. His duties included translating documents and acting as an intermediary during diplomatic visits. Marvell's appointment launched his political career, and in 1659 he was elected to Parliament. It is a testament to Marvell's ability to cut his politics to fit each administration that his career survived the fall of Cromwell and the restoration of the monarchy. Marvell died in 1678. His collected poems were published in 1681 under the title *Miscellaneous Poems*.

ON THE VICTORY OBTAINED BY BLAKE OVER THE SPANIARDS

IN THE BAY OF SANTA CRUZ, IN THE ISLAND OF TENERIFF. (1657)

Now does Spains Fleet her spatious wings unfold,
Leaves the new World and hastens for the old:
But though the wind was fair, the slowly swoome
Frayted with acted Guilt, and Guilt to come:
For this rich load, of which so proud they are,
Was rais'd by Tyranny, and rais'd for war;
Every capatious Gallions womb was fill'd,
With what the Womb of wealthy Kingdomes yield,
The new Worlds wounded Intails they had tore,
For wealth wherewith to wound the old once more.
Wealth which all others Avarice might cloy,
But yet in them caus'd as much fear, as Joy.
For now upon the Main, themselves they saw,
That boundless Empire, where you give the law,
Of winds and waters rage, they fearful be,
But much more fearful are your Flags to see
Day, that to these who sail upon the deep,
More wish't for, and more welcome is then sleep,
They dreaded to behold, Least the Sun's light,
With English Streamers, should salute their sight:
In thickest darkness they would choose to steer,
So that such darkness might suppress their fear;
At length theirs vanishes, and fortune smiles;
For they behold the sweet Canary Isles.
One of which doubtless is by Nature blest
Above both Worlds, since 'tis above the rest.
For least some Gloominess might stain her sky,
Trees there the duty of the Clouds supply;
O noble Trust which Heaven on this Isle poures,
Fertile to be, yet never need her showres.

A happy People, which at once do gain
The benefits without the ills of rain.
Both health and profit, Fate cannot deny;
Where still the Earth is moist, the Air still dry;
The jarring Elements no discord know,
Fewel and Rain together kindly grow;
And coolness there, with heat doth never fight,
This only rules by day, and that by Night.
Your worth to all these Isles, a just right brings,
The best of Lands should have the best of Kings.
And these want nothing Heaven can afford,
Unless it be, the having you their Lord;
But this great want, will not along one prove,
Your Conquering Sword will soon that want remove.
For Spain had better. Shee'l ere long confess,
Have broken all her Swords, then this one Peace,
Casting that League off, which she held so long,
She cast off that which only made her strong.
Forces and art, she soon will feel, are vain,
Peace, against you, was the sole strength of Spain.
By that alone those Islands she secures,
Peace made them hers, but War will make them yours;
There the indulgent Soil that rich Grape breeds,
Which of the Gods the fancied drink exceeds;
They still do yield, such is their pretious mould,
All that is good, and are not curst with Gold.
With fatal Gold, for still where that does grow,
Neither the Soyl, nor People quiet know.
Which troubles men to raise it when 'tis Oar,
And when 'tis raised, does trouble them much more.
Ah, why was thither brought that cause of War,
Kind Nature had from thence remov'd so far.
In vain doth she those Islands free from ill,
If fortune can make guilty what she will.
But whilst I draw that Scene, where you ere long,
Shall conquests act, your present are unsung,
For Santa Cruz the glad Fleet takes her way,

And safely there casts Anchor in the Bay.
Never so many with one joyful cry,
That place saluted, where they all must dye.
Deluded men! Fate with you did but sport,
You scap't the Sea, to perish in your Port.
'Twas more for Englands fame you should dye there,
Where you had most of strength, and least of fear.
The Peek's proud height, the Spaniards all admire,
Yet in their brests, carry a pride much higher.
Onely to this vast hill a power is given,
At once both to Inhabit Earth and Heaven.
But this stupendious Prospect did not neer,
Make them admire, so much as they did fear.
For here they met with news, which did produce,
A grief, above the cure of Grapes best juice.
They learn'd with Terrour, that nor Summers heat,
Nor Winters storms, had made your Fleet retreat.
To fight against such Foes, was vain they knew,
Which did the rage of Elements subdue.
Who on the Ocean that does horror give,
To all besides, triumphantly do live.
With hast they therefore all their Gallions moar,
And flank with Cannon from the Neighbouring shore.
Forts, Lines, and Sconces all the Bay along,
They build and act all that can make them strong.
Fond men who know not whilst such works they raise,
They only Labour to exalt your praise.
Yet they by restless toyl, because at Length,
So proud and confident of their made strength.
That they with joy their boasting General heard,
Wish then for that assault he lately fear'd.
His wish he has, for now undaunted Blake,
With winged speed, for Santa Cruz does make.
For your renown, his conquering Fleet does ride,
Ore Seas as vast as is the Spaniards pride.
Whose Fleet and Trenches view'd, he soon did say,
We to their Strength are more obilg'd then they.

Wer't not for that, they from their Fate would run,
And a third World seek out our Armes to shun.
Those Forts, which there, so high and strong appear,
Do not so much suppress, as shew their fear.
Of Speedy Victory let no man doubt,
Our worst works past, now we have found them out.
Behold their Navy does at Anchor lye,
And they are ours, for now they cannot fly.
This said, the whole Fleet gave it their applause,
And all assumes your courage, in your cause.
That Bay they enter, which unto them owes,
The noblest wreaths, that Victory bestows.
Bold Stainer Leads, this Fleets design'd by fate,
To give him Lawrel, as the Last did Plate.
The Thund'ring Cannon now begins the Fight,
And though it be at Noon, creates a Night.
The Air was soon after the fight begun,
Far more enflam'd by it, then by the Sun.
Never so burning was that Climate known,
War turn'd the temperate, to the Torrid Zone.
Fate these two Fleets, between both Worlds had brought.
Who fight, as if for both those Worlds they fought.
Thousands of waves, Thousands of men there dye,
Some Ships are sunk, some blown up in the skie.
Nature never made Cedars so high a Spire,
As Oakes did then. Urg'd by the active fire.
Which by quick powders force, so high was sent,
That it return'd to its own Element.
Torn Limbs some leagues into the island fly,
Whilst others lower, in the Sea do lye.
Scarce souls from bodies sever'd are so far,
By death, as bodies there were by the War.
Th'all-seeing Sun, neer gaz'd on such a sight,
Two dreadful Navies there at Anchor Fight.
And neither have, or power, or will to fly,
There one must Conquer, or there both must dye.
Far different Motives yet, engag'd them thus,

Necessity did them, but Choice did us.
A choice which did the highest forth express,
And was attended by a high success.
For your resistless genious there did Raign,
By which we Laurels reapt ev'n on the Mayn.
So prosperous Stars, though absent to the sence,
Bless those they shine for, by their Influence.
Our Cannon now tears every Ship and Sconce,
And o're two Elements Triumphs at once.
Their Gallions sunk, their wealth the Sea does fill,
The only place where it can cause no ill,
Ah would those Treasures which both Indies have,
Were buryed in as large, and deep a grave,
Wars chief support with them would buried be,
And the Land owe her peace unto the Sea.
Ages to come, your conquering Arms will bless,
There they destroy, what had destroy'd their Peace.
And in one War the present age may boast,
The certain seeds of many Wars are lost,
All the Foes Ships destroy'd, by Sea or fire,
Victorious Blake, does from the Bay retire,
His Seige of Spain he then again pursues,
And there first brings of his success the news;
The saddest news that ere to Spain was brought
Their rich Fleet sunk, and ours with Lawrel fraught.
Whilst fame in every place, her Trumpet blowes,
And tells the World, how much to you it owes.

W. Somerset Maugham

(1874–1965)

Novelist, playwright, and short story writer William Somerset Maugham was the highest-paid author in the world in the 1930s. Maugham himself said that he was "in the very first row of the second-raters . . . I never pretended to be anything but a story teller. It has amused me to tell stories and I have told a great many."

Born in Paris, Maugham was orphaned at ten and went to live in England with his uncle, a vicar. He wanted to be a doctor and studied medicine until he was in his midtwenties. Emboldened by his early writing success, Maugham quit medicine and moved back to Paris to live the life of a struggling author. Although he had some plays produced, his breakthrough novel was *Of Human Bondage* (1914), the story of a young man with a clubfoot who overcomes his physical limitations to become a doctor. After World War I (in which he tried to serve in intelligence on the Russian front, but was dismissed because of poor health), Maugham set off on exotic travels: Mexico, the Pacific Islands, eastern Asia, and Pago Pago.

Some critics feel that Maugham's prose was at its best in his travel writing, and his books include *On a Chinese Screen* (1923) and *Don Fernando* (1935, from which this is excerpted), in which he described his Seville neighborhood. "If you went out in the morning you might see a lady in black, with her maid, going to mass; sometimes a huckster passed along with his donkey, his wares in great open panniers; or a beggar, stopping at house after house, who raised his voice at each *reja*, the wrought iron gate that led into the patio, and begged for alms with the phrase of immemorial usage. At nightfall the ladies who had been driving in the Paseo in a landau drawn by two horses came home again and the streets resounded with the clatter of the horses' hooves. Then all grew silent." Maugham was so convinced of the benefit of travel to the young writer that he established the Somerset Maugham Award for that purpose. He died just short of his ninety-second birthday at his home in France.

From DON FERNANDO

I was living in Seville at the time, in the street called Guzman el Bueno, and whenever I went out or came home I passed Don Fernando's tavern. When, my morning's work done, I had gone for a stroll down the gay and crowded Sierpes, I found it very pleasant to drop in for a glass of manzanilla on my way back to luncheon; and in the cool of the evening, walking my horse over the dangerous cobbles after a ride in the country, I would often stop, call the boy to hold the horse, and step in. The tavern was no more than a long low room with doors on two sides of it, for it was at the corner of a street; the bar ran down the length of the room and behind it were the barrels of wine from which Don Fernando served you. From the ceiling hung bunches of Spanish onions, strings of sausages and hams from Granada, which Don Fernando always said were the best in Spain. I think his custom was chiefly among the servants of the neighbourhood. This district of Santa Cruz was then the most elegant in Seville. Tortuous white streets, with large houses, and here and there a church. It was strangely deserted. If you went out in the morning you might see a lady in black, with her maid, going to mass; sometimes a huckster passed along with his donkey, his wares in great open panniers; or a beggar, stopping at house after house, who raised his voice at each reja, the wrought iron gate that led into the patio, and begged for alms with the phrase of immemorial usage. At nightfall the ladies who had been driving in the Paseo in a landau drawn by two horses came home again and the streets resounded with the clatter of the horses' hooves. Then all again grew silent. This was many years ago. I write now of the last years of the nineteenth century.

Don Fernando was small even for a Spaniard, but he was very fat. His round brown face shone with sweat and he had always two days' growth of beard. Never more and never less. I do not know how he managed it. He was incredibly dirty. He had long black shining eyes, with extremely long lashes, and they were at the same time sharp, good-natured and gay. He was a wag and he enjoyed his own dry humour. He spoke in the soft Andalusian Spanish from which the

Moorish influence has eliminated the harshness of Castile and it was
not till I had learnt the language pretty well that I found him easy to
understand. He was an aficionado of the bull-ring and it was his
boast that the great Guerrita came in now and then to drink a glass
of wine with him. He was a bachelor and lived alone with a scrubby,
pale-faced boy whom he had got from the orphanage and who did
the cooking, washed the glasses and swept the floor. This boy had
the most pronounced squint I ever saw.

But Don Fernando did not only sell you as good a glass of manzanilla as you could get in Seville; he also dealt in curios. That was
why I dropped in to see him so often. You never knew what he might
have to show you. I suppose the things came through a confidential
servant from the houses in the neighbourhood. Their owners, tem-
porarily embarrassed, were too proud to take them to a shop. They
were for the most part small and easily portable, pieces of silver, lace,
old fans with sticks of mother-of-pearl decorated with gold, crucifixes, paste ornaments and antique rings of baroque design. Don
Fernando seldom acquired a piece of furniture; but when he did, a
bargueño or a pair of straight-backed chairs, with leather seats and all
studded with nails, he would keep it upstairs in the bedroom he
shared with the foundling. I had very little money and he knew I
could only buy trifles, but he loved to show his purchases and two or
three times he took me up into his room. The windows were closed
to keep out the heat by day and the noxious airs by night and it was
very dirty. It stank. In opposite corners of the room were two small
iron beds, unmade at whatever time of day you went in, and the
sheets looked as though they had not been washed for months. The
floor was strewn with cigarette-ends. Don Fernando's eyes would
shine more brightly than ever when he passed his grubby, podgy
hand over the wood of a chair that had been polished by the usage of
three centuries. He would spit on the dusty gilt surface of a taberna-
cle and rub the place with his finger to show you with delight the
exquisite quality of the gold. Sometimes, while you stood at the bar,
he would fish out from behind it the pieces of a pair of ear-rings,
those old heavy Spanish ear-rings in three tiers, and assemble them
delicately so that you might admire the beauty of the paste and the

elegance of the setting. He had a way of handling these things, sensual and tender, that showed you more than any words he might have spoken how profound a feeling he had for them. When he flicked open an old fan, with the peculiar click that the Spanish woman gives, and fanned himself, an old fan a great lady in her mantilla had flaunted at a bull-fight when Charles III was King of Spain, you could not but feel that, ignorant though he was, he had some vague, delightful emotion of the past.

Don Fernando bought cheaply and sold cheaply; and so, after bargaining for days, often for weeks, which I think we both enjoyed, I was able to get from him little by little a number of objects which were not of the smallest use to me, but which I hankered after because their associations appealed to my fancy. So I bought the fans that pretty women, dead a hundred and fifty years ago, had flirted, the ear-rings they wore in their ears, the fantastic rings they wore on their fingers and the crucifixes they hung in their rooms. It was junk and in the passage of time it has all been stolen, lost or given away. Of all I bought from Don Fernando I have now nothing but a book, and that I did not want and bought against my will. One day as I stepped across the threshold Don Fernando addressed me forthwith.

"I've got something for you," he said. "I bought it especially for you."

"What is it?"

"A book."

He opened a drawer in the bar and brought out a little squat volume bound in dirty parchment. My face fell.

"I don't want that."

"But look at it. It's an old book. It's more than three hundred years old."

He opened it and showed me the title page. There it was all right, the date 1586, with the imprint of Madrid and the publisher's name: Por la viuda de Alonso Gomez Impressor de la C.R.M.

"It doesn't cost anything," he went on. "I'll give it you for fifty pesetas."

"But I don't want it at any price."

"It's a celebrated book. When it was brought to me I said to myself: Don Guillermo will like that. He's an educated man."

"My eye and Betty Martin." (Not many people know the Spanish for that.) "Sell it to somebody else. I'm not a book collector. I only buy books to read."

"But why shouldn't you read this? It's very interesting."

"Not to me."

"A book three hundred years old? Come, man, don't say things like that to me. Look, there's writing on the margins in places and there's writing on the back page. That shows you it's old."

It was true that some reader had written notes here and there in a hand that might very well have been of the seventeenth century, but I could not decipher a word. I turned a few pages. It was beautifully printed on strong, fine paper, but the type was so close-set that it was difficult to read. The old spelling, the abbreviations I noticed, made it hard to understand. I shook my head firmly and handed the book back to Don Fernando.

"You can have it for forty pesetas. I paid thirty-five for it myself."

"I wouldn't have it as a gift."

He shrugged his shoulders with a sigh and put the book away.

A few days later I happened to pass the tavern on horseback and Don Fernando, who was standing at the doorway sucking a toothpick, called me.

"Come in a moment; I've got something to say to you."

I dismounted and gave the bridle to the boy. Don Fernando put the book in my hands.

"I'll give it to you for thirty pesetas. I lose five on it, but I want you to have it."

"But I don't want the book," I cried.

"Twenty-five pesetas."

"No."

"You needn't read it. Put it in your library."

"I haven't got a library."

"But you ought to have a library. Start your library with this book. It's a beautiful book."

"It isn't a beautiful book."

And it wasn't. Even though I knew I should never read it I might have been tempted if it had been bound in leather with a coat of arms in gold, a handsome folio with wide margins. But it was an ugly little volume, much too thick for its height, and the parchment with which it was bound was crinkled and yellow. I was determined not to have the book. Don Fernando, I do not know why, was determined that I should; and after that I never went into the tavern without his attacking me. He flattered me, he cajoled me, he threw himself on my mercy, he appealed to my sense of justice; he came down in his price to twenty pesetas, to ten, but I stood firm. Then one day he got hold of a wooden statuette of St. Anthony, obviously of the seventeenth century, beautifully carved and painted, that I immediately set my heart on. We bargained over it for several weeks until at last we arrived somewhere near the price that he was prepared to let it go for and that I was able to pay. The difference between us was only twenty pesetas. I forget the exact sum. I think he was asking a hundred and thirty pesetas and I was offering a hundred and ten.

"Give me a hundred and thirty for the statue and the book," he said, "and you'll never regret it."

"Curse the book," I cried in exasperation.

I paid for my drink and walked to the door. Don Fernando called me back.

"Listen," he said.

I turned round. He came towards me, an ingratiating smile on his fat, red lips, with the statuette in one hand and the book in the other.

"I'll give you the statuette for a hundred and twenty pesetas and I'll make you a present of the book."

A hundred and twenty pesetas was the price I had all along made up my mind to give.

"I'll pay that," I said, "but you can keep the book."

"It's a present."

"I don't want a present."

"But I want to make you one. It's a pleasure for me. You can't refuse a present. Come, man."

I sighed. I was beaten. I was a trifle ashamed.

"I'll give you twenty pesetas for the book."

"Even at that it's a present," he said. "You could sell it in Madrid for two hundred."

He wrapped it up in a dirty piece of newspaper; I paid my money, and with the book in my hand and the statuette under my arm, walked home.

James A. Michener

(1907–1997)

"I think young people ought to seek that experience that is going to knock them off center," said novelist James Michener. He was speaking from firsthand knowledge. By the time he was twenty he had hitchhiked across the country, traveled by boxcar, worked in a carnival, and visited all but three of the United States. Then he entered Swarthmore College on a scholarship for his formal education. Michener taught in private schools and eventually entered publishing, a career that was interrupted by World War II. The navy sent him to the Solomon Islands, the basis for his first book, *Tales of the South Pacific* (1947), a Pulitzer Prize winner that was adapted into the musical *South Pacific*. Michener was forty when it was published.

During his long writing career, Michener specialized in the sprawling novel that illuminated one part of the country or the world: these included *Hawaii* (1957), *The Source* (1963, about Israel), *The Covenant* (1980, about South Africa), and *Texas* (1985). There were four dozen books in all, including five art books. Almost all of them sold millions and were far more popular with the public than with critics. Michener employed a team of researchers, and the hallmark of his work is the entwining of fact and fiction.

Iberia (1968) is an atypical Michener book. Nearly a thousand pages, it is a travelogue of impressions made on Michener's many visits to Spain. Michener is a charming and opinionated, if undisciplined, guide. A chance encounter with a friend (and he seems to know everyone in Spain) will send his narrative careening off into a new direction. He is a hopeless name-dropper—Orson Welles, Jacqueline Kennedy, Tennessee Williams, Ernest Hemingway, Rita Hayworth. Michener defends his fellow tourist and reviles the British writers who report bad American behavior in Spain. "In the latest English travel books on Spain there was a constant procession of American boors and boobs, but the authors were well-versed men and must surely have come into contact somewhere with the kinds of Americans I knew . . . I cannot charge them with planned falsehood, but I can query their powers of observation . . ."

Michener died at ninety at his home in Austin, Texas.

From IBERIA

BADAJOZ

Badajoz still lay forty miles to the north. In a hot bus that talked back
to itself I was plodding through the vast region called Extremadura,
that empty, rocky section of Spain lying southwest from Madrid
along the Portuguese border. It was a day of intense heat, with the
thermometer well above a hundred and ten. For as far as I could see
there were no towns, no villages, only the brassy, shimmering heat
rising up from the plains and the implacable sky without even a wisp
of cloud. When dust rose, it hung in the motionless air and required
minutes to fall back to the caked and burning earth. I saw no animals,
no birds, no men, for they refused to venture forth in this remorse-
less heat.

In fact, the only thing in nature that moved was the sun, terrible
and metallic as it inched its way across that indifferent sky. I was
relieved therefore when the bus descended a long hill and we came to
a meadowland filled with trees, but such trees I had not seen before.
They were not tall like elms, nor copious like maples. They were low,
extremely sturdy, with dark gray trunks and gnarled branches that
reached wide, so that each tree was given a considerable area to itself.
The meadowland in between was filled with small yellow flowers, as
if it were a carpet of gold, accented here and there with concentra-
tions of white daisies and punctuated by the massive trees with their
dark crowns.

I had barely inspected this pleasing landscape when the trees
changed radically. Their trunks, up to a height of perhaps ten feet,
turned suddenly bright orange, as if they had been painted that
morning. And before I could adjust to orange-colored trees they
were replaced by trunks of angry russet, then by trunks of a dark and
heavy brown, and finally by trees whose trunks were the original gray
I had seen at first; but all the trees, whether orange or gray, sent their

limbs twisting and turning in the hot air as if they were gasping for breath.

"What is it?" I asked the driver.

"Cork forest. The bright orange means a tree that was stripped of its cork a few days ago. Enough time and the bark grows gray again." We saw a low shed back among the spacious trees but no sign of life. "The cork harvesters are taking a siesta," the driver explained.

We next came to a grove with quite different trees; the trunks were badly shattered, as if the trees were dying; in some there were holes through which I could see; the branches were low and carried delicate leaves that were dark on top, silvery gray on bottom, with clusters of small black fruit. "Olive grove," the driver said. "When the breeze comes through, the leaves flutter. Beautiful." But this day there was no breeze.

Most of the land was barren, with no trees at all. The soil was rocky and red from decomposing ferrous elements. At times a stream-bed, empty of water for the past five months, crawled like a wounded snake across the plain, but often there was not even this to watch. I longed for at least a buzzard to mark that merciless sky, but none appeared. "Sleeping," the driver said. "Everything is sleeping."

We came to a village, a truly miserable collection of adobe huts clustered about an unpaved square. One bar was open, apparently, for its doors were not closed, but no men were visible behind the strands of beads that served as a curtain for keeping out the flies. Farther on there was a town, and since it was now nearly five in the afternoon people were beginning to move about, but the heat was so intense that no work was being done. It was a town that had little to commend it except its longevity; Roman legions had known this town, and when their expeditions had ended in the years before the birth of Christ, Caesar Augustus had allowed the oldest veterans to take up land here. Over the ravine at the edge of town ran a stone bridge that had been used in its present form for more than two thousand years.

"You want to stop for a drink?" the driver asked.

"Not in this town," and we pushed on.

We came now to fields that looked as if they might have been cultivated and to a series of oak and olive forests that were well tended.

"We're getting close to Badajoz," he said, pronouncing the word with respect. As evening approached, the heat grew more bearable and in one river valley we actually felt a breeze. We climbed a hill, turned west and saw below us the Río Guadiana, which farther on would form the border between Portugal and Spain, and in its valley stood a city without a single distinction: no towers, no ancient walls, no exciting prospects. The eastern half looked old and unrepaired; the western half, new and unrelated to the rest; and there was no apparent reason why a man in good sense would descend the hill to enter that particular city, for this was Badajoz, the nothing-city of the west. "Precisely what I wanted," I said.

In America when I had explained to my friends that I was heading for Badajoz, they had shrugged their shoulders because they had never heard of it, and when I told my Spanish friends they grimaced because they had. "For the love of Jesus, why Badajoz? It has absolutely nothing." In Spanish this last phrase sounds quite final: "Absolutamente nada," with the six syllables of the first word strung out in emphasis. They tried to dissuade me from going, explaining that Badajoz was a mere depot town along the border, that it was lost in the emptiness of Extremadura, and that if I was determined to visit a remote town, why not a beauty like Murcia near the Mediterranean, or Jaén in the mountains, or Oviedo, where the relics of Christ were kept. "Why Badajoz?"

Why indeed? I had not tried to explain, but there was an explanation and a good one. When I heard the word Spain, I visualized not kings and priests, nor painters and hidalgos, nor Madrid and Sevilla, but the vast reaches of emptiness, lonely uplands occupied by the solitary shepherd, the hard land of Spain stretching off to interminable distances and populated by tough, weatherbeaten men with never a ruffle at their throats nor a caparisoned horse beneath them. In short, when I thought of Spain, I thought primarily of Extremadura, the brutal region in the west, of which Badajoz was the principal city.

There was a reason. Apart from my first brief visit to Castellón de la Plana and Teruel as a student, my introduction to Spain had come in the American southwest, in the empty areas of New Mexico, Arizona, Texas and California, where the Spanish impact had been great. To me, a Spaniard was a man like Coronado, who had ventured into Kansas in 1541. Hernando de Soto and Cabeza de Vaca were my Spaniards and the unknown men who settled Santa Fe and Taos. The Spain I had known in the western United States was a heroic Spain, the Spanish landscape with which I was familiar reached at least four hundred miles in any given direction over largely empty land. To have been a Spaniard in those early days in New Mexico and Arizona signified, and the closest approach to that Spain in the home country was Extremadura.

My second contact with Spain was different. I had spent considerable time in Mexico and at one period or another had lived in all but two of its states, always seeing Mexico as a land that had been discovered, occupied, developed and ruined by Spaniards. I knew well the routes traveled by Hernán Cortés in his conquest of the Aztecs, and I had studied those haunting plateresque churches built by his followers in towns where silver was mined. There were few Spanish buildings in Mexico that I had not explored, and some of the happiest days of my youth were those spent in drifting across the plateaus of Chihuahua or exploring the jungles west of Vera Cruz. But whenever I looked at Mexico, I saw Spain. Mexican culture was meaningful only as an extension of Spanish culture, and the cyclones of Mexican political history were merely a reflection of the home country.

Early in my study I discovered that most of the Spanish heroes who had operated in the Americas had come from Extremadura. The New World was won for Spain not by gentlemen from Toledo and Sevilla but by a group of uneducated village louts who, realizing that they had no future in their hard homeland, had volunteered for service overseas, where their Extremadura courage proved the most valuable commodity carried westward by the Spanish galleons.

Extremadura was my Spain, and no one who had missed my experiences in New Mexico and Old could appreciate what Badajoz meant to me, but when I saw this unlovely, battered town, called Pax Augusta by the Romans, and when I saw about me the suspicious, dour Extremadurans, whose ancestors had conquered not cities but whole nations and continents, I felt that I had come back to my own land.

My first experience in the city proved that I was in Extremadura. The hotel to which I had been sent was dark and mean and tucked away on a side street. The clerk growled, "We can let you have a small room for tonight. Fifty pesetas." This was eighty-three cents and I judged I could go a little higher, so I said, 'I'll be here for a month, so if you have a larger room . . .'"

"A month! In that case the room will be sixty pesetas."

This confused me, and I started to explain that elsewhere if a man stayed for a month the price went down, not up, but he stopped me. "We don't want people coming here. We have too many already." I looked about the dark lobby and saw no one. I was about to point this out when he snapped, "You can't have a room for a month. Nobody can have a room for a whole month." He looked at me suspiciously, as if to ask, "Why would a foreigner want to stay in Badajoz for a month?"

My second experience was one that I look back upon with affection. Through the warm night I walked to the main square and asked a policeman where a hungry man could get a decent meal, and he took me by the arm and said, "There's only one place—Restaurante Colón. And you'll thank me later." He led me to an old narrow building whose face had recently been lifted with purple plastic, chrome and neon. I hesitated but he pushed me in, and I found a menu which offered a bewildering selection: green plate, gray plate, black plate, ivory plate and white plate, each for about a dollar twenty. When the waiter came, a very tall, thin Extremaduran, he grabbed the menu away and whispered, "If you want the best, take the zarzuela." I was pretty sure I knew what a zarzuela was, so I asked, "How's that again?" And he growled, "Take the zarzuela."

A zarzuela, unless I was out of my mind, was what I had seen in Castellón de la Plana, a short Spanish-type musical comedy in which the songs are closer to opera than those of an American musical. I had seen some good zarzuelas and had enjoyed them, but now I was being asked to eat one.

I must have shown my apprehension, because the waiter said an extraordinary thing: "My friend, if you trust in the goodness of God, take the zarzuela." Such advice I could not ignore, so I nodded, fearing the worst.

Instead I got the best: a ramekin containing olive oil, a judicious amount of garlic, some baked potatoes, chopped onions, pimientos, tomatoes and a heavenly assortment of shrimp, crayfish, squid, octopus, hake and filet of sole, all done to a golden brown and served with croutons and an effervescent white wine. It was a savory introduction to Badajoz and I had to agree with the waiter that sometimes the goodness of God must be trusted.

When I finished, it was still light and I had no intention of going back to my gloomy hotel. I decided instead to stroll through the streets of Badajoz and to see with a fresh eye how a Spanish city looked. I wanted, as it were, to build a base of understanding to which I could add as I visited the nine other cities of my projected tour, and in retrospect I am glad that I did this, because if one understands Badajoz he will understand Spain.

The Restaurante Colón stood on the main plaza, and as I left it I faced the cathedral, a low, squat ugly building built many centuries ago and one of the least attractive in Spain. It carried a square tower of no distinction, decorated by nine urns on each side, looking like the battlements of a fortress and not a cathedral. Eight bells hung in the tower, but during my stay I did not hear them ring. The massive walls had no Gothic windows, nor did they carry any ornamentation to relieve their drabness. The building was entered by a sadly inappropriate door flanked by four Ionic columns which some architect had added in the eighteenth century in an attempt to dress up the façade, and on the great slab-sided front facing the plaza appeared the two words which I would see carved into the walls of churches all across Spain: JOSÉ ANTONIO. The letters were accompanied by seventeen laurel wreaths cast in rusting iron.

Although the cathedral was unusually ugly it conveyed a sense of dignity, for it was a frontier church-fortress, and only the security which it provided had allowed Badajoz to survive its sieges and attacks. It was then and remained now the center of Badajoz life, and the society which it supervised was much like it: ancient, unornamented, solid and well able to protect itself.

The plaza which the cathedral dominated was small and awkward and as undistinguished a main square as I would see in Spain. There were old buildings of no quality and others like the Restaurante Colón whose face-lifted façades gleamed garishly in plastic and neon. The Banco Mercantil had recently been redone in ultramodern style and looked rather handsome. Its windows were low, and to keep idlers from sitting on the sills, the latter were decorated with sharp, tall spikes. The six white columns of the Palacio Municipal supported a balcony ready for an orator who never came.

What was the chief characteristic of the plaza? That it was jammed with automobiles and had the same parking problem as Rome, London or New York. The parking of cars was supervised by a corps of crippled war veterans who collected their fee whenever a car drew up to the curb. Traffic through the very narrow streets leading into the plaza was constant and was guided by policemen with a good sense of humor. Every four or five minutes large buses passed through the square on various routes which took them to all parts of the suburbs. The buses hauled large numbers of passengers, as they did throughout Spain.

Having completed a rapid survey of the plaza, I closed my eyes and asked, "Is there anything here that would prove I am in Spain?" I looked again, and apart from the obvious signs in Spanish, saw nothing that would betray the origin of this city. It could have been Italy, or southern France, or even rural Texas. I want to make this point secure because travelers often expect strange cities to look a certain way, but with modern technology, architecture and traffic most of them look alike. If I had tried this test of "Where am I?" in the plazas of the villages and towns of southern Extremadura the answer would have been, "This can only be Spain," but in the cities, no. They are international.

Tim Moore

(1964 –   )

Tim Moore was put on the path of travel writing by the death of his grandfather, who left him two thousand pounds on the condition that he use it for a trip. It was 1989; Moore was twenty-four and set out for Eastern Europe by bus. He has since written books following well-worn routes of previous travelers: the European Grand Tour and its first tourist, Thomas Coryate, who walked across Europe in 1608 (*The Grand Tour*, 2000), the Tour de France (*French Revolutions*, 2001), and the pilgrimage to the cathedral of Santiago de Compostela (*Travels with My Donkey*, 2004), from which this is excerpted.

In addition to his books, Moore has been published in *Esquire*, *The Sunday Times*, and *The Observer*. Sometimes described as the "next Bill Bryson," he follows Bryson's tested formula: go on a trip, meet interesting people, make fun of them, make more fun of yourself. Moore acknowledges Bryson: "He made it possible for the ordinary self-deprecating writer to get read, without having to do something dramatic and hairy chested, which, at my size, would not be easy."

Moore is not alone in his pilgrimage to Santiago de Compostela; he takes with him a donkey, Shinto (to whom he dedicates his book). The writer and his ass have a love/hate relationship: Shinto relieves himself at inopportune times "extruding a large bunch of khaki briquettes," balks at going over wooden bridges (of which there are many), and unexpectedly rears up like a bronco tossing luggage like confetti all over the *camino*. Ultimately, Moore and Shinto put aside their tortured personal relationship and forge "a professional understanding" that they were going to get to Santiago together. This selection details the end of their pilgrimage.

From TRAVELS WITH MY DONKEY

Today Santiago is a city of 95,000, and the literature warned that urban sprawl and an ill-sited copse had combined to obscure the bell towers and so denude Monte de Gozo of its visually dramatic symbolism. By now a link in a strung-out chain of toiling walkers, we topped the hill and found ourselves on the lip of a huge and hazy hollow, filled with rush-hour traffic and vertically conspicuous commercial structures. "Well, there it is," said Simon, and I sucked in a long, steadying draught of hot air. Then a taxi rounded us with a derisive toot, lurched to a halt by a gate down the road and deposited a fat hot man and his rucksack.

The last time I'd seen those buttocks, they'd sat untrousered upon a tissue-less latrine, and if this had the effect of portent-management, then so did the complex that opened up beyond that gate. Bungalow bunkers as long as streets, dozens and dozens striped up a hefty swathe of hillside, the empty concrete boulevards between them pierced by the vegetation of neglect. At the conclusion of every forlorn vista, lichen-streaked statuary corroded into the undergrowth.

We clopped between two of these pilgrim prison blocks, both clearly empty, and presently found ourselves in a desolate plaza bordered by facing parades of self-service canteens and largely moribund retail units. Unsynchronised wisps of Celtic pipery echoed from Tannoy stalks. Here was the dominant legacy of Galicia's efforts to commemorate and facilitate the 1993 Holy Year, when the Pope visited Santiago, yet it had all the soulful ambience of a holiday camp for low-ranking party officials in the Chernobyl exclusion zone. "This is *awful*," I said, hands on hips in front of a whitewash-windowed ex-launderette.

My two companions were wanly scanning the urban horizon in underwhelmed concurrence when the biped froze. "There," said Simon, simply, quietly, half-raising a finger to a gap in the trees atop a block-studded middle-distance hillock. I narrowed my eyes, scanned the relevant area of smogged horizon, and saw it. Them. Rising gin-

gerly through the sunlit urban fuzz, the tapering baroque rockets of
the cathedral of Santiago de Compostela.

Well, I can't tell you how that helped. One of the few active enterprises around us was a souvenir shop, and suddenly its glib offerings
seemed not an insult to our achievement but a celebration. For days
now the images of Santiago Peregrino, St. James as a pilgrim to his
own tomb, had been gathering in profusion: a statue in a church, a
sticker on a bumper, and now in this window a keyring, a corkscrew,
an ashtray. Scrutinising them I felt a pulse of fraternal affection for
this mild apostle of gourd and staff, a perfect study in mournful,
pious sincerity: "It's just so tragic," he always seemed to sigh. "If only
I could even begin to find the words to explain what a great, great
guy I am."

And those blue tiles glazed with yellow arrows or stylised scallop
shells: we'd been following those for forty days, and I wanted people
to know that we had. I'd have one each of those for my garden wall,
though not yet. Not just yet. The converging lines on the scallop
shell were said to represent the converging pilgrim routes to Santiago, and we weren't quite at that auspicious confluence. I didn't get
one for the same reason that I hadn't yet worn my scallop shell, the
one Nicky had given me before I'd left. You acquired your shell in
Santiago as an indication to medieval contemporaries that you'd been
and gone and done it, a medal of achievement, not intent.

Reanimated we went down to check in at hut twenty-one, my fêted
jackass entered beneath us in the register by a happy young *hospitalero*
as Shinto Moore, travelling on foot, aged eleven. ("Is *mínimo* here for
peregrino ten years old," he explained with a tickled wink.) Shinto was
led as instructed into an adjacent strip of meadow by the laundry
lines, and watching him settle down to his Last Supper we went off
for ours. There was only the one option, and this involved celebrating the imminent remission of my sins by pushing a tray along a
stainless-steel counter, watching as a succession of blank-faced
women filled it with small plates of shrink-wrapped food. It was
abysmal, so abysmal as to be excellent. Sucking on Capri-Suns we
scanned this strip-lit environment and its scattering of smartly car-
diganed Spanish *peregrinos*, the handbag-carrying hundred-clickers

sharing our hallowed penultimate ponderings. And we laughed, and were still laughing when we slid our trays into the rack of empties and retired to our room.

This was an airless, fetid eight-bunker, one of fifteen such in each barrack block, and our six fellow last-nighters were already locked into the gentle, automatic snoring of the hot and weary. Simon tutted quietly, but I felt oddly comforted, almost nostalgic: it had been four days since last I'd shared my sleep with pilgrims. And, I thought, as the mattress planks took my weight with a splintered sigh, at least an earthly lifetime before I ever would again.

Walking in a cell crowded with grubby, mumbling strangers, pulling on underwear foot-laundered in last night's shower and still perhaps four hours from comfortable dryness, shampooing with household detergent: it seemed that almost everything I was doing I'd never do again, unless I took my trousers down at a North Korean border post.

Or unless this whole business had indeed left me strangely changed beyond repair. Maybe I'd return and decree bed linen a satanic extravagance. And hot water. Certainly there was a worrying moment when Simon dropped his old socks and pants in the bin—his wife Catherine had dispatched him with a disposable wardrobe—and I restrained only with difficulty an urge to retrieve them.

Bright eyed and, yes, bushy tailed, there was the large grey animal who had earlier conducted another of these last rites, for the final time drawing his master from unconsciousness with that klaxon reveille.

Shinto fixed me with a look hungry for adventure, eager, almost intelligent. Bareback in the hock-high meadow grass, he called to mind a gold-rimmed, hand-retouched collector's plate in a colour-supplement advert: "Alert to the Call: a fresh spring morn, and this lively little Pyrenean jack has been exploring. (Penis not to scale.)" Scrutinising him with a sense of potent déjà vu I suddenly recalled the dream his braying had cut short: Shinto had been awarded a prize for special achievement at some sort of pet pageant, but as I led him through the crowd with applause in my ears and a Tobleroned lump of pride in my throat, there between us and the podium stood a taunting trio of stairs . . .

For the last time I squatted down by his side, upturned hoof in lap and scraper in hand, the submerged percolations of that huge, warm stomach bubbling in through my ear. I might not quite have fulfilled Hanno's prediction by eating from the same bowl as my donkey, but for a week now his chaff and my crusts had shared the same sack. Sighing and puffing I packed and repacked the bags, and brushed and rebrushed Shinto, trying not to think that this was The End, the final installment of a forty-one-day life within my life, but at the same time unavoidably aware that it was and willing myself into a suitable climactic frame of mind.

At the mouth of every hut behind us were groups of pilgrims facing the same inner turmoil, grooming themselves for an appointment with eternity like corpses in a coffin. An ironed shirt kept flat-packed at a rucksack's fundament now retrieved for the benefit of St. Jim, a comb pulled through sun-mangled hair. Simon nudged me and inclined his head, and through a bathroom window I saw two faces pressed close to a mirror: an elderly man shaving his middle-aged Down's Syndrome son.

It wasn't until 9:00 that we left, exchanging knowing, bracing nods and half-smiles with those around us, like students massing outside the hall of their final examination. It was a steep descent round the perimeter of the Monte de Gozo complex, and as our strides lengthened with the gradient so the skies above suddenly darkened. No sooner had we broached the outskirts of Santiago proper than those guiding towers were smeared out by a flash downpour, one so violent that by the time I'd extracted and unfurled my poncho Shinto had slammed in the anchors. "Um," I said, through a curtain of hood drips; then there was a creak and a crank and a big up-and-over garage door beside us pivoted aloft.

Inside the dim void thus revealed stood a blasé, full-faced mechanic, who thumbed us in whilst critically assessing the tiny cigarette stub pinched between his thumb and forefinger. In a minute there were half a dozen of us in there, and in another the one with four legs had somehow sniffed out a sack of grain. Still addressing himself to his dwindling fag end the mechanic palmed out a scoop and let Shinto snuffle it up from his hand. Then a young chap in a red cagoule held a tentative hand out into the open, morphed it into a thumbs-up and in a moment we were all waving our gruff protector farewell.

The pocket storm was merely the first of a sequence that in three swift stages formed a perfect microcosm of every alarum of the previous six weeks, every phobia nurtured by Shinto in those 770 clicks gone slowly by. We'd been on the wet pavement less than a minute when it fell away down a hefty flight of stairs. The backtracking detour was moderate by the standards of many endured, but at its conclusion lay a busy, narrow road bridge whose bolt-on pedestrian portion was assembled from wooden planks. For the last time I saw Shinto assess the middle distance with that look of mildly perplexed helplessness, as if a direct causal link existed between this obstacle and the sudden inactivity of his limbs, as if it wasn't a bridge but a force field. Look, said his eyes, I can assure you that this is just as frustrating for me as it is for you.

These days I almost agreed. As our marriage had matured so those stand-up rows had mellowed into gentle bickering, and I squeezed the three of us on to the tarmac, between guard rail and elbow-flicking wing mirrors, with an air of fond indulgence. My affection for Shinto had now reached a level where it seemed a poignant tragedy that those splendid genes lay nowhere but his own ageing body (though given a good innings, that body had every chance of outlasting mine). He was Shinto the First, and Shinto the Last. My passage through the pilgrimage literature had been regularly enlivened by the descriptive appellations of medieval monarchs: Sancho the Fat, "the hunch-backed Orduno IV the Evil." It was all a question of spin: with bad PR you were Henry the Impotent, with good PR Alfonso the Chaste. So here, before me, was King Shinto the . . . Beige.

The bridge proved the last of the morning's To-be-a-Pilgrim trinity of trials, and our approach thereafter was not one designed to nurture tearful portent. A construction site half-staffed with idle donk-baiters, receding batteries of slightly scabby housing estates, waiting for the little green man with my little grey donkey: had it not been for the tiny and diminishing digits on those camino marker posts and an unusually jaded citizenry, this could just have been another of those surreal and stressful trans-metropolitan experiences.

We drew breath for the final assault with just one more of those inadequate bar breakfasts of cake and *café con leche*, then headed across our last dual carriageway and into the cloistered alleys of the old town. Walls narrowed and houses rose, shielding the cathedral towers from view and making every rounded corner a mouth-drying, spine-fizzing anticlimax: this was surely it, and if not then this, and if not then this. The last yellow arrow led us down a flagstoned hill, and sensing that this really was it Simon respectfully melted forward into the morning shoppers. I contemplated the rope in my calloused hands and what it led to, and in doing so felt pride abruptly tempered by a gauche self-consciousness, like a boy wearing a school uniform for the first time, a reprise of the sensation that had for so long dominated my every moment at Shinto's side.

Tightening my grip on the rope and breathing hard I felt rather than saw a moss-stoned ecclesiastical structure looming up to our left; but as the street ahead passed down towards it and beneath a grand archway so it devolved into a stairway. A final, numb-limbed diversion round a circling, anti-clockwise road to the right, a road which a minute later ejected me into the bottom right-hand corner of a belittling cobbled sea, a great, broad square sparsely populated by tiny mortals and imperiously dominated by the lichened, mildewed, florid might of my destination.

With my overborne faculties condensed into a reedy, whistling tinnitus and the sensation of wet heat on my cheeks I apparently continued walking, distantly aware of the swelling crowd I was dragging across the grey stones. At any rate there I soon found myself, in the shadow of that swoon-inducing façade, at the foot of the weighty double staircase that accessed its lofty entrance. "Photo, photo!" piped a shrill voice in my ear, not caring that the head to which it belonged now lay buried in a warm, soft neck, not knowing that through that head spooled a messily spliced loop tape of mud and sun and barley, of treble bunks and double brandies, of flan and friend and midnight bray, of trial and tribulation. "Photo, photo, photo!"

My brother was watching from the Plaza del Obradoiro's distant opposite bank, and later reported that my tourist entourage had all exchanged shrugs—and, in one case, swivelled-fingers-in-temples—before clicking away regardless. When I raised my head and blinked out the last tear one snapper came up and pressed a euro in my hand; I contemplated it blankly, too fraught and drained to protest. I'd had this down as a humble alms offering until an unkempt man in a brown felt cape and scallop-brimmed hat shuffled into shot for a piece of the action—his outfit was set off with a staff and gourd in one hand and a cig and a multilingual note in the other: "Foto with me €2." Simon had crept up unseen with my camera and captured the scene as my rent-a-pilgrim struck a photogenic pose with his head arched down to Shinto's, and looking at the result now I'm rewarded to note those long ears flattened back in sour hostility.

I walked on before I began to feel like the false medievalist, or that caped and gourded dog with the same notice over there, or those Pentax-toters sticking their head through the comedy pilgrim cut-outs over there. Still the crowd surged and eddied around, shouting out all the old questions in French, in English, in Spanish, but always now in retrospect: what did he eat, where did he sleep. I again had the certain feeling that Shinto knew this was an important, defining moment in his life both as ass and pilgrim, and again I was right. The oohs and aahs morphed into ohs and urghs, and sure enough when I looked back he'd laid down a dozen hot markers on those holy cob-bles.

Simon jogged up just before a pair of finger-raised policemen, and together we crinklingly dispatched the unwanted souvenirs with plastic-bag mittens. Returned to earth more literally than ever before we stood, sagging crap bags in hands, and embraced carefully. "I'll stay with him," said Simon when we'd finished, "and you go off for your certificate." The compostela—my Get Out of Hell Free card, and I'd forgotten all about it.

Obtaining this might have held more significance had the process felt a little less like renewing a TV licence during a water shortage. Queuing in the strip-lit Pilgrim Office at the end of a long line of unwashed, unfamiliar arrivals—snorers to a fat-bellied, big-nosed man—I felt a suggestion of the anticlimax that many pilgrims had written about. Half an hour later I was dictating my name to a bored official, who after a little scribbling handed me a small scroll. Topped by a sepia depiction of Santiago Peregrino and fulsomely bordered with scallop shells, in a Latin rubric unchanged from the fourteenth century this detailed the devoted ambulatory achievements of Dnum Timoteum Moore. *"Compostela por mi burro?"* I asked, in an unexpectant tone that perhaps made the ensuing refusal too easy.

Jubilation was what I'd wanted, and happily it had taken hold in the streets by the time I bounded outside. Simon and Shinto were already beleaguered by familiar and now ecstatic faces: English Sara, Jean-Michel, the Scottish couple who had rescued my donkey from suicidal garrotting at Ribadiso. Our hugs were cut short by the dull gonging of huge bells; midday, and the daily Pilgrims' Mass. Leaving Shinto in Simon's care once more, outside a bar with the singing gay Italians, I trotted up the double staircase and into the cathedral's dim but thronged interior, a majestic Romanesque cavern encased beneath that baroque icing.

In that buffeting crush of rucksacks and day-trippers, it was never going to be easy to work myself up to the spiritual orgasm this moment seemed to demand. Too restless and hassled for insight or manifestation; no statues here you could imagine sweating blood. Perhaps the closest I came was while pressing my hand into the column supporting the welcoming image of Santiago, into five finger holes worn deep in the marble by the grateful, weary touch of pilgrim digits over 900 years. Yes, that was a moment.

More of a moment, certainly, than my contact with the brashly gilded representation of St. James that loomed up behind the altar. Only after twenty minutes in a significance-sapping queue, jostled throughout by nattering, nonchalant tourists, was I granted my swift embrace, clasping those giant golden shoulders from behind as if trying to blag a saintly piggyback. Two impatient schoolkids nudged me onwards, down through the crypt for a quickstep shuffle past the silver casket, inside it the bones that had brought so many millions all this way.

But then they hadn't really brought me, or in fact more than a handful of us. In the literature, medieval relic worship was consistently paralleled with today's veneration of celebrity memorabilia, and if so then St. James wasn't shifting many albums. Shuffling back down the teeming aisle in search of an empty pew I saw occasional religiously overwhelmed pilgrims genuflecting or crossing their chests: they were Jim fans, and in the final analysis, we weren't. All this was certainly spectacular, but wedging myself between two gossiping Hispanics near the back I felt slightly removed, as if watching a grand sporting finale in whose outcome I had no particular interest.

A squad of sombrely resplendent clerics took their positions in front of the apostle, and when the first took his place at the mike and spoke it all got better immediately. In a Eurovision-judge drone he began to recite the nationalities and their point of pilgrim departure, and when the words "*Valcarlos, Inglaterra*" echoed out of the Tannoy I felt my features tighten. At length a tiny nun took his place, and when she unexpectedly filled the world with soaring, mellifluous hosannas I couldn't restrain a wet blink. Looking ahead I noted the backs of two familiar heads three rows up: Evelyn and Petronella, the latter once more twitching with fluid-faced emotion, but this time by no means alone.

Incoming tourists squeezed into my pew as the mass trundled on, as we stood, and sat, and kneeled, and stood and sat. The collection plate came round and I clanged down the euro I'd been given in the square outside; a queue began to form for the bread and wine. A sudden exhaustion had pinned me to my seat, and I'm glad it did because as I belatedly sidled towards the exit my attention was drawn to a conspicuous phalanx of robed curates. They staggered to the altar bearing upon their shoulders an arresting burden: an enormous and elaborate silver receptacle, an FA Cup the size of a dustbin. Everyone rushed to the front: this was the *botafumeiro*, Catholicism's largest dispenser of holy incense, only brought out on days of especial religious import.

Its contents ignited, this glinting quarter-tonner was laboriously lashed to a rope and hoisted high into the vaulted darkness; then, yanking the cord like tattooed bosuns, the clergymen began a process originally intended to neutralise the stench of a thousand filthy, footsore walkers. Twenty fat-armed heave-hos had the smoke-belching colossus swinging from one side of the distant, vaulted roof to the other, whooshing between the aisles with dreadful momentum: one degree either side and we'd have had a messy strike of pilgrim ninepins. It later transpired that the bishop had authorised this astounding spectacle at the financial behest of a party of visiting Germans; some were outraged, but I figured that the hard-nosed mercenaries who ran the medieval Church could only have approved.

I emerged overwhelmed and smelling of holy mothballs, exhausted at this unseemly rush of events and experience after all those long weeks of measured toil. It was worse for my poor donkey: back at our table outside the bar I found him enduring the worst excesses of Shintomania, patted and petted by a three-deep throng. Evelyn and Petronella arrived, then Sara, and Barbara and Walther, and Janina and Anna, then Donald, who'd somehow got lost on the run-in and spent half a day circumnavigating the ring road. Simon shooed away the more persistent paparazzi, and as the fearsome clamour subsided we all slumped wordlessly round a big tin table.

Beers arrived and our weathered, rural faces crumpled in silent joy and wet-faced disbelief: we had made it. We had all done what at various times we all thought we never would. In the eyes of pilgrim history, we had lived through what so many did not. Glasses were raised in triumphant toast, but before mine reached my mouth I rushed inside the bar with Shinto's bowl. "*Tengo un burro,*" I rasped emotionally at the barman, wondering if I'd ever hear these words pass my lips again. I realised I would, and quite soon, when the barman pushed the bowl slightly further down his counter and carefully placed a large cigar beside it.

Simon was gathering up his belongings when I at last emerged with Shinto's aquatic reward. I looked at my watch: he had less than an hour to get to the airport.

"A million steps," he said, shouldering that vast rucksack.

"Sorry?"

"I worked it out last night. That's what you've done. A man's pace is around 75 centimetres, and you've done just over 750 kilometres." I tried to look intelligent. "So that's a million."

"If they told you that at the start," piped up Donald, already on beer two, "you'd turn round and go straight home." I just nodded blankly, then looked down at Shinto, hosing up the last dregs by my feet. A million for me, and double for him. One small step for a man was two for his donkey. In fact more like eight, the way mine had been going.

Jan Morris

(1 9 2 6 –   )

Travel writer, journalist, and historian Jan Morris has had many journeys, both personal and geographical. Born James Morris of Anglo-Welsh parents in Somerset, England, he attended boarding school until World War II, when he enlisted in the army at the age of seventeen. He served in Italy, Egypt, and Palestine, and returned to England, met his future wife, Elizabeth, and married in 1949. The couple had five children. In 1951 he became the foreign subeditor of the *Times* (London) and made his reputation when he covered the expedition to Mount Everest in 1953.

In the 1960s Morris became a well-known travel writer with books like *Venice* (1960), *Cities* (1963), and *Spain* (1964, from which this excerpt is taken). His personal life was undergoing a transformation as well. From 1964 through 1972 Morris began the process of a sex change, culminating in an operation. Morris says that he was the "victim of a genetic mix-up" and details his journey from man to woman in the book *Conundrum* (1974). However, his marriage endured.

Morris's admirers noted a change in sensibility from the macho James Morris to Jan Morris. She herself wrote that she has a "softer prose style, perhaps of softer judgments." Her writing is marked by a combination of journalism and history. In later works she reevaluated places she had visited before. "I seldom go to a city now, after so many years, that I have not written about before: I know the shape of a place, I have inner comparisons to make." In recent years her work has become more impressionistic, and she strives to get what she calls "a wanderer's response."

From SPAIN

FOUR CITIES

It is especially in the interior of Spain that the faith still rings true, for though Christianity is more ebullient in the south, the stern landscapes of the tableland are like sounding-boards for the spirit. Here, though your voice often falls flat upon a dry soil, or is whisked away by the bitter wind, ideas seem to echo and expand, visions form in the great distances, and man, all alone in the emptiness, seems only the agent of some much greater Power. No wonder the Spaniards, at once oppressed and elevated by the character of the place, have built upon this plateau some of the grandest of all human artifacts, the cities of the centre. They are grand not so much as collections of treasures, or gatherings of people, but as things in their own right: all different, all indeed unique, all instantly recognizable for their own savour and design, but all touched by this same resonance of setting, and thus, one feels, by something nobler still. Let us visit four of them now, and see how powerfully this combination of variety and inner cohesion contributes to the presence of Spain.

Salamanca, on the western edge of the *meseta*, is made of sandstone. One does not often specify the raw material of a city, but Spain likes to be explicit: Santiago is granite, Salamanca is sandstone. She is the calmest of the famous cities of the tableland, set more tranquilly than most beside the River Tormes, insulated by age and culture against the fierce intensity of the country. Salamanca is above all a university city—"Mother of the Virtues, the Sciences, and the Arts"—and though her scholarship has long been shrivelled, her colleges decimated in war or emasculated by autocracy, still she has the special poise that marks a place both learned and long admired.

You approach her, if you come the right way, by foot across a fine Roman bridge, and this in itself is a kind of sedative. The bridge is old, stout, and weather-beaten; the river below is wide and steady; groves of larches and poplars line the banks; and if you pause for a moment at the alcove in the middle, you will find that life around you seems wonderfully simple and assured, as though the big trucks pounding along the ring road are only some transient phenomenon from another civilization. In the thicket immediately below the bridge, perhaps, a solitary student is deep in his book at a trestle table, supported by a bottle of pop from the shanty-café along the path, and inspired by flamenco music from the radio beneath his chair. Downstream the bourgeoisie washes its cars in the river water. Across the river a small boy canters around on a pony. A mill-wheel turns at the weir upstream; sheep graze the fields beyond; in the shallows an elderly beachcomber is prodding the mud with a stick.

Raise your eyes only a little, and there above you, scarcely a stone's throw away, stand the two cathedrals of Salamanca—so close is the Spanish country to the Spanish town, so free from peevish suburbs are these old cities of the interior. It is rather like entering Oxford, say, in the Middle Ages. The city is the heart and the brain of its surrounding countryside, so dominant that the olive trees themselves seem to incline their fruit towards its market, and the mules and asses pace instinctively in its direction. Yet the physical break is instant, and complete. One side of the river is the country, the other side is the city, and there is no straggle to blur the distinction.

Almost immediately, too, the meaning of Salamanca becomes apparent, and you seem to know by the very cut or stance of the place that this is a city of scholars. Here is the old courtyard of the university, where generations of students have written their names in flowery red ochre; and here are bookshops, those rarities of contemporary Spain, heavily disguised with magazine racks and picture postcards, but still recognizably university shops; and here is the great mediaeval lecture-room of Luis de León, still precisely as he knew it, still bare and cold and dedicated, with his canopied chair just as it was when, reappearing in it after four years in the cells of the Inquisition, he began his lecture with the words "*Dicebamus hesterna die . . .*"—"As we were saying yesterday . . ."

Salamanca University was founded in the thirteenth century, and for four hundred years was one of the power-houses of European thought. Columbus's schemes of exploration were submitted to the judgement of its professors. The Council of Trent was a product of its thinking. The concept of international law was virtually its invention. The first universities of the New World, in Mexico and Peru, were based upon its statutes. It was while serving as Professor of Greek at Salamanca that Miguel de Unamuno, driven out of his mind by the atrocities of the Spanish Civil War, rushed into the street one day shouting curses on his country, later to die of grief.

Around this institution, over the centuries, a noble group of buildings arose, and stands there still in golden splendour. The gorgeous plateresque façade of the Patio de las Escuelas, with its dizzy elaborations, its busts of Ferdinand and Isabel, and its lofty inscription— "The King and Queen to the University and the University to the King and Queen"—is a reminder of the importance of this place to the State, the Crown and the Church throughout the grand epoch of Spanish history. The New Cathedral, pompous and commanding, was opened in 1560 to express the grandeur of a university that then boasted twenty-four constituent colleges, six thousand students, and sixty professors of unsurpassed eminence. One of the most delightful buildings in Spain is the House of the Shells, built at the end of the fifteenth century for a well-known Salamanca sage, and covered all over with chiselled scallops. And nothing in Europe better expresses a kind of academic festiveness than the celebrated Plaza Mayor, the drawingroom of Salamanca: its arcaded square is gracefully symmetrical, its colours are gay without being frivolous, its manner is distinguished without being highbrow, and among the medallions of famous Spaniards that decorate its façade there have been left, with a proper donnish foresight, plenty of spaces for heroes yet to come.

It is a lovely city, but like many lovely Spanish things, it is sad. Its glories are dormant. Its university, once the third in Europe, is now classed as the seventh in Spain, and seems to have no life in it. Few outrageous student rebels sprawl in the cafés of the Plaza Mayor, no dazzling philosophical theories are emerging from these libraries and lecture-rooms. Expect no fire from Salamanca. The Inquisition dampened her first, and in our own time Franco's narrow notions fatally circumscribed her. The genius of this tableland is not friendly to liberty of thought: and just as Spain herself is only now headily experimenting with the freedom of ideas, so it will be a long time, I fear, before Salamanca rejoins the roster of Europe's intellectual vanguard.

There is sadness too in Ávila, though of a different kind. This is a soldier's city, cap-à-pie, and when you approach it from the west over the rolling plateau almost all you see is its famous wall: a mile and a half of castellated granite, with eighty-eight round towers and ten forbidding gates. It looks brand new, so perfect is its preservation, and seems less like an inanimate rampart than a bivouac of men-at-arms, their helmeted front surveying the *meseta*, their plated rear guarding some glowing treasure within. It looks like an encampment of Crusaders on the flank of an Eastern hill: a city in laager, four thousand feet up and very chilly, with the smoke rising up behind the walls where the field kitchens are at work.

But inside those watchful ranks, no treasure exists. Ávila is like an aged nut, whose shell is hard and shiny still, but whose kernel has long since shrivelled. Her main gate is by the mottled cathedral, whose apse protrudes into the wall itself, and around whose courtyard a dozen comical lions—the only light relief in Ávila—hold up an iron chain, their rumps protruding bawdily over the columns that support them. At first the shell feels full enough, as you wander among the mesh of mediaeval streets inside, through the arcades of the central plaza, and down the hill past the barracks; but presently the streets seem to peter out, the passers-by are scarcer, there are no more shops, the churches tend to stand alone in piles of rubble, and the little city becomes a kind of wasteland, like a bomb-site within the walls, several centuries after the explosion.

Ávila was always a mystic city, but this wasted presence gives her a gone-away feeling. The snow-capped sierra stares down at her, the plain around seems always to be looking in her direction, the little River Adaja runs hopefully past her walls; but when you knock at her gate, there is nobody home—and even those knights-at-arms turn out to be made of stone, and are floodlit on festival days. The life of the city has escaped the ramparts, and settled among the shops and cafés of the modern town outside; and from there, sitting with an omelette at a restaurant table, or wandering among the country buses, you may look up at the Gate of Alcazar and the city walls, and think how false, indeed how slightly ludicrous, a defensive posture can look when there is nothing at all to defend.

So emaciated does the old part of Ávila feel today that sometimes it is difficult to imagine how virile she must have been in her palmy days. Was it really here that St. Teresa was born, that most robust of mystics, whose very visions were adventure stories, who jogged all over Spain in a mule wagon, and who did not even scruple to answer back Our Lord? ("That's how I treat My friends," she once heard a divine voice remark, when she was complaining about a flooded river crossing, and unperturbed she retorted: "Yes, and that's why You have so few!") Was it really this pale outpost of tourism that young Prince Juan, only son of the Catholic Monarchs, was trained to rule the earth's greatest empire—only to die before his parents, and thus pass the crown to the house of Austria, to Philip II and his successors of the Escorial? Was it really in Ávila, this city without a bookshop, that the great Bishop Alfonso de Madrigal, the Solomon of his time, wrote his three sheets of profound prose every day of his life—to be immortalized in the end by an alabaster figure in the cathedral that shows him halfway through his second page of the day? Was it here in Ávila that the martyr St. Vincent, having stamped upon an altar of Jupiter, was beheaded on a rock with his two loyal sisters?

It all feels so remote, so long ago, so out of character: in the Civil War, the last great historical event in which Spain played a part, Ávila fell bloodlessly to the Nationalists, and never thereafter heard a shot fired in anger. For me she is like a superb plaster cast of a city, all hollow. There is only one place in Ávila in which the pungency of the past really seems to linger, and that is the crypt of the Church of San Vicente, just outside the walls on the eastern side. Here you may see the very rock on which that family of martyrs died, and beside it in the wall there is a small sinister hole. On October 27, 303, St. Vincent was executed, and his body was thrown to the dogs who prowled and yapped about the rock. A passing Jew paused to make fun of the corpse, but instantly there flew out of that small hole in the rock face an angry serpent, which threw itself upon the Hebrew and frightened him away. This episode was gratefully remembered by the

Christians. For several centuries it was the custom of the people of Ávila, when they wished to take an oath, to crowd down the steps of the crypt of San Vicente, and place their hands in that orifice as they swore; and to this day it is easy to see them down there in the dark, beside that rough old rock—awestruck peasant faces, queer hats and thonged sandals, a smell of must, earth, and garlic, a friar to supervise the solemnities and the slow words of the oath echoing among the shadows.

The Jew was so glad to escape with his life that it was he who built the church upstairs, and an inscription beside his tomb in the west transept tells the tale. As for the serpent, when Bishop Vilches took a false oath at the hole in 1456, out it popped again and stung him.

A world away is Segovia, and yet she stands only forty miles to the north-east, in the lee of the same mountains. If Ávila is only a shell, Segovia is all kernel: she feels the most complete and close-knit of Castilian cities, as though all her organs are well nourished, and nothing is atrophied. The gastronomic speciality of Ávila is a little sweet cake made by nuns; but the speciality of Segovia is roast suckling pig, swimming in fat and fit for conquerors.

Segovia is the most beautifully organized of cities. She is a planner's dream. She lies along an elongated rocky knoll, with the sparse little River Clamores on the south side, and the more affluent Eresma to the north, and to get the hang of her you should first walk up to the little Calvary which stands, lonely and suggestive, on a hillock beside the Ávila road. From there you can see the whole city in silhouette, and grasp its equilibrium. Very early in the morning is the best time, for then, when the sun rises over the plateau, and the city is suddenly illuminated in red, it loses two of its three dimensions, and looks like a marvellous cut-out across the valley. In the centre stands the tall tower of the cathedral, the last of the Gothic fanes of Spain. To the left there rise the romantic pinnacles of the Alcazar, most of it a nineteenth-century structure in the Rhineland manner, all turrets, conical towers, and troubadour windows, properly poised above a precipice (down which a fourteenth-century nanny, when she inadvertently dropped the baby, instantly threw herself too). And at the other end, forming a tremendous muscular foil to this fantasy, there strides across a declivity the great Roman aqueduct of Segovia, looking from this distance so powerful and ageless that it might actually be a strut to hold the hill up. Between these three bold corner-posts—fortress, church, and aqueduct—Segovia has filled herself in with a tight, steep, higgledy-piggledy network of streets, sprinkled with lesser towers, relieved by many squares, and bounded by a city wall which is often blended with houses too, and looks, from your brightening Calvary, rather like the flank of a great ship. She seems, indeed, to sail across her landscape. She looks like a fine old clipper ship, there in the morning sun, full-rigged, full-blown, ship-shape and Bristol-fashion.

A sense of strength or defiance infuses her. It was in the Alcazar that Isabel, recently proclaimed Queen of Castile, found herself besieged by a furious mob, but rode so bravely into the thick of it, alone upon her charger, that the crowd fell back subdued by her very presence. It was in the Alcazar too that the daring King Alfonso the Wise actually ventured to doubt, poring over his books one day, whether in fact the sun moved round the earth: instantly, such was the effect of this proposition, there was a flash of lightning, and the King, hastily dismissing the whole idea from his mind, ever afterwards wore a rope of St. Francis around his waist, a perpetual penance for a rash thought. It was in the queer little Church of Vera Cruz, beneath the castle, that the Knights Templar performed their secret rites of chivalry, standing vigil over their arms all night, in all the mysterious splendour of seneschal, gonfalon, and accolade. It was the image of Our Lady of Fuencisla, in the Carmelite convent, that was officially made a Nationalist Field-Marshal in the Civil War; she still carries a Marshal's baton, and it is said that when Hitler was told the story, he swore that nothing on earth would induce him to visit Spain. Even the calamities of Segovia have a boisterous air: the old palace of the Alcazar, which was burnt down in 1862, was destroyed, it is said, by the cadets of its artillery school, because they wanted the school to be moved to Madrid. Even her miracles are thoroughgoing: one night in November 1602 an intense light shone over the convent of Santa Cruz, and the crowd that hastened there was gratified to find an eminent Dominican theologian, Melchor

Cano, lost in prayer upon his knees, but suspended a good four feet above the level of the ground.

The finest sight in Castile is how Segovians sweepingly define the first appearance of their city, and I agree with them: there can be a few urban compositions on earth to equal the impact of Segovia, when you cross the last ridge on the approaching road, and see her bulk riding there above the fields. For myself, though, I remember with no less pleasure a stroll I took inside the city on my first evening there. It was a wet night, the lamplight shining damply on the streets, and as I wandered aimlessly through the drizzle I came upon a small plaza down the hill from the cathedral, called in the vernacular the Place of the Sirens. It is set upon a flight of steps, rather like the Scala d'Espagna in Rome, and feels like some slightly overpainted opera set—so theatrical that you almost expect it to revolve beneath your feet, to carry you onstage. To its left stands the lovely Romanesque atrium of San Martín, with a tall square tower above it; in its centre there stands the effigy of a well-known Segovian patriot, waving a flag; on the right, as you climb the steps, there is a row of enchanting small houses, ferns and flowers dripping over their balconies; above the rooftops there looms a four-square fortified palace, where Wellington stayed when he took Segovia; and at the top of the steps there is a small courtyard, enclosed on three sides by walls.

It was very shadowy in this yard that night, and I could not see very well. The street lights behind me, reflected in the puddles, only made the darkness darker. On the left-hand side, however, close to the wall, I could just make out two squat, plump stone shapes, crouching in the dark; and when I cautiously stumbled over to them, I found them to be a pair of queer primitive animals, with snouts, tails, and very solid bellies. Were they pigs? Were they lions? Were they gods? Were they devils? Nobody really knows, but I took no risks that evening, and hastily backed away from them: I was in Segovia, a city of spirit, and I thought they might bite.

Lastly Toledo, which stands to Spain as Kyoto to Japan—a repository of all that is proudest, oldest, and most private in the national consciousness. When you think of Old Spain, you think of Toledo—

"a clear and illustrious nightmare," as the poet Garcilaso de la Vega once irreverently described her. Toledo was once the capital of Spain, and is still the seat of the Spanish Primate, and within her walls the Castilian, Jewish, and Moorish cultures, productively co-existing for several centuries, created a rich and tolerant civilization of their own. Everybody knows what Toledo looks like, from El Greco's famous idealization of the place, and even the most determinedly flippant tourist, taking an afternoon excursion from Madrid, usually feels it necessary to cast an eye over this celebrated city, provided of course she can get back by cocktail time.

If you believed the old travellers you would imagine Spain to be one uninterrupted desert, absolutely denuded of vegetation; but Toledo is one city that really does live up to their descriptions— "girdled in," as Augustus Hare put it, "by the indescribable solitude of its utterly desolate hills." She stands only forty miles from Madrid, but there *is* a kind of indescribable solitude to her flavour, and the desolation of her hills, if scarcely utter, still is severe. If Segovia often feels like a flat backcloth, Toledo is heavily in the round. She is built on a rocky mound in a bend of the Tagus, and is thus surrounded on three sides by a deep gorge, with shingle and grey rock running down to the water's edge. The river runs fast here, with a clutter of old stone mills and two excellent bridges; a castle stands sentinel across the stream; harsh grey hills are all about: the setting of Toledo is all abrasion—nothing soft, nothing amusing, nothing hospitable. This is the Spanish character at its most intractable. If a city can be said to look like a person, then Toledo looks just like one of those El Greco characters who were in fact conceived here—towering, handsome, humourless, sad, a little bloodless.

The Church dominates this city, and reminds us that the archbishops of Toledo have often been men more powerful than the State itself: the formidable Cardinal Jiménez de Cisneros not only paid all the expenses of an expeditionary force to Africa, but actually led it himself, in the crimson. On the flank of Toledo's hill stands the fortress of the Alcazar, still recognizably large enough to hold, as it used to, two thousand horses in its subterranean stables. Unmistakably dominating it, though, its tower rising effortlessly above a tawny muddle of roofs and minor pinnacles, stands the cathedral. At night it is floodlit, and then the great luminous finger of this church, peremptory against the sky, makes even the transient sceptic think for a moment about immortality.

Inside the city, too, things of the spirit seem pre-eminent. They may be Jewish devotions that are remembered, in the haunted synagogues of this once-great Jewish city. They may be Muslim, in the adorable little mosque now called Cristo de la Luz—a tiny Córdoba, with its own small copse of horseshoe arches and its silent dusty garden. They may be memories of the Mozarabs, those Christians who retained their faith throughout the Moorish occupation, and thus kept alive the ancient liturgy of Gothic Christianity. When Toledo was recaptured from the Moors in 1085, a dispute arose as to whether the old Mozarabic rites should be retained, or replaced by the Gregorian rites from Rome—adopted in northern Spain during the years of the occupation. The issue was put to trial by fire. The rival prayer books were placed simultaneously in the flame, but the Roman was whisked to safety by a heavenly wind, while the Mozarabic simply did not burn; and because of this stalemate, which both sides claimed as a victory, the old Gothic ritual is still celebrated, every day of the week, in one chapel of Toledo Cathedral. (They keep the doors closed during the service, and when I chanced to open it one day I found myself almost at the priest's side on the steps of the altar: so severely did he turn to stare at me, so disapprovingly did his acolytes look up, so long and empty did the chapel extend behind him, that I instantly closed that door again, and allowed the Mozarabic ritual to continue its survival without me.)

But Roman or Gothic, Gregorian or Mozarab, above all it is Spanish Catholicism, that imperial creed, that is honoured and reflected in this imperial city. This is the city of the Toledo blade—"a sword of Spain," as Shakespeare called it, "the ice-brook's temper"; nowadays the swordsmiths make matador's swords and paper knives, but once they were kept busy making swords for Christian knights. In the Church of Santo Tomé there hangs El Greco's celebrated picture *The Burial of Count Orgaz*, which epitomizes the alliance between God and the Spanish ruling classes. Count Orgaz was a Toledan so distinguished for piety that when he died the young St. Stephen and the old St. Augustine personally descended from Heaven to bury him.

The painting shows them doing so, but more striking than their saintly figures are the Spanish gentlemen who stand behind. They look sorry indeed, but not surprised: they seem to represent a class of society that expect miracles as a matter of policy, and they are watching the saints at work rather as they might watch, with a certain patronizing interest, the technique of any foreign expert sent to do a job under reciprocal arrangements. To the right of the picture a priest appears to be checking the operation in some instruction handbook. High above, Philip II, though still alive when the painting was done, is already among his peers in Heaven. It is a beautiful picture, most richly composed, most haunting in portraiture, given an unexpected twinkle by El Greco's signature—Domenico Theotokopouli—delicately embroidered on the hem of a page's handkerchief; but it seems to record, not an instance of divine grace but the payment of a national due.

You may sense the same air of high collusion all over Toledo. At one end the Church of San Juan de Los Reyes, above the bridge of San Martín, is a resplendent monument to the Reconquest. Its architecture, the most delicate and elaborate kind of Gothic, is like a smile of gentle triumph across the prostate art of the infidel, and upon its golden walls there hang the chains of Christian captives released from Moorish camps and galleys. At the other end of the city the ruined Alcazar is a memorial, in many Spanish minds, to the last of the Crusades. "The heroic epic," said a message from the young woman of Burgos to the defenders of the fortress in 1937, "which your valour for God and Spain has written in our glorious Alcazar will be the pride of Spanish chivalry for ever": seventy priests had been murdered in Toledo, and when the Army of Africa fought its way in at last, the main street ran with blood, several wounded men were killed in their beds in hospital, and forty anarchists, trapped in a seminary, set fire to the building and burnt themselves to death.

And surveying all, the culmination of this city, Toledo Cathedral stands like a vast testimonial of Spain's divine destiny. The streets of Toledo are unbelieveably tortuous, so narrow that along most of them a car cannot pass, and even a hand-trolley of oranges blocks the way; but when you have manoeuvred your baffled way along them, have discovered the unremarkable outer walls of the cathedral, and have entered its unobtrusive cloister gate, then the immense expanse of the interior, its nave of seven bays and its twenty-eight chapels, seems to express the ultimate escape of the Spaniard from himself, *via* glory, to infinity. "Valour for God and Spain" fills this great church like incense; and as witness to the working relationship between the two you may be shown a small white stone, preserved behind a grille, upon which Our Lady actually set foot during a royal visit in 666.

Soldiers, saints, heroes, and great churchmen seem to populate Toledo Cathedral, and when there is a service at the high altar, with all the swift formality of its ritual, the bowing priests, the genuflecting servers, the bewigged attentive vergers, the clink of the censers, the gorgeous shimmer of copes and jewelled monstrances, the exchange of plainchant between altar, *coro*, and thundering organ— when the heart of the cathedral is filled with the sights and sounds of that tremendous spectacle, this really does feel like the nerve-centre of some formidable war machine, a bunker or a Pentagon, disposing its unseen forces in distant strategies. From the transept ceilings the Cardinals' hats hang rotting like battle-flags. In the Chapter House the faces of all the archbishops look back at you from their portraits like generals in a war museum. In the treasury the silver spheres, rings, breastplates, censers, and crucifixes glitter beneath their bright lights like State jewels. Above the high altar there stands the figure of a mysterious shepherd who, sent by God to help Spain, guided the Christians to victory over the Moors through the mists of Las Navas de Tolosa in 1212; only King Alfonso VIII saw the face of this man, and the King it was, we are told, who carved the figure.

It is a great hall of triumph, a victory paean for the Christian culture. A superb assembly of treasures here upholds the Christian ethos—grilles by the great Spanish masters of wrought iron; sculpture and stained glass by virtuosos from Holland, Italy, and France; paintings by Rubens, Velázquez, Van Dyck, Goya, El Greco, Bassano, Giovanni Bellini; multitudes of stone angels, tombs of kings and prelates, sudden shafts of sunlight through stained glass, a vast, tumbled, restless, infinitely varied museum of the faith. Nothing in Christendom, I suspect, better expresses the militancy of the Church than the *retablo* or reredos of Toledo, which rises in serried magnifi-

cence from the high altar to the roof. It is fretted everywhere with
stone canopies and niches, and in a series of elaborate stone tableaux,
like the set of an experimental theatre, tells the New Testament story;
with an endless profusion of detail, and an inexhaustible imagination—with saints on guard at each flank, and angels fluttering everywhere—with a gleaming gold, and blue, and a glow of old stone—
with an almost physical movement upwards, up through the sweet
mystery of the Nativity and the splendour of the Ascension, up
through a glittering field of stars in a deep blue sky—up to the very
rafters of the cathedral, where your dazed eye reaches at last the
supreme symbol of Calvary, portrayed there in immense tragic grandeur at the very apex of Christian Spain.

With such a cause, one feels, with such a champion, no Christian
soldier could lose. We are, however, in Spain, where the last victory is
death itself—"*Viva la Muerte!*" was the battle-cry of the Falange in
the Civil War. A few feet away from that glorious reredos there
stands the tomb of the Cardinal-Archbishop Portocarrero, Viceroy
of Sicily, Cardinal Protector of the Spanish Nation, Regent and Primate of Spain. He died in 1719, and has been described as "incapable, obstinate, and perfectly selfish"; but on his tomb, by his own
orders, there was inscribed the dry Spanish epitaph *Hic Jacet Pulvis,
Cinis, et Nihil*—"Here Lies Dust, Ashes, Nothing."

Incomparable old cities of the interior! No other towns on earth are
anything like them. They have no peers, no rivals, no imitators. A circle a hundred miles across would contain them all; but you can stand
ten thousand miles from their walls, close your eyes and think of
Spain, and see them clear as sunlight still.

Favell Lee Mortimer

(1 8 0 2 – 1 8 7 8)

Mrs. Favell Lee Mortimer was born in London, the daughter of a banker. Her first book, *The Peep of the Day or a Series of the Earliest Religious Instruction the Infant Mind is Capable of Receiving* (1833), instructed young children about correct behavior and their relationship to God. (Mrs. Mortimer was both unmarried and childless at the time of publication.) Her advice seems bizarre to modern parents and she addressed the child reader directly, like an omniscient but invisible teacher. "Will your bones break?—Yes they would, if you were to fall down from a high place or if a cart were to hover over them . . . If you were not to eat some food for a few days, your little body would be very sick, your breath would stop, and you would grow cold, and you would soon be dead."

Having conquered child rearing, Mrs. Mortimer decided to instruct her audience on the ways of other lands. *Near Home or Europe Described* (1849) was the first book in her trilogy about the world. She informed children about what to expect abroad. No country measured up to Mrs. Mortimer's high standards. "What country do you love best?" she asked rhetorically. "Your own country. I know you do."

And Mrs. Mortimer wanted to keep it that way, for she has nothing good to say about any country other than England. Italians are wicked and ignorant, the Portuguese are indolent, the Russians are civil but sly, and the Greeks love singing, but sing badly. Of Spain she wrote, "The Spaniards are not only very idle, they are cruel." As evidence, she cited bullfights, enjoyed by both men and women and even priests who ought to know better.

Favell Mortimer's reputation endures as a literary curiosity and evidence of Victorian England's xenophobia. The author's voice is opinionated, confident, self-righteous, and authoritative. Mrs. Mortimer did exhaustive research for her books, although much of the material on which she relied was decades old. Despite her wide-ranging knowledge of foreign lands, Mrs. Mortimer left Great Britain only twice, on short trips. Mrs. Favell Lee Mortimer died in 1878 in England, of course.

This is excerpted from *Near Home or Europe Described*.

From NEAR HOME OR EUROPE DESCRIBED

SPAIN

The Country.—Is Spain a beautiful country? Yes, it is very beautiful. There are high mountains and very wide plains, and fine trees, and a clear blue sky.

The plains are not flat and smooth, but uneven. Children love to run down steep banks and to clamber among hillocks. Now you would like to play at hide-and-seek among the brushwood and bushes of a Spanish plain, but once you would not have dared to play there for fear of meeting a terrible playfellow—I mean a robber.

There used to be robbers in Spain, who hid themselves among the caves in the mountains, and among the thickets in the forests. If you travelled through Spain, you would often see black crosses set up by the roadside, with some writing on them. What are these crosses for? Read what is written upon one—"A man, named Charles was murdered here in May, 1840." Read what is written upon the next—"A woman, named Julia, and her children, were murdered here in January, 1736." Whenever a person has been murdered by the roadside, a cross is set up to mark the place.

Sometimes, as you went along, you would hear the tinkling of bells, with the deep sound of men's voices singing. You need not fear that robbers are coming, for *they* make no noise. The bells are tied round the necks of mules, with burdens on their backs, and the men are driving them, and singing to amuse themselves by the way.

Look at that great waggon drawn by oxen—how slowly it moves along!

The Animals.—There are some wild beasts in the north of Spain—boars and wolves. The shepherds are more afraid of a wolf than a boar, because their large dogs would sooner fight with a boar than with a wolf. And why? Because a wolf has such sharp teeth and claws, and because it is so cunning. It knows what part to lay hold of in each animal. When it sees a bullock, it seizes it by its throat, but when it sees a horse, it flies at its haunches.

There are large herds of horses feeding in the valleys of Spain. When the mares see a wolf coming, they know what to do. They put their foals all together, and they stand all round with their tails towards the foals. As soon as one of the mares sees a wolf coming towards her, she stands on her hind-legs, ready to trample it under her feet. The wolves, finding they cannot approach, are at last obliged to go away.

But when a horse is *alone*, it is very much terrified at the wolves. A gentleman was riding among the mountains, when suddenly his horse stopped and trembled all over. He could not think what was the matter with the poor beast. At first he supposed the horse was taken ill, but, on listening, he heard some squeaking and growling among the bushes. He pointed his gun towards the place whence the noise came and fired. Then a scampering was heard—the wolves were running away as fast as they could. The poor horse did not recover his health for several days, so dreadfully had he been frightened.

Men are sometimes frightened at wolves as well as horses. Two Spaniards were once walking along among hills, when they saw a whole troop of wolves coming along; one large, fierce grey wolf led the way, and the rest followed. They were galloping fast, with their tails lifted up, and their eyes looking fiery. The poor men tried to get out of the way, as well as they could. They turned out of the path, and stood on the side of a hill among the vines, and there they waited trembling, and hoping the wolves would not see them. But the first wolf turned that very way, and the rest came after it. The wolf passed by one of the men without noticing him, though it came so near him that its bristly hair brushed the man's legs. When it came to the other man, who was standing a little higher up the hill, it passed by—almost—then turned half round, and snapped at him, without biting him. That was a sign to the pack of wolves to eat him. They understood the sign, and in a few moments tore the man limb from limb, howling all the while most dreadfully, and leaving nothing but bones.

It is not often that wolves get hold of a man, but they often devour sheep.

There are large flocks of sheep in Spain, with very fine wool, called merinos. There are goats leaping amongst the mountains, and there are tame goats, and they are milked as cows are milked in England.

You have often seen a flock of sheep, but did you ever see a flock of pigs? In Spain you might see one. All the people in a village who keep pigs, send them out under the care of one man every day, to feed in the plains. The man is called a swineherd. He has a troublesome charge, for pigs are not as quiet and gentle as sheep. One evening, a traveller saw the swineherd returning with his pigs. The man wore a ragged cloak, and a hat in the shape of a sugar loaf. In one hand he held a cow-horn, with which he made a horrible noise; in the other, he held a stick with a nail at the end, and with this stick he pricked those pigs that did not mind the sound of the horn. The pigs followed the man very steadily, till they came close to the village; then they set up a loud grunt, and set off in a fast gallop; one went one way, and another went another way; each knew the way to his own home, and was in such a hurry to reach it, that he bolted through the open door and jumped over the threshold, frightening off the little children as he rushed by. It was the thought of supper, I think, which made the pigs so eager.

If the Spanish pigs are such active creatures what must the horses, ponies, and donkeys be? They are all very spirited, and can gallop very fast. I will tell you a story about a Spanish pony.

A gentleman wanted a pony to ride up over the mountains. He met a gipsy, who said he had one to sell. The gipsy said, "My pony is the best in Spain." But when the gentleman saw the animal, he did not think so much of it, for it seemed weak, and it had the marks of a rope upon its poor thin sides, as if it had been beaten a great deal. Yet its eye was bright and lively.

"It looks weak," said the gentleman.

"You cannot ride him," replied the gipsy. "If you mount him, he will run away, and nothing will stop him, but the sea."

The gentleman did not believe the gipsy; so, sitting upon the pony with only a halter, and just a bridle, in its mouth, he set off. Oh! How the creature did gallop! It seemed, indeed, as if he never would stop till he should come to the sea. But the sea was a long, long way off; no pony could have gone so far. At last the pony came to a very wide ditch; it jumped over it, the halter broke, and the rider fell off, and rolled in the dust. He soon got up, for he was not hurt.

Where was the pony? Glad to find it had got rid of its burden, it was rioting in the fields, kicking its heels into the air. The gipsy had seen all that had happened. He now whistled, and the obedient beast, giving a gentle neigh, trotted back to him.

There are also bulls in Spain. I shall tell you then the cruel manner in which they are treated.

FOOD.—The Spaniards do not breakfast till the middle of the day. They take something in their bed-rooms before they dress, but it is only a very small cup of chocolate, and a little bit of bread without butter (for very little butter is made in Spain). They drink water or cold sugar and water several times in the day.

At their noon-day breakfast, the favourite dish is called puchero, or olla. It is made of stewed beef and chickens, cut small, and peas, and beans, and other vegetables, and a little bit of pork or bacon. Then there are roasted hares, and rabbits, and kids, and pigeons, and cheese, and eggs, and cakes, and fruits.

The Spaniards dine about six o'clock. At their dinner they often have stewed beef and tomatoes, or love-apples, dressed in oil.

You would think many of the Spanish dishes were spoiled by the oil and garlic with which they are mixed. The oil is the juice of the olive. There are a great many olive-trees in Spain, fine spreading trees; and the olive is a little dark round fruit about the size of a plum. The Spaniards eat a great many olives with bread. Poor people sometimes dine on olives and bread.

There are many other fruits you like better than olives. Oranges and figs are more plentiful than apples are in England, and great quantities are sent to other countries.

Spanish grapes are very beautiful and very cheap. Many of them are dried and sent to England. They are called raisins. Have you ever eaten Malaga raisins?

Wine is so common in Spain that poor men drink it in earthen cups, as English people drink beer; but the Spaniards do not keep it in barrels, as we do beer, but in skins. A pig-skin is easily turned into a bottle, and laid upon a donkey; a barrel would not be half as convenient to travel with.

The famous sherry wine, so often seen in England, comes from Xeres, in Spain.

A traveller, with his guide, called one day, on a priest, in his little cottage, in the country. Over the door grew a beautiful vine. The traveller knocked, but no answer was returned. The truth was, the old priest, as well as his old servant and his favourite cat, had all fallen asleep after dinner. But, at last, the knocking was heard, and the door was opened. The old man, thinking that the visitors had dined, desired cakes and sweetmeats to be placed on the table, but when he found they had not, he said he must give them some dinner. Yet what to give them he knew not, for he had no meat in the house. So he took them to his pigeon-house, to see whether he had a pigeon fit to kill; but the pigeons were too young to be eaten. Then he looked unhappy, and after showing his visitors his bed, he led them into some empty rooms, where flitches of bacon were hanging from the ceiling. Looking up, he said, "I am sorry I have nothing better to offer you than this bacon, and some fresh eggs; for my hens lay every day." The traveller thought this dinner quite good enough. The old priest gave a great deal away to the poor, and kept two clean beds for any travellers who might need a place to rest.

RELIGION.—The religion in Spain is the Roman Catholic. The priests do not read the Bible much, nor do they advise the people to read it, though the Bible is the book which can make us wise, and save our souls.

There was a good man who wished to give Bibles and Testaments to the Spaniards. He hired a donkey, and loaded it with a bag of books. As he went along, a young woman passed, leading a little boy by the hand. She stopped him, and said, "Uncle, what have you got on your ass?"

Why did she call him uncle? It is a name which the Spaniards always give out of politeness to people whom they don't know. The young woman said, "Have you got soap on your ass?"

The stranger told the young woman that he sold good books, and he showed her a Testament. She began to read out loud, and at last cried out, "What beautiful, what charming reading!" Then she inquired the price of the book. Though it was very cheap, she said she had not money enough to buy it; so she put it down, and went away. But soon the little boy came running back, shouting out, "Stop, uncle! The book, the book!" The little fellow had got the money for it in his hand, but it was all in copper, not in silver.

A few of the priests, when they saw the good man's Bibles, praised them, and bought some; but most of the priests were angry, and spoke against the holy books. Poor people bought them. Many of them had never seen a Testament before. Sometimes a poor man would sit under the shade of a great tree, while his neighbors would gather round and listen attentively to the history of the Lord Jesus. You have heard that history. You have a Bible or a Testament of your own. Do you love it? Do you think it "beautiful and charming reading?"

COTTAGES.—Some of the cottages are very miserable indeed. A gentleman, travelling amongst the mountains with his guide, came to a village where there were a few black huts. He knocked at the door of one. A man opened it, holding a burning piece of wood in his hand, instead of a candle. The gentleman asked to be allowed to sleep in the hut that night. The poor man let him in, and led him first through a room full of straw, then through a stable, into the room where the family lived. After providing bacon and eggs for supper, he pointed to a small door in the roof, and told the gentleman he might sleep there upon some clean straw.

"Is there no bed in the cottage?" asked the gentleman.

"No," replied the poor man. "I never slept in a bed in all my life, nor have my children nor did my father and mother before me. We sleep on the hearth by the fire, or else among the cattle in the stables."

In some parts of Spain there are rows of neat white cottages, with red-tiled roofs. But when the door of a cottage is open, you see at the end of the narrow passage, an image of the Virgin Mary upon an altar. On the steps of the altar, there are little candles and candlesticks and tiny vases of artificial flowers, which are no bigger than peas.

In Spain the Virgin Mary is worshipped more than God. How much grieved the blessed Mary would be, could she hear the prayers and praises that are offered up to her! She would say, "Go to my Son; He saved *me*, and He is able to save *you*."

AMUSEMENTS.—The favourite amusement of the young people is dancing. Generally there is a place, near the church, where the grass is smooth, and there the people assemble to dance, and play at games. They are very fond of playing on the guitar, and singing songs as they play. In summer evenings the guitar may be heard in the streets long after it is dark. Very few people like reading, or any useful employment.

The Spaniards are cruel, for they delight in bull-fights. There is a large building in every town for fighting bulls. Seats are placed all round, and in the middle is a large place for the bulls, with rails to keep them from hurting the people. The people are glad when they see the bull driven in. Generally he is teased before he comes into the place, and a sharp iron is sticking in his neck all the time he is there. Showers of iron arrows are thrown at him. Sometimes as many as fifty arrows are hanging from his neck. There are men on horseback with long spears who attack the bull. Very soon the bull with his horns gores one of the horses; the rider gets away as quickly as he can, and the people help him to get over the rails, while some men in red cloaks rush forward and frighten the bull. The man whose horse is killed gets another horse, and comes back again to torment the bull. Sometimes the men are killed by the bull, but this happens very seldom. The poor horses suffer most. They are generally old and worn-out. It must be dreadful to behold the poor blind-folded creatures, with streams of blood pouring from their breasts, and their bodies gashed and torn to pieces whilst they are yet alive.

When the bull has been tormented for a long while, a man on horseback enters, with a sword to kill him. This man is called the "Matador." While the bull puts down its head, in order to try to hurt with its horns, the matador pierces its neck with his sword. As soon as he has done it, the people give a shout of joy. The bull does not die immediately, but runs backwards and forwards in an agony, till he drops down dead. Then the trumpets sound, as if some great thing had been done. Mules are brought in, ropes are tied to the bull's horns, and the mules drag out the dead body. Sometimes six bulls are killed one after another. The more bulls are killed, the better the people like the fight. If only a few are killed the people *hiss*. A matador is paid fifty or sixty pounds for every bull he kills, and sometimes more.

And can women like to see such bloody sights? Yes, they do—and priests, who ought to show the people what is right, are pleased to view these wicked deeds. How angry the merciful God must be to see men thus torment His poor dumb creatures!

When the Prince of Wales visited Spain, he did not go to see a bull-fight.

H. V. Morton

(1892–1979)

Henry Canova Vollam Morton was a British travel writer of the old school. Publicity photographs show him with a pencil mustache, a jaunty fedora, and a suit and tie. He entered journalism at sixteen when it was considered a career taken up instead of college, rather than after it. Morton honed his reporting skills writing Fleet Street feature stories. His career was disrupted by service during World War I, but he returned to journalism in time to cover the discovery of the tomb of Tutankhamen at Luxor, Egypt, reports of which made him famous.

He stayed close to home with a series of articles—"word pictures"—about London that were later anthologized into a book, *Heart of London* (1925). It became a bestseller. In 1926, behind the wheel of a Morris, he set out to "discover" England, "to see what lies off the beaten track. I will, as the mood takes me, go into towns and unknown hamlets, I will shake up the dust of kings . . ." The result was the immensely popular *In Search of England* (1926).

From his native England Morton branched out: Scotland (*In Search of Scotland*, 1929), Wales (*In Search of Wales*, 1931), and then to the Middle East, Europe, and South Africa. He became so entranced by Capetown that he and his wife emigrated there, buying a farm with a view of Table Bay. It was there that he died. Morton's books sold millions during his lifetime and he is appreciated still for his literate, meticulous reportage. This excerpt is from *A Stranger in Spain* (1955).

From A STRANGER IN SPAIN

I

The aircraft descended upon a landscape that was just as I had expected it to be. The trees had vanished centuries ago, much of the top soil had gone, and the bones of the land lay stark and bare in various shades of brown. There was a lonely dignity about it as there is about most wide, uncluttered landscapes, and blue and purple hills rose far off on the edge of the sky. Three or four small feathers of cloud, which I was to learn are characteristic of Castile, hung in the sky as if puffed there by a locomotive; but perhaps that is too earthy a metaphor, for they also suggested the wing feathers of cherubim and seraphim. Against the undulations of the plain the Madrid airport wore the gay and impertinent look of a pleasure steamer upon a sombre lake.

A glass partition and a door guarded by two armed men in sage green uniforms, wearing hats of black patent leather and of a shape that recalled Napoleon, separated the travellers from a café which overflowed to a strip of lawn and white railings. Here Spaniards were sipping drinks and pointing to the sky as the aluminum shells came gliding down from Lisbon, Paris and Rome. The Customs House smelt like a night club. A South American plane had just come in, and many a shrill and costly-looking female was unlocking her neat air luggage, watched by the two Civil Guards, who had the eyes of melancholy stags.

I was impressed by the white cotton gloves which the Customs officers drew on before they probed into the luggage. I was soon to learn that white gloves are a symbol of the Spanish sense of fitness. A glove is an aristocratic symbol, and was once worn only by kings and bishops. As the world becomes more democratic one sees fewer gloves, and the clenched fist, of course, is always bare.

There were Mexicans, Peruvians and other South Americans in the queue at the passport window, *conquistadores* in reverse, returning to visit the old country, and I watched them, thinking that Spain is one of the few places where America does not mean the United

States. All the *Americanos* were, of course, tourists, and so was I. The word *turista* is to modern Spain much as *peregrino* was in the Middle Ages. It is entirely comprehensible.

"Why have you come to Spain?"

"*Turista!*"

The stamp descends immediately upon the passport, a pair of dark eyes pass sadly over you, loaded with the vast melancholy of those who have to deal with the public; and you are free to step into Spain.

II

My rooms were featureless and might have been in London, Paris or Rome, indeed the only touch of a Spanish hand was a picture of the Crucifixion above the bed. The afternoon sun shot in and took possession when, after a struggle with one of those webbing bands unknown in less sunny climes, I lifted the wooden shutters a yard or two and revealed what lay beyond. I saw a low huddle of roofs beautifully covered with mulberry-coloured tiles, long and semi-circular in shape, of the kind seen on Byzantine churches all over Greece. Beyond was a hideous concrete block of flats, every window shuttered and no doubt in every room a slumbering Spaniard. To the left was evidently a large seminary, where a solitary priest was slowly pacing a corridor, breviary in hand. He was the only sign of life in Madrid's *siesta*, or rather in that portion of it visible from my window. He was young and sallow and his lips were moving. His soutane was new and well-cut, perhaps the best soutane one could buy. He had evidently been recently ordained and was the pride of his family, who had all gathered to hear him say his first Mass. As the black figure paced up and down he became for me symbolic of Spain: this tireless spirit of Orthodoxy scorning repose on a hot, sunny afternoon. So might he have paced beside the heretic, and so did Philip II pace the corridors of the Escorial.

More than once I stretched my hand to the telephone, then, remembering where I was, withdrew it. What a fearful solecism it would be to shatter a friend's *siesta*! It would be at least an hour before I could ring up anyone. What should I do? Should I go out and walk along the shady side of the street, past the shuttered shops? No; the lethargy which is Spain's first gift to the stranger was already taking control, and I thought the best thing was to smoke a cigarette and wait until Madrid became perpendicular again.

I have sometimes wondered whether other nations are as ignorant of our history as we are of theirs. The story of Spain, so unlike that of any other nation in Europe, is little known in England except to the student, and even those who have absorbed a lot of Spain, who have read Cervantes and have heard the music of Manuel de Falla, who have seen the paintings of Velázquez and El Greco, perhaps even Goya in reproduction, would be hard put to it to tell you anything of the history of Spain except at one or two points where it touched ours: when Henry VIII married Catherine of Aragon and when Philip II tried to conquer Elizabethan England with the Spanish Armada. It is surprising to realize that the great St. Ferdinand of Castile, who warred against the Moors so stoutly, had an English grandmother; or that Edward II, the first Prince of Wales, had a Spanish mother; that the Black Prince brought from Spain the huge ruby now set in front of the Imperial State Crown of England; that John of Gaunt used to call himself "Monseigneur d'Espagne" and fancied himself the King of Castile; or that Spanish blood ran in the veins of Richard III, Edward IV, Elizabeth of York, and, thin no doubt by that time, of Henry VIII and Elizabeth. . . .

The telephone rang. The *siesta* was over. The traffic policemen's whistles would be blowing again, and the crowded tramcars and antique taxis circulating once more; the steel shutters would be coming down from the shop windows.

"Hello," said the voice of a friend. "Welcome to Spain! Will you have dinner with me tonight? Good! Then I'll call for you round about ten."

"About *ten?*"

"Yes, or is that a bit too early?"

"No, I'll expect you then."

And I, who regard it as one of life's greatest pleasures to be in bed at ten, groaned inwardly.

III

I went out into the warm streets. All strange cities seem enormous until you have become acquainted with them, and Madrid is no exception. I thought the Calle de Alcalá one of the finest avenues in Europe. The hub of Madrid's wheel is the Puerta del Sol—the Gate of the Sun, of Moorish Madrid—at first a confusion and then, when you have become more familiar with the city, a fascination. It is a magnet. Somehow you always find yourself there; if you are lost, you go there and recover your bearings.

It was delightful to move with the crowds as this summer day was ending, and to glance into the good-looking shop windows—especially admirable shoe shops—and to hear all round the rattle and volley of Castilian. How different a language seems when you hear it spoken rapidly, loudly, confidently and colloquially in its native land. I took a chair on the pavement outside a café and ordered a *café con leche*. The people who passed and re-passed were well dressed. There was a high proportion of sun-glasses among the men, and I noticed with interest the Spanish habit of wearing the jacket hung from the shoulders with the arms swinging loosely, a relic I suppose of the Spanish cloak. The women were hatless and their hair was beautifully tended. All these people had made an effort. They were not dressed up or flamboyant, neither had they that rich look one used to notice in Bond Street, but they were living up to a certain standard of fitness. As I looked at them I remembered the white cotton gloves in the Customs House.

When I had finished my coffee I walked slowly along the Avenida de José Antonio, where the crowds were thicker, the shops continuous, and the smell of petrol and oil from the oldest motors in use in the world more penetrating. José Antonio! In the days to come I was to be haunted by that name. There are hundreds of streets called after him. You see his name in huge letters above war memorials outside churches. It is everywhere. No one can be in Spain for even a few days without becoming familiar with it. There must come a moment in every stranger's visit to Spain when, unable to bear it any longer, he goes up to the first Spaniard he sees and asks, "Who was José Antonio?" And the answer is perfectly simple. He is the yet uncanonized saint of Nationalist Spain. He was the son of General Primo de Rivera. He founded the Falangist movement and was shot by Communists eighteen years ago during the Civil War.

As I strolled on, glancing into the shop windows, wondering who could possibly want a little model of a *banderillero* in the act of sticking darts into a bull, a young man attached himself to me and walked beside me whispering. Imagining him to be a tout, I told him sharply to go away in what I believed to be good Castilian, and was consequently humiliated when he replied in English, asking me to buy a fountain pen, which he furtively withdrew from his breast pocket. These whispering pen vendors haunt the streets of Madrid. The pens they offer appear identical with the American original, but are made in Barcelona. The pen men are never rude and are easily shaken off. They just replace the pen in a breast pocket and with a philosophical sigh, as if they had been doing it as a wager, fade into the crowds. But you soon get to know them and they soon get to recognize you.

Such people, also taxi-drivers and hotel porters, are a stranger's first contacts in a foreign capital. And I must not forget the dear old black-market cigarette women of Madrid, highly respectable little old women in black dresses and aprons who have a regular beat on the pavements and carry trays full of American cigarettes. There is nothing at all furtive about them. They will sell you their technically forbidden goods under the eye of a policeman.

When darkness fell Madrid began to take seats as if for a nocturnal pageant or procession. Every pavement chair was occupied. Offices and shops had let down their shutters and the day's work was over. Then into the main avenues thousands of men and women came from a hundred tributaries, by underground, bus and on foot, to stroll about and walk up and down, and down and up. This was the nightly *paseo*, that queer relic of the seventeenth century when the aristocracy took the air in the evening along the Paseo del Prado. The same thing used to happen in St. James's Park in the eighteenth century, when the whole of London society could have been seen strolling up and down, dressed for dinner. I tried six or seven cafés before I was able to pounce on a vacated seat from which I could watch this parade. The crowds were different from the hungry, hunt-

ing crowds which shamble along Piccadilly towards Leicester Square
at night: they were a more decorous crowd, a crowd dressed neatly
for the occasion, and they reminded me of an old-fashioned church
parade.

It was extraordinary to see a large proportion of the population of
a modern city circulating in this way and I thought it a pleasant sight.
There was nothing vulgar about it, no cat-calls or whistles, or obvious casual encounters; on the other hand no women would have put
on those neat little frocks, black patent leather shoes, and have made
sure that their hair was looking right, had they not expected to be
noticed and admired. No doubt they were, but they did not seem
conscious of it. If they heard a compliment they did not turn round
and smile: they passed on in the lamplight, often three or four
together, heads well up, backs straight, dignified and serious.

It took me a week to get used to the fantastic hours of eating. In
the 'twenties Primo de Rivera tried to make Spain eat at European
times, but even a dictator could not do this. When the habit began I
do not know, but it is not an ancient one. In 1786 when Dr.
Townsend, rector of Pewsey, in Wiltshire, visited Spain, the king and
members of the royal family dined about midday, the old-fashioned
courtiers dined at one-thirty, and the more modern at two o'clock. A
German named Fischer, who toured Spain about ten years later and
had a keen eye for such things, does not mention unusual mealtimes,
and neither does Richard Ford, who never missed a Spanish peculiarity. It is impossible to imagine these late hours in any city before the
arrival of street lighting, and I suppose Spain's habit of dining at ten
is perhaps no older than the gas lamp.

By the time my friend arrived at the hotel I was tired and would
much rather have had a sandwich and have gone to bed. For him the
evening was just beginning, and in his cheerful company I revived
and we went out together.

IV

We dined at a small restaurant in surroundings which reminded me
vaguely of the old Café Royal. It belonged to the red plush and
gilt cupid era of restaurant décor. There were massive sideboards, gilt

mirrors, silver candelabra, and some of the waiters had perhaps been selected to match this atmosphere. I was shown a little Chinese room at the back which is pointed out as one in which the scandalous Isabel II sometimes came by a back stair to meet her latest lover.

We ordered *langostinos*, which are Dublin Bay prawns, cold in may-onnaise, *tournedos* with mushrooms and port wine sauce, and *fraises du bois* flavoured with orange juice. We drank a pale dry sherry and a red wine of La Rioja.

"I haven't seen such well-dressed crowds in any European capital since the last war," I said.

"Ah, but you must remember," replied my friend, "that every Spaniard is at heart a grandee, and his last economy would be in out-ward show. Thousands of the well-dressed men you've noticed tonight, wearing well-cut suits and shoes made by hand in Majorca, have only one suit and they go back to a bed-sitting room. You may be as poor as a church mouse in Spain, but you must put up a show. It's the same with the girls. They are not expensively dressed, but they are very neat. Salaries are desperately low, so low that Spaniards who can't get into some racket or other, or pull down a sinecure job, have to take on extra work, like teaching languages, in their spare time. I know a man who has six different jobs! It's said the Spaniard is lazy. You ought to see the way some of them work! When Spaniards are never to be found at their offices the foreigner jumps to the conclusion that they're still in bed, but the truth is that they're probably trying to earn an honest peseta somewhere else."

"Shall I see the awful poverty which English people are told exists here?"

"No, not this year. You see, we've had two good harvests. The trouble with Spain is that she has no fat stored away. She lives from harvest to harvest. A bad harvest and the country is on the bread line. The poverty stories that everyone has read were written two years ago after a run of bad harvests. Also the European press loves to exaggerate Spanish difficulties. You will never convince the aver-age Spaniard that the foreign editors of some of the best known English newspapers are not secret Communists."

"Is Franco popular?"

"No one is ever popular in Spain. It's an old Spanish custom!

Franco is respected for having ended the Civil War and for having got Spain to work again, and in my opinion his feat in steering the country through post-war Europe is a miracle. I think it would be right to say that the average man admires Franco—as much as any Spaniard can admire any other Spaniard—as an honest man, but as always in Spain, the people round him, who began by doing good, have done well. All Governments in this country feather their own nests and everybody knows it."

"What is Franco like?"

"He's a soldier, and a God-fearing one like Cromwell. The sword in one hand and a holy relic in the other. Actually he would have been perfectly happy in a garrison town. He has no dynastic ambitions. He has no son. His only daughter is married and he lives a quiet domestic life with his wife in the old palace of the Prado, about sixteen miles out of Madrid. He isn't a dictator in the European sense at all. He's just a soldier who has put down a rebellion and proclaimed military law and intends to see the law kept."

"What do you think of the future?"

"Can anyone in the world think of the future? The future of Spain is anyone's guess. People in England and America don't realize that the late Don Alfonso XIII never abdicated. He just cleared out and went into exile. Spain is really a monarchy without a king. Franco is the Head of the State and he is pledged to bring back a king someday. Should anything happen to Franco, and providing the whole country didn't blow up, he would be succeeded by a Regency Council pledged to the same purpose. This was decided by a referendum held in 1947, when the vote in favour of a return of the monarchy was something like fourteen millions to one."

"And who is to be the new King of Spain?"

"Well, nobody knows for certain. Don Alfonso left a son, Don Juan, now a middle-aged man, who lives in Portugal. He has a son, a boy of sixteen, Don Juan Carlos, who is being educated by the Jesuits, and most people believe that he will be chosen king someday."

"And then?"

He lifted his arms like a Spaniard and let them fall limply and despairingly.

"Who can say? There are some who believe that Spain is naturally a monarchist country, and others who think that the return of the king—of any king—will start another civil war. But who knows?"

We discussed American Aid and Spain's need of agricultural machinery and other things. He told me that some Spaniards were opposed to American Aid. They feared that Spain, having avoided the two world wars, might be drawn into the third.

We changed the subject. We talked about Spanish women. I told him that the thousands of *señoritas* I had seen that night wandering about freely in the streets did not tally with the still accepted idea that women in Spain were closely guarded.

"All that began to go during the Republic," he said, "and the Civil War ended it. At one time during the War, when Franco's troops were besieging Madrid, they were opposed by a battalion of women who opened fire on them with rifles and machine guns."

"What happened to the old Spanish gallantry?"

"Well, as a matter of fact," he replied, "I don't think the girls were fired on when they were running away! Why I mentioned this is to show you that a country can't go through what Spain has experienced and still keep its women in purdah. Women were given the vote and they still have it. The Republic allowed divorce, but the Church has, of course, now put a stop to that. The *duenna* is a more or less spiritual inhibition, a kind of ghostly presence. I'd say that women in Spain today are very much as they were in Victorian England. There was a time in England when it was not done to dine alone with a man or to travel alone in a hansom with him. It's like that here. Girls are well behaved. They know that if they weren't, no man would ever marry them! And marriage and a large family is the dream of every normal Spanish female. Having married, she then disappears from life and begins to rule her family. The only people in Spain more powerful than the mothers are the grandmothers."

"Do tell me," I said, "why old brown palm trees are tied to so many balconies in Madrid."

"That's easy," he replied. "They come from the date palms at Elche, in the south-east near Alicante. Every Easter they are tied into bundles which are blessed by the priests and sold all over Spain as a protection against lightning."

My friend rushed off to attend some party. It was just after midnight. I walked back through the Puerta del Sol, which was as crowded as ever. The police whistles shrilled in the night. Hundreds of old cars were changing gear and backfiring. How anyone sleeps in this part of Madrid I cannot imagine. I noticed the number of small children, dressed up as if for a party and in the last stages of exhaustion, who were being dragged along by their parents. This was the first time I noticed the Spanish passion for *los niños*, those pale-faced little creatures drooping on shoulders, or trying to keep up, who should have been in bed five hours ago. I noticed a father carrying a little boy who had fallen asleep. A look of adoration crossed the man's face and he kissed the child awake. Its eyes focused him with difficulty, its face struggled into a smile, then down went the head again upon his shoulder. In Spain children seem to be treated either as dolls or adults.

As I neared my hotel I became conscious of a whispering shadow beside me and there before me, moving with me, was another of those horrid pens.

Eric Newby

(1919–2006)

When he was eighteen Eric Newby signed on to crew one of the last four-masted commercial sailing ships, the *Moshulu*. His eight-month round-trip from Europe to Australia provided material for his first travel book, *The Last Grain Race* (1956). Like Newby's other books, it told a tale of incredible adversity met with pluck and good humor. The survival skills that he learned on the *Moshulu* stood him in good stead during World War II when he was captured by the Nazis in Italy and then escaped, spending months on the run sheltered by sympathetic Italian villagers. He came out of the war with the Military Cross and a wife, Wanda, an Italian partisan of Slovenian extraction who had aided his escape.

Wanda and Eric Newby are one of the great travel teams. Eric is good-natured, optimistic, and sometimes illogical; Wanda is unsentimental, irascible, and practical. Her low grumble can be heard, sotto voce, throughout most of Newby's books—a counterpoint to his soaring tenor. They have traveled 1,200 miles down the Ganges (*Slowly Down the Ganges*, 1966), into Afghanistan (*A Short Walk in the Hindu Kush*, 1958), on the Trans-Siberian railroad (*The Big Red Train Ride*, 1985), and (well into their sixties) cycled through Ireland, in winter (*Round Ireland in Low Gear*, 1985).

"'You've had some pretty crazy ideas in your life, Newby,' Wanda said, rather unfairly I thought, while we were pouring water on our nettle stings, getting the herbage out of our transmissions, scraping cowshit off our trousers, swatting horseflies rendered torpid by overindulgence in our blood and generally smartening up, 'but this towpath idea of yours is the craziest of the lot.'"

In the 1980s the Newbys took on the Mediterranean, starting in Tuscany and working their way through Libya, Jerusalem, Istanbul, Naples, Montenegro, and Spain. Uninterested in the traditional holiday spots of the Riviera, they went for the tough places and ended up, exhausted, in Spain. This excerpt is from *On the Shores of the Mediterranean* (1984).

Eric Newby died in 2006 at home in England. Wanda survives him.

From ON THE SHORES
OF THE MEDITERRANEAN

HOLY WEEK IN SEVILLE

Late in the afternoon of Holy Saturday, 2 April 1983, the seventh and last day of Holy Week, we lay on a rooftop high above the Plaza Jerónimo de Córdoba near the Church of Santa Caterina in the eastern part of Seville, soaking up the sun which was shining down from a deep blue cloudless sky. Although it was still only the first week of April, here it was already as hot as English midsummer day.

We were exhausted. We had arrived in Seville seven days previously, early on the morning of Palm Sunday, the first day of Holy Week, in time to see the Procesión de Las Palmas, headed by the Archbishop and the Chapter carrying palms which they later placed on a *paso*, a processional float, with a statue on it depicting Christ on an ass entering Jerusalem.

This float, popularly known as La Borriquita, was escorted on its four-hour journey from the Church of San Salvador, where it was housed, to the Cathedral, and back again, by children wearing long white robes, belts of woven grass and hoods embellished with the red cross of Santiago. Many spectators carried olive branches as symbols of peace during this procession of the Archbishop.

During these seven days we had seen at least part, in some cases the major part, of fifty-one processions escorting one hundred and three separate *pasos*; fifty-two if the first part, the children's procession, is considered separate from the second part, the procession of the Sacred Christ of Love, Our Lady of Succour and St. James the Apostle, popularly known as El Amor, which is escorted by black-hooded brothers wearing the shield of their Hermandad or Cofradía, as these Brotherhoods are known. None of these processions had lasted for less than four hours. The longest, La Macarena, had lasted for twelve and a half hours, another, Jesús Cautivo, Jesus Captive, had lasted for twelve hours, and that of Cristo de la Sed, Christ of the Thirst, otherwise known as Nervión, after the Barrio, the quarter of Seville from which it comes, eleven and a half hours.

Night and day, except for an hour or so after midday, the great floats, all of them enormously heavy, embellished with silver, some decorated with flowers and bearing sumptuously dressed figures of the Virgin, costing thousands of pounds each year to decorate (the floats and figures are of inestimable worth, a Virgin's clothing and accessories alone valued at £100,000 [$140,000]), other effigies depicting events in the last six days of the life of Christ, had swayed through the streets, those of the Virgins like great ships illuminated by masses of candles, all borne on the backs of hordes of sweating porters invisible beneath the velvet draperies, some macabre, some beautiful, some very old, some made as late as the 1970s. If it rains during the procession, the floats are taken back either to their own churches or the nearest available one and the whole thing is called off.

All these figures, however old or new, have been carved and coloured by what can only be described as a school of artists who have always devoted themselves to producing what the Spanish call *simulacros imágenes*, with a skill that they have inherited from the craftsmen of Greece and Rome, who themselves inherited it from Babylon, Egypt and Phoenicia. This art form is based on such exact observation that the end products have somehow ceased to have the attributes of statuary as we think of it but rather resemble waxworks or dead bodies wearing clothing, for these figures, except those of Christ Crucified, are almost always clothed, usually very richly, with real not sculpted clothing.

Looking at these figures, so many of them similar in intention and execution, it is difficult for the layman to know whether he is looking at a work of the sixteenth century, such as the Cristo de Burgos, the oldest documented image, carved by Juan Bautista Vásquez in 1573, one by Marcos de Cabrera, carved in 1575, a seventeenth-century work by Juan de Mesa, Pedro Roldán or Juan Martínez Montañés, or a modern work, done in the fifties, such as the masterly figures carved for the procession of Jesús Cautivo by José Paz Vélez.

In the course of these fifty-two processions, besides seeing Jesus riding into Jerusalem, we had seen him instituting the Eucharist of the Last Supper, kissed by a Judas dressed in yellow, the colour of anathema, while watched by Peter, James, Thomas and John, and praying in the olive grove at Gethsemane.

Arrested, presented to the people by Pilate in the presence of
Claudia, his wife, and a band of Negro servants, Roman soldiers and
Jews. Slapped by a Jew at his trial in the palace of Annas, who is seen
seated on a throne flanked by a bearer of false witness, another Jew.
Sentenced to death surrounded by Roman soldiers and Jews, while
Pilate washes his hands and Claudia looks on thinking of something
else (Holy Week in Spain is something to be avoided by practising
Jews like the Plague). Mocked by Herod.

Scourged. Having the Crown of Thorns placed on his head.
Receiving the Cross and embracing it. Falling to the ground unable
to support its weight. Helped by Simon of Cyrene. Carrying the
Cross, consoling a number of women, among them St. Veronica,
who has just wiped his face with a cloth that miraculously retains his
image. Sitting on a rock while soldiers gamble for his robe. Waiting to
be crucified with the two thieves, meanwhile converting one of
them.

Crucified. Raised to a vertical position by four Jews. Speaking his
last seven words on the Cross, listened to by the Virgin of the Remedies, St. John the Evangelist and the Three Marys, Magdalene,
Salome and Cleophas. Dying on the Cross, with Mary Magdalene
kneeling at the foot of it. Having his side pierced by a soldier
mounted on horseback, while others watch. Dead on the Cross,
which rises from a bed of red carnations. Removed from the Cross
by Joseph of Arimathea and Nicodemus and slung in a sheet. Held
in her outstretched arms by the Virgin, dead below the empty Cross.
Taken to the burial grounds.

So many scourgings, so many crucifixions, so much agony. Too
much for us, day after day, although there is no commitment to witness any of it. The Brotherhoods gain nothing at all out of the hundreds of thousands of spectators. No collections appear to be made.
Only those who set up stands and provide chairs along the route,
presumably the Municipality, and those with good points of view to
offer, make anything out of it; these and the providers of food and
drink, sleeping accommodation and souvenirs. In this way the Semana Santa is rather like an extended coronation; but although there is
no obligation to watch the processions one can scarcely ignore them,
for they quarter the city with a persistence that is unparalleled else-

where in the Catholic world, even in Spain, outside Andalucía. Here, even the most devout have been known to confess to a surfeit.

Most difficult to become fed up with, and almost impossible for the Spaniards, who are virtually Mariolatrists, are the fifty-two Virgins we have seen up to now (there are more to come), most of them lone figures, all of them with their own floats, some of them accompanied on these always sumptuous vehicles by a diffident, usually moustached, disciple, John.

There are so many Virgins for both men and women to go overboard about, Virgins of Peace, the Broom Bush, Grace and Hope, the Star, Grief, Succour, of the Dew, the Mercies, Health, the Sadnesses, the Afflictions, of Guadelupe, of the Waters, of Grace and Protection, of the Abandoned Ones, of the Anguishes (two of them), the Incarnation, of the Candles, of the Sweet Name, the Sufferings, the Remedies, of Protection, the Palm Leaf, the Rule, of Charity, of the Palm, of the Good End, of the Angels, the Tears of Victory, of Mercy, of the Conception, of Great Pain and Grief, of Hope, of the Presentation, of Montserrat, of Great Pain in her Loneliness, of Protection, of the O (from antiphons, prayers sung on the Feast of Expectation, all of which begin "O, Maria . . ."), of Loreto, of Villaviciosa, of Pity and so on, almost *ad infinitum*. As Wanda said, something of a confession for a practising member of the Church to make, "I've had enough Virgins for a bit."

Even up here on the rooftops, almost level with the belfries of half a dozen churches, one or two of which had been built by the Moors as minarets, it was difficult to get away from them. From far below and far off, in the deep canyons which were the streets of a city that was still partly Moorish, with its pillared inner patios surrounding fountains that were for them as secretive as anything in Fez (that is if the occupants wanted to be secretive) rose the fanfares of bugles and trumpets and the rolling of drums which accompany the playing of the marches which are peculiar to Holy Week. In this case one of the bands was playing a march called the *Armagura* which was originally composed for the Crowned Virgin of Grief, La Armagura Coronada, and which is played so often that it might almost be regarded as the theme music of the Semana Santa.

These bands were accompanying two of the Brotherhoods that

had both set off at 3:30 P.M. from their respective churches where they kept their *pasos*. One, the Brotherhood of the Order of Servitas of Our Lady of Pain, Sacred Christ of Providence, Holy Mary of Loneliness and St. Mark the Evangelist, otherwise known as Los Servitas, was by this time, 5:00 P.M., one and a half hours outward bound from its mother church, the Capilla de los Dolores, near the Plaza de San Marcos in the Barrio of the same name, and was now about to enter the Plaza Encarnación on its convoluting course to the Cathedral, which it would reach, unless the procession in front of it was running late, around 6:50 P.M.

The other, La Esperanza de la Trinidad, the Sacramental Brotherhood of the Sacred Decree of the Holy Trinity, Sacred Christ of the Five Wounds, Sacred Mary of the Conception, whose church was La Trinidad in Calle María Auxiliadora off the ring road, was now in Calle Juan de Mesa, bound on what appeared to be a collision course with the floats of Los Servitas, an encounter that would take place, unless the organizers averted it, which they would probably succeed in doing, at the entrance to the Sierpes, the narrow tortuous Bond Street of Seville which is also at the beginning of what is known as the Carrera Official, Official Route, to the Cathedral, which every procession must follow whatever route it has taken previously. According to the ultra-Catholic, ultra-Establishment newspaper, the *ABC*, which I was at this moment trying to read, they were due to arrive at this point within five minutes of one another, around 6:15 P.M.

It was time to get ready for the procession of La Real Hermandad Sacramental del Santo Entierro de Nuestro Señor Jesucristo y María Santísima de Villaviciosa, which promised to be rather different from those we had previously seen, as I was to be a participant.

"Are you sure you want to go?" I said to Wanda. "You've seen so many."

"I'll tell you what," she said. "I may have had enough Virgins and crucifixions, and I don't care if I never eat another *pescado frito* or drink another glass of manzanilla, but I wouldn't miss you in the procession for anything."

With Wanda clasping the *laissez-passer* signed by the Hermano Mayor, the elected head of the Royal Sacramental Brotherhood of the Holy Burial of Our Lord Jesus Christ and Sacred Mary of Villaviciosa, popularly known as the Santo Entierro, the Holy Burial, in case I lost it, we set off on foot—which is the only way of arriving anywhere on time in Seville in Holy Week—for the church where its images are kept, the Convent of San Gregorio in Calle Alfonso XII.

It was from this same street, or rather a turning off it, that we had seen the floats of the Primitive Brotherhood of Our Father Jesus the Nazarene, the Holy Cross of Jerusalem and Sacred Mary, otherwise known as El Silencio, emerge from the Chapel of San Antonio Abad in the early morning, 1:05 A.M., on Good Friday, Viernes Santo Madraguarda.

The first of its two great *pasos* bore the figure, probably carved at the beginning of the seventeenth century, of Jesus the Nazarene embracing the cross which he had just received into his hands for the journey to Golgotha, with the blood streaming down his face from beneath the crown of thorns. The second bore the Virgin of the Conception standing on a bed of orange blossom, looking down on the dense crowd through a forest of white candles from beneath a gold-embroidered *palio*, a velvet canopy embellished with precious stones. Weeping, with the simulated tears coursing down her face which was framed in fabulous ivory lace beneath a golden crown, her immense embroidered velvet mantle streaming away behind her, she was apparently unconscious of the absurdly young-looking, conventionally moustached St. John who stood by her side looking anxiously at her as though she might faint away. And as the thirty-six Costaleros, the porters who were carrying it, invisible beneath the float, made the difficult shuffling turn towards Calle Alfonso XII, the *palio* and the twelve slender silver columns with its hangings began to oscillate, so that the whole construction appeared to be about to take off into the air.

This was the moment when in other processions of a more popular character, such as that of the Sacred Mary of Hope, known as La Esperanza de Triana, or that of her rival, the Sacred Mary of Hope known as La Macarena, the Virgin would have been greeted with cries of *"Guapa! O Guapaguapaguapa!"* ("O beautiful, beautiful, beautiful girl!") and the air would have been filled with fanfares and the rolling of drums. But because this was El Silencio, the Silent, the oldest of all but one of the Cofradías in Seville, founded in 1340, all that was heard was what are known as the Whistles of Silence, a series of eerie sixteenth- and seventeenth-century airs rendered on oboes, bassoons and clarinets.

Then the *paso* had come to a halt and someone had begun to sing a *saeta*, launching it, like the arrow from which it takes its name, from a balcony high overhead, a form of *cante hondo* and a more austere, ancient form of the flamenco which is itself Andalusian. The origins of the *saeta* have been sought, largely unsuccessfully, among the Moors, the Jews, the gypsies and in the Christian liturgy. They are songs which express faith, hope, desire, remorse, repentance and, above all, love. An unearthly performance which here in Seville during Holy Week is received either with extravagant enthusiasm or with derision, according to whether it is approved or not approved. There is no middle way.

Then the Capataz, the foreman of the Costaleros, dressed in a black suit, banged with a gavel on a metal plaque set on the first of the two *pasos*, the one with Jesus the Nazarene embracing the Cross, at the same time shouting, "*Elevar!*" and when the Costaleros had raised it had banged on it again, this time with the words "*Adelante! Marcha!*" ("Go on! Forward march!"), and the forty-two Costaleros, having stood up with the dreadful load poised on the napes of their necks, moved forward, together with two files of Nazarenos, the name applied to members of the Brotherhood who were taking part in the procession, wearing black hoods and tunics, wide belts woven from esparto grass and carrying purple candles.

Then the second float was raised and set in motion, that of the Virgin of the Conception and St. John, escorted by Nazarenos carrying white candles and preceded by a Hermano, a brother, bearing a drawn sword, a warning that all the members of this Brotherhood are dedicated to defend the doctrine of the Immaculate Conception, even at the cost of their lives, and were so-dedicated centuries before it became dogma. Then the Whistles of Silence began again and the procession swayed out of sight.

*　　　*　　　*

There was an elegant crowd in the Convent of San Gregorio when we reached it around six o'clock. There were young men in dark suits and black ties and white collars who looked as if they might be bankers. (There is in fact a Brotherhood largely made up of bank employees, Our Father Jesus before Annas, Sacred Christ of the Great Pain, and Holy Mary of the Sweet Name, popularly and perhaps appropriately known as La Bofetada, The Slap, also as the Dulce Nombre, Sweet Name.) Or they could have been accountants, *negociantes de vino*, landowners, lawyers on the way up. Even those who looked as if they might still be on the lowest rungs of whatever ladder they were on, showed unmistakable signs that they would eventually rise to the top of it providing they didn't make a boob of whatever ritual they might be called upon to carry out, in this, La Real Hermandad Sacramental del Santo Entierro de Nuestro Señor Jesucristo y María Santísima de Villaviciosa.

And there were older men wearing morning coats and the sort of grumpy expressions that seem to come as second nature to members of the Spanish upper crust, with the medallions of the Hermandad slung round their necks. They were already at the top, presidents of corporations, and that was what they looked like; one or two of them sufficiently groggy-looking to make one think that they might suddenly fall off their particular ladder, thus giving younger members a chance to go up a rung or two.

Conspicuous among this resplendent band, the younger of whom had not yet started to change into their ceremonial gear, were the wives and girl friends, all dressed up to the nines, some also in black, but all subfusc and as smart as guardsmen. In fact the whole thing was reminiscent of a gathering of officers and their girl friends and madams in the Guards Chapel for a memorial service. They certainly did not look like the sort of women who were employed to dress and undress the Virgin before and after the procession, and they were not, this delicate task being entrusted to those who are usually themselves virgins, but of a certain age. No man is permitted to take this liberty, not even a priest.

This was a Brotherhood of the Establishment, the oldest of all the Brotherhoods of Seville, founded in 1248 by King Ferdinand III of Castile. Known as El Santo, although he was not canonized until

1671 and twenty years after his death, Ferdinand was a Catholic ruler of such extraordinary religious zeal that he not only helped to pile the faggots around the followers of the Albigensian heresy who were sentenced by an early form of Inquisition to suffer the equivalent of the auto-da-fé, but himself applied the torch to them with his own hands. He founded the Brotherhood three hundred years before the Semana Santa began to be celebrated as it is today, which was in the sixteenth century, in order that his newly liberated subjects might have their faith reinforced by an annual procession. The second most ancient of the Brotherhoods of Holy Week was El Silencio, which was founded on 14 March 1340, in what are known as the Carnestolendas, those last three days of carnival when the prohibition against eating meat becomes imminent with the onset of Lent. It was founded with the intention of perpetuating the memory of the journey to Calvary and at that time and for long afterwards its members carried crosses, walked barefoot and wore crowns of thorns, practices which together with flagellation and the wearing of chains did not become extinct among some penitents until after the last war, although all the Brotherhoods always have a number of voluntary penitents who still carry heavy crosses and walk barefoot. The members of El Silencio, by virtue of their devotion to Jesus the Nazarene, were known as Nazarenos, the name by which all members of Brotherhoods who take part in the processions of Holy Week in memory of the penitential progression of Christ to Calvary are known, and notwithstanding the existence of the Brotherhood of Santo Entierro, which pre-dates it by nearly a hundred years, El Silencio is known as Madre y Maestra, Mother and Mistress, of all the Hermandades or Cofradías which make up the Brotherhoods of Seville.

Soon after six o'clock those members of the Santo Entierro who were going to take part in the procession began to transform themselves into Nazarenos in the sacristy of the convent which belongs to the Padres Mercedarios, the Mercedarians, the Fathers of the Order of St. Mary. They put on their long black tunics, attaching the long black sleeves, which were separate, with safety pins, of which there were not enough to go round until someone was sent out to buy some. Then they rolled up their trousers so that they would not show below the hems of their tunics, for although the legs of the trousers must not be seen the trousers must not be taken off, as I was told. A host of Nazarenos, emulating the journey to Calvary and escorting the Virgin of Villaviciosa without trousers, would be not only unthinkable but positively scandalous.

When all this was done to their satisfaction, they scrutinized themselves in the one clouded mirror with which the sacristy was provided, crowding round it rather like model girls taking a last look at themselves before beginning to show a spring collection. Then they donned the immensely tall black pointed hoods, which completed the disguise, turning them in an instant from keen, conservative, ambitious young men into strange, unearthly, eerie figures, with only the eyes flickering behind the twin eyeholes in the hoods to show that hidden behind them was not some sort of foul fiend but a human being. These were the Nazarenos. In a sense they were Penitentes; but the real Penitentes wore hoods that hung loose down their backs, walked barefooted and carried heavy wooden crosses on their shoulders.

Of all the Brotherhoods the Santo Entierro was the smallest. Altogether it only had 100 members and of these 80 were taking part in the procession. Some Brotherhoods were enormous. La Estrella, founded in 1566 by shipyard workers of Seville, Cadiz and other ports trading with the New World, had 2,260 brothers of whom 1,000 Nazarenos took part in the procession; El Gran Poder, 4,894 brothers with almost a thousand participants; La Macarena had 5,893 members, 1,007 of whom were Nazarenos; La Esperanza de Triana 3,542 brothers, 800 of whom were Nazarenos.

It was now 6:25 P.M. In five minutes the procession was due to begin. It was a strange scene. The body of the church was now crowded with Nazarenos, some swinging thuribles of incense, some carrying wands and silver crosses or else lighting their big four-foot-long candles, barefooted Penitentes trying the weight of their heavy crosses and the ninety-six Costaleros (others were in reserve) of the Cuadrilla de Domingo Rojas. It was they who would carry the three floats of the Brotherhood. Rough-looking members of the working class, dressed in white vests and wearing canvas shoes, some of them bottle-nosed, some with huge paunches, they were the sort of men who until the introduction of containers and automation into the port area of the city had earned their living as stevedores. What they did now, apart from lugging the *pasos* of El Santo Entierro round Seville once a year, was unclear. Perhaps they had been declared redundant, as had the stevedores at Naples and almost everywhere else, and given such massive severance pay that they no longer had to bother. Or perhaps they were members of a union who were unsack-able even if their jobs had disappeared. Whatever they were, they were not the kind of men of whom I was anxious to ask such questions.

On their heads they wore turbans of white cloth wound in such a way that a thick pad, sometimes stuffed with sand and sawdust, protected the nape of the neck on which almost the entire weight of the enormously heavy *paso* has to be supported. The weight is taken on a wooden bar, one of a number of such bars beneath the float, one behind the other, sufficient for whatever number of men are needed to carry it, which varies between twenty-five and forty-eight and exceptionally, to carry the huge first float of the Brotherhood of Sacred Christ of Exaltation and Our Lady of Tears, known as Los Caballos, fifty-four men. These headcloths gave the Costaleros a distinctly biblical air, but of those who mocked the Saviour rather than of those who supported him. Paid to do this work, presumably handsomely, they were a race apart. Few members of the Brother-hood appeared to take much notice of them, but nevertheless they were the most important participants in the entire procession, for without them the floats could not form part of it. They well deserved whatever they earned, for however thick the wrappings, by the time they returned to the church, around a quarter-to-eleven that night, many of them would have deep wounds in the backs of their necks.

In recent years it has become so difficult to recruit Costaleros, and so expensive, that the majority of the Brotherhoods now employ their own members to carry the *pasos*. It was difficult to imagine the brothers of the Santo Entierro agreeing to do this but as it would be impossible anyway, in a Brotherhood numbering only one hundred members, the question does not arise.

One of the first Cofradías to carry its own float was the very large

Brotherhood of the Christ of the Good Death (de la Buena Muerte), otherwise known as Los Estudiantes, founded in 1924 by professors and students of Seville University which is housed in what used to be the Royal Tobacco Factory, an immense eighteenth-century building and the scene of the first act of Bizet's *Carmen*. There is a Cofradía of Tobacco-workers, Las Cigarreras, Our Father Jesus Tied to the Column, and Holy Mary of Victory, founded in 1562, which had for its head, its Hermano Mayor, King Alfonso XIII, grandfather of the present King Juan Carlos, who until his abdication in 1930 himself used to take part in the procession. They keep their two floats in the Chapel of the New Tobacco Factory, on the other side of the river in the district called Los Remedios. There is also a Brotherhood of Gypsies, Los Gitanos, whose women dance the flamenco outside their church of San Román while waiting for the *pasos* bearing Christ walking towards Calvary and the Virgin of the Anguishes to appear; of Negroes, Los Negritos, formed in 1390 by a group of black Africans, although there are very few black Africans now; two Brotherhoods of Bullfighters, one, El Baratillo, named after its church at the bull-ring, the other San Bernardo. There is a Brotherhood of Bakers, Los Panaderos, and of Hotel and Restaurant Workers, known as Santa María. There is even a Brotherhood of Judges, Lawyers, and members of the Guardia Civil, the Siete Palabras, The Seven Words; and of Travel Agents, Our Father Jesus of Health and Good Voyage, known as Buen Viaje.

High overhead, dominating everything else in the chapel of the Convent of San Gregorio, were the three floats of the Santo Entierro. The first, La Muerte, otherwise known as La Canina, represents the Triumph of the Holy Cross over Sin and Death. At the foot of the now-vacant cross, with the ladders used to lower the body of the dead Christ from it still in position and with long strips of funereal drapery hanging from it, a skeleton, Death, sits on a globe of the world which is enfolded by a serpent bearing in its mouth an apple, the emblem of Original Sin, Death itself in an attitude of despair and dejection, its skull bent, supported by a skeletal hand. This, the most macabre of all the *pasos*, made its first appearance in 1693 and this present skeleton was carved in 1829 by Juan de Astorga. Among all the 112 *pasos* paraded by the fifty-six Brotherhoods in Holy Week,

La Muerte is unique, the only one that has this particular allegorical character.

The second *paso* bears La Urna, Cristo Yacente, Christ Recumbent in a great gilded, crystal panelled, Gothic casket, wearing only a loin-cloth. The figure was carved in the seventeenth century by Juan de Mesa. This is the Santo Entierro, the Holy Burial, from which the Brotherhood takes its name.

The third and last *paso* carries El Duelo, the Mourning. The figure of the Virgin of Villaviciosa carved by Antonio Cardoso Quirós in 1691, tearful, with head bowed, wears a golden halo instead of a crown, a black mantle embroidered with gold thread and carries in her hands the Crown of Thorns. With her are John the Evangelist, St. Joseph of Arimathea, Nicodemus and the Three Marys, carved at the same time as La Muerte by Juan de Astorga.

At half past six the great doors of the Convent were flung open and, together with some half dozen Nazarenos, some carrying red candles, one, Guillermo Mira Abaurrea, the Diputado Mayor of the Brotherhood, a tall imposing figure, carrying the leading cross of the Brotherhood, I emerged in the beautiful soft evening light of Seville in spring into a street packed with people who miraculously gave way as we advanced towards them, making a passage for us.

Meanwhile the Costaleros waited invisible beneath the *pasos*. Then the Capataz banged on the metal plaque with his gavel, at the same time shouting, "*Elevar!*" and forty-two Costaleros struggled to their feet beneath their macabre load, bearing the first of the three *pasos*, La Muerte. Then he banged again, this time shouting, "*Adelante! Marcha!*" and they began to shuffle forward. The upright of the empty cross was higher than the archway of the church door and they only cleared it because they bent their knees in what must have been an agonizing position, bowed beneath the awful weight of the *paso*. Then it, too, was in the open air with its funereal hangings moving in the light air and with the skeleton's ribs trembling horribly. There were none of the cheers that would have greeted the successful accomplishment of such a difficult manoeuvre had this been a less austere, more popular float, such as one of those of the Triana or La Macarena. Instead, as had been El Silencio, it was greeted with silence. You cannot cheer Death, however much you might welcome him. In the 733rd year of its existence the procession of the Santo Entierro was once more on its way.

The main body of the procession had been waiting in the street and now the first part of it formed behind La Muerte. This was composed of hooded Nazarenos from twenty-seven of the fifty-two Cofradías and Hermandades which had already passed through the Cathedral in Holy Week, each in the costume of his Brotherhood, the youngest of these being the Brotherhood of Nuestro Padre Jésus Despojado de Sus Vestiduras, Christ despoiled of his Clothing, which was only 13 years old. The oldest, Los Negritos, was 584 years old.

The Nazarenos were dressed in white and purple for Christ, white and blue for the Virgin, white and crimson, cream with black facepieces, purple with the cord belt of the Franciscans, white with woven belts of gold cord, and in the black of the Nazarenos of the Gran Poder and Santa Cruz.

I never saw the procession. I was in the worst place to see any procession, in it and at the front of it. I never even saw La Urna or El Duelo leave the Convent, so I do not know what sort of welcome they got from the crowd, whether cheers or silence, for by that time I was already far away, beginning the Carrera Oficial, moving ghostlike through the Calle Sierpes which in places is so narrow that, with chairs placed on either side for spectators, each of which costs 220 pesetas, it fits the processions closely round the hips.

I didn't see the members of the Council or General of Hermandades and Cofradías, the representative of the Comendador of the Order of Mercy, Padre Luis Cid, the Censor of the Order, or the President of the Council of Cofradias, José Sánchez Dubé, or the Municipal Band, directed by Maestro José Albero Francés, although I certainly did hear it when it entered La Campana, the big square before the Sierpes, when it struck up the march *Cristo Yacente*, from its position behind La Urna con El Cristo Yacente, when it practically took the tiles off the roofs.

Neither did I see the acolytes dressed in eighteenth-century clothing who were carrying a black canopy raised on silver poles in respect for the dead Christ in La Urna. Neither did I see the troop of Roman soldiers with plumed helmets who preceded it; nor the representa-

tives of the Real Maestanza (whatever that is); the Delegate of the
Government of Andalucía (Leocadio Marín); the Second in Command of the Military Government (General Juan Ollero); the President of the Sala de lo Contencioso, Fernando Rubiales, representing
the Audencia Territorial; the Chief Inspector of Taxes, Hipólito
Hernández; nor the Rector of the University, Guillermo Jiménez
Sánchez. Nor did I see Fernando de Queral Müller, Captain-General
of the Second Air Region nor his Band and Guard of Honour; he
was taking part in the procession as representative of King Juan
Carlos. (By a rule of the Brotherhood promulgated in 1805, future
kings of Spain would automatically assume the title of Hermano
Mayor. In 1940 General Franco took part in the procession, having
interpreted the rule of the Brotherhood perhaps too literally.) Nor
did I see that indefatigable figure, the Archbishop of Seville, Mon-
señor Carlos Amigo Vallejo, or the Mayor of Seville, Luis Urfiuela
Fernández, or the members of the Council of the Brotherhood,
although I had already seen them, the men at the top of the ladder,
in the church before we left. Nor did I see the officials of the Municipal and Provincial Governments of Seville, but I didn't feel any the
worse off for that.

Well, what did I see as a pseudo-Nazareno, now one of the sup-
porters of this Real Hermandad Sacramental del Santo Entierro, this
Brotherhood with its massive display of temporal and spiritual
power which had kindly provided me with their *laissez-passer*, as I
walked, one of the front-runners of the procession? I saw a sea of
people in front of me which I now knew would open up to let me
through without the aid of policemen or the Guardia Civil, would
part like the waters of the Red Sea before the Children of Israel, in
the circumstances perhaps an unfortunate simile, as I drew near
them.

What did they feel, what were they thinking about, these thousands of people, the adventurous people up trees and lampposts, the
ladies in mantillas and tall combs on the balconies, some of whom
would have been well advised to forgo this way of dressing in which
success and failure is measured by a hair's breadth, the bourgeoisie
sitting in the seats in the Sierpes, those members of the Establishment not taking part in the processions who were sitting in the boxes

faced with red velvet, outside the Casa del Ayuntamiento, the City Hall? What were they thinking about, I wondered, making the most of this heaven-sent gift of anonymity, seeing the Sevillans crossing themselves, drinking beers and manzanillas, picking at their *tapas*, the snacks that come with the drinks, picking their noses, flirting—all in the beautiful Sevillan gloaming? What are *you* all thinking about, I wondered, looking in through what would normally have been an expanse of plate glass, now opened up for the occasion, into a fashionable men's club in the Sierpes, face to face with its assembled members gazing incuriously out at me and the procession, a band of grumpy-looking General Francos, elegantly swathed in dark grey flannel and Harris tweed. Was this the same club referred to as "Les Laboureurs," the Labaradori, I wondered, that Nancy George, writing in French, looked into through a similar open window in Holy Week, 1931? "The Labourers have one thing in common," she wrote. "They do not labour. It is the best known of all the clubs, the most aristocratic, its members follow the Christ of the Gran Poder barefooted and their wives, filled with ennui, leave them at this hour to run around in their sumptuous automobiles." Well, if this was what they were still up to, no wonder their husbands looked grumpy.

Such a procession as this was very restful to take part in, at least for the hooded Nazarenos, much less so for the barefooted Penitentes lugging their heavy crosses, but nothing like as heavy as the Cross Christ carried, and much much less for the wretched Costaleros. Hooded, a unique anonymity is conferred on the wearer. Forbidden to speak, a merciful prohibition, the only external distractions are the small boys and girls who continually demand wax from your candle to add to what by now at the end of Holy Week amounts to a large ball of the stuff, and occasionally a girl comes very close who is either brazen or genuinely attempting to identify a friend or relation. The only other obligation a Nazareno has, an unofficial one, is to distribute sweets, of which he should have laid in a large store before leaving on his journey, to children or anyone else who takes his fancy. For the rest of the time he is a privileged voyeur, a ghost arrayed in ghostly clothing.

Halts were frequent. This was because the Costaleros were only able to carry their *pasos* for a comparatively short distance before being allowed to sink down on the road for an obligatory rest. Then they were brought water by an *aguador*, a water carrier, who would lift up the velvet hangings which concealed them from view and give them a drink from an earthenware pitcher. Sometimes during one of these halts one or two of them would rush off to a bar to drink a couple of beers in quick succession and relieve themselves, while others, either overcome by heat or worn down by the enormous weights they were called on to carry, were replaced by reservists.

Our procession was held up because the procession in front of ours, La Esperanza de la Trinidad, was behind time, having been on the road three hours longer than ours. This was because they could not leapfrog over the procession in front of them, that of Los Servitas, which was also running late. These were the two Brotherhoods whose bands we had heard trumpeting away up on the roof in the afternoon. And because of all this we of the Santo Entierro were impeding the progress of the fifty-sixth and last procession, the Papal and Royal Sacramental Brotherhood of Our Lady of Rocamadour, Blessed Souls and Ancient Brotherhood of Nazarenes of Our Lady of Loneliness, La Soledad, which had nothing behind it to hold up. For this was the last procession of Holy Week. There is, in fact, another procession on the morning of Resurrection Sunday, El Resucitado, but it is a new procession, its first appearance was in 1982, and it is not really part of Holy Week.

Now we paced solemnly through the Plaza San Francisco, otherwise Plaza de la Falange, where the top brass were sitting in stands draped in red and no one was going exactly crazy about our austere procession, and on into the Avenida José Antonio and the Avenida Queipo de Llano, otherwise Avenida de la Constitución (where it got the same reception), wishing that the administration would decide once and for all what they are going to call their streets. The vast bulk of the Cathedral was beginning to loom ahead on the port bow, and the sun was sinking swiftly, for it was now long after eight. It illuminated the float ahead already lit by innumerable candles, which was carrying the beautiful Virgin of Esperanza, the masterpiece of Juan de Astorga, as it halted at the junction of the Alemanes, on the north side of the Cathedral, with Calle García de Vinuesa, the way down to the bull-ring and the Guadalquivir, evoking enthusiastic cries and applause as its Costaleros executed a sort of side step, making the slender silver poles supporting her green and gold embroidered velvet canopy shiver like aspens in a breeze.

How would they have looked at me and any companions I might have had, these people of Seville, if we had been Jews or Moors, the Jews symbols of wealth, the Moors of skill in agriculture, on our way to the Quemadero, the burning place of the heretics in the Prado de San Sebastián, the flat plain beyond the southern walls where the auto-da-fé, the execution of the sentence of the Inquisition, was carried out now by the Dominican inquisitors, the instruments of the Holy Office who would have wrung the confessions from us in the Moorish citadel at Triana beyond the bridge, but by the civil power?

Would they have done what they had done today as El Santo Entierro went by, crossed themselves, shed a tear, applauded, picked at their noses or at their *tapas*, continued to sip their manzanillas, climbed trees to see us, put on their best clothes for the event, while we passed in procession dressed in the *san benite*, the yellow fool's caps and tunics of the condemned heretics, the colour of Judas Iscariot, the colour in those days of the dress of the common criminal on his way to execution?

What I was taking part in here in Seville—and I was impressed by what I was taking part in—is something far older than the processions of the Christian Church. The processions of Holy Week are not only an echo of pagan antiquity. They are a direct continuation, thinly disguised, of the processions of images of gods and goddesses, carried on the shoulders of common men in the ancient world. In ancient times this perhaps was Tarshish, the furthest known habitation in Europe, at the western end of the Mediterranean, the uttermost part of the known world in Europe, as was Morocco in Africa, a place which the Phoenicians wished and tried to keep secret to themselves.

Here, in Spain, these processions continued as a Christian ritual under the Visigoths until they were interrupted by the Moors, but they started up again long before the Muslims left the peninsula for ever.

For us, watching them take place, and at the same time reading accounts of similar processions in the ancient world, time was annihilated. One might have been witnessing the procession of the Phoenician Astarte, otherwise the Egyptian Ashtaroth, goddess of the heavens, the Roman Juno Coelestis, her name everywhere signifying star, imported here in Seville from the eastern Mediterranean to comfort those Phoenician traders who were so far from home. Just as she was worshipped and carried through the streets crowned with stars, as are the Virgins today, in Babylon, Tyre, Sidon, Memphis, Carthage, Rome, in the same way as was the Sacred Boat of Osiris, the Shrine of Isis, the Ark of the Covenant of the Jews, wherever their temples were to be found, so she was here as late as the third century A.D.

With a truly dramatic flourish the last two *pasos* of La Esperanza de la Trinidad was made to perform a ninety-degree turn by her Costaleros and the Virgin of Hope of the Trinity went swaying up the ramp into the Cathedral through the Puerto San Miguel at the south-west end to the accompaniment of drums and bugles and trumpets and the applause of what here was a vast assembled multitude. We followed her in shortly afterwards with La Muerte, but again it was very noticeable that Death did not have the box office appeal of Virgins, especially Virgins of the calibre of Our Lady of Hope of the Trinity.

The Cathedral was built on the site of the mosque of the Almohad Sultan, Abu Yousef Mansur. He started to build it in 1163 and completed it fifteen years later, in 1178. In 1248 Seville was reconquered by the Christians, and for the next 153 years it was a Christian place of worship. Then, in 1401, it was pulled down and the present building constructed. Nothing was left of the mosque of Abu Yousef to remind the Christian worshipper of the place where his apostatized forefathers had worshipped, suitably circumcised, except for the Patio de los Naranjos, the rather sad-looking Court of Oranges, in which they had carried out their ritual ablutions at what was a fountain originally built by the Visigoths, and the Giralda, the great minaret, soaring more than 300 feet into the heavens, now part of Captain-General Müller's airspace.

Here in Seville a clean sweep was made, and the unknown French architect who built the Cathedral (the influence is said to be that of

St. Ouen at Rouen, one of the most beautiful Gothic churches ever built) carried out the resolution made by the Chapter at its first conference, "to construct a church such and as good that it never should have its equal. Let Posterity," said its members, "when it admires it complete, say that those who dared to devise such a work must have been mad."

And indeed, standing in it before La Muerte among the guttering red candles borne by the Nazarenos of El Santo Entierro, all of whose *pasos* were now stationed in it, and those members of all the other Cofradías who accompanied them, awaiting the Blessing at the Station of the Holy Sacrament, hearing the murmurings of what was a vast congregation within its great choir and its chapels, all largely invisible in the ever-increasing murk—for it was now nine o'clock—it would have been difficult not to agree that they had triumphantly succeeded.

And now the Capataces of all three *pasos*, La Muerte, La Urna and El Duelo, banged with their gavels on the metal plaques, and once more the Costaleros, who had profited by this long halt to rush off and relieve themselves in a hard-to-find lavatory in a sacristy on the south side, raised themselves up, some of them bleeding from deep wounds beneath their neck pads, and to the shouts of "*Adelante! Marcha!*" surged forward yet again as they had done innumerable times in the last two hours and a half.

It was now 9:05 P.M. The *pasos* of the Santo Entierro were once more back on time and they had only another hour and ten minutes before re-entering the Convent at 10:15 P.M., for this is a very short procession and all the processions of Holy Saturday have to be back in their temples before Resurrection Sunday begins at midnight.

I went forward with them, the Nazarenos, the *aguador*, the man who walks behind each float with a ladder in case a sudden puff of wind snuffs out the candles, the Penitentes with their crosses causing them real discomfort now, as they intended they should, some of them deliberately carrying them with the lower part of the cross, instead of the point of balance, on their shoulders.

Then we went through the Puerto de los Palos at the east end of the Cathedral into the Plaza de la Virgen de los Reyes with its Christian and Moorish monuments, where the crowds were waiting in the soft night air, leaving behind us nothing but the wax we had spilled on the stone slabs, as had every Nazareno here and throughout the city in the last seven days and nights. Tomorrow or the day after, no doubt it would be scraped away. Tomorrow afternoon, the afternoon of Easter Sunday, the bullfights would begin, and with them another celebration, the Feria, with dancing and music and feasting and pretty girls carried side-saddle behind their men on horseback. And it would be as if we and our procession, and all the other processions, like the Muslims, had never existed.

Kate O'Brien

(1897-1974)

Born in Ireland and convent-educated, Kate O'Brien was one of nine children. She studied English and French at University College, London, and then at the age of twenty-three took a job as a governess for a family in Bilbao. From then on Spain had a special place in her heart, and she returned to it often in her work. She wrote, "I was pleased in my roots with the unexpected Spain I had found—and glad to the extent that I would not realize for years to have opened up acquaintance with a country I was to love very much . . ." Returning to London, she married a Dutch journalist, but the union lasted less than a year.

Best known as a novelist, O'Brien tread a dangerous literary and political path and her work was condemned both in her native Ireland and in Spain. Her third novel, *Mary Lavelle* (1936), was banned for obscenity in Ireland as it involved both extramarital love and lesbianism. Set in Madrid and Toledo, it is the story of a young Irishwoman who becomes a governess for a wealthy Spanish family, a clear parallel to O'Brien's own life. Her next book, *Farewell Spain* (1937), from which this excerpt is taken, is an impressionistic travelogue, written just as Spain was about to descend into political collapse. O'Brien was so critical of the Franco regime that she was banished from that country for twenty years.

Although she could not travel to her beloved Spain, it continued to be part of her work. Her most successful novel, *That Lady* (1946), details the romance of Ana de Mendoza and Antonio Pérez in the sixteenth-century court of Philip II of Spain; it was later made into a Broadway play and ensured O'Brien a measure of financial security. She bought a house in Ireland, but sold it in 1960 and never returned to her homeland. O'Brien died in England at seventy-six.

From FAREWELL SPAIN

LA MONTAÑA

And as I go I shall say a few words, well or ill-chosen, on methods of travel in the Peninsula. Words of advice, I mean. For long, main-route journeys one must naturally take the train. And the trains are all right. Perhaps they are not so fast as all that, but they serve. They are roomy and have fine, big windows. You can get good meals on the trains—good, that is, as railway meals are judged anywhere. And do not think it a waste of time to travel by day. It is never a waste of time to watch the Spanish landscape marching past. Even if the weather is very hot, travel by day. At any cost it's a pity to move about Spain in the dark. If you sit still on the shadier side—the trains are very rarely crowded—you won't die of the heat. And even if you do, your last sight of earth will have been very noble. But the conductor won't let you die. At every stop he'll fetch you the coldest, loveliest beer you've ever gulped. But you must offer him a cigarette, and indicate that you would be honoured if he would smoke it with you in your carriage and talk with you a little. For among the well-bred peoples of this Peninsula there is, in everyday intercourse, none of that "Colonel's lady and Judy O'Grady" *embarras* that still goes on in other quarters of the globe. So far as one can make out there never has been in Spain. Never mind the trouble that exists there now—the class war. It is indeed a class war, and no error. But its cause, its causes, have always been vigorously living too, side by side with this other thing, this natural ease which every individual feels in the company of every other. The wars, injustices, miseries and delays which too long have maddened Spain have never impinged, as it were, upon this deep individual sense of pride and its complementary courtesy, nor would it ever strike oppressor or oppressed that they might do so. It is a difficult thing to explain, but so are many Spanish paradoxes, which nevertheless remain true. Still it is as well for the socially inhibited Northerner to be prepared for the straightforward politeness of Spanish porters, washerwomen and newspaper boys. I once saw a very distinguished English female don nearly choke with stuttering embarrassment when an English countrywoman, providing an extempore meal during a car breakdown, asked her "If she wouldn't like a nice bit of lettuce to her tea?" Why that good idea should be so remote from the understanding of any healthy English scholar I don't know, but there are people who cannot, without grave risk, be even mildly surprised. So be warned—if the dirtiest and most illiterate old man in Santiago de Compostela (and he'll be dirty and illiterate) takes your bag from your lodging to the bus, at parting he will take your hand and shake it warmly and kindly in good-bye. That is, if he likes you. And no matter how exquisitely elegant you may look, he'll shake hands with you and pat your shoulder—if he likes you. If the *botones* of your hotel ("buttons," "bell-hop") sees you sitting bored in the empty verandah, he will come and sit with you and tell you interesting things about his life at home and his funny old grandmother, and will ask you questions about life in England. And if—as once actually happened to me—you are distressed by some news in a letter just collected at the Poste Restante, and are so indiscreet as to sit on a bench in a park and shed tears, a woman selling sweets will sit down beside you, give you a kiss and thrust a packet of burnt almonds into your hand.

But to return to my views on methods of travel. For distances that can be covered in two, three, or even four hours, always take an autobus in Spain. For one thing, they go all over the place and they're cheap. Most of them are quite comfortable, and, like the trains, they are rarely crowded. You'll strike up amusing acquaintanceships on them, though of course you'll do that on the trains, too. But in this very matter of going from Santander to Burgos. As the crow or the bus flies, it is, as far as I remember, an affair of three hours and about eighteen pesetas first class. Ten shillings. By train—well, I've forgotten the price, but the crazy mileage you cover makes it a great deal more—and it takes all day. Nine hours—or ten, I think. You jolt away down, hour after hour, to an astoundingly uninteresting place called Venta de Baños (Inn of Baths). There you can get out of your train—but *not* to take a bath. I can't imagine that anyone was ever so blithe as to take a bath at Venta. You spend two or maybe three hours in a bedraggled little garden café outside the station. (That café and one petrol pump are the whole of Venta.) There is certain to be a wedding party going on in the café. You take photographs of the whole party, by request, and write down all the addresses of the photographed. When this amusement palls you walk over to the station and re-consult your kindly porter about trains for Burgos. But he shakes an amused head at you. You try the *manzanilla* in the station canteen, but, after a bit, abandon it to the flies. You ask for the key of the *señoras* (or the *caballeros*, as the case may be). A senior official in gold braid crosses the line with you, key in hand. It will not turn in the lock. Some lesser officials arrive to advise. Some women arrive to assist. Some children have a try. Your porter tells you proudly that the children are his. Just as the door of the *señoras* is burst open, your train sails in. A mercy actually. You get to Burgos at dead of night— too late to see those lovely girlish spires rise lightly from amid shivering trees.

Meantime, as I counsel, my bus is rattling on. Up and down hills, through villages bitterly ennobled by centuries of starvation, over the river Paz, where delicious trout are to be caught, they tell me. The fields of maize look mostly dull and ugly, as cabbage-fields, with their repetitions of rose-curves, never look, but here and there, sloping oddly to the sun, they seem like fields of blue swords. Eucalyptus woods climb the hills gracefully, and groves of umbrella pines stand stylised and composed, all ready for John Nash. Rainy clouds race in from the north, from the sea; away ahead, west and south, the teeth of the great Picos glitter snowily.

The domestic architecture of these Cantabrian provinces is one of Spain's minor triumphs. Anyone travelling by road from Irun to Oviedo, or for that matter to Vigo, must be impressed by the beauty, harmonious variety and functional fitness of the older farmhouses, manors and cottages he will pass. Basque architecture has the most excellent mannerisms, and here in Montaña, where the weather is of the rainy, uncertain kind that is good for pasturage and mixed farming, how sane it seems to have kept faithful as the parish church to romanesque strength and sturdiness, alleviating it practically—since the sun does often come out and must be used and enjoyed—by purposeful suggestions of the sixteenth and seventeenth centuries; balconies, arcades and hooded courts. How faultless in these villages, against the grey, blue-grey and blue-green of the land, against the dead buff of the *Parroquia*, is the cottagers' centuries-old knack of mixing bluish whitewash and whitish blue! There are farm gateways to be observed in this region, there are cottage-porches overhanging *solanas*, which are so right and beautiful that, seeing their age and that inevitably they must soon be replaced, one groans in anxiety. For here in Spain too, and necessarily, they have the building fever, and have it as badly—I use the word with precision—as everywhere else. They are building deplorable houses all over the Peninsula—and even where they are building fairly good ones, they're not so hot, if you get me. We talk a great deal about functionalism nowadays, as if we had discovered it—God help us!—when all we are doing is to snaffle it. We think that a boot-factory erected in Vladivostok in 1936, granted that it looks and works exactly as a boot-factory is expected to, should be just as perfect a thing if erected in Torquay, did they happen to require a boot-factory there. We divorce the idea of function completely from its external conditions. And so we hope to internationalise, uniform and, I think, strait-jacket the world. God help us! Eighteenth-century Englishmen knew a good deal about the function of a house, for England. So, for Castile, did the feudal and renaissance Spanish lords. So do many twentieth-century Americans, and no doubt, if the world hangs on awhile, some more good ways of building houses for special conditions will be found. But I believe that there must be a limit to the number of ways in which a house, shop or garage should be designed, and so I dread the consequences of allowing peaceful regions all over the globe to be startled out of their traditional good sense by armies of mass-producing gimcrackers, who will blithely take away from the timid and the innocent in one generation conceptions which have stood up gently to hundreds of years, while giving them in return a few notions which very likely would be rubbish anywhere, and ten to one are rubbish as and where applied.

These people of the Montaña could very well build their own new houses now, as their ancestors did, if they were let alone. Not slavishly imitating, but carrying on in their own terms, without affectation, the Montaña idea of a suitable house. But there is not a vestige of a hope that they will do so. Horrors are springing up everywhere—so well-disseminated are all our rotten new ideas—horrors

and hybrids without health or steadiness or a vestige of grace or reju-
venation. Things made out of every kind of absurd brick and tile,
brought from God knows where to the land of granite and sandstone.

And now we are passing through Torrelavega—a little wild industrial town in a wide, wet valley. Practically owned by a Belgian firm
which extracts some chemical or other from the river-bed. The Belgian farm has built houses here for its Belgian clerks and foremen.
To make them feel more at home. Funny little rows of flat, thin
houses, of purply brick with slate-coloured shutters. Exactly such
small flat houses as you see from the train on the drearier outskirts of
Brussels and Antwerp. Houses built to front neatly on a neat street in
a neat little country. They look exiled and wretched here in this
muddy, fertile Spanish valley. Torrelavega itself is a poor and desperate place, but it is strongly built, its big square is comfortably arcaded,
its workmen's cafés are vast and warm. And I think that in winter,
when rain sweeps across this open stretch and plane-trees thrash on
roofs, the Belgians, slipping into their slight little houses out of the
mud, must suspect that the wild Spaniards, in their old shabby, thick-
walled houses, deep-porched and deep-windowed, are warmer and
more secure than they.

Anyway—we'll be at Santillana in a minute, where no one has laid
a stone upon a stone this many a day.

George Orwell

(1903–1950)

Born Eric Arthur Blair in Motihari, India, the son of a British civil servant, George Orwell took his pseudonym before the publication of *Down and Out in Paris and London* (1933), a description of his impoverished life in Britain and France. Orwell felt that his account of homelessness would embarrass his parents, whom he once described as "lower-upper-middle class." Orwell not only rejected their traditional values, but embraced radical socialism. During the Spanish Civil War, he enlisted as part of the Independent Labour Party contingent, a group of twenty-five Britons who supported the defeat of Franco and the overthrow of capitalism.

Homage to Catalonia (1937, from which this is excerpted) details Orwell's disillusionment with the Spanish Communist Party and his conversion to anti-Stalinism. He witnessed the communist suppression of the Workers' Party of Marxist Unification (P.O.U.M.). Nearly fatally wounded when he was shot through the neck, he barely escaped from Barcelona to France. In an introduction to *Homage to Catalonia*, Lionel Trilling wrote, "[Orwell] made no effort to show that his heart was in the right place, or the left place . . . He was interested only in telling the truth. Not very much attention was paid to the truth—his book sold poorly in England, it had to be remaindered, it was not published in America, and the people to whom it should have said most responded to it not at all." In 1946 Orwell wrote, "Every line of serious work that I have written since 1936 has been written, directly or indirectly, against totalitarianism and for democratic Socialism, as I understand it."

Although Orwell's health declined in the 1940s, he wrote his most enduring novels during this time: the allegorical *Animal Farm* (1944) and the dystopian *1984* (1949). The success of those novels provided Orwell with financial security for the first time. He died in 1950 from tuberculosis, probably contracted during his "down-and-out" years. At his request he was buried by Anglican rite. Orwell's epitaph reads, "Here lies Eric Arthur Blair."

From HOMAGE TO CATALONIA

In trench warfare five things are important: firewood, food, tobacco, candles and the enemy. In winter on the Zaragoza front they were important in that order, with the enemy a bad last. Except at night, when a surprise-attack was always conceivable, nobody bothered about the enemy. They were simply remote black insects whom one occasionally saw hopping to and fro. The real preoccupation of both armies was trying to keep warm.

I ought to say in passing that all the time I was in Spain I saw very little fighting. I was on the Aragon front from January to May, and between January and late March little or nothing happened on that front, except at Teruel. In March there was heavy fighting round Huesca, but I personally played only a minor part in it. Later, in June, there was the disastrous attack on Huesca in which several thousand men were killed in a single day, but I had been wounded and disabled before that happened. The things that one normally thinks of as the horrors of war seldom happened to me. No aeroplane ever dropped a bomb anywhere near me, I do not think a shell ever exploded within fifty yards of me, and I was only in hand-to-hand fighting once (once is once too often, I may say). Of course I was often under heavy machine-gun fire, but usually at longish ranges. Even at Huesca you were generally safe enough if you took reasonable precautions.

Up here, in the hills round Zaragoza, it was simply the mingled boredom and discomfort of stationary warfare. A life as uneventful as a city clerk's, and almost as regular. Sentry-go, patrols, digging; digging, patrols, sentry-go. On every hill-top, Fascist or Loyalist, a knot of ragged, dirty men shivering round their flag and trying to keep warm. And all day and night the meaningless bullets wandering across the empty valleys and only by some rare improbable chance getting home on a human body.

Often I used to gaze round the wintry landscape and marvel at the futility of it all. The inconclusiveness of such a kind of war! Earlier, about October, there had been savage fighting for all these hills; then, because the lack of men and arms, especially artillery, made any

large-scale operation impossible, each army had dug itself in and settled down on the hill-tops it had won. Over to our right there was a
small outpost, also P.O.U.M., and on the spur to our left, at seven
o'clock of us, a P.S.U.C. position faced a taller spur with several small
Fascist posts dotted on its peaks. The so-called line zigzagged to and
fro in a pattern that would have been quite unintelligible if every
position had not flown a flag. The P.O.U.M. and P.S.U.C. flags were
red, those of the Anarchists red and black; the Fascists generally flew
the monarchist flag (red-yellow-red), but occasionally they flew the
flag of the Republic (red-yellow-purple).* The scenery was stupendous, if you could forget that every mountain-top was occupied by
troops and was therefore littered with tin cans and crusted with dung.
To the right of us the sierra bent south-eastwards and made way for
the wide, veined valley that stretched across to Huesca. In the middle
of the plain a few tiny cubes sprawled like a throw of dice; this was
the town of Robres, which was in Loyalist possession. Often in the
mornings the valley was hidden under seas of cloud, out of which
the hills rose flat and blue, giving the landscape a strange resem-
blance to a photographic negative. Beyond Huesca there were more
hills of the same formation as our own, streaked with a pattern of
snow which altered day by day. In the far distance the monstrous
peaks of the Pyrenees, where the snow never melts, seemed to float
upon nothing. Even down in the plain everything looked dead and
bare. The hills opposite us were grey and wrinkled like the skins of
elephants. Almost always the sky was empty of birds. I do not think
I have ever seen a country where there were so few birds. The only
birds one saw at any time were a kind of magpie, and the coveys of
partridges that startled one at night with their sudden whirring, and,
very rarely, the flights of eagles that drifted slowly over, generally followed by rifle-shots which they did not deign to notice.

At night and in misty weather patrols were sent out in the valley
between ourselves and the Fascists. The job was not popular, it was
too cold and too easy to get lost, and I soon found that I could get

---

*An errata note found in Orwell's papers after his death: "Am not now completely
certain that I ever saw Fascists flying the republican flag, though I *think* they sometimes flew it with a small imposed swastika."

leave to go out on patrol as often as I wished. In the huge jagged ravines there were no paths or tracks of any kind; you could only find your way about by making successive journeys and noting fresh landmarks each time. As the bullet flies the nearest Fascist post was seven hundred metres from our own, but it was a mile and a half by the only practicable route. It was rather fun wandering about the dark valleys with the stray bullets flying high overhead like redshanks whistling. Better than nighttime were the heavy mists, which often lasted all day and which had a habit of clinging round the hill-tops and leaving the valleys clear. When you were anywhere near the Fascist lines you had to creep at a snail's pace; it was very difficult to move quietly on those hill-sides, among the crackling shrubs and tinkling limestones. It was only at the third or fourth attempt that I managed to find my way to the Fascist lines. The mist was very thick, and I crept up to the barbed wire to listen. I could hear the Fascists talking and singing inside. Then to my alarm I heard several of them coming down the hill towards me. I cowered behind a bush that suddenly seemed very small, and tried to cock my rifle without noise. However, they branched off and did not come within sight of me. Behind the bush where I was hiding I came upon various relics of the earlier fighting—a pile of empty cartridge-cases, a leather cap with a bullet-hole in it, and a red flag, obviously one of our own. I took it back to the position, where it was unsentimentally torn up for cleaning-rags.

I had been made a corporal, or *cabo*, as it was called, as soon as we reached the front, and was in command of a guard of twelve men. It was no sinecure, especially at first. The *centuria* was an untrained mob composed mostly of boys in their teens. Here and there in the militia you came across children as young as eleven or twelve, usually refugees from Fascist territory who had been enlisted as militiamen as the easiest way of providing for them. As a rule they were employed on light work in the rear, but sometimes they managed to worm their way to the front line, where they were a public menace. I remember one little brute throwing a hand-grenade into the dug-out fire "for a joke." At Monte Pocero I do not think there was anyone younger than fifteen, but the average age must have been well under twenty. Boys of this age ought never to be used in the front line, because they cannot stand the lack of sleep which is inseparable from trench warfare. At the beginning it was almost impossible to keep our position properly guarded at night. The wretched children of my section could only be roused by dragging them out of their dug-outs feet foremost, and as soon as your back was turned they left their posts and slipped into shelter; or they would even, in spite of the frightful cold, lean up against the wall of the trench and fall fast asleep. Luckily the enemy were very unenterprising. There were nights when it seemed to me that our position could be stormed by twenty Boy Scouts armed with air-guns, or twenty Girl Guides armed with battledores, for that matter.

At this time and until much later the Catalan militias were still on the same basis as they had been at the beginning of the war. In the early days of Franco's revolt the militias had been hurriedly raised by the various trade unions and political parties; each was essentially a political organization, owing allegiance to its party as much as to the central Government. When the Popular Army, which was a "non-political" army organized on more or less ordinary lines, was raised at the beginning of 1937, the party militias were theoretically incorporated in it. But for a long time the only changes that occurred were on paper; the new Popular Army troops did not reach the Aragon front in any numbers till June, and until that time the militia-system remained unchanged. The essential point of the system was social equality between officers and men. Everyone from general to private drew the same pay, ate the same food, wore the same clothes, and mingled on terms of complete equality. If you wanted to slap the general commanding the division on the back and ask him for a cigarette, you could do so, and no one thought it curious. In theory at any rate each militia was a democracy and not a hierarchy. It was understood that orders had to be obeyed, but it was also understood that when you gave an order you gave it as comrade to comrade and not as superior to inferior. There were officers and N.C.O.s, but there was no military rank in the ordinary sense; no titles, no badges, no heel-clicking and saluting. They had attempted to produce within the militias a sort of temporary working model of the classless society.

Of course there was not perfect equality, but there was a nearer approach to it than I had ever seen or than I would have thought conceivable in time of war.

But I admit that at first sight the state of affairs at the front horrified me. How on earth could the war be won by an army of this type? It was what everyone was saying at the time, and though it was true it was also unreasonable. For in the circumstances the militias could not have been much better than they were. A modern mechanized army does not spring up out of the ground, and if the Government had waited until it had trained troops at its disposal, Franco would never have been resisted. Later it became the fashion to decry the militias, and therefore to pretend that the faults which were due to lack of training and weapons were the result of the equalitarian system. Actually, a newly raised draft of militia was an undisciplined mob not because the officers called the privates "Comrade" but because raw troops are *always* an undisciplined mob. In practice the democratic "revolutionary" type of discipline is more reliable than might be expected. In a workers' army discipline is theoretically voluntary. It is based on class-loyalty, whereas the discipline of a bourgeois conscript army is based ultimately on fear. (The Popular Army that replaced the militias was midway between the two types.) In the militias the bullying and abuse that go on in an ordinary army would never have been tolerated for a moment. The normal military punishments existed, but they were only invoked for very serious offences. When a man refused to obey an order you did not immediately get him punished; you first appealed to him in the name of comradeship. Cynical people with no experience of handling men will say instantly that this would never "work," but as a matter of fact it does "work" in the long run. The discipline of even the worst drafts of militia visibly improved as time went on. In January the job of keeping a dozen raw recruits up to the mark almost turned my hair grey. In May for a short while I was acting-lieutenant in command of about thirty men, English and Spanish. We had all been under fire for months, and I never had the slightest difficulty in getting an order obeyed or in getting men to volunteer for a dangerous job. "Revolutionary" discipline depends on political consciousness—on an understanding of *why* orders must be obeyed; it takes time to diffuse this, but it also takes time to drill a man into an automaton on the barrack-square. The journalists who sneered at the militia-system seldom remembered that the militias had to hold the line while the Popular Army was training in the rear. And it is a tribute to the strength of "revolutionary" discipline that the militias stayed in the field at all. For until about June 1937 there was nothing to keep them there, except class loyalty. Individual deserters could be shot—were shot, occasionally—but if a thousand men had decided to walk out of the line together there was no force to stop them. A conscript army in the same circumstances—with its battle-police removed—would have melted away. Yet the militias held the line, though God knows they won very few victories, and even individual desertions were not common. In four or five months in the P.O.U.M. militia I only heard of four men deserting, and two of those were fairly certainly spies who had enlisted to obtain information. At the beginning the apparent chaos, the general lack of training, the fact that you often had to argue for five minutes before you could get an order obeyed, appalled and infuriated me. I had British Army ideas, and certainly the Spanish militias were very unlike the British Army. But considering the circumstances they were better troops than one had any right to expect.

Meanwhile, firewood—always firewood. Throughout that period there is probably no entry in my diary that does not mention firewood, or rather the lack of it. We were between two and three thousand feet above sea-level, it was mid-winter and the cold was unspeakable. The temperature was not exceptionally low, on many nights it did not even freeze, and the wintry sun often shone for an hour in the middle of the day; but even if it was not really cold, I assure you that it seemed so. Sometimes there were shrieking winds that tore your cap off and twisted your hair in all directions, sometimes there were mists that poured into the trench like a liquid and seemed to penetrate your bones; frequently it rained, and even a quarter of an hour's rain was enough to make conditions intolerable. The thin skin of earth over the limestone turned promptly into a slippery grease, and as you were always walking on a slope it was impossible to keep your footing. On dark nights I have often fallen half a dozen times in twenty yards; and this was dangerous, because it meant that the lock of one's rifle became jammed with mud. For days together clothes, boots, blankets and rifles were more or less coated with mud. I had brought as many thick clothes as I could carry, but many of the men were terribly underclad. For the whole garrison, about a hundred men, there were only twelve great-coats, which had to be handed from sentry to sentry, and most of the men had only one blanket. One icy night I made a list in my diary of the clothes I was wearing. It is of some interest as showing the amount of clothes the human body can carry. I was wearing a thick vest and pants, a flannel shirt, two pull-overs, a woollen jacket, a pigskin jacket, corduroy breeches, puttees, thick socks, boots, a stout trench-coat, a muffler, lined leather gloves, and a woollen cap. Nevertheless I was shivering like a jelly. But I admit I am unusually sensitive to cold.

Firewood was the one thing that really mattered. The point about the firewood was that there was practically no firewood to be had. Our miserable mountain had not even at its best much vegetation, and for months it had been ranged over by freezing militiamen, with the result that everything thicker than one's finger had long since been burnt. When we were not eating, sleeping, on guard or on fatigue-duty we were in the valley behind the position, scrounging for fuel. All my memories of that time are memories of scrambling up and down the almost perpendicular slopes, over the jagged lime-stone that knocked one's boots to pieces, pouncing eagerly on tiny twigs of wood. Three people searching for a couple of hours could collect enough fuel to keep the dug-out fire alight for about an hour. The eagerness of our search for firewood turned us all into botanists. We classified according to their burning qualities every plant that grew on the mountain-side; the various heaths and grasses that were good to start a fire with but burnt out in a few minutes, the wild rose-mary and the tiny whin bushes that would burn when the fire was well alight, the stunted oak tree, smaller than a gooseberry bush, that was practically unburnable. There was a kind of dried-up reed that was very good for starting fires with, but these grew only on the hill-top to the left of the position, and you had to go under fire to get them. If the Fascist machine-gunners saw you they gave you a drum of ammunition all to yourself. Generally their aim was high and the bullets sang overhead like birds, but sometimes they crackled and chipped the limestone uncomfortably close, whereupon you flung yourself on your face. You went on gathering reeds, however; nothing mattered in comparison with firewood.

Beside the cold the other discomforts seemed petty. Of course all of us were permanently dirty. Our water, like our food, came on mule-back from Alcubierre, and each man's share worked out at about a quart a day. It was beastly water, hardly more transparent than milk. Theoretically it was for drinking only, but I always stole a pannikinful for washing in the morning. I used to wash one day and shave the next; there was never enough water for both. The position stank abominably, and outside the little enclosure of the barricade there was excrement everywhere. Some of the militiamen habitually defecated in the trench, a disgusting thing when one had to walk round it in the darkness. But the dirt never worried me. Dirt is a thing people make too much fuss about. It is astonishing how quickly you get used to doing without a handkerchief and to eating out of the tin pannikin in which you also wash. Nor was sleeping in one's clothes any hardship after a day or two. It was of course impossible to take one's clothes and especially one's boots off at night; one had to be ready to turn out instantly in case of an attack. In eighty nights I only took my clothes off three times, though I did occasionally manage to get them off in the daytime. It was too cold for lice as yet, but rats and mice abounded. It is often said that you don't find rats and mice in the same place, but you do when there is enough food for them.

In other ways we were not badly off. The food was good enough and there was plenty of wine. Cigarettes were still being issued at the rate of a packet a day, matches were issued every other day, and there was even an issue of candles. They were very thin candles, like those on a Christmas cake, and were popularly supposed to have been looted from churches. Every dug-out was issued daily with three inches of candle, which would burn for about twenty minutes. At that time it was still possible to buy candles, and I had brought several pounds of them with me. Later on the famine of matches and candles made life a misery. You do not realize the importance of these things until you lack them. In a night-alarm, for instance, when everyone in the dug-out is scrambling for his rifle and treading on everybody else's face, being able to strike a light may make the difference between life and death. Every militiaman possessed a tinder-lighter and several yards of yellow wick. Next to his rifle it was his most important possession. The tinder-lighters had the great advantage that they could be struck in a wind, but they would only smoulder, so that they were no use for lighting a fire. When the match famine was at its worst our only way of producing a flame was to pull the bullet out of a cartridge and touch the cordite off with a tinder-lighter.

It was an extraordinary life that we were living—an extraordinary way to be at war, if you could call it war. The whole militia chafed against the inaction and clamoured constantly to know why we were not allowed to attack. But it was perfectly obvious that there would be no battle for a long while yet, unless the enemy started it. Georges Kopp, on his periodical tours of inspection, was quite frank with us. "This is not a war," he used to say, "it is a comic opera with an occasional death." As a matter of fact the stagnation on the Aragon front had political causes of which I knew nothing at that time; but the purely military difficulties—quite apart from the lack of reserves of men—were obvious to anybody.

To begin with, there was the nature of the country. The front line, ours and the Fascists', lay in positions of immense natural strength, which as a rule could only be approached from one side. Provided a few trenches have been dug, such places cannot be taken by infantry, except in overwhelming numbers. In our own position or most of those round us a dozen men with two machine-guns could have held off a battalion. Perched on the hill-tops as we were, we should have made lovely marks for artillery; but there was no artillery. Sometimes I used to gaze round the landscape and long—oh, how passionately!—for a couple of batteries of guns. One could have destroyed the enemy positions one after another as easily as smashing nuts with a hammer. But on our side the guns simply did not exist. The Fascists did occasionally manage to bring a gun or two from Zaragoza and fire a very few shells, so few that they never even found the range and the shells plunged harmlessly into the empty ravines. Against machine-guns and without artillery there are only three things you can do: dig yourself in at a safe distance—four hundred yards, say—advance across the open and be massacred, or make small-scale night-attacks that will not alter the general situation. Practically the alternatives are stagnation or suicide.

And beyond this there was the complete lack of war materials of every description. It needs an effort to realize how badly the militias were armed at this time. Any public school O.T.C. in England is far more like a modern army than we were. The badness of our weapons was so astonishing that it is worth recording in detail.

For this sector of the front the entire artillery consisted of four trench-mortars with *fifteen rounds* for each gun. Of course they were far too precious to be fired and the mortars were kept in Alcubierre. There were machine-guns at the rate of approximately one to fifty men; they were oldish guns, but fairly accurate up to three or four hundred yards. Beyond this we had only rifles, and the majority of the rifles were scrap-iron. There were three types of rifle in use. The first was the long Mauser. These were seldom less than twenty years old, their sights were about as much use as a broken speedometer, and in most of them the rifling was hopelessly corroded; about one rifle in ten was not bad, however. Then there was the short Mauser, or *mousqueton*, really a cavalry weapon. These were more popular than the others because they were lighter to carry and less nuisance in a trench, also because they were comparatively new and looked efficient. Actually they were almost useless. They were made out of reassembled parts, no bolt belonged to its rifle, and three-quarters of them could be counted on to jam after five shots. There were also a few Winchester rifles. These were nice to shoot with, but they were wildly inaccurate, and as their cartridges had no clips they could only be fired one shot at a time. Ammunition was so scarce that each man entering the line was only issued with fifty rounds, and most of it was exceedingly bad. The Spanish-made cartridges were all refills and would jam even the best rifles. The Mexican cartridges were better and were therefore reserved for the machine-guns. Best of all was the German-made ammunition, but as this came only from prisoners and deserters there was not much of it. I always kept a clip of German or Mexican ammunition in my pocket for use in an emergency. But in practice when the emergency came I seldom fired my rifle; I was too frightened of the beastly thing jamming and too anxious to reserve at any rate one round that would go off.

We had no tin hats, no bayonets, hardly any revolvers or pistols, and not more than one bomb between five or ten men. The bomb in use at this time was a frightful object known as the "F.A.I. bomb," it having been produced by the Anarchists in the early days of the war. It was on the principle of a Mills bomb, but the lever was held down not by a pin but a piece of tape. You broke the tape and then got rid of the bomb with the utmost possible speed. It was said of these bombs that they were "impartial"; they killed the man they were thrown at and the man who threw them. There were several other types, even more primitive but probably a little less dangerous—to the thrower, I mean. It was not till late March that I saw a bomb worth throwing.

And apart from weapons there was a shortage of all the minor necessities of war. We had no maps or charts, for instance. Spain has never been fully surveyed, and the only detailed maps of this area were the old military ones, which were almost all in the possession of the Fascists. We had no range-finders, no telescopes, no periscopes, no field-glasses except a few privately-owned pairs, no flares or Very lights, no wire-cutters, no armourers' tools, hardly even any cleaning materials. The Spaniards seemed never to have heard of a pull-through and looked on in surprise when I constructed one. When you wanted your rifle cleaned you took it to the sergeant, who possessed a long brass ramrod which was invariably bent and therefore scratched the rifling. There was not even any gun oil. You greased your rifle with olive oil, when you could get hold of it; at different times I have greased mine with vaseline, with cold cream, and even with bacon-fat. Moreover, there were no lanterns or electric torches—at this time there was not, I believe, such a thing as an electric torch throughout the whole of our sector of the front, and you could not buy one nearer than Barcelona, and only with difficulty even there.

As time went on, and the desultory rifle-fire rattled among the hills, I began to wonder with increasing scepticism whether anything would ever happen to bring a bit of life, or rather a bit of death, into this cock-eyed war. It was pneumonia that we were fighting against, not against men. When the trenches are more than five hundred yards apart no one gets hit except by accident. Of course there were casualties, but the majority of them were self-inflicted. If I remember rightly, the first five men I saw wounded in Spain were all wounded by our own weapons—I don't mean intentionally, but owing to accident or carelessness. Our worn-out rifles were a danger in themselves. Some of them had a nasty trick of going off if the butt was tapped on the ground; I saw a man shoot himself through the hand owing to this. And in the darkness the raw recruits were always firing at one another. One evening when it was barely even dusk a sentry let fly at me from a distance of twenty yards; but he missed me by a yard—goodness knows how many times the Spanish standard of marksmanship has saved my life. Another time I had gone out on patrol in the mist and had carefully warned the guard commander beforehand. But in coming back I stumbled against a bush, the startled sentry called out that the Fascists were coming, and I had the pleasure of hearing the guard commander order everyone to open rapid fire in my direction. Of course I lay down and the bullets went harmlessly over me. Nothing will convince a Spaniard, at least a young Spaniard, that fire-arms are dangerous. Once, rather later than this, I was photographing some machine-gunners with their gun, which was pointed directly towards me.

"Don't fire," I said, half-jokingly as I focused the camera.

"Oh, no, we won't fire."

The next moment there was a frightful roar and a stream of bullets tore past my face so close that my cheek was stung by grains of cordite. It was unintentional, but the machine-gunners considered it a great joke. Yet only a few days earlier they had seen a mule-driver accidentally shot by a political delegate who was playing the fool with an automatic pistol and had put five bullets in the mule-driver's lungs.

The difficult passwords which the army was using at this time were a minor source of danger. They were those tiresome double passwords in which one word has to be answered by another. Usually they were of an elevating and revolutionary nature, such as *Cultura—progreso*, or *Seremos—invencibles*, and it was often impossible to get illiterate sentries to remember these highfalutin words. One night, I remember, the password was *Cataluña—heroica*, and a moon-faced peasant lad named Jaime Domenech approached me, greatly puzzled, and asked me to explain.

"Heroica—what does heroica mean?"

I told him that it meant the same as valiente. A little while later he was stumbling up the trench in the darkness, and the sentry challenged him:

"Alto! Cataluña!"

"Valiente!" yelled Jaime, certain that he was saying the right thing.

Bang!

However, the sentry missed him. In this war everyone always did miss everyone else, when it was humanly possible.

David Plante

(1940–   )

David Plante's memoir, *American Ghosts* (2005), revealed how closely his novel *The Foreigner* (1984, from which this excerpt is taken) follows his autobiography. Plante is the sixth of seven sons born to a French Canadian family in Providence, Rhode Island. His narrow family life was circumscribed by the Catholic Church. At nineteen Plante had an opportunity to study abroad. On the boat to Europe he met a mysterious woman and expected to have an affair with her. Instead, his world changed when he lost his virginity to her young male acquaintance. Although Plante distanced himself from his French Canadian roots (he and his partner live in London), it is material he has mined again and again in his fiction. Plante is an experimental writer and his work is characterized by spare prose. His characters are often gay or sexually ambiguous men.

Like Plante, the main character of *The Foreigner* grows up French Canadian. The novel begins, "I was born in two countries. The outer country, vast, was America. I belonged to another, a small one within the large; the French Parish, in Providence, Rhode Island, into which I was born." Travel abroad brings friendship with two unpredictable and dangerous people: Angela, a black American woman whom he follows to Spain, and Vincent, another American. Spain is a vibrant player in *The Foreigner*: it is light, exciting, and dangerous in comparison to the predictability of Providence.

Plante has written many other books, including his Francoeur trilogy—*The Family* (1978), *The Country* (1981), and *The Woods* (1982)—and his novel *The Accident* (1991) also set in Spain.

From THE FOREIGNER

At the Tarragona station, I spoke in French to a man who said that to get to Almería I must first go to Valencia, and gave me the times of the trains. I left the station with my bag and crossed the street to a café where it was hot and the ceiling fans were not working. I stood at the bar, which was covered with dust, and asked for a cerveza. The bar woman, thin and white, in a dry dusty black dress, didn't understand me. I repeated. She frowned. I repeated, showing my teeth, "Cerveza." Frowning, she brought me the bottle of beer and a glass. I drank, paid, picked up my bag and went into the hot August afternoon. I walked slowly up the cement steps from the station to the Ramblas, wide and lined on both sides with palm trees in wooden tubs, and I walked slowly down it, to where it ended in a plaza with a bronze statue of a general on a horse and a low wall. Beyond the wall was the sea. In the plaza I sat at an outdoor café to have another beer and to eat a sandwich jamón.

I sat facing the sea. It was black blue. It appeared to be a dark flat plane, vertical, against which stood the sunlit statue and palm trees.

The sun was still up when I went to the harbor. I walked past many houses with Habitaciones painted in black on the front, and made myself go into one. My room was small and had an enamel basin on a stand in one corner and an enamel bidet in another corner. I lay on the bed. The late sunlight shone about the edges of the closed curtains. I rose from the bed and opened the curtains.

In the town, I took a walkway, arbored with a vine, up to a ruined castle, and from the ramparts of the castle looked down at the roofs and walls with shadows against the plane of the sea.

I read the menu outside a restaurant, but could not make myself go in.

When it was dark, I went back to my room, undressed and got into bed.

With a start, I woke. I heard my mother and father talking in their bedroom, next to mine. I could hear their voices.

In the morning, a sharp wind blew. I walked through the wind to the station where I found a long line at the ticket window, closed, behind the grille, by a wooden shutter. I joined the line and put the bag between my feet. Fifteen minutes before the train was to arrive the shutter opened and the line pressed forward. The people who got tickets went out on to the platform with their rope-tied bags, cardboard boxes, baskets. I shuffled closer to the window, and looking past the three people before me saw the shutter slam. The person in front of me, an old woman in a wrinkled black suit, turned to me, set her mouth, and went off.

I said to myself, "What happened?"

I stood among people going out for the train.

The consigna where you could leave your luggage was shut, so I had to carry my bag. In the dusty bar across from the station I sat at a corner table and had coffee, bread and butter and jam. I sat for a long while after the empty cup and the plate and knife were cleared. Outside, the wind blew up dust in the street.

Again, when I went to the station, there was a line. I was early, though, and after I joined the line other people did too. Shifting my weight from foot to foot, I waited; I looked often at my watch. A short time before the train was due, the ticket window opened. It closed in the face of the woman standing in front of me. People moved about me, but I for a time did not move.

I walked up and down the Ramblas. Hungry, I felt I could not make myself go into a restaurant. But I must eat. The meal and the wine made me sleepy. I could hardly focus when I counted out the money on to the saucer, and as I went out of the restaurant I lurched with the weight of my bag. I did not know which way to go. The wind had stopped.

At three o'clock I returned to the station. I had an hour and a half to wait for another train, and I was third in line. The shutter did not open.

A little nauseated, I sat on a bench in the station. My body tensed when I saw a young man, three hours before the train was to come, take a place before the shuttered ticket window, and I took a place behind him. The light and the heat in the outside stillness were thickening. The young man kept looking round at me; he was thin, and wore a suit. I was in a short-sleeved shirt, slacks, and sandals. The young man asked me something which I understood to be, "Where are you going?" and when I said, "Almería," the young man pressed his lips together and stuck them out and said, "C'est loin, c'est très loin."

We talked in French.

A line formed behind us. As the time approached for the shutter to open, my body tensed more. The shutter didn't open; with a shuddering burst, the train passed the station.

"Why?" I asked the young man.

The young man, who was a student, made a face.

He invited me to have a beer with him at the bar across from the station. The student held out his thumb. He explained to me how to hitchhike.

In the room, I lay sweating on the bed. As it got dark, I fell asleep; but I woke from time to time with a jerk. When it came to me where I was, I rubbed my body hard.

I missed the local train to Salou, where I would start to hitchhike, and, again, waited in the Tarragona train station. The still heat brought out flies; they settled on my neck, cheeks, forehead, and on my hands as I tried to brush them from my head. A woman and a boy, at the end of the long bench I sat on, let the flies settle on them, and only blinked, and I stopped trying to keep the flies off myself.

When I got out at Salou, I went from the station, past rough stone buildings, to a country road. On one side of the road, beyond parched fields, were twisted red mountains, and on the other side of the road, beyond the low and eroded headlands, was the sea. Cactus plants grew along the road and cast spiky shadows. Changing my bag from hand to hand, I walked. I was not sure this was the road I should be on, or if I was going in the right direction. I often turned round to see if a car was coming along. When I saw an advancing cloud of dust, I stood to the side and held out my thumb. As an old truck passed me a woman sitting next to the driver pointed down, and I guessed that she meant that they were stopping soon. I walked on. I walked round a mountain about which the road curved, and beyond which the landscape was vast; the mountains were high and far back, and the open land before them was covered with great boulders, and, on the sea side, the sloping land was, too, covered with enormous boulders. At times, though, they appeared to me small, and the mountains not high and far but low and near. Distorting heat waves rose from the tarred and oiled road; the smell rose. Another truck came along and stopped, and the driver leaned over to open the door for me to get in. The driver's hands were stubby and calloused; he said, only, that he was going twenty kilometers, or so I understood, and drove the rattling truck in silence. The windshield was covered with dust which, because of the vibrations of the truck, was striated; the striations shifted. The truck stopped before turning off into a dirt road, and I jumped down and slammed the door.

The road went through countryside that was flat; the road was straight, so, before me and behind me, it disappeared to points, and glared. I was weak from lack of food and water. The bag was heavy.

I was picked up by an American in a rented car who was driving all the way to Valencia. The American was bald. He didn't ask me where I was from.

The American said, "You just traveling around?"

"Yes," I said.

Hot wind blew in the open window.

"Alone?"

"Yes, alone."

"I'm not sure I'd travel on my own in this country."

"Why?"

"You never know."

By the side of the road two women were selling grapes. The grapes were piled on an old door laid across benches. The American stopped the car beyond them and got out. I got out, too. As we approached, a woman held up a large bunch of grapes.

"Let me buy," I said.

"No," the American said, "I will."

"But you're giving me a lift."

"No, I will."

I stood away as the American paid one woman while the other wrapped the great bunch of grapes in newspaper. In the car, he placed the bundle on the seat between us and opened the newspaper. The grapes were large, bright; some were crushed, and juice oozed from them.

"Help yourself," the American said.

I broke off a small bunch. The grapes were filled with cool liquid, I put a number in my mouth and ate them together, swallowing the seeds. The liquid rose out on my lips.

The American started the car.

"Aren't you going to have any?" I asked.

"I bought them for you."

"Why?"

"I thought you'd like them."

I said, "Thanks."

On the outskirts of Valencia the road widened and was divided by trolley tracks and trees. The American pulled up at a trolley stop and told me he was not going into the center of the city.

At the train station I asked, in French, for the next train to Almería. It was at nine o'clock in the morning. I asked if I could buy a ticket. "Bien sûr," the ticket man said. I asked for a second-class ticket, but there was no second-class on the train, only first and third. I bought a third-class ticket, and examined it carefully in the late sunlight outside the station to make sure it was for Almería.

In a hotel near the station I took a room with a bath, and I lay in the lukewarm water. My body tingling, I washed my socks and underwear.

The hotel restaurant was still empty, though to me it was late. I ate a tortilla, paella, a thin veal steak with fried potatoes, a salad; I drank a bottle of wine.

It seemed to me my skin was taut and smooth, and sometimes I reached into my shirt to touch my body.

I walked along the street, lit by globes, crowded with Spaniards taking their evening paseo. Sometimes I bumped into them, and I felt the momentary impact of their bodies on mine, and I retained the impact. The strollers crowded about me.

I left them by turning into a quiet side street, and as I walked I imagined, at moments, that my body stepped out from me into a space and walked beside me, and I could reach out and touch it.

Back in the crowd, I imagined, more, that my body was outside me in the crowd, and I bumped into it.

I couldn't sleep. I twisted and turned in the sheet, which wrapped about me. Then I was not sure if I was asleep or awake. When I woke, not sure where I was, I rubbed my body. I rubbed my chest, my thighs.

I was waiting on the platform for the train at eight o'clock. Passengers gathered about me. When, a little before nine, the train came into the station, the passengers ran to open the doors before it stopped; bags and bundles raised above their heads, they struggled to get on against the passengers getting off. Women shouted. By the open windows, suitcases and boxes were handed out of the train and handed in. A man held up a cage of chickens to another man who took it in. I hung back and looked down the platform; I ran to the end of the train where the crowd was less, and boarded after a fat woman was helped up the metal steps by a man pulling her by the arms.

Boxes were piled outside the w.c., and people were sitting on the lower ones. My bag held against me so my knees kicked it as I walked, I went down the corridor alongside the compartments; the corridor was crowded, and as I went I looked into each compartment, where, in thick cigarette smoke, the Spaniards sat pressed together. There was no space to stand in the corridor. I pressed my way through and came to the w.c. at the other end of the carriage, and, among others, I was able to stand by a dirty window.

The train was shunted. The passengers lurched. A woman grabbed my shoulder and laughed; I smiled at her.

I pointed down to the floor of the train. "Almería?" I asked.

I frowned too.

The woman turned to talk to the man next to her. They had a long discussion. Then she turned to me and said, "Si, Almería."

"Muchas gracias," I said. I turned a little away from her.

The train was stationary. I heard steam hissing, and metallic clinking, and I thought the train was about to start, but the hissing and clanking stopped, the train remained stationary. I was sweating. A voice over a loudspeaker on the platform made an announcement which I did not understand, but as no one reacted to it I imagined it was to say the train was departing. The train remained still, and, in the heat, the passengers settled into the stillness. A bell rang and I thought it must be a signal for the train to go, but it didn't go. I tried to open the dirty window; it wouldn't open. In the hot still silence I heard a whistle. I stared at the gray concrete platform through the dirty glass. Another bell sounded, a tingling bell. I continued to look out at the platform, where, in the bright light, was a crate. After a long silence the crate moved; it was the train, which moved very slowly out of the station.

Mary Lee Settle

(1918–2005)

At the age of eighty-two Mary Lee Settle explored Spain. She drove her rental car and took only a few things: *Don Quijote*, the poems of St. John of the Cross, St. Teresa's autobiography, a topographical map, and plastic cutlery so that she could eat in her room by herself. "To be alone by choice is one of the great luxuries of the world," she wrote. "I went to Spain alone. I wanted to discover it, not have it pointed out to me by friends."

Mary Lee Settle led a traveler's life. Born in West Virginia and grounded in the culture of the South, she moved to New York after two years of college to model and act, even testing for the role of Scarlett in *Gone with the Wind*. During World War II she lived in England and worked for the U.S. Office of War Information, returned to New York, and then to London again, writing plays, articles, fiction, and even an etiquette column. She finally found fame with her five related novels, the Beulah Quintet. The first, *The Love Letters*, was published in 1954 and the last, *The Killing Ground*, was published in 1982.

Settle continued to travel and left the United States for five years in 1969, living in Turkey and England. "I said if Nixon was elected president I was going back to Europe," she said. "He was and I did." The result of her years in Turkey was the impressionistic travel book *Turkish Reflections: A Biography of a Place*. *Spanish Recognitions* (2004, from which this is excerpted), was one of her last books and she hoped it would be a companion to *Turkish Reflections*. Despite her peripatetic life Settle still felt the pull of the South. "I am a Southerner," she wrote, "and there is bred in us, as carefully as if we were prize hounds, a sense of betrayal in leaving our roots."

From SPANISH RECOGNITIONS

HOLIDAY

It was time to stop and stay a while—someplace easier, unknown, unimportant, and that did not remind me of death and civil war. I had known the facts and much of the propaganda of the war since I was young; but knowing it was clean and mental, and something far away. Intelligence is bloodless.

I hadn't known about Lorca, only facts. Now I had made myself walk in his streets, from his boyhood home to a lush forest of pine trees, and it was familiar in a different way, as if a dear friend had died. I saw him as he had seen Granada.

I found out, driving alone west across Andalucía, what "Mine eyes dazzle" meant. For when I thought of Granada from time to time along that featureless highway I was engulfed in what I had seen, and then my eyes would dazzle, tears but not crying, like rain left on a window. I would have to slow the car until the moment passed. I prayed that my favorite city would become beautiful again in my mind, as it had been before I had gone up on that terrible mountain. It has now. As always, I want to go back.

I was tired of sorrow. I wanted to do nothing for a little while. Having followed war, kings, queens, caliphs, saints, and then one I had been close to by reading since I was eighteen, I wanted to go where no place was. A rest. A week; it sounded like the luxury of the world, no driving, no past, just sea and sun. Lovely. There was only one problem. I hate the Costa del Sol.

It is the most un-Spanish of places. It has been invaded for too long by the northern Europeans escaping fog, rain, and puritanism. Oh, the buildings are there, and buried deep below the sand, a fascinating past obscured by beautiful Swedish girls in their topless bikinis, and pale English girls imitating beautiful Swedish girls. Hard rock, soft rock—no, not sandstone, limestone, marble—but music, and commercial *flamenco*, the noise of tourism at its worst over the beaches. It is the only part of Spain I know where Spaniards have, through fatigue and exposure, learned to be rude. Crowds are so

thick in summer and early fall that they seem not so much to move as
to be stirred. I have just described a perfect holiday for an eighteen-
year-old modern Visigoth.

I was already in the south, so there was no going to the English
Channel for a little restful mist, or to the Bay of Biscay for saints,
shrines, and treacherous sea. I consulted the map and the guidebooks
I carried. I found it. I thought I found it, a small resort referred to
condescendingly as a place where Spanish families went in the season.

It was a long way from Granada, all the way across the south of
Spain. I didn't care. Between Córdoba and Seville, I found the drive
was too long, and stopped, I thought, just for the night, at Carmona.
I stayed three days. I found the minor road that passed through
where the two-hundred-year frontier had been in the thirteenth century. That was the reason why the towns I passed through were called
Arcos de la Frontera, Jerez de la Frontera, and, later, Palos de la
Frontera. I remember best the mile after mile of sunflowers; all their
heads watched in one direction, regimented by the sun.

Sanlúcar was not on the Mediterranean coast but on that Atlantic
shore between the frontier of Portugal and the Pillars of Hercules,
now called the Straits of Magellan. It sounded wonderfully uninteresting. Little to do. Not really recommended. Perfect. A place where
there might be the sun and the silence I craved.

In a great half-circle of shore in southern Atlantic Spain, fed by
three rivers, is the Costa de la Luz, a lovely name, the Coast of Light.
There is, they say, so little there to see. Sanlúcar de Barrameda
sounded, and it was meant to sound, like a boring little resort. Imagine it! Dull, quiet, and pastless, not fascinating. I couldn't wait. I
drove west from Arcos de la Frontera, still driving away from
Granada, not toward anything, but gradually, after Carmona, I began
to be in the present again, avoiding fascinating cities.

There was no sign for Sanlúcar de Barrameda; I was prepared for
that by my trusty dragoman, a Michelin atlas of every road in Spain
there had ever been, and I saw that if I got off at the sign for a place
called Lebrija, and headed southwest on a little pencil line on my
map, I would finally arrive at Sanlúcar.

I couldn't find it. For mile after mile it simply wasn't there. I passed
sand dune after sand dune. I was lost in a space of sand and sky and a

hint of the sea. Sanlúcar was nowhere, signs but no city. I finally got to a traffic circle in the road. Those circles in Spain have to be learned and, once familiar, are a godsend. Driving around the circle I almost missed another small sign, Sanlúcar, and had to go around again. This time I made the turn at the sign that said I had arrived in Sanlúcar.

There was still nothing there. Oh, there were some filling stations, a few roadside eating places, a few houses. Nothing else. No sea, no resort. I knew it had to exist, or had arrived at hope, which is the stop before knowledge. After all, I had a reservation at a hotel, and any traveler knows that means a place exists. Behind hope I found fatigue, and behind that, a little touch of despair. I pulled into a filling station. One of those blessed, well-dressed English-speaking college girls came out to the car. She smiled. "You are looking for Sanlúcar, are you not?" she said before I could speak. I simply nodded.

She gave me perfect directions into the town, the turning toward the hotel, the hotel itself, with a warning that it was in the center of a cat's cradle of Moorish walking streets, off to the side of a large church, across from a nunnery, behind the *plaza mayor*. Of course. I followed her directions exactly and was lost for three hours in a little Moorish Christian medieval ancient town. At first I was fool enough to try to drive around to find my hotel. Then I parked at a little square and walked. I realized later that for at least one of those hours I had been within a hundred feet of the hotel. Once, I passed it. How could I get so lost in a little, old mild resort where nothing happened?

I was to find out later that it wasn't little, it wasn't medieval, and it had one of the most fascinating pasts in all of Spain. So many roads I had followed led there, from the *Reconquista*, the Indies, the *conquistadores*.

Then, quite suddenly, I recognized the hotel, a blank white wall across from a high, blank brick wall, behind the blank white stucco of an ancient church with one small baroque circular window in a monastery plaza. It was the time of *siesta*. There was not a soul around in the street. In the hot part of the day Sanlúcar was, sensibly, asleep.

I tried the only large double door I could find, and there it was, a small sign, *Los Helechos*, The Ferns. I walked into the door that led to two Moorish houses combined into a hotel, with two white courtyards filled with plants, an old well, a quiet within it that I could not believe. It was as pure an *Arabian Nights* scene as I could have found, a simple hotel, with a lobby full of plants, a desk where another young college student spoke enough English to guide me. I followed him through a corridor to an opening into a lovely white courtyard with a fountain and green, tree-sized plants. This was what my room looked out on from a barred window with a green plant of my own on the sill. I had found an ideal place just to be for a while after the hurly-burly of wars and mountains and all that I had hoped for in Spain except a place to sit and think. I was to find out that I had arrived at the best hotel, the most attractive, and the cheapest of all the places where I had been living.

Every evening after their classes were over a group of young college students, men and women, made the unassuming hotel bar their *tertulia*. They drank very little. They played chess and Chinese checkers and discussed quietly whatever they were discussing. I began later to see the *tertulias* all over the town, always at the same table: businessmen in one of the outdoor restaurants, the farmers at the medieval market, the retired fishermen who have had their own meeting place since the fourteenth century. I saw them in the mornings, always at the same time.

In the early evening on my first day there, when the sun was low, I walked back out of the magic door to see where I was. I wandered into the *plaza mayor*, where the people of Sanlúcar sat all evening, some with baby carriages beside them, with contented, sleeping babies. For the first time in Spain after dark I was not a stranger. Everybody around me knew everybody else around me and included me in the smiles, the greetings.

There were discussions and soft laughter. The half-light of lamps from the little local bars and restaurants was just beginning to color the twilight. Down a narrow street I walked toward a second plaza and, dividing the two plazas from one another, a small palace which had been turned into a hotel, not grand, just another genteel old house the color of age and neglect beside a street too small for cars, so narrow that I could touch both walls that bound it. A man with his dog seemed to live in a doorway. I thought of Unamuno's story of two sisters, a family seething with silent passion, marooned in parlors with heavy curtains, the pathetic notion of local snobbery, the same theme as Lorca's *The House of Bernarda Alba*.

I escaped into the second plaza, where there was a breeze that promised the sea. In front of me was a quarter-of-a-mile walk on an elegant, almost formal esplanade as wide as the city blocks that had been laid out between the medieval town and the sea. It was lined with trees, with fine modern houses. It was another city, new and white, this one with beautiful gardens, this far south; semitropical blooming plants that leaned over white walls.

Sanlúcar was not one town. It was two. They lay beside each other. Nothing seemed to have been destroyed to build new buildings. The medieval town where I had wandered, lost, was still there, behind me, where I lived.

Ahead of me the water was turned white by evening. I could hear it, and I walked toward it, aware of the Atlantic Ocean. But it was not the ocean in this deceptive, ancient, magic town. It was the estuary of the largest river in Spain, the Guadalquivir, its name from the Arabic name for great river. Away in the distance was the vague shore of the largest natural habitat in Europe, the Doñana National Park, a place of birds, wild animals, islands, swamps, old paths, and, I found out later, where Goya spent the summer with the Duchess of Alba in what was then the most famous aristocratic watering place in Spain.

I also learned, in that first evening, that the food there was perfect, that Sanlúcar was the center for the finest, lightest sherry blushed with gold in that ring of towns, including Jerez de la Frontera, that make most of the sherry that comes from Spain. It is called manzanilla; to me it is to most sherries as single malt is to ordinary Scotch whiskey. I knew none of this. I only knew that I was where I most wanted to be, and that the air was clean, the little town the right size for a kind of gentle wanderlust, and that there was little to discover.

There is the most honest pamphlet about the Costa de la Luz. It simply says, under gastronomy, that the best dish there is fried fish. (No complicated sauces, no fabulous traditional local messes.) So every evening after sharing the *siesta*, I ate the finest fried fish in all the Mediterranean, red mullet, *barbounia* in Turkey, *triglia di fango* (slime mullet!) in Italy, *salmonete* in Spain. This superb fish was so fashionable in ancient Rome that people lost fortunes buying it to impress their guests at banquets. There was, at one time, a law that only the emperor could eat it.

So there I sat in the evenings at an outdoor restaurant on the esplanade in the gathering darkness as the night came down, alone but never lonely, eating red mullet, the emperor's fish, drinking manzanilla, the lightest sherry known. To paraphrase Thoreau, it was not sherry I drank nor I who drank sherry; it was the wine of the Hesperides and I was served it by the wind from the west.

As I began to learn to be in Sanlúcar, the place where nothing happened, I was finding out that it seemed to contain all that I had begun to learn in my traveling—unsought, secret roads of the past and the historic changes of Spain, as if all those roads led to it. I was more and more aware that I was in one of the places in Spain that I would go back to again and again.

I had, on that first evening, seen two cities. Now, in the daylight I found the third. Overlooking the medieval and the modern cities, the *barrio alto* had once been the aristocratic summer resort of Imperial Spain. The long, high palisade followed the eastern shore of the river, a steep sentinel over the lower cities. There was the castle, there the once-great houses, on watch over the markets, the fishing boats, all the way to the sea, where the ships from the new world crossed the bar of the Guadalquivir.

Sanlúcar lay at the main entry from the Atlantic Ocean to the rich, newly discovered Indies, America. It had been there that the ships laden with gold and silver crossed the bar at last after the dangerous Atlantic crossing, the entry to what Fernand Braudel called the most ancient and treacherous of all the shores of the Atlantic, the nursery of Atlantic exploration.

Instead of a quiet town, I had discovered once again that, like Columbus, I had found what I had not looked for—the beginning of the upriver voyage to the city of Seville where every ship from the Spanish Main had to report at the *Casa de Contratación*, the government register and customs house. What a relief it must have been to cross the bar at Sanlúcar after the perilous Atlantic voyage, to moor at last beyond the danger of the pirates from England and North Africa, gathered offshore like flies around honey. No wonder Sanlúcar had the reputation of being a wild port, the place in Spain where the vagabonds gathered in bands. In the days of the American voyages, poets, runaway students, thieves, the poor, the starving, and those called by a new word in the sixteenth century, *pícaros*, all sought passage on the outgoing ships, and gathered in the riotous taverns.

Crossing the bar. It is one of those phrases we use without considering what it means. It has been a metaphor for death and turned into a joke . . . Tennyson's "and may there be no moaning of the bar when I put out to sea." No. Not a pub or a café or a down-and-dirty bar. It was a sandbar, and it was at the ocean entry to a river where the current flowing into the tidal estuary moved the underwater sand into, literally, a high sandbar the ships had to cross to get into port. The bar at Sanlúcar controlled the size of the ships that plied to and from Seville for well over a hundred years from 1500, just after the discovery of America, to the late seventeenth century when the great galleons came into service and the *Casa de Contratación* was moved to Cádiz. No ship over two hundred tons could cross the Sanlúcar bar; the great galleons that we are so familiar with from movies and popular stories were built for a thousand or more tons.

A ton is a huge barrel, as high as my head, for freight and, in Sanlúcar, for aging the manzanilla sherry. I saw a huge display of sherry barrels one evening when marquees were put up along the esplanade. The *bodegas*, the sherry factories, showed their wares in barrels black with age, with the *bodega*'s names of their sherries on them. The one I remember is Goya.

The reputation of Sanlúcar as a major port for ships to Seville and for fishing still has hints of its more fashionable past, not only the memory of a famous love affair of Goya. The past is still represented in the names of the owners on the racing forms for one of the oldest and most famous horse races in Spain. The race is on one day in August. Spanish people come from all over the country to see it and bet on it. Sanlúcar is never more crowded. It is claimed to be the oldest horse race in Spain. There, as they would have when the races began in the mid-nineteenth century, the fishermen, the street poor, the punsters, the vagabonds, the poets, the *hidalgos*, the *caballeros* gather. Groups share ownership of many of the entries—"*Los Insolventes*," the broke, have entered a gelding called Sir Castrates; "The Fishermen," a horse called Philippi. The Count, a horse called

Olmeda. The horse belonging to the group called *Picota*, the pillory, is named "The Winds of the South."

The races are run near sunset at the evening low tide for over a mile along the flat sand shore of the Guadalquivir. Thousands of spectators stand in the shallow water on one side and the sand beach on the other. It must be one of the most beautiful sports events in the world. And it was started by a group that may no longer exist, the Aristocrats, at least not as the powerful, arrogant Goths they were for so long. It was in Sanlúcar that I had the greatest clue to what had happened to so many of them as they began to die out.

There is yet another of those narrow streets that goes toward the high bluff. I went there first without an idea of going up the hill. I was trying to find the market. The outside wall of it was forbidding, dark, a low, medieval doorway, a carved escutcheon over it. I thought it might have been a monastic building or at least a charity hospital. A woman entered the door, and I followed her.

Inside, busy women fingered vegetables and fruit under bright lights. Someone haggled over a chicken. The place had all the noise and color of an Andalucian market, the smell of raw meat, fresh vegetables, of figs and apricots and oranges. I wondered how long it had been there. Once again, everybody seemed to know everybody else, sharing the morning. The walls, the ceiling, the large counters seemed very old, but the flowers, the vegetables, the fruit were so fresh they must have been picked that morning, and not far away. Even better was the friendliness, good coffee, and the fifty-cent lunch. I tried it because I reasoned that the people who brought vegetables and meat to the market would not be satisfied with bad food. I was right.

The street beyond the market was so steep that it had wide steps, and to go onto it was to sink back into a deep and unexplained past of ancient gargoyle carvings on columns against a wall or a building at the beginning of the long flight of steps; maybe it was an abutment that must have been fourteenth century, rising against a perpendicular bluff. I had to guess. There was no way of knowing.

At first at the top, I went to the right of the road, where a grand Mudejar folly had been built, probably in the late eighteenth century. It was more "Moorish" than any Moorish building ever was. Neat and gaudy, wonderful colors, and a sneaking look at a plant-gorged courtyard, it tells much about the secret, ironic attitude of Sanlúcar toward its own past, that it is this building that has been chosen as the *ayuntamiento*, the town hall. It was a pleasant, lively place; the people lounged around it, walked in the fantasy of a garden of old trees.

Not so beyond it. On the crest of the hill, there was a sense of frailty, of death, decay, neglect in the once-fine houses. Some of the carved doors sagged, some of the windows were broken, some of the houses had obviously been broken into. There was one house with a sign so old that it, too, sagged with rain and wind and age; I think it was called the *Caballeros* club. A faded sign put there some years before said, "closed for repairs."

The people who had made the hill the power center of the town of Sanlúcar had gone away, or died or grown old or gone broke, or some of them may have moved down into the shore city and built fine houses there. Whatever had happened to them, it was for me a memorial to a way of living that shut out the common world, and drew its fatal strength from a privilege that every year in Spain before the civil war had meant less and less.

But the center around which they had clustered was still there, still cared for, still lively. It was the seat of one of the greatest land owners ever in Spain, the Duke of Medina Sedonia. It was the ninth Duke (and first of a new line), who had been dragged kicking and screaming by Philip II into being the Admiral of the Glorious Armada, and still, in that house, there are archives of probably the greatest value to Spain's history outside of officialdom.

The ducal palace, which looked attractive but unassuming on the street side, the rear of the estate, must have been bordered by the strange creatures like gargoyles on the decorated wall I had passed when I climbed the stairs of the street. Above it must have been wonderful gardens and a spacious ducal lawn. But that could only be imagined. All I could know of the present Dukes of Medina Sedonia, if indeed they lived there, was that they had clung to a place they loved while all around them was desertion and loss, and because they had done it, they had presented Sanlúcar with a grand presence that was, to outsiders like me, a well-kept secret. I honored that, for it was this house where the archives have been opened to leading European historians, perhaps for centuries, notably in the twentieth century to Fernand Braudel.

Behind the evasive, unassuming side of the ducal palace was a church that told the story of the last years of the *Reconquista*, that two-hundred-year secession of any but border raids in the thirteenth and fourteenth century. It had been built by Moorish artisans, and its door was of Mudejar carving.

But even more for me, in what I had thought was a dead place, was the Discalced Carmelite Convent. It keeps the most authentic copy, made by nuns during the lifetime of St. John of the Cross, of his writing. He had read it and copyedited it, so his imprimatur shows how valid a text it is.

On the last day I was there I decided that I really ought to have seen Cádiz, not see but have seen, or "done" as some tourists say, marking off lovely old after lovely old, museum after museum, capital after capital. So I drove for an hour to Cádiz, east of Sanlúcar, the port of the high galleons of the Spanish Main. Before new archeological evidence was found, it was reputed to be the oldest city in Europe.

In the museum I saw what I expected, the slightly fat-faced Phoenicians with their tightly curled hair, carved on the lids of their coffins. These were the first known traders to open up the Costa de la Luz to the Middle East. Before they ventured beyond the Straits of Magellan into the Atlantic, it was believed that if you went beyond the Pillars of Hercules, you were in danger of falling off the edge of the world. Here and there were mysterious figures that were not Phoenician, and when I examined them I saw, again, the word Tartessan. The carving was more delicate, the wit more evident, but their identity was still a mystery to me—Tartessan. It brought back the first time I had seen the name, at a stop on my way someplace else. It was to lead me into yet another Spain.

I wandered into the park that was the main square in front of the museum and I found the huge monument, with almost photographic life-sized images, of the men who had met in Cádiz during the Napoleonic Wars when the rest of Spain was torn apart, and had written the first constitution for a republic. Can a huge marble monument be touching? Yes, it can. This tribute is to a republic that was destroyed by the heavy foot of reaction after Napoleon's exile.

On the way home, for I thought of my hotel room as home by then, I remembered a story that I had heard of a soldier from World War II who had been caught by the retreat from Dunkirk in 1940. He had hiked with his company twenty miles to Dunkirk in new boots, and his feet hurt "something awful." When asked years later what he had done when he got to the English Channel, while the defeated British Army was being strafed and dive-bombed by Stukas as they waited for boats, he said, "Ooh, I took off me boots and I had meself a lovely paddle."

It gave me an idea. So when I got back to Sanlúcar in the early evening, I went down to the wide, beautiful, nearly empty sand beach where there had been through the day so many swimmers, took off my shoes, rolled up my pants, and had myself a lovely mile-long paddle where the horse races were run, and the ships of Magellan had set out to the Spice Islands in 1529 and ended up circling the world.

I had found the place that, having opened the rest of the south to strangers, the Spanish wanted to keep to themselves. So don't go to Sanlúcar when you are "doing" Europe. There is nothing there to do.

Chris Stewart

(1951–   )

Before becoming a bestselling author, Chris Stewart was the drummer for Genesis (he quit when he was seventeen, after they cut their first album), a sheep shearer, a travel writer, and an expat farmer in the tiny Andalusian town of Orgiva. He and his wife, Ana, bought El Valero, a farm with olive, almond, and lemon groves, but no access road, water supply, or electricity. For twelve years they struggled to survive. "We worked damn hard seven days a week and really struggled to make ends meet . . . it was genteel poverty if you know what I mean. But of course, no matter how nice your particular poverty is, it's always a constant, nagging worry."

And then *Driving Over Lemons* (1999, from which this was excerpted) was published and the Stewarts' lives changed dramatically, as have the lives of the people of Orgiva. There are more than 350,000 copies in print in Britain, and Stewart's fans make a pilgrimage to his home. "There's a big influx of Brits," he said, "and the blame is all being laid at my door . . . it's not of plague proportions but we do get people from all over the world. If they're nice and lucky they get a cup of tea."

In his book Stewart focuses on the relationships that he formed in Spain. Domingo, a resourceful neighbor, becomes his valued ally. The Stewarts also befriend a group of eccentrics who long ago left the mainstream to live their days in Spain. "However much you may fight against it, if you live abroad where there are other expatriates, you become part of what is known as the Foreign Community." In this excerpt, Stewart sketches some of the people in the Foreign Community who become important parts of his family's life.

The sequel to *Driving Over Lemons* is *A Parrot in the Pepper Tree* (2002). Stewart, his wife, Ana, and daughter, Chloë, continue to live in El Valero.

From DRIVING OVER LEMONS

FRIENDS AND FOREIGNERS

However much you may fight against it, if you live abroad where there are other expatriates, you become part of what is known as the Foreign Community. Initially, I struggled hard against this notion but as the years passed I grew more relaxed about my status as a foreigner and more willing to appreciate the ties that, by language, humour and shared experience, bound me to my compatriots.

Being a part of a foreign community is a bit like being at school. Among other things seniority bestows respect. In our part of the Alpujarras, the most senior member by age, time served, and a natural proclivity towards seniority, was Janet. She had moved here in the early Seventies and built a large house on the outskirts of Tijolas, at the beginning of our valley, which she proceeded to enclose with a highly imposing wall.

Romero once told me with a smirk of how a horsedealer of his acquaintance had once scaled these walls. He tethered his horse nearby and swung himself up with the aid of a stout creeper and a handy tree. His intention, once inside the garden, was undoubtedly to surprise the lady occupant, but his plan went badly wrong. As he dropped from the wall into the shrubbery, he was set upon by Janet's pack of Appenzeller dogs, one of which gave him a nasty bite in the arse. He flew back over the wall and rode painfully into town where he promptly denounced Janet to the police for keeping a dangerous animal.

For those with less nefarious intentions there's a small blue door that you can knock upon. Ana and I, having been invited to lunch by Janet the summer after we moved to El Valero, knocked and waited politely, as befits newcomers visiting the gentry. The top half of the door flew open to reveal her pack of slavering dogs. Janet stood amongst them, knuckles clenched round the handle of a long leather whip which she flailed to left and right, cursing the dogs roundly.

"Come in, come in, quickly, quickly, and don't mind the dogs. Just keep your hands above your heads, they'll get used to you. Down,

you bugger!" And with a deft boot and a lash of the whip she floored
a particularly disagreeable specimen that was hovering around our
throats.

We shuffled in, hands up, and the door slammed behind us. "Welcome, my dears!" shouted Janet above the awful din. "Wait there a
minute while I deal with these brutes. Some meat should keep them
quiet." She disappeared with the dogs at her heels, leaving us trembling by the door. Soon she returned with half a dozen split cow's
heads, red and meaty, which she hurled onto the lawn. The dogs
crashed through the shrubbery and leapt in slobberous delight upon
the head-bones.

"These are my children, you see," beamed Janet as she discarded
her whip. "Now, what shall we drink before lunch?"

We settled for wine and sat down at the table beneath a vine-
covered trellis—one of a sequence of DIY-looking follies. Lawns
dotted with exotic trees rolled across to a huge stone-flagged pool
with a classical gazebo at the end. We sipped our wine and gasped
politely at the garden.

"You must excuse me a minute, I'm just putting the finishing
touches to the lunch. Help yourselves to more wine."

We helped ourselves and went to admire a fish-pond, full of fish
and frogs, among them a tiny green tree-frog that Janet had imported
from exotic climes. Sitting down again I noticed a snake lying by the
pond contentedly eating a fish.

"Now there's a most singular phenomena," I remarked to Ana.

"Perhaps we should say something . . ."

"Janet, is there supposed to be a snake eating fish by the pond?"

"What?" from the kitchen.

"A snake, there's a snake eating your fish."

She shot out of the kitchen. "A snake? Where? . . . so there is. I
know him—he's been taking all the fish for the last couple of
months. This time I'm going to fix the bastard. Wait, Chris, hold him
there while I get something to kill him with. I know what'll settle his
hash! Hang on there, don't whatever you do let him go!" and she shot
back into the kitchen.

I looked quizzically at Ana, and back at the snake.

"How the hell am I supposed to keep it there?"

The snake fortunately didn't seem much disposed to move. It was still peacefully eating its fish . . . or rather Janet's fish. I could hear a frenzied rummaging in the kitchen, and furious cries.

"Where oh where is the bloody meat tenderiser? Where in the name of hell has the thing gone?! . . . there it is! Is he still there, Chris? You still got him?"

"Yes, still here."

She came hurtling out of the kitchen, brandishing the meat-tenderiser, leapt into the bushes and lunged for the snake with her weapon, whereupon the head of the utensil fell off.

"Buggery! Now the head's come off! Can't they make decent tools in this accursed country? And now the bloody snake's slithered off again."

She sat down at the table and took a slug of wine.

"Oh well, it was a damn good try. Perhaps I'll get him next time. Right, let there be luncheon!"

And she produced a sumptuous six-course Indian meal, all freshly prepared. As we worked our way through it she told us the story of her life. How she was thwarted by the Mau Mau uprising in her attempts to qualify as a vet in Kenya, and forced instead to study the subject at home, coming through with a pretty thorough knowledge of animal ailments and their treatment. She now runs a free clinic from her home and does a first-rate job of fixing up all the local cats, dogs and horses. Doing this she enjoys her happiest hours.

When she is not attending to sick animals, Janet told us, she studies. She was currently working through maths and physics and veterinary science, and in order to prevent her outlook on life becoming too earnest, was reading Swiss satirical magazines in French and German. Try as I might, I found it impossible to imagine the Swiss as a fund of satirical humour. I said as much to Janet. "Yes . . . yes, Chris, you're perfectly right. They don't have any humour at all. In fact, the Swiss have the sort of sense of humour you'd expect a dog to have!"

Thank heavens for Janet, she's a true eccentric and, for all her bluffness, unfailingly generous. She has also become a staunch friend of Chloë's. "I've never had much time for babies, Ana," she boomed on her first visit after Chloë's birth. "Animals are a lot less trouble and serve you better too as a general rule. But I have to say that's a damn fine baby you've got there. I'll tell you what I'm going to do, I'm going to knit it a parrot. Nice little fellow like that, what it needs is a proper woollen parrot. I used to be pretty good at knitting years ago, you know, but it got in the way of the veterinary studies, so I stopped it."

Sure enough, within a couple of weeks a bright woollen parrot, an amorphous woollen bag with a couple of flaps on the side and two buttons for the eyes, turned up. Janet had also knitted a white tam-o-shanter—to keep the little fellow's head warm. Stuffed with straw it would have made a handy pack-saddle for a donkey. But that was not all: she had also carpentered a beautiful high-chair with the seat upholstered apparently in some rare tribal cloth, and made a wooden chest to keep Chloë's clothes in. Treasured gifts.

There seems to be a preponderance of eccentric women among the foreigners here. Some of them have husbands in tow, but they tend to be vapid creatures who fade into the background and are of little account. Amanda and Malcolm are one such couple: typical, in their way, of the Orgiva New Agers. Malcolm has long white hair and a penchant for loose flowing clothes. Rodrigo, whose flock of goats ravages the wilderness around Amanda and Malcolm's land, is unable to accept that Malcolm is a man. Rodrigo always refers to them, and he refers to them a lot, as there are constant disputes between them, as "those two Englishwomen."

Before coming to Spain, Amanda made a living as an organic farmer on the Welsh borders, and in the Alpujarras she was soon recognised among the ex-pat community as the person to consult on all matters horticultural and botanical. I sought her out one hot June morning to ask her advice about *Lavatera olbia*, a flowering shrub that is indigenous to central and western Andalucía. A friend in England, who is a seed-merchant, had started giving us the odd order for wild flower seeds, and had asked for a kilo of the *lavatera*. Try as I might, I couldn't find a single specimen of the plant. So I set out with Chloë gurgling away on the seat beside me, on an expedition to try Amanda's botanical expertise.

I came upon her, clad in white muslin, thumping away with a mattock in her vegetable patch. As I bounced along the rough mountain track that led to her home, she straightened up as she saw me, swept the hair from her eyes and asked: "Who is this that comes to visit me when the moon is rising in Aquarius?"

People had told me about Amanda's enthusiasm for astrology but even so the question caught me off my guard. I looked down to see if Chloë could shed any light on the issue, but she had succumbed to the noonday heat and fallen fast asleep.

"Er . . . my name's Chris, Chris Stewart. I'm told you're an expert botanist. I need some information about some plants that might grow around here."

"People are very kind to say that. I'm sure it's not true, but let's have some tea anyway and I'll see if I can help you out."

Amanda had not come across any of the *lavatera* I was after but was clearly a repository of knowledge on Alpujarran flora. We drank tea beneath a rose-covered arbour and talked about botany, the mountains and Rodrigo, as we gazed across the Mediterranean at the faint outline of the Rif in Morocco. Chloë, meanwhile, dozed on in my lap.

"Rodrigo is too bad, you know, his goats are absolutely destroying the countryside. I've told him about it time and again but he takes not a blind bit of notice. Soon Rodrigo and his wretched goats will have us living in a desert. You do know, don't you, that the Sahara Desert was a green and fertile garden until Rodrigo and his ilk started having their way with it?"

"I had heard of such a thing, yes."

"Well, the answer, I'm convinced, is to plant retama all over the dry parts of the mountains. Retama will put up with pretty much anything . . . except goats."

"Retama? You can't be serious!"

Retama is a tall woody shrub with long silver leaves and deep roots. In spring it scents the hills and valleys throughout southern Spain with its pendulous showers of yellow blooms. There's an awful lot of it about and it's of little apparent use. Persuading Rodrigo to plant retama on the hills would be like trying to get a British dairy-farmer to sow docks and thistles.

"I'm perfectly serious," she insisted. "Retama is the thing. I have actually had a talk with Rodrigo about my idea, and I do believe he is slowing coming round to it."

"I'm the first one to approve of a bit of original thinking," I said, trying not to be dismissive, "but I can't really see the idea taking root, so to speak. Retama is pretty, and it's drought-resistant with those long long roots, but beyond providing a bit of seed and frond for the goats to . . ."

"Wretched goats! I'm not going to plant it for the goats, Chris. In order to build up a viable ecology in this area we must start to get the goats out of the equation."

We talked around the subject until it was exhausted, Chloë was awake, and her supper beckoned. I made my excuses, casting a lunch invitation for Sunday as I started the Landrover. "Oh—and bring your . . . bring, er . . ."

"Malcolm, you mean Malcolm, I take it. Yes, I'll bring him, too."

"That," said Amanda, pushing back the sleeves of her muslin dress and jabbing at the fly-trap that I'd hung on the stable wall, "that is a disgusting contraption. How could you do that?"

The offending trap was an American patent and a device of which I was rather proud. It consisted of a plastic bag full of water and some mephitic muck that is apparently so irresistible to flies that they crawl happily through a plastic funnel in order to drown themselves alongside a sodden and evil-smelling mass of their peers. I was lured into buying it by the bizarre testimonial emblazoned across the packet: "With your wonderful fly-trap we were able to enjoy our annual barbecue without flies. Where we have our barbecue is right by the hogpens!"

"Surely, Amanda, one has to draw the line somewhere," I protested, "and flies fall a long way beneath the line I've drawn. Look at the misery they cause the horses and sheep, to say nothing of the misery they cause us."

"Us? You, you mean. Flies don't bother me at all, nor Malcolm." A snort of assent sounded behind my left shoulder. "If you're at peace with yourself and the world around you, then the flies won't trouble you. It's as simple as that."

Now I knew that Amanda was serious about the flies because I had heard from a woman who had once stayed at her house that she experienced similar tender feelings towards scorpions. Scorpions do not as a rule like water but for some reason they would come scuttling in from all corners of the surrounding country to fall into Amanda's pond and drown. So distressed was Amanda by this that she had a net prepared to fish out the poor mites, as she called them, and return them to the world of stones and scrub from whence they came.

My informant had good reason to be impressed by these actions. She had been stung on the mouth by one of Amanda's poor mites in bed. This was despite the fact that she was a woman at peace with herself and her surroundings, although naturally anyone would lose a certain amount of faith in their surroundings after an event like that. It did seem a shame that not all creatures shared Amanda's vision of the universe.

Amanda and Malcolm had arrived early for lunch and we had been showing them around Ana's vegetable patch. Ana edged the conversation tactfully away from our wanton slaughter of flies and onto the safer ground of natural fertilisers, as we pried Chloë from her sandpit and walked up to the house.

"Isn't it one of God's greatest miracles that the dung of the beasts carries all the elements essential to the growth of the plants that feed the very creatures that produce the manure that feeds the plants . . . and so on," I rabbitted, anxious to display my organic credentials. "The more I think of that particular fact, the more delighted I am by the organisation of the universe."

"Being vegans, of course, we don't use animal manure," Malcolm replied, "only our own excreta—and seaweed."

There was a pause.

"You're making a bit of a rod for your own back there, aren't you, Malcolm?" I suggested. "I mean, importing seaweed when you're living in the mountains surrounded by copiously dunging animals?"

"Yes, it makes things much more difficult, of course, but we try not to use the products of any animal that is exploited. Animals should be wild and free like us."

I looked hard at Malcolm. Wild and free were not the first two adjectives I would have hit upon.

"We don't wear leather shoes or woollen clothes, either."

"Well, it certainly is a hard path you choose. But lunch must be ready now. Ana has prepared a meal that we hope will be acceptable in every way. It's amazing how you have to think to do it."

Ana had indeed excelled herself. She presented us with a delicious-looking dish of aubergines, peppers, tomatoes, potatoes and garlic, all bubbling together in a spicy sauce of soya-milk yoghurt.

"I'm afraid we can't possibly eat that."

"You what?!"

"We don't eat peppers or aubergines or tomatoes or potatoes. All those vegetables are *Solanaceae*, members of the deadly nightshade family. They're poisonous."

"You'll enjoy the garlic then, just pick around the rest."

The first thing you hear is a whistle that sounds like a tutubia, except that tutubias rarely come down to the river, preferring the scrub high in the hills. Then comes a rolling river of bells and you realise that it's Rodrigo calling to his goats. Up the river they come, in a dozen or more streams, picking their way over ledges and boulders or browsing by the water's edge while Rodrigo waits above the bank, keeping watch from beneath the brim of his ancient straw hat.

There's truth in what Amanda says about the destructive capacity of goats. Sheep are bad enough but goats are in a different league. A goat will stand on its back legs and reach eight feet in the air, ripping all the leaves and branches off the trees to that height. They are prodigious climbers and scramblers, sure-footed and fearless beyond belief, and their delicate pointed feet are like little jackhammers, scrabbling away earth banks, stone walls and the edges of terraces.

Kid, however, is delicious to eat, fetching a higher price than lamb, and on terrain where no other creature could survive, goats sustain themselves and produce a couple of litres of milk a day—not just ordinary milk, but milk with almost miraculous properties of healing and nourishment. So, in spite of the opposition of the ecologists there will always be goats and their goatherds in the Alpujarras.

I often walk across the lemon terrace and down the rocky ramp into the riverbed to pass the time of day with Rodrigo.

"Hola!" I greet him.

"Qué?" he asks.

That "qué?" means "what?", but not just an ordinary "what?" It is delivered expansively, the head cocked, the palms upturned and stretched wide, and spoken loud and long. It means "How are you doing? How's the wife and the little one? How's your life and how is the farming and the crops?" I can't say it like Rodrigo does. It takes many years of walking with only goats and your own thoughts for company before you can manage the delivery of that particular "qué." I have to be more specific.

"How's your wife, Rodrigo?"

"Ay, Cristóbal, she's bad, very bad. She can hardly walk now, she's had a hard life."

"I'm sorry to hear that."

"You see, Cristóbal, life is but a breath. We come into this vale of sorrow, we're here four days, and if we get a chance to do some little good, do someone a favour, then we've done well and we can be a little happy perhaps. But then we're cut down and gone, just bones and dust. In truth we're no different from the dumb beasts, these goats I walk with."

A pronouncement like this is best received in silence. I know Rodrigo well enough by now to respect the sincerity behind his awkward philosophising. Rodrigo has a truly generous spirit.

"I saw you talking with the Englishwomen yesterday. Were they saying things about me and the goats?"

"Well, mainly they were talking about the goats, Rodrigo. They don't like them at all, that's sure. It appears that they busy themselves out on the hill planting retama and then your goats come along and eat it."

"Cristóbal, why would anyone want to plant retama in the *secano*? I can't see it."

"It's strange, I know, but they say it is good for the soil—it stops the erosion. Anyway, I think they'd rather you didn't take your goats near their place."

"There is a Via Pecuaria there and I have to pass it to get to the land above El Picacho. One is entitled to graze the Via Pecuaria. Look, Cristóbal, I don't want to be a bad neighbour to them—if they want to plant retama on the hill then that's fine with me, but there's not so much grazing about that I can afford to leave a *secano* like El

Picacho. As the goats pass they will of course eat the young retama; it's only natural. You see my point?"

"I do, I do."

And thus continues the endless battle between the ecologists and the pastoralists.

Rodrigo gets lonely in the river. He walks all day every day of the year with his goats, and he's done so in these mountains and valleys for fifty years. He has seen whole weather cycles change the face of his world. Years of drought when his pencil-thin animals had to scuff in the dust for the tiniest shoot—years when he needed all his herder's skill to seek out the places where, after months or even years without rain, some barely perceptible mist of moisture might remain. And years when for months at a time he couldn't get his horse across the swollen river, and had to go all the way down to the Seven-Eye bridge to get to his goat stable. Those were the easy years, he told me, when he could sit on a stone not a mile from his stable, with a couple of fertiliser bags tied over his head and shoulders—the preferred way of keeping off the lashing rain—and watch his goats gorge themselves.

Rodrigo had resigned himself to this harsh and lonely existence. It would never have occurred to him that one day his load might be lightened by someone to help—and least of all a frail-looking Dutch sculptress. But that's how it worked out.

Antonia, the Dutchwoman in question, had begun spending her summers at La Hoya, a crumbling farmhouse, just down the valley from El Valero. The day we met her, on her first summer in the valley, she had walked up the riverbed with her big smelly old dog and was trailing from terrace to terrace behind our ram, looking out from a wide-brimmed hat and moulding his shape in a lump of wax that she was working with her fingers.

"I'll separate him and shut him in for you if you like," I offered.

"No, I prefer to watch him moving around with the flock. I get a more natural result that way."

The ram seemed to take a dim view of being modelled, moving off as soon as Antonia got a good vantage, and leading her on a stumbling trail around the stony meadow. The business was further complicated by the heat of the day, because the wax kept melting, and every fifteen minutes or so Antonia had to dip it in the cooling water of the *acequia*. When she got back, of course, the flock had disappeared, and by the time she had found them the wax had started melting again. So I gave her a bucket which she filled with water and carried around with her.

By this method Antonia was able to make a certain amount of progress, and slowly the models took shape. She made a lot of sheep that summer, along with some bulls and goats—and a wonderful rendering of Domingo's donkey, Bottom. When she returned to Holland to cast some of her models in bronze, she left a little menagerie of wax figures in a drawer in our house, to the great delight of Chloë.

Rodrigo lives high above La Hoya at La Valenciana, about an hour and a half on horseback, but stables his goats at the lower farm. Each morning, having seen to the needs of the cows, the pigs, the chickens and the horse, he saddles up and moves off down the steep hill. Arriving at La Hoya, he ministers to any goats that need attention, then takes them out into the river or up onto the hills. Even in the scorching heat of summer he never takes a siesta; there'd be no time to fit it in. Goats don't mind the heat at all.

All of a sudden a slight variation appeared in the monotony of Rodrigo's existence. La Antonia, as he called her, took to walking with him in the river, occasionally fashioning an animal in wax as they progressed. Rodrigo must be the only goatherd in Spain with a model of a billy-goat cast personally for him in bronze; it's an expensive process. When there was goatwork to be done, injections, wormings, washings and so on, Antonia would often spend the whole morning helping, and goatwork is a lot easier with two people than with one. On the odd occasion when it was necessary to put an animal out of its misery for one reason or another, Antonia would even kill goats for Rodrigo with a knife. Alpujarreños do not like to kill animals. I have to do the same on occasion for Domingo.

Antonia made a difference to Rodrigo's life, day to day, but when Rodrigo's wife, Carmen, fell ill and was rushed to hospital in Granada, her presence became vital. After shutting the goats in for the night, Antonia would drive Rodrigo home, help him tend to the other animals, then take him to Granada and stay there while he spent the whole night sitting beside his sick wife's bed. This is the custom here, the family is expected to deal with much of the nursing.

The vigil continued for nine days, and then Carmen came home, at least a little better. Since then La Antonia has become an adored honorary member of their family. When she goes to spend the night with them at La Valenciana it's only with the greatest reluctance that they let her go. I've never been inside Carmen and Rodrigo's home but Ana has. She went up there one day with Antonia and of course Carmen invited them in. It proved impossible to escape without eating and drinking all of the most delicious and precious consumable items in the house. Ana said it was like visiting with the queen.

Antonia spends long spells in Holland, earning money for her work in Spain, drumming up patronage and commissions, and doing the bronze castings for the figures she makes. When she leaves the valley on these trips, Rodrigo walks with his goats and weeps a little. "I think God sent me the Antonia, Cristóbal," he confided to me. While she's away he besieges us for news of her and judges minutely when a postcard might be expected.

Antonia is a real artist and she puts as much energy and artistry into her life as she does into her work. She gives and gives, and despite the fact that she's not very robust, nothing is too much trouble for her. And so life repays her, people love her. She's the only foreigner I know here who simply by being true to herself has become a part of the Alpujarra.

Calvin Trillin

(1 9 3 5 –)

When asked to elaborate on his statement that food writers are obsessive and crazy, Calvin Trillin said, "For one thing, obviously, people literally become obsessive about eating. There are actual pathologies having to do with eating, as opposed to say, being a sportswriter . . . There were food writers in New York who would actually think that if you liked or didn't like the Coach House—an old-style American kind of restaurant in Greenwich Village—it wasn't simply that you were mistaken or perhaps had a different opinion. It was your character. You were a flawed human being." Trillin's view of food—and the world—is expansive. As a writer for *The New Yorker*, he is more likely to tout the virtues of a deli in the East Village than a four-star French restaurant on the Upper West Side. Trillin once campaigned to change the national dish of Thanksgiving to something more tasty—spaghetti carbonara.

But Trillin does not limit his culinary adventures to New York. In *Feeding a Yen* (2003, from which this is excerpted), he traveled to New Mexico to sample *posole*, Ecuador for *ceviche*, Nice for *pan bagnat*, and northern Spain for *pimientos de Padrón*. On his quests Trillin was usually accompanied by his wife, Alice. (Like Eric Newby's Wanda, Alice was Trillin's sensible foil. Trillin said that readers were often surprised that she did not sport a bun and oxford shoes.)

In addition to food essays, Calvin Trillin has authored many books, including *Remembering Denny* (1993), a well-received memoir about a Yale classmate who committed suicide, and *Tepper Isn't Going Out* (2001), "the first novel about a parking space." Trillin lives in Greenwich Village; Alice died on September 11, 2001, of natural causes.

From FEEDING A YEN

PEPPER CHASE

I'm aware that I tend to go on about *pimientos de Padrón*. They are on a list I keep in my head of the victuals that, despite being my favorite dishes in one part of the world or another, rarely seem to be served outside their territory of origin—a list I sometimes refer to as the Register of Frustration and Deprivation. I have always assumed that a lot of people have such a list, no matter where they live. Now and then, I try to comfort myself with the thought that, given the fact that I live in New York, my Register of Frustration and Deprivation is much shorter than it would be if I lived anywhere else. That doesn't seem to help much.

When I think of food I've enjoyed in Tuscany, for instance, I think of the grain called farro—something that almost never seems to turn up on the menus of those Tuscan trattorias that gradually became more prevalent in Manhattan than delis. Of all the things I've eaten in the Cajun country of Louisiana—an array of foodstuffs which has been characterized as somewhere between extensive and deplorable— I yearn most often for boudin. Except when a kindly friend of mine from New Iberia arrives in New York carrying his ice chest, I've never had Cajun boudin outside of Louisiana. During long New York winters, no such kindly friend arrives from Nova Scotia, where I live in the summer, carrying an ice chest full of Lunenburg sausage, which is strong on the herb summer savory and can be grilled like a hot dog or eaten with Lunenburg County sauerkraut or crumbled in a pasta dish that has always been called at our house *spagatinni Lunenburgesa*. Lame versions of tapas are served all over New York, but none of the city's markets sell that bread rubbed with tomatoes that you get at La Boqueria, the splendid public market of Barcelona. My register is filled with dishes like that. On gray afternoons, I go over it, like a miser who is both tantalizing and tormenting himself by poring over a list of people who owe him money.

When, at the tag end of a long meal, people began talking about their unsatisfied food cravings, my tale is often about *pimientos*. It always starts in Santiago de Compostela, which has been one of the world's great pilgrimage destinations for more than a millennium—the goal of pilgrims who demonstrate their devotion by walking for miles down El Camino de Santiago. The market, just a few blocks from the magnificent Romanesque cathedral that is said to hold the remains of St. James the Apostle, is about to open. It's early in the morning. The fishmongers are still lining up their sardines, and a butcher is using something that looks like a blowtorch to singe the last hairs from a hog's head. Scattered along one edge of the market, a dozen women from the town of Padrón itself, which is only fifteen miles away, sit behind huge baskets of digit-sized green peppers. They sort constantly, setting aside the peppers that they can distinguish, simply by touch, as unsuitably piquant, and preparing a couple of hundred-*pimiento* bags on the off chance that some customer in a terrible hurry will not want to witness the selection being counted out, pepper by pepper. I'm standing with something akin to a religious feeling in that lovely market, whose vaulted stone market sheds are actually called naves. I'm thinking about how the very peppers I'm observing are going to taste in a few hours, after they've been fried in olive oil and sprinkled with coarse salt, and my distress at having to wait those few hours is such that I have to nip over to the market-café across the street and buck myself up with some fresh *churros* dipped in *café con leche.*

"Peppers!" says someone at the table who has been itching to describe the exquisite pleasure of eating something drizzled with something on a bed of something else. "You're making all this fuss about some little green peppers cooked in oil? You *yearn* for peppers?"

I do. They're on the register.

By putting *pimientos de Padrón* on the list, I don't mean to imply that the region of Spain that Santiago serves as spiritual and political capital—Galicia, which the less sophisticated geographers usually describe as the bit above Portugal—is a one-dish spot. Galicians (*gallegos* in Spanish) gave the world, among other dishes, *caldo gallego*, the soup that is often the first item Cubans, many of whom are grandchildren of Galician migrants, put on their restaurants' menus. Galicians are renowned for their *empanadas*—absolutely flat pies that are filled with a layer of tuna or sardines or lamprey eel or pork. The

Galician version of turnip greens provides a glorious piece of evidence that Galicia may have been visited in the past not only by the Vikings and Romans and Visigoths and Arabs and Normans and Celts mentioned in the guidebooks but also by some honest dirt farmers from Alabama.

Above all, Galicia has seafood of a variety and quality unmatched by any place I've ever been. In Galicia, a neighborhood café might offer among its snacks mussels, oysters, scallops, crawfish, three kinds of lobster, razor clams, spider crabs, ordinary crabs, octopus, squid, baby cuttlefish, clams, gooseneck barnacles (which, I have to say in the spirit of constructive criticism, might have been better off choosing another part of a goose to look like), and two or three varieties of shrimp. At practically any celebration, the presence of octopus is understood. I once read in a guidebook, for instance, that toward the end of June every year, at a shrine near a village called Silleda, people who feel themselves possessed by demons go through a ritual to exorcise the demons, and then everyone gathers for a feast of octopus. In Las Nieves, there is an annual celebration during which the families and friends of people who had a close brush with death the previous year march in a procession carrying tiny coffins and then join the assembled for a serious octopus feed. If bar mitzvahs are held in Galicia, I would expect to find octopus at the reception.

The seafood comes as a sort of surprise. In fact, the first time Alice and I were in that part of Spain—this was in the middle sixties, and we were driving through on our way to Portugal—we somehow remained oblivious to the sorts of marine creatures that could be put on our plate. Maybe we were moving too fast to eat, although I remember stopping in Santiago at the Hostal Reyes Católicos, which was built in the sixteenth century as a shelter for pilgrims. What we had read and heard about Galicia was how green it was and how picturesque. In those days, it was, in fact, almost shamelessly picturesque. In Galicia, a haystack is conical—the point on top finished off with a flourish, like the top of a soft-ice-cream cone. Galician farmers have always managed to make works of art out of the necessities of farming—stone walls, for instance, and haystacks and, most of all, the simple granary. The granaries, or *hórreos*, are like small stone houses on stilts, with pitched tile roofs that are almost always adorned with stone crosses. At the time of that first visit, Franco had just appointed as tourist minister a man named Manuel Fraga Ibarne, who was said to be taking a more modern approach to marketing Spain's attractions, and a lot of what we saw looked perfect enough to have been staged by him personally. "Ah, clever of you to place that *hórreo* in silhouette against that stand of pine trees, Fraga Ibarne," we'd find ourselves commenting as we drove along a mountain road in Galicia. Passing an old woman who was dressed completely in black and was pulling along a cart of twigs, we might say, "Ah, back in your hardy-peasant drag, Fraga, you sly devil."

It was on our next trip, maybe twenty-five years later, that we got the full impact of the seafood. I felt like some traveler who, having put off visiting Italy for many years because he has a limited interest in old churches and restored hill towns, finally shows up and discovers, for the first time, that the Italians have a way with pasta. The temptation is to ask, Why didn't anybody tell me about this before?

By that second trip, of course, Fraga Ibarne's machinations were less in evidence. We had arrived in Vigo, a city of about 250,000 people, most of whom were honking their horns. It was lunchtime, and we had found an outdoor café in the port, on a short block called Calle Pescadores. Fraga Ibarne would have shuddered at the ambience. On one side of a narrow street were three or four cafés, with tables that permitted the customers to stare straight into the cement back wall of a hotel that looked ugly enough from the front. There were jagged holes in the wall where pipes came through. The only thing breaking the view of the cement wall was the stand of a clothes vendor who was selling what looked like Kmart castoffs. There were four vendors of a different sort on our side of the street, just in front of the cafés—women who stood behind marble tables and shucked oysters. They acted as independent operators, bringing oysters to customers at any of the cafés. It was the café operators' responsibility to furnish the lemons. Ours did bring lemons, along with a huge spider crab and some grilled shrimp and some bread and an order of *pimientos de Padrón*. I looked around at the view. Then I had another bite of crab, which was delicious. Then I had some more peppers. The peppers were truly wondrous. "You know," I finally said to Alice, "this place is beautiful in its own way."

Galicia, we discovered, is a grazer's paradise. In the narrow streets off Santiago's cathedral square, it is common to stop at a restaurant to have a *ración* (a healthy portion) of, say, razor clams and a *ración* of octopus and of sardines and, of course, of *pimientos de Padrón*—and then move on to the place next door or across the street, where the cuttlefish had seemed particularly succulent the previous evening, even though the *pimientos* were merely spectacular. It was in Galicia that I said to Alice, after what I suppose you might call a series of meals one evening, "Alice, I think we should break out of that old breakfast-lunch-dinner trap."

Galicians are great celebrators of food—actually, they're pretty good at celebrating just about anything—and it's not unusual for a town to have, say, a razor clam festival or a sardine festival or an *empanada* festival. Our second visit to Galicia was in late July, which should have been at the height of the festival season, but we'd apparently chosen the week when the celebrators paused to catch their breath. The blow that I found hardest to bear during that trip of lost opportunities was missing the *pimientos de Padrón* festival, held every year just outside Padrón in the tiny village of Herbón—the place whose monastery was where Franciscans apparently first tried growing the pepper seeds they'd brought back from the New World in the eighteenth century and the place that remains the heart of the *pimientos de Padrón* belt.

After we returned to New York, I would daydream about what that festival might have been like. In those dreams I see myself with an unlimited supply of *pimientos*, grown and cooked by the masters. I am drinking wine. I am eating octopus, of course. People keep bringing more *pimientos* to my table. Just before I leave, a stranger sits down. He speaks perfect English. He tells me that he's importing the seeds of *pimientos de Padrón* to America—returning them to their hemisphere of origin. He's an entrepreneur, of course, but his interest in *pimientos* is much broader than that: he views what he's doing as a sort of repatriation project. Oddly enough, he tells me, north-central New Jersey has precisely the same soil conditions as Herbón. He already has orders from Spanish restaurants in New York, a list of which he shows me. I glance at his list, noting that several of the restaurants are in my neighborhood. This man displays a wide knowledge of peppers, and he seems to be what my father would have called a real go-getter—someone who wouldn't hesitate to tackle any project. I ask him if he's familiar at all with Cajun boudin.

Before Alice and I left for our next visit to Galicia, ten years later, we confirmed that the *pimientos de Padrón* festival was definitely scheduled for the first Saturday of August. We arrived in Santiago a week before that. Why take a chance? Also, we intended to do some pepper research, not all of it at the table. I'd arranged to meet with Julio Martín, long the agricultural extension agent for an area that includes the patch of land around Padrón and Herbón. Señor Martín was not encouraging about the possibility of my being able to cross *pimientos de Padrón* off my Register of Frustration and Deprivation anytime soon. The peppers I yearn for, he said, amount to a relatively small crop produced on small family holdings—perhaps a hundred families have been granted numbers that they can put on their pepper bags signifying authentic *pimientos de Padrón*—and no export system has ever been put together. Thirty percent of the crop is consumed in Galicia, and virtually all of the rest is distributed to other parts of Spain. Given the fact that *pimientos de Padrón* are harvested in Galicia only in the summertime, Señor Martí told me, the innocent who has a plate of peppers at a Madrid tapas bar in January is actually eating a legume produced in southern Spain or even North Africa.

But we were in Galicia, in August, and we could eat the real article, sometimes three times a day. For a week, I watched myself living out pepper dreams. There we are eating *pimientos de Padrón* along with razor clams and Serrano ham in a *jamonería* (ham specialist) not far from the cathedral square in Santiago. We are eating peppers and cuttlefish and sardines at a table outside one of the restaurants lining a sort of alleyway in the graceful old quarter of Pontevedra. We are eating *pimientos de Padrón* and sardines in an outdoor café on the harbor of Barqueiro, a fishing village along the fjords known as the Rias Altas. In Lugo, we are eating peppers in one of those distinguished Spanish restaurants that line the walls with photographs of the celebrated who have dined there—including, in this case, the pope. The pope! There's no stopping us. Across the bay from Ferrol, in a fishing town called Mugardos, we are eating peppers in a *pulpería*—an octopus restaurant—along with *pulpo de Mugardesa*, a version of octopus served nowhere else. In bars, we're eating dollar-and-a-half plates of peppers, biting them off while holding them by the stem; in fancy restaurants, we're eating six-dollar-a-plate peppers, with their stems removed, presumably to encourage the customer to use a knife and fork. At times, I thought I could hear my mother saying, "Eat your vegetables!" Then I remembered something Julio Martín had told us: If *pimientos de Padrón* were allowed to stay on the vine, they would grow large and red and inappropriately spicy. We weren't just eating vegetables, I reminded Alice; we were eating baby vegetables.

Did we reach any critical conclusions? At times we had the feeling that peppers eaten some distance from Padrón tended to be less reliably marvelous, although, to be honest about it, I don't recall seeing any left on our plates. In Porto do Barqueiro, for instance, our peppers didn't seem quite as tasty as usual, although that could have been simply in comparison with the fat sardines that we had at the same time. In Betanzos, in a restaurant where the razor clams were stupendous, the number of spicy peppers seemed particularly high, leading me to speculate that there might be a little joke among *pimientos de Padrón* people to send the hot ones to Betanzos. On the other hand, in Lugo, an interior city where it was difficult to find authentic *pimientos de Padrón* in the city market, the peppers at lunch were excellent. With no certain pattern emerging, there was nothing to do but keep eating. Toward the end of the week, I used the calculator mode of my pocket-sized electronic Spanish-English dictionary to estimate that Alice and I had consumed about seven hundred peppers.

Julio Martín had kindly agreed to accompany us to the *pimientos de Padrón* festival. We were to meet across from the Padrón city market. It was a landmark we knew, since we had been there the previous Sunday to inspect the shellfish and to snack in one of the eating tents on barbecue pork ribs and octopus—the octopus snatched out of the bubbling water of a huge pot, then held on a wooden block and snipped into bite-sized pieces with a scissors, then doused with salt, paprika, and olive oil. (They don't pretty up octopus in Galicia. If you've always wondered whether those little suction-cup thingees might adhere to the tongue while you were trying to get them masticated, Galicia is the place to find out.) Three friends of ours, two from London and one from Paris, had arrived in Santiago to join us for the festival. Alice said she felt some echoes of *The Sun Also Rises*, when Jake Barnes and Lady Brett and that bunch went to the festival in Pamplona, except that this time the group was focused on tiny green peppers instead of bulls.

On Saturday morning, the rain was coming down in sheets. It occurred to me that our festival jinx might have held. The previous Sunday, we'd arrived at Isla de Arousa for the mussel festival only to discover that we were there a week early. The Viking festival at Catoira—a celebration that features the disembarkation of some reenactors with horns on their hats and then, I'd been told, a lot of octopus and other Viking grub—was so jammed with traffic that we'd turned tail without getting out of the car. The only festival we'd actually managed to attend was the little town of Laro's celebration of *tortillas*—which in Spain are flat, pie-shaped potato omelets. The *tortillas* were free, unless you count having to listen to an exceedingly long speech before they were distributed, and they were good *tortillas*. But townspeople, who arrived carrying baskets of foodstuffs to supplement the *tortillas* (and octopus) being offered on the grounds, had reserved all of the picnic tables, so we had to bolt our food before the true owners of our table arrived. Also, to be direct about it, I do not yearn for potato omelets.

Although it was possible that the entire pepper festival would have to be suspended, Señor Martín remained calm. We all repaired to a bar called Casa Diós, which would be on the parade route if the rain lifted enough to permit the procession of farm implements that customarily moves out around noon to provide the festival's kickoff. As it turned out, the proprietors of the bar were pepper growers themselves—someone said that the grandmother, in her eighties, still went to the Santiago market every morning with her basket—so we asked for a couple of orders, along with a salt cod *empanada* and some sliced pork. The *pimientos de Padrón* were the best I'd ever tasted—soft, juicy, obviously snatched from the pot just before they turned brown. "I'm okay now," I said to Alice, "even if the rain doesn't stop."

But it did. There was still a strong drizzle as a line of tractors and plows pulling homemade floats—models of the original monastery in one case, three-foot-high peppers with arms in another—passed in front of the Casa Diós, but not long after that the sun came out. And not long after that, we were at the *pimientos de Padrón* festival. It was held in a sort of community picnic grounds out in the country, next to a graceful old convent that, I gathered, was on the site of where the Franciscans had their inspired stroke of agronomy centuries before. Peppers, in thick, shoulder-high plants that looked too dense to walk through, were visible in adjoining fields. In a little valley, picnic tables had been set out under gnarled oak trees. The tractors and plows from the procession were parked in front of the stage. Someone was selling octopus and barbecued pork. A mountain of *broa*, the dense cornmeal bread I'd always identified with Portugal, stood on a large table. Not far away, in three huge black pots suspended over an open fire, *pimientos de Padrón* were being fried in oil.

Before I knew what was happening, Señor Martín had pulled me up on the stage, where the mayor and other dignitaries were gathered to award parade trophies and do some speechifying. I hadn't noticed any other outsiders around, and I suppose he'd called me forward in the spirit that high school reunion organizers give a small prize to the person who's come the farthest. Alice and our friends were pointing to me on the stage and laughing; it was as if Jake Barnes had jumped into the bullring, tearing off his sport coat to use as a cape. Still, I thought about giving a little speech, and I patted my pocket to make sure the Spanish-English dictionary was in place. "You could say that I'm sort of a pilgrim myself," I might begin. But when the time came for me to be introduced, all I could muster was "*Muchas gracias.*" I wanted to get to the peppers.

After the ceremony, the mayor invited us to share his table. There was wine. There was, it almost goes without saying, octopus. There were *empanadas*. There was *broa*. People kept bringing more and more plates of peppers. Nobody came up to talk about a scheme to grow *pimientos de Padrón* in America, it's true, but I had four packets of seeds in my suitcase. An essay on *pimientos de Padrón* that I'd read in a book about eating in Galicia had reported rumors of success growing the peppers in California. I happen to have a friend in California who is adventurous in such matters. I had not given up.

When I got back from Galicia, I turned over the four packets of seeds to my friend in California, but the report of a successful crop—a crop, I'd been thinking, that was so bountiful it merited a festival of its own—never came. Occasionally, I would get vague reports of *pimientos de Padrón* sightings at a farmers' market someplace out there. Once, I received a letter from a woman who said that in New Jersey—where, not that far from the place my imaginary acquaintance had chosen as the scene of the pepper's repatriation to the Western Hemisphere, there happens to be a substantial Galician community—some of her relatives and their neighbors are obsessed with raising *pimientos de Padrón* in their backyard gardens. She invited me to join members of the community at a Galician feast built around the crop of *pimientos*. Unfortunately, the feast was in July, when I'm in Nova Scotia and have a reluctance to return to the United States which is somewhere between a policy and an article of religious belief. The next July found me back in Nova Scotia, wondering whether I'd made a mistake in not being a bit more flexible about my travel restrictions. Fortunately, I had Lunenburg sausage to soothe my feelings. Also Lunenburg pudding—a completely different foodstuff that looks like a sausage but is ready to eat, usually on a cracker with drinks. I love Lunenburg pudding. I've never seen Lunenburg pudding outside of Nova Scotia.

Anthony Trollope

(1815 – 1882)

Born the fourth of six into a poor family, Anthony Trollope suffered at the hands of other schoolchildren. He was a strange-looking child who showed little promise of the enormously popular novelist he would become. Trollope wrote, "I was big and awkward and ugly and had no doubt skulked about in a most unattractive manner. Of course I was ill-dressed and dirty. But ah! How well I remember the agonies of my young heart." It was his mother who reversed the family fortunes when her book *Domestic Manners of the Americans* (1832) became a bestseller. After a career with the post office, first in England and then in Ireland, Trollope followed his mother into the literary life. He wrote his first novel, *The Macdermots of Ballycloran*, in 1847.

Trollope was one of the most popular writers of the mid-nineteenth century. His forty-seven books included *Barchester Towers* (1857), the Palliser novels series, and *The Way We Live Now* (1874). He was also a prodigious travel writer. This short story, "John Bull on the Guadalquivir," is based on Trollope's six-day trip around southern Spain to inspect postal operations in Gibraltar. Trollope later recalled that, as the character in the story, he had once mistaken a Spanish duke for a bullfighter.

When he was with the post office in Ireland Trollope met a young Englishwoman, Rose Heseltine, and married her. She was invaluable, as she copied his work (his handwriting was almost indecipherable) and dealt with his literary affairs. Her loyalty was unshakable. Late in life, Trollope fell in love with Kate Field, the intrepid young American reporter also represented in this volume. Rose Trollope became her friend as well. When he died of a stroke in 1882, Anthony Trollope's literary fortunes were on the wane, only to be revived by critical reappraisals in the twentieth century. The novelist Joanna Trollope is not a direct descendant but is of the same family as Anthony Trollope.

JOHN BULL ON THE GUADALQUIVIR

I am an Englishman, living, as all Englishman should do, in England, and my wife would not, I think, be well pleased were any one to insinuate that she were other than an Englishwoman; but in the circumstances of my marriage I became connected with the south of Spain, and the narrative which I am to tell requires that I should refer to some of those details.

The Pomfrets and Daguilars have long been in trade together in this country, and one of the partners has usually resided at Seville for the sake of the works which the firm there possesses. My father, James Pomfret, lived there for ten years before his marriage; and since that and up to the present period, old Mr. Daguilar has always been on the spot. He was, I believe, born in Spain, but he came very early to England; he married an English wife, and his sons had been educated exclusively in England. His only daughter, Maria Daguilar, did not pass so large a proportion of her early life in this country, but she came to us for a visit at the age of seventeen, and when she returned I made up my mind that I most assuredly would go after her. So I did, and she is now sitting on the other side of the fireplace with a legion of small linen habiliments in a huge basket by her side.

I felt, at the first, that there was something lacking to make my cup of love perfectly delightful. It was very sweet, but there was wanting that flower of romance which is generally added to the heavenly draught by a slight admixture of opposition. I feared that the path of my true love would run too smooth. When Maria came to our house, my mother and elder sister seemed to be quite willing that I should be continually alone with her; and she had not been there ten days before my father, by chance, remarked that there was nothing old Mr. Daguilar valued so highly as a thorough feeling of intimate alliance between the two families which had been so long connected in trade. I was never told that Maria was to be my wife, but I felt that the same thing was done without words; and when, after six weeks of somewhat elaborate attendance upon her, I asked her to be Mrs. John Pomfret, I had no more fear of a refusal, or even of hesitation on her part, than I now have when I suggest to my partner some commercial transaction of undoubted advantage.

But Maria, even at that age had about her a quiet sustained decision of character quite unlike anything I had seen in English girls. I used to hear, and do still hear, how much more flippant is the education of girls in France and Spain than in England; and I know that this is shown to be the result of many causes—the Roman Catholic religion being, perhaps, chief offender; but, nevertheless, I rarely see in one of our own young women the same power of a self-sustained demeanour as I meet on the Continent. It goes no deeper than the demeanour, people say. I can only answer that I have not found that shallowness in my own wife.

Miss Daguilar replied to me that she was not prepared with an answer; she had only known me six weeks, and wanted more time to think about it; besides, there was one in her own country with whom she would wish to consult. I knew she had no mother; and as for consulting old Mr. Daguilar on such a subject, that idea, I knew, could not have troubled her. Besides, as I afterwards learned, Mr. Daguilar had already proposed the marriage to his partner exactly as he would have proposed a division of assets. My mother declared that Maria was a foolish chit—in which by-the-bye she showed her entire ignorance of Miss Daguilar's character; my eldest sister begged that no constraint might he put on the young lady's inclinations— which provoked me to assert that the young lady's inclinations were by no means opposed to my own; and my father, in the coolest manner suggested that the matter might stand over for twelve months, and that I might then go to Seville, and see about it! Stand over for twelve months! Would not Maria, long before that time, have been snapped up and carried off by one of those inordinately rich Spanish grandees who are still to be met with occasionally in Andalucía?

My father's dictum, however, had gone forth; and Maria, in the calmest voice, protested that she thought it very wise. I should be less of a boy by that time, she said, smiling on me, but driving wedges between every fibre of my body as she spoke. "Be it so," I said, proudly. "At any rate, I am not so much of a boy that I shall forget you." "And, John, you still have the trade to learn," she added, with her deliciously foreign intonation—speaking very slowly, but with perfect pronunciation. The trade to learn! However, I said not a word, but stalked out of the room, meaning to see her no more before she went. But I could not resist attending on her in the hall as she started; and, when she took leave of us, she put her face up to be kissed by me, as she did by my father, and seemed to receive as much emotion from one embrace as from the other. "He'll go out by the packet of the 1st April," said my father, speaking of me as though I were a bale of goods. "Ah! that will be so nice," said Maria, settling her dress in the carriage; "the oranges will be ripe for him then!"

On the 17th April I did sail, and felt still very like a bale of goods. I had received one letter from her, in which she merely stated that her papa would have a room ready for me on my arrival; and, in answer to that, I had sent an epistle somewhat longer, and, as I then thought, a little more to the purpose. Her turn of mind was more practical than mine, and I must confess my belief that she did not appreciate my poetry.

I landed at Cádiz, and was there joined by an old family friend, one of the very best fellows that ever lived. He was to accompany me up as far as Seville; and as he had lived for a year or two at Xeres, was supposed to be more Spanish almost than a Spaniard. His name was Johnson, and he was in the wine trade; and whether for travelling or whether for staying at home—whether for paying you a visit in your own house, or whether for entertaining you in his—there never was (and I am prepared to maintain there never will be) a stancher friend, choicer companion, or a safer guide than Thomas Johnson. Words cannot produce a eulogium sufficient for his merits. But, as I have since learned, he was not quite so Spanish as I had imagined. Three years among the bodegas of Xeres had taught him, no doubt, to appreciate the exact twang of a good, dry sherry; but not, as I now conceive, the exactest flavour of the true Spanish character. I was very lucky, however, in meeting such a friend, and now reckon him as one of the stanchest allies of the house of Pomfret, Daguilar, and Pomfret.

He met me at Cádiz, took me about the town, which appeared to me to be of no very great interest;—though the young ladies were all very well. But, in this respect, I was then a Stoic, till such time as I might be able to throw myself at the feet of her whom I was ready to

proclaim the most lovely of all the Dulcineas of Andalucía. He carried me up by boat and railway to Xeres; gave me a most terrific
headache, by dragging me out into the glare of the sun, after I had
tasted some half a dozen different wines, and went through all the
ordinary hospitalities. On the next day we returned to Puerto, and
from thence getting across to St. Lucar and Bonanza, found ourselves on the banks of the Guadalquivir, and took our places in the
boat for Seville. I need say but little to my readers respecting that far-
famed river. Thirty years ago we in England generally believed that
on its banks was to be found a pure elysium of pastoral beauty; that
picturesque shepherds and lovely maidens here fed their flocks in
fields of asphodel; that the limpid stream ran cool and crystal over
bright stones and beneath perennial shade; and that every thing on
the Guadalquivir was as lovely and as poetical as its name. Now, it is
pretty widely known that no uglier river oozes down to its bourn in
the sea through unwholesome banks of low mud. It is brown and
dirty; ungifted by any scenic advantage; margined for miles upon
miles by huge, flat, expansive fields, in which cattle are reared—the
bulls wanted for the bullfights among others; and birds of prey sit
constant on the shore, watching for the carcases of such as die. Such
are the charms of the golden Guadalquivir.

At first we were very dull on board that steamer. I never found
myself in a position in which there was less to do. There was a nasty
smell about the little boat which made me almost ill; every turn in the
river was so exactly like the last, that we might have been standing
still; there was no amusement except eating, and that, when once
done, was not of a kind to make an early repetition desirable. Even
Johnson was becoming dull, and I began to doubt whether I was so
desirous as I once had been to travel the length and breadth of all
Spain. But about noon a little incident occurred which did for a time
remove some of our tedium. The boat had stopped to take in passengers on the river; and, among others, a man had come on board
dressed in a fashion that, to my eyes, was equally strange and picturesque. Indeed, his appearance was so singular, that I could not but
regard him with care, though I felt at first averse to stare at a fellow-
passenger on account of his clothes. He was a man of about fifty, but
as active apparently as though not more than twenty-five; he was of

low stature, but of admirable make; his hair was just becoming griz-
zled, but was short and crisp and well cared for; his face was prepossessing, having a look of good humour added to courtesy, and there
was a pleasant, soft smile round his mouth which ingratiated one at
the first sight. But it was his dress rather than his person which
attracted attention. He wore the ordinary Andalucian cap—of which
such hideous parodies are now making themselves common in
England—but was not contented with the usual ornament of the
double tuft. The cap was small, and jaunty; trimmed with silk velvet—as is common here with men careful to adorn their persons; but
this man's cap was finished off with a jewelled button and golden fil-
igree work. He was dressed in a short jacket with a stand-up collar;
and that also was covered with golden buttons and with golden
button-holes. It was all gilt down the front, and all lace down the
back. The rows of buttons were double; and those of the more
backward row hung down in heavy pendules. His waistcoat was of
coloured silk—very pretty to look at; and ornamented with a small
sash, through which gold threads were worked. All the buttons of his
breeches also were of gold; and there were gold tags to all the
button-holes. His stockings were of the finest silk, and clocked with
gold from the knee to the ankle.

Dress any Englishman in such a garb and he will at once give you
the idea of a hog in armour. In the first place he will lack the proper
spirit to carry it off, and in the next place the motion of his limbs will
disgrace the ornaments they bear. "And so best," most Englishmen
will say. Very likely; and, therefore, let no Englishman try it. But my
Spaniard did not look at all like a hog in armour. He walked slowly
down the plank into the boat, whistling lowly but very clearly a few
bars from an opera tune. It was plain to see that he was master of
himself, of his ornaments, and of his limbs. He had no appearance
of thinking that men were looking at him, or of feeling that he was
beauteous in his attire;—nothing could be more natural than his
foot-fall, or the quiet glance of his cheery gray eye. He walked up to
the captain, who held the helm, and lightly raised his hand to his
cap. The captain, taking one hand from the wheel, did the same, and
then the stranger, turning his back to the stern of the vessel, and
fronting down the river with his face, continued to whistle slowly,

clearly, and in excellent time. Grand as were his clothes they were no burden on his mind.

"What is he?" said I, going up to my friend Johnson with a whisper.

"Well, I've been looking at him," said Johnson—which was true enough; "he's a—an uncommonly good-looking fellow, isn't he?"

"Particularly so," said I; "and got up quite irrespective of expense. Is he a—a—a gentleman, now, do you think?"

"Well, those things are so different in Spain that it's almost impossible to make an Englishman understand them. One learns to know all this sort of people by being with them in the country, but one can't explain."

"No; exactly. Are they real gold?"

"Yes, yes; I dare say they are. They sometimes have them silver gilt."

"It is quite a common thing, then, isn't it?" asked I.

"Well, not exactly; that—Ah! yes; I see! of course. He is a torero."

"A what?"

"A mayo. I will explain it all to you. You will see them about in all places, and you will get used to them."

"But I haven't seen one other as yet."

"No, and they are not all so gay as this, nor so new in their finery, you know."

"And what is a torero?"

"Well, a torero is a man engaged in bull-fighting."

"Oh! he is a matador, is he?" said I, looking at him with more than all my eyes.

"No, not exactly that;—not of necessity. He is probably a mayo. A fellow that dresses himself smart for fairs, and will be seen hanging about with the bull-fighters. What would be a sporting fellow in England—only he won't drink and curse like a low man on the turf there. Come, shall we go and speak to him?"

"I can't talk to him," said I, diffident of my Spanish. I had received lessons in England from Maria Daguilar; but six weeks is little enough for making love, let alone the learning of a foreign language.

"Oh! I'll do the talking. You'll find the language easy enough before long. It soon becomes the same as English to you, when you live among them." And then Johnson, walking up to the stranger, accosted him with that good-natured familiarity with which a thoroughly nice fellow always opens a conversation with his inferior. Of course I could not understand the words which were exchanged; but it was clear enough that the "mayo" took the address in good part, and was inclined to be communicative and social.

"They are all of pure gold," said Johnson, turning to me after a minute, making as he spoke a motion with his head to show the importance of the information.

"Are they indeed?" said I. "Where on earth did a fellow like that get them?" Whereupon Johnson again returned to his conversation with the man. After another minute he raised his hand, and began to finger the button on the shoulder; and to aid him in doing so, the man of the bull-ring turned a little on one side.

"They are wonderfully well made," said Johnson, talking to me, and still fingering the button. "They are manufactured, he says, at Osuna, and he tells me that they make them better there than anywhere else."

"I wonder what the whole set would cost?" said I. "An enormous deal of money for a fellow like him, I should think!"

"Over twelve ounces," said Johnson, having asked the question; "and that will be more than forty pounds."

"What an uncommon ass he must be!" said I.

As Johnson by this time was very closely scrutinising the whole set of ornaments I thought I might do so also, and going up close to our friend, I too began to handle the buttons and tags on the other side. Nothing could have been more good-humoured than he was—so much so that I was emboldened to hold up his arm that I might see the cut of his coat, to take off his cap and examine the make, to stuff my finger in beneath his sash, and at last to kneel down while I persuaded him to hold up his legs that I might look to the clocking. The fellow was thoroughly good-natured, and why should I not indulge my curiosity?

"You'll upset him if you don't take care," said Johnson; for I had got fast hold of him by one ankle, and was determined to finish the survey completely.

"Oh, no, I shan't," said I; "a bull-fighting chap can surely stand on

one leg. But what I wonder at is, how on earth he can afford it!"
Whereupon Johnson again began to interrogate him in Spanish.

"He says he has got no children," said Johnson, having received a
reply, "and that as he has nobody but himself to look after, he is able
to allow himself such little luxuries."

"Tell him that I say he would be better with a wife and a couple of
babies," said I—and Johnson interpreted.

"He says that he'll think of it some of these days, when he finds
that the supply of fools in the world is becoming short," said Johnson.

We had nearly done with him now; but after regaining my feet, I
addressed myself once more to the heavy pendules, which hung
down almost under his arm. I lifted one of these, meaning to feel its
weight between my fingers; but unfortunately I gave a lurch, probably through the motion of the boat, and still holding by the button,
tore it almost off from our friend's coat.

"Oh, I am so sorry," I said, in broad English.

"It do not matter at all," he said, bowing, and speaking with equal
plainness. And then, taking a knife from his pocket, he cut the pendule off, leaving a bit of torn cloth on the side of his jacket.

"Upon my word, I am quite unhappy," said I; "but I always am so
awkward." Whereupon he bowed low.

"Couldn't I make it right?" said I, bringing out my purse.

He lifted his hand, and I saw that it was small and white; he lifted
it and gently put it upon my purse, smiling sweetly as he did so.
"Thank you, no, señor; thank you, no." And then, bowing to us both,
he walked away down into the cabin.

"Upon my word he is a deuced well-mannered fellow," said I.

"You shouldn't have offered him money," said Johnson; "a
Spaniard does not like it."

"Why, I thought you could do nothing without money in this
country. Doesn't every one take bribes?"

"Ah! yes; that is a different thing; but not the price of a button. By
Jove! he understood English, too. Did you see that?"

"Yes; and I called him an ass! I hope he doesn't mind it."

"Oh! no; he won't think anything about it," said Johnson. "That sort of fellows don't. I dare say we shall see him in the bull-ring next Sunday, and then we'll make all right with a glass of lemonade."

And so our adventure ended with the man of the gold ornaments. I was sorry that I had spoken English before him so heedlessly, and resolved that I would never be guilty of such gaucherie again. But, then, who would think that a Spanish bull-fighter would talk a foreign language? I was sorry, also, that I had torn his coat; it had looked so awkward; and sorry again that I had offered the man money. Altogether I was a little ashamed of myself; but I had too much to look forward to at Seville to allow any heaviness to remain long at my heart; and before I had arrived at the marvellous city I had forgotten both him and his buttons.

Nothing could be nicer than the way in which I was welcomed at Mr. Daguilar's house, or more kind—I may almost say affectionate—than Maria's manner to me. But it was too affectionate; and I am not sure that I should not have liked my reception better had she been more diffident in her tone, and less inclined to greet me with open warmth. As it was, she again gave me her cheek to kiss, in her father's presence, and called me dear John, and asked me specially after some rabbits which I had kept at home merely for a younger sister; and then it seemed as though she were in no way embarrassed by the peculiar circumstances of our position. Twelve months since I had asked her to be my wife, and now she was to give me an answer; and yet she was as assured in her gait, and as serenely joyous in her tone, as though I were a brother just returned from college. It could not be that she meant to refuse me, or she would not smile on me and be so loving; but I could almost have found it in my heart to wish that she would. "It is quite possible," said I to myself, "that I may not be found so ready for this family bargain. A love that is to be had like a bale of goods is not exactly the love to suit my taste." But then, when I met her again in the morning I could no more have quarrelled with her than I could have flown.

I was inexpressibly charmed with the whole city, and especially with the house in which Mr. Daguilar lived. It opened from the corner of a narrow, unfrequented street—a corner like an elbow—and, as seen from the exterior, there was nothing prepossessing to recommend it; but the outer door led by a short hall or passage to an inner door or grille, made of open ornamental iron-work, and through that we entered a court, or patio, as they called it. Nothing could be more lovely or deliciously cool than was this small court. The building on each side was covered by trellis-work; and beautiful creepers, vines, and parasite flowers, now in the full magnificence of the early summer, grew up and clustered round the windows. Every inch of wall was covered, so that none of the glaring whitewash wounded the eye. In the four corners of the patio were four large orange-trees, covered with fruit. I would not say a word in special praise of these, remembering that childish promise she had made on my behalf. In the middle of the court there was a fountain, and round about on the marble floor there were chairs, and here and there a small table, as though the space were really a portion of the house. It was here that we used to take our cup of coffee and smoke our cigarettes, I and old Mr. Daguilar, while Maria sat by, not only approving, but occasionally rolling for me the thin paper round the fragrant weed with her taper fingers. Beyond the patio was an open passage or gallery, filled also with flowers in pots; and then, beyond this, one entered the drawing-room of the house. It was by no means a princely palace or mansion, fit for the owner of untold wealth. The rooms were not over large nor very numerous; but the most had been made of a small space, and everything had been done to relieve the heat of an almost tropical sun.

"It is pretty, is it not?" she said, as she took me through it.

"Very pretty," I said. "I wish we could live in such houses."

"Oh, they would not do at all for dear old fat, cold, cozy England. You are quite different, you know, in everything from us in the south; more phlegmatic, but then so much steadier. The men and the houses are all the same."

I can hardly tell why, but even this wounded me. It seemed to me as though she were inclined to put into one and the same category things English, dull, useful, and solid; and that she was disposed to show a sufficient appreciation for such necessaries of life, though she herself had another and inner sense—a sense keenly alive to the poetry of her own southern chime; and that I, as being English, was to have no participation in this latter charm. An English husband might do very well, the interests of the firm might make such an arrangement desirable, such a mariage de convenance—so I argued to myself—might be quite compatible with—with heaven only knows what delights of superterrestrial romance, from which I, as being an English thick-headed lump of useful coarse mortality, was to be altogether debarred. She had spoken to me of oranges, and having finished the survey of the house, she offered me some sweet little cakes. It could not be that of such things were the thoughts which lay undivulged beneath the clear waters of those deep black eyes—undivulged to me, though no one else could have so good a right to read those thoughts! It could not be that that noble brow gave index of a mind intent on the trade of which she spoke so often! Words of other sort than any that had been vouchsafed to me must fall at times from the rich curves of that perfect mouth.

So felt I then, pining for something to make me unhappy. Ah, me! I know all about it now, and am content. But I wish that some learned pundit would give us a good definition of romance, would describe in words that feeling with which our hearts are so pestered when we are young, which makes us sigh for we know not what, and forbids us to be contented with what God sends us. We invest female beauty with impossible attributes, and are angry because our women have not the spiritualised souls of angels, anxious as we are that they should also be human in the flesh. A man looks at her he would love as at a distant landscape in a mountainous land. The peaks are glorious with more than the beauty of earth and rock and vegetation. He dreams of some mysterious grandeur of design which tempts him on under the hot sun, and over the sharp rock, till he has reached the mountain goal which he had set before him. But when there, he finds that the beauty is well-nigh gone, and as for that delicious mystery on which his soul has fed, it has vanished for ever.

I know all about it now, and am, as I said, content. Beneath those deep black eyes there lay a well of love, good, honest, homely love, love of father and husband and children that were to come—of that love which loves to see the loved ones prospering in honesty. That noble brow—for it is noble; I am unchanged in that opinion, and will go unchanged to my grave—covers thoughts as to the welfare of many, and an intellect fitted to the management of a household, of servants, namely, and children, and perchance a husband. That mouth can speak words of wisdom, of very useful wisdom—though of poetry it has latterly uttered little that was original. Poetry and romance! They are splendid mountain views seen in the distance. So let men be content to see them, and not attempt to tread upon the fallacious heather of the mystic hills.

In the first week of my sojourn in Seville I spoke no word of overt love to Maria, thinking, as I confess, to induce her thereby to alter her mode of conduct to myself. "She knows that I have come here to make love to her—to repeat my offer; and she will at any rate be chagrined if I am slow to do so." But it had no effect. At home my mother was rather particular about her table, and Maria's greatest efforts seemed to be used in giving me as nice dinners as we gave her.

In those days I did not care a straw about my dinner, and so I took an opportunity of telling her. "Dear me," said she, looking at me almost with grief, "do you not? What a pity! And do you not like music either?" "Oh, yes, I adore it," I replied. I felt sure at the time that had I been born in her own sunny clime, she would never have talked to me about eating. But that was my mistake.

I used to walk out with her about the city, seeing all that is there of beauty and magnificence. And in what city is there more that is worth the seeing? At first this was very delightful to me, for I felt that I was blessed with a privilege that would not be granted to any other man. But its value soon fell in my eyes, for others would accost her, and walk on the other side, talking to her in Spanish, as though I hardly existed, or were a servant there for her protection. And I was not allowed to take her arm, and thus to appropriate her, as I should have done in England. "No, John," she said, with the sweetest, prettiest smile, "we don't do that here; only when people are married." And she made this allusion to married life out, openly, with no slightest tremor on her tongue.

"Oh, I beg pardon," said I, drawing back my hand, and feeling angry with myself for not being fully acquainted with all the customs of a foreign country.

"You need not beg pardon," said she; "when we were in England we always walked so. It is just a custom, you know." And then I saw her drop her large dark eyes to the ground, and bow gracefully in answer to some salute.

I looked round, and saw that we had been joined by a young cavalier—a Spanish nobleman, as I saw at once; a man with jet black hair, and a straight nose, and a black moustache, and patent leather boots, very slim and very tall, and—though I would not confess it then—uncommonly handsome. I myself am inclined to be stout, my hair is light, my nose broad, I have no hair on my upper lip, and my whiskers are rough and uneven. "I could punch your head though, my fine fellow," said I to myself, when I saw that he placed himself at Maria's side, "and think very little of the achievement."

The wretch went on with us round the plaza for some quarter of an hour talking Spanish with the greatest fluency, and she was every whit as fluent. Of course I could not understand a word that they said. Of all positions that a man can occupy, I think that this is about the most uncomfortable; and I cannot say that, even up to this day, I have quite forgiven her for that quarter of an hour.

"I shall go in," said I, unable to bear my feelings, and preparing to leave her. "The heat is unendurable."

"Oh dear, John, why did you not speak before?" she answered. "You cannot leave me here, you know, as I am in your charge; but I will go with you almost directly." And then she finished her conversation with the Spaniard, speaking with an animation she had never displayed in her conversations with me.

It had been agreed between us for two or three days before this, that we were to rise early on the following morning for the sake of ascending the tower of the cathedral, and visiting the Giralda, as the iron figure is called, which turns upon a pivot on the extreme summit. We had often wandered together up and down the long dark gloomy aisle of the stupendous building, and had, together, seen its treasury of art; but as yet we had not performed the task which has to be achieved by all visitors to Seville; and in order that we might have a clear view over the surrounding country, and not be tormented by the heat of an advanced sun, we had settled that we would ascend the Giralda before breakfast.

And now, as I walked away from the plaza towards Mr. Daguilar's house, with Maria by my side, I made up my mind that I would settle my business during this visit to the cathedral. Yes, and I would so manage the settlement that there should be no doubt left as to my intentions and my own ideas. I would not be guilty of shilly-shally conduct; I would tell her frankly what I felt and what I thought, and would make her understand that I did not desire her hand if I could not have her heart. I did not value the kindness of her manner, seeing that that kindness sprung from indifference rather than passion; and so I would declare to her. And I would ask her, also, who was this young man with whom she was intimate—for whom all her volubility and energy of tone seemed to be employed? She had told me once that it behoved her to consult a friend in Seville as to the expediency of her marriage with me. Was this the friend whom she had wished to consult? If so, she need not trouble herself. Under such circumstances I should decline the connection! And I resolved that I would find out how this might be. A man who proposes to take a woman to his bosom as his wife, has a right to ask for information— ay, and to receive it too. It flashed upon my mind at this moment that Donna Maria was well enough inclined to come to me as my wife, but—. I could hardly define the "buts" to myself, for there were three or four of them. Why did she always speak to me in a tone of childish affection, as though I were a schoolboy home for the holidays? I would have all this out with her on the tower on the following morning, standing under the Giralda.

On that morning we met together in the patio, soon after five o'clock, and started for the cathedral. She looked beautiful, with her black mantilla over her head, and with black gloves on, and her black morning silk dress—beautiful, composed, and at her ease, as though she were well satisfied to undertake this early morning walk from feelings of good nature—sustained, probably, by some undercurrent of a deeper sentiment. Well; I would know all about it before I returned to her father's house.

There hardly stands, as I think, on the earth, a building more remarkable than the cathedral of Seville, and hardly one more grand. Its enormous size; its gloom and darkness; the richness of ornamentation in the details, contrasted with the severe simplicity of the larger outlines; the variety of its architecture; the glory of its paintings; and the wondrous splendour of its metallic decoration, its altar-friezes, screens, rails, gates, and the like, render it, to my mind, the first in interest among churches. It has not the coloured glass of Chartres, or the marble glory of Milan, or such a forest of aisles as Antwerp, or so perfect a hue in stone as Westminster, nor in mixed beauty of form and colour does it possess anything equal to the choir of Cologne; but, for combined magnificence and awe-compelling grandeur, I regard it as superior to all other ecclesiastical edifices.

It is its deep gloom with which the stranger is so greatly struck on his first entrance. In a region so hot as the south of Spain, a cool interior is a main object with the architect, and this it has been necessary to effect by the exclusion of light; consequently the church is dark, mysterious, and almost cold. On the morning in question, as we entered, it seemed to be filled with gloom, and the distant sound of a slow footstep here and there beyond the transept inspired one almost with awe. Maria, when she first met me, had begun to talk with her usual smile, offering me coffee and a biscuit before I started. "I never eat a biscuit," I said, with almost a severe tone, as I turned from her. That dark, horrid man of the plaza—would she have offered him a cake had she been going to walk with him in the gloom of the morning? After that little had been spoken between us. She walked by my side with her accustomed smile; but she had, as I flattered myself, begun to learn that I was not to be won by a meaningless good nature. "We are lucky in our morning for the view!" that was all she said, speaking with that peculiarly clear, but slow pronunciation which she had assumed in learning our language.

We entered the cathedral, and, walking the whole length of the aisle, left it again at the porter's porch at the farther end. Here we passed through a low door on to the stone flight of steps, and at once began to ascend. "There are a party of your countrymen up before us," said Maria; "the porter says that they went through the lodge half an hour since." "I hope they will return before we are on the top," said I, bethinking myself of the task that was before me. And indeed my heart was hardly at ease within me, for that which I had to say would require all the spirit of which I was master.

The ascent to the Giralda is very long and very fatiguing; and we had to pause on the various landings and in the singular belfry in order that Miss Daguilar might recruit her strength and breath. As we rested on one of these occasions, in a gallery which runs round the tower below the belfry, we heard a great noise of shouting, and a clattering of sticks among the bells. "It is the party of your country-men who went up before us," said she. "What a pity that Englishmen should always make so much noise!" And then she spoke in Spanish to the custodian of the bells, who is usually to be found in a little cabin up there within the tower. "He says that they went up shouting like demons," continued Maria; and it seemed to me that she looked as though I ought to be ashamed of the name of an Englishman. "They may not be so solemn in their demeanour as Spaniards," I answered; "but, for all that, there may be quite as much in them."

We then again began to mount, and before we had ascended much farther we passed my three countrymen. They were young men, with gray coats and gray trousers, with slouched hats, and without gloves. They had fair faces and fair hair, and swung big sticks in their hands, with crooked handles. They laughed and talked loud, and, when we met them, seemed to be racing with each other; but nevertheless they were gentlemen. No one who knows by sight what an English gen-tleman is, could have doubted that; but I did acknowledge to myself that they should have remembered that the edifice they were treading was a church, and that the silence they were invading was the cher-ished property of a courteous people.

"They are all just the same as big boys," said Maria. The colour instantly flew into my face, and I felt that it was my duty to speak up for my own countrymen. The word "boys" especially wounded my ears. It was as a boy that she treated me; but, on looking at that befringed young Spanish Don—who was not, apparently, my elder in age—she had recognised a man. However, I said nothing further till I reached the summit. One cannot speak with manly dignity while one is out of breath on a staircase.

"There, John," she said, stretching her hands away over the fair plain of the Guadalquivir, as soon as we stood against the parapet; "is not that lovely."

I would not deign to notice this. "Maria," I said, "I think that you are too hard upon my countrymen?"

"Too hard! no; for I love them. They are so good and industrious;

and come home to their wives, and take care of their children. But why do they make themselves so—so—what the French call gauche?"

"Good and industrious, and come home to their wives!" thought I. "I believe you hardly understand us as yet," I answered. "Our domestic virtues are not always so very prominent; but, I believe, we know how to conduct ourselves as gentlemen: at any rate, as well as Spaniards." I was very angry—not at the faults, but at the good qualities imputed to us.

"In affairs of business, yes," said Maria, with a look of firm confidence in her own opinion—that look of confidence which she has never lost, and I pray that she may never lose it while I remain with her—"but in the little intercourses of the world, no! A Spaniard never forgets what is personally due either to himself or his neighbours. If he is eating an onion, he eats it as an onion should be eaten."

"In such matters as that he is very grand, no doubt," said I, angrily.

"And why should you not eat an onion properly, John? Now, I heard a story yesterday from Don —— about two Englishmen, which annoyed me very much." I did not exactly catch the name of the Don in question but I felt through every nerve in my body that it was the man who had been talking to her on the plaza.

"And what have they done?" said I. "But it is the same everywhere. We are always abused; but, nevertheless, no people are so welcome. At any rate, we pay for the mischief we do." I was angry with myself the moment the words were out of my mouth, for, after all, there is no feeling more mean than that pocket-confidence with which an Englishman sometimes swaggers.

"There was no mischief done in this case," she answered. "It was simply that two men have made themselves ridiculous for ever. The story is all about Seville, and, of course, it annoys me that they should be Englishmen."

"And what did they do?"

"The Marquis D'Almavivas was coming up to Seville in the boat, and they behaved to him in the most outrageous manner. He is here now and is going to give a series of fetes. Of course he will not ask a single Englishman."

"We shall manage to live even though the Marquis D'Almavivas may frown upon us," said I, proudly.

"He is the richest, and also the best of our noblemen," continued Maria; "and I never heard of anything so absurd as what they did to him. It made me blush when Don —— told me." Don Tomás, I thought she said.

"If he be the best of your noblemen, how comes it that he is angry because he has met two vulgar men? It is not to be supposed that every Englishman is a gentleman."

"Angry! Oh, no! he was not angry; he enjoyed the joke too much for that. He got completely the best of them, though they did not know it; poor fools! How would your Lord John Russell behave if two Spaniards in an English railway carriage were to pull him about and tear his clothes?"

"He would give them in charge to a policeman, of course," said I, speaking of such a matter with the contempt it deserved.

"If that were done here your ambassador would be demanding national explanations. But Almavivas did much better;—he laughed at them without letting them know it."

"But do you mean that they took hold of him violently, without any provocation? They must have been drunk."

"Oh, no, they were sober enough. I did not see it, so I do not quite know exactly how it was, but I understand that they committed themselves most absurdly, absolutely took hold of his coat and tore it, and—; but they did such ridiculous things that I cannot tell you." And yet Don Tomás, if that was the man's name, had been able to tell her, and she had been able to listen to him.

"What made them take hold of the marquis?" said I.

"Curiosity, I suppose," she answered. "He dresses somewhat fancifully, and they could not understand that any one should wear garments different from their own." But even then the blow did not strike home upon me.

"Is it not pretty to look down upon the quiet town?" she said, coming close up to me, so that the skirt of her dress pressed me, and her elbow touched my arm. Now was the moment I should have asked her how her heart stood towards me; but I was sore and uncomfortable, and my destiny was before me. She was willing enough to let these English faults pass without further notice, but I would not allow the subject to drop.

"I will find out who these men were," said I, "and learn the truth of it. When did it occur?"

"Last Thursday, I think he said."

"Why, that was the day we came up in the boat, Johnson and myself. There was no marquis there then, and we were the only Englishmen on board."

"It was on Thursday, certainly, because it was well known in Seville that he arrived on that day. You must have remarked him because he talks English perfectly—though by-the-bye, these men would go on chattering before him about himself as though it were impossible that a Spaniard should know their language. They are ignorant of Spanish, and they cannot bring themselves to believe that any one should be better educated than themselves."

Now the blow had fallen, and I straightway appreciated the necessity of returning immediately to Clapham where my family resided, and giving up for ever all idea of Spanish connections. I had resolved to assert the full strength of my manhood on that tower, and now words had been spoken which left me weak as a child. I felt that I was shivering, and did not dare to pronounce the truth which must be made known. As to speaking of love, and signifying my pleasure that Don Tomás should for the future be kept at a distance, any such effort was quite beyond me. Had Don Tomás been there, he might have walked off with her from before my face without a struggle on my part. "Now I remember about it," she continued, "I think he must have been in the boat on Thursday."

"And now that I remember," I replied, turning away to hide my embarrassment, "he was there. Your friend down below in the plaza seems to have made out a grand story. No doubt he is not fond of the English. There was such a man there, and I did take hold—"

"Oh, John, was it you?"

"Yes, Donna Maria, it was I; and if Lord John Russell were to dress himself in the same way—" But I had no time to complete my description of what might occur under so extravagantly impossible a combination of circumstances, for as I was yet speaking, the little door leading out on to the leads of the tower was opened and my friend, the mayo of the boat, still bearing gewgaws on his back, stepped up on to the platform. My eye instantly perceived that the one pendule was still missing from his jacket. He did not come alone, but three other gentlemen followed him, who, however, had no peculiarities in their dress. He saw me at once and bowed and smiled; and then observing Donna Maria, he lifted his cap from his head, and addressing himself to her in Spanish, began to converse with her as though she were an old friend.

"Señor," said Maria, after the first words of greeting had been spoken between them; "you must permit me to present to you my father's most particular friend, and my own—Mr. Pomfret; John, this is the Marquis D'Almavivas."

I cannot now describe the grace with which this introduction was effected, or the beauty of her face as she uttered the word. There was a boldness about her as though she had said, "I know it all—the whole story. But, in spite of that you must take him on my representation, and be gracious to him in spite of what he has done. You must be content to do that; or in quarrelling with him you must quarrel with me also." And it was done at the spur of the moment— without delay. She, who not five minutes since had been loudly condemning the unknown Englishman for his rudeness, had already pardoned him, now that he was known to be her friend; and had determined that he should be pardoned by others also or that she would share his disgrace. I recognised the nobleness of this at the moment; but, nevertheless, I was so sore that I would almost have preferred that she should have disowned me.

The marquis immediately lifted his cap with his left hand while he gave me his right. "I have already had the pleasure of meeting this gentleman," he said; "we had some conversation in the boat together."

"Yes," said I, pointing to his rent, "and you still bear the marks of our encounter."

"Was it not delightful, Donna Maria," he continued, turning to her; "your friend's friend took me for a torero?"

"And it served you properly, señor," said Donna Maria, laughing, "you have no right to go about with all those rich ornaments upon you."

"Oh! quite properly; indeed, I make no complaint; and I must beg your friend to understand, and his friend also, how grateful I am for their solicitude as to my pecuniary welfare. They were inclined to be severe on me for being so extravagant in such trifles. I was obliged to explain that I had no wife at home kept without her proper allowance of dresses, in order that I might be gay."

"They are foreigners, and you should forgive their error," said she.

"And in token that I do so," said the marquis, "I shall beg your friend to accept the little ornament which attracted his attention." And so saying, he pulled the identical button out of his pocket, and gracefully proffered it to me.

"I shall carry it about with me always," said I, accepting it, "as a memento of humiliation. When I look at it, I shall ever remember the folly of an Englishman and the courtesy of a Spaniard"; and as I made the speech I could not but reflect whether it might, under any circumstances, be possible that Lord John Russell should be induced to give a button off his coat to a Spaniard.

There were other civil speeches made, and before we left the tower the marquis had asked me to his parties, and exacted from me an unwilling promise that I would attend them. The señora, he said, bowing again to Maria, would, he was sure, grace them. She had done so on the previous year; and as I had accepted his little present I was bound to acknowledge him as my friend. All this was very pretty, and of course I said that I would go, but I had not at that time the slightest intention of doing so. Maria had behaved admirably; she had covered my confusion, and shown herself not ashamed to own me, delinquent as I was; but, not the less, had she expressed her opinion, in language terribly strong, of the awkwardness of which I had been guilty, and had shown almost an aversion to my English character. I should leave Seville as quickly as I could, and should certainly not again put myself in the way of the Marquis D'Almavivas. Indeed, I dreaded the moment that I should be first alone with her, and should find myself forced to say something indicative of my feelings—to hear something also indicative of her feelings. I had come out this morning resolved to demand my rights and to exercise them—and now my only wish was to man away. I hated the marquis, and longed to be alone that I might cast his button from me. To think that a man should be so ruined by such a trifle!

We descended that prodigious flight without a word upon the subject, and almost without a word at all. She had carried herself well in the presence of Almavivas, and had been too proud to seem ashamed of her companion; but now, as I could well see, her feelings of disgust and contempt had returned. When I begged her not to hurry herself, she would hardly answer me; and when she did speak, her voice was constrained and unlike herself. And yet how beautiful she was! Well, my dream of Spanish love must be over. But I was sure of this; that having known her, and given her my heart, I could never afterwards share it with another.

We came out at last on the dark, gloomy aisle of the cathedral, and walked together without a word up along the side of the choir, till we came to the transept. There was not a soul near us, and not a sound was to be heard but the distant, low pattering of a mass, then in course of celebration at some far-off chapel in the cathedral. When we got to the transept Maria turned a little, as though she was going to the transept door, and then stopped herself. She stood still; and when I stood also, she made two steps towards me, and put her hand on my arm. "Oh, John!" she said.

"Well," said I; "after all it does not signify. You can make a joke of it when my back is turned."

"Dearest John!"—she had never spoken to me in that way before—"you must not be angry with me. It is better that we should explain to each other, is it not?"

"Oh, much better. I am very glad you heard of it at once. I do not look at it quite in the same light that you do; but nevertheless—"

"What do you mean? But I know you are angry with me. And yet you cannot think that I intended those words for you. Of course I know now that there was nothing rude in what passed."

"Oh, but there was."

"No, I am sure there was not. You could not be rude though you are so free hearted. I see it all now, and so does the marquis. You will like him so much when you come to know him. Tell me that you won't be cross with me for what I have said. Sometimes I think that I have displeased you, and yet my whole wish has been to welcome you to Seville, and to make you comfortable as an old friend. Promise me that you will not be cross with me."

Cross with her! I certainly had no intention of being cross, but I had begun to think that she would not care what my humour might be. "Maria," I said, taking hold of her hand.

"No, John, do not do that. It is in the church, you know."

"Maria, will you answer me a question?"

"Yes," she said, very slowly, looking down upon the stone slabs beneath our feet.

"Do you love me?"

"Love you!"

"Yes, do you love me? You were to give me an answer here, in Seville, and now I ask for it. I have almost taught myself to think that it is needless to ask; and now this horrid mischance—"

"What do you mean?" said she, speaking very quickly.

"Why this miserable blunder about the marquis's button! After that I suppose—"

"The marquis! Oh, John, is that to make a difference between you and me?—a little joke like that?"

"But does it not?"

"Make a change between us!—such a thing as that! Oh, John!"

"But tell me, Maria, what am I to hope? If you will say that you can love me, I shall care nothing for the marquis. In that case I can bear to be laughed at."

"Who will dare to laugh at you? Not the marquis, whom I am sure you will like."

"Your friend in this plaza, who told you of all this."

"What, poor Tomás!"

"I do not know about his being poor. I mean the gentleman who was with you last night."

"Yes, Tomás. You do not know who he is?"

"Not in the least."

"How droll! He is your own clerk—partly your own, now that you are one of the firm. And, John, I mean to make you do something for him; he is such a good fellow; and last year he married a young girl whom I love—oh, almost like a sister."

Do something for him! Of course I would. I promised, then and there, that I would raise his salary to any conceivable amount that a Spanish clerk could desire; which promise I have since kept, if not absolutely to the letter, at any rate, to an extent which has been considered satisfactory by the gentleman's wife.

"But Maria—dearest Maria—"

"Remember, John, we are in the church; and poor papa will be waiting breakfast."

I need hardly continue the story further. It will be known to all that my love-suit throve in spite of my unfortunate raid on the button of the Marquis D'Almavivas, at whose series of fetes through that month I was, I may boast, an honoured guest. I have since that had the pleasure of entertaining him in my own poor house in England, and one of our boys bears his Christian name.

From that day in which I ascended the Giralda to this present day in which I write, I have never once had occasion to complain of a deficiency of romance either in Maria Daguilar or in Maria Pomfret.

Joanna Trollope

(1 9 4 3 –   )

Born in her grandfather's rectory in the Cotswolds, Joanna Trollope wrote that she always felt like an outsider, a perception that helped her become a writer. She went to Oxford, became a teacher, and began writing in the evening "to fill the long spaces after the children had gone to bed. I don't think we should ever underestimate the power of story—story is how we negotiate with each other, how we build up relationships, how we learn. And nothing is so fascinating as good narrative—nobody of any age can resist 'What Happens Next . . . ?'"

Joanna Trollope has been writing for over thirty years and her novels have earned her great commercial success as well as an appointment to the Order of the British Empire in 1996. *A Spanish Lover* (1993), from which this is exerpted, is the story of two sisters—Lizzie, married and with a stable family, and Frances, single and searching for change. Frances shocks Lizzie when she becomes involved with a Spanish businessman who is not only married, but has no intention of leaving his wife.

When asked about Anthony Trollope, her distant relative, Joanna Trollope said, "I admire him hugely, and take several things he said about writing very much to heart, especially his description of his own kind of fiction which he said were chronicles of 'those little daily lacerations upon the spirit.'"

From A SPANISH LOVER

Luis Gómez Moreno waited at Málaga Airport. Dressed in the male-European casual summer uniform of cotton trousers, linen jacket, and polished loafers, he stood in the arrivals hall, his briefcase between his feet, and read a newspaper article about the growing dissatisfaction of the enormous number of Spaniards living in the Basque country. A Spanish town councillor in a Basque town said that Basque behaviour in council meetings was a lesson in racism.

"They only allow their own language in council meetings. They won't even allow simultaneous translation!" Basque, said the writer of the article, is a language older than Latin with nothing in common with Spanish. The Basque country is a rural paradise and its invasion by the Spanish is bitterly resented. "These," said the reporter with relish, "are a most tenacious people."

As a small boy, Luis had been told, furtively, about the bombing of Guernica, the Basques' sacred city, by Hitler's Condor Legion. He had been told this by a young uncle, his mother's brother, and furtively, because in Luis's childhood, General Franco was an object of undiluted veneration. "Your mother," the young uncle had said disapprovingly, "your mother, my sister, was taught to obey Franco, God and your father, in that order!" That uncle was the first taste of rebelliousness in Luis's life, the first glimpse of his dominating mother as other than irreproachable. When Luis was twelve, the uncle took his radical political ideas to America; the family story was that he chose to go, but Luis rather thought otherwise, and his mother once, in a temper, confirmed his suspicion.

"Your uncle Francisco," she had shouted, "was a traitor to Spain!"

There had been a good deal of shouting in Luis's childhood. As in most post-war Spanish households, Luis's father's authority over them all was absolute, but this authority had to take into account the size of Luis's mother's personality and the strength of her will. She knew her duty and she rebelled against it all the time, buoyed up by the deeply Spanish belief that strength was to be gained through suffering. Her very frustration would, she knew, in the end be rewarded. Luis and his sister, Ana, instead of enjoying the home life propounded by Franco, a life of rhythm, discipline and order, lived in fact in a quarrelsome bear-garden. By the time he was fourteen, Luis dared to admit to himself that he disliked his mother and by the time he was a father himself, watching his relationship with baby José's mother disintegrate, he was beginning to wonder if he disliked all mothers; that motherhood was a state likely to turn any woman into a possessive, unbalanced monster. His own mother had screamed at him; now his wife, the minute she was a mother, was doing the same thing. His mother had wanted him to obey her implicitly, especially in matters of religious devotion; his wife wanted something else, something to do with freedom and esteem.

"It is not easy," she had once said to him with deadly emphasis, "to try and be a feminist in this land of machismo."

The effect of it all was to make Luis wary of profound relationships with women. He could see that some of his mother's generation felt cheated after lifetimes spent as virtual slaves in the house; he could see equally well that subsequent generations of Spanish women wished to have the freedom to work and to mix, but it was the handling of women with either of those grievances that seemed so difficult; the barrage of their resentment and mockery seemed to make any kind of mutual understanding almost impossible. He strongly disapproved of hearing his father say—as his father often did—"Give a woman freedom, and you get anarchy," but he equally disapproved of the violence with which the opposite view was expressed.

Despite those early seductive whisperings from his political uncle, Luis knew he was not a radical. Indeed, there were times when the notion of a life of rhythm, discipline and order seemed not only attractive but civilised and better able to ensure a general level of happiness than the seemingly progressive pursuit of self-fulfilment. As a citizen of one of the more socialist cities of Spain, he sometimes felt out of step with the way things seemed determined to move, while at the same time being unable to share completely a feeling common to many of his countrymen, that General Franco had, in many ways, been no bad thing for Spain. A foreigner, an American businessman with whom he was having dealings, had once said, after an exhausting meeting they had both attended, "Luis what *excessive* people the Spanish are!" Perhaps, Luis thought afterwards, it's the excessiveness of Spanish women that makes them such a big deal to live with. Too big a deal. For fifteen years Luis had lived, apart from visitors, alone.

Above his head, a clear female voice announced over the loudspeaker system that the flight from London Gatwick had just landed. Luis looked at his watch. The airport was quite full so the baggage wouldn't be through for at least twenty minutes. He considered going to buy a cup of coffee, and then reconsidered it. Even if it took thirty minutes for her to emerge, Luis decided he would not chance not being there when Frances Shore came through customs.

When he had said good-bye to her at Seville Airport on Christmas Eve, Luis had not thought he would hear from her again. Briefly, he was mildly sorry about this, partly because he was furious with José for being so incompetent—José's continued incompetence was the source of many new quarrels between Luis and José's mother—and partly because Frances Shore was quite unlike anybody he had ever done business with in twenty-five years. He had known many Englishwomen during his time at the London School of Economics, but they had, on the whole, been a politically determined breed and not much interested in a young man from what they saw as the land of bull fights, religious bigotry and fascism. In the years since the sixties, he had never done business with an Englishwoman and met very few. His sense of adventure and taste for novelty had been aroused by the thought of defying Christmas and taking this Miss Shore to his three *posadas*. Then José had effectively scuppered the whole plan and when Frances had said good-bye at the airport—politely but not with any particular warmth—he had thought that was that. Miss Shore, in her unmistakably English mackintosh, would have other travel fish to fry.

But she had telephoned him. He had been in Brussels, discussing the EEC regulations for the setting up of organic farms—he was planning one, with an Andalusian consortium—and arrived back in Seville, to find a message from Frances. It was February. He rang her back immediately, and she said she would like to re-open negotiations with the Posadas of Andalucía. He said he would be charmed.

She said sharply, "I don't want you to be charmed, I just want you to be there, when you say you will be."

"I will be here in May."

"May is hopeless, I've got far too much business in May."

"Five days only. Andalucía is at its best in May. Or September. You fly to Málaga and I will meet you."

"Not in May."

"Then September."

"September is worse."

"Then—"

"All right," Frances said. "I'll juggle things. I'll come in May." And here she was, in the baggage hall of Málaga Airport. He felt pleased. In fact, he felt more than pleased, he felt a kind of quickened interest, as at the prospect of something unknown, but attractively unknown.

He folded up his newspaper—if the Spanish were excessive, what adjective was left for the Basques?—put it in his briefcase, and moved across to the space of dusty floor in front of the doors that led to the customs hall. They were opening constantly, disgorging passengers with baggage trolleys and the mildly disorientated expressions that are the inevitable effect of air travel. Luis watched them closely; a few Spaniards came through but mostly they were English, and a lot of them the loudly confident, commercial English whose requirements had filled southern Spain with high-rise blocks of flats and mock Moorish villages, to the increase of its prosperity and to the detriment of its spirit. Then, suddenly, there was Frances. She wore a blue linen skirt and a white T-shirt with a cardigan tied over her shoulders, and she carried her own suitcase. She came straight over to him and held out her hand to him, smiling.

"Mr. Gómez Moreno," she said. "I hope you realise that I intended never to come back to Spain."

Having stowed her in his car, and climbed into the driver's seat, he asked if she would mind if he took off his tie.

"I cannot drive in a tie, somehow. I think I will strangle."

"Of course," Frances said, startled at the courtesy of being asked. She folded the lengths of her blue skirt around her legs. "It's so lovely to be warm."

"Twenty-two degrees," Luis said with satisfaction, as if he had arranged it especially for her. He started the car, and turned to look at her briefly, with a broad smile. "Well, here you are, Miss Shore, back in Spain."

"Frances."

"Thank you," he said. "Frances. Then Luis also."

He pulled the car out of the wired-off compound of the airport carpark. Above Frances hung the same strong blue sky she had seen on Christmas Eve in Seville, but this sky was full of warmth, not just light.

"I don't want us to have any more confusions," Luis said, "but I am curious to know why you changed your mind, why you decided to telephone me. Of course, I am pleased—"

"It rankled," Frances said, looking out of the window. "It wouldn't stop."

"Rankled?" he said, not understanding.

"Yes. It irritated me that it hadn't worked, that it was a good idea that went wrong. And a lot of my clients, the ones who have been with me since the beginning, were beginning to hint that they would like new horizons. Where are we going?"

"Mojas," he said. "I am taking no chances this time." He was laughing.

"Mojas? I've never heard—"

"You wouldn't have. It's a village. It's a tiny village in the mountains between Granada and the sea. It has my best *posada*, my favourite. We are too late, though, for the almond blossoms."

"Almonds—"

"The village used to live by its almonds. Even now, the almond season is the busy season, the village streets full of donkeys with baskets, every house sounding with the tapping of the women and children shelling. We can hardly take the car into the village, the streets are so small. Donkeys are fine, cars are not."

"My clients," Frances said carefully, "would like that." She thought of them, cultivated, capable, respectful of the places they visited, repelled by the violation caused by mass tourism. "They are quite quiet people," she said to Luis. "They are the sort of people who will read seriously about Spain before they come, and who would never buy dolls dressed as flamenco dancers."

He laughed again. He was driving very fast through the shade-dappled suburbs of Málaga, slipping in and out of lanes of traffic as if he didn't need to think about it. Every so often, in bright glimpses between buildings to the right of the road, came a flash of the sea.

Frances thought, with a sudden little inward clutch of pleasure: I'm liking this!

It had been truthful to say she had been irked by the Seville episode. Once it was over, she hadn't meant to think about it anymore, but it kept popping up in her mind as something not only bungled, but unfinished. The newspapers seemed to be unnaturally full of pieces about Spain—surely they never were before?—and the telly seemed absolutely obsessed with the place all of a sudden, with programmes about Spanish women and crime and Catholicism, about Spanish gambling and food and drink and about the Spanish army. Frances had turned the television on one day soon after Christmas, quite idly, while wandering about with a mug of coffee and a slice of toast, and there, instead of a chat show or a police drama or a politician, was a very young Spanish army recruit, stooping in reverence to kiss the Spanish flag. Frances was amazed. It was such a theatrical, passionate, serious thing to do. Imagine telling an English squaddie he had to kiss the Union Jack!

In the end, Frances had given in. Spain was clearly campaigning for her, and so, in a quieter way, was Mr. Gómez Moreno Senior, whose business card, wherever she tucked it away, wormed itself to the surface of drawers and piles of paper like a fragment of broken china in a flowerbed.

"I'm jinxed," Frances said to Nicky. "Bloody Spain."

"Ring him, then," Nicky said. "Go and see his hotels. If they're great, hurray, and if they're grotty you'll defeat the jinx."

"They're in wonderful places—"

"I know. I read that piece about the cathedral in Córdoba that's inside a mosque."

"And it's a much better spring and autumn climate than Italy—"

"Ring him," Nicky said.

"And flights to Málaga are frequent and reasonable—"

"Then ring him."

"And the hotel that's in the mountains sounds as if it would be good for the flora and fauna lot—"

"Frances," Nicky said, raising her voice almost to a shriek, "ring him!"

So she did, and he said he would be charmed to see her. Then he

wrote and said he would escort her personally to all three *posadas*, that
he would show her the countryside and the glories of Granada, Córdoba and Seville. He said, in his letter, that he would devote himself
to her.

"Wow," said Nicky.

"Don't be silly—"

"You watch it. Mediterranean men—"

"He's a middle-aged, married Catholic and I hardly know him."

"Do you disapprove of associating with married men?"

"Yes," Frances said.

Nicky pecked a bit at her typewriter. "Trouble is, there aren't many
others. If they aren't married, they're either gay or they're goofy."

Frances gave a quick glance sideways at Luis. He didn't look at all
goofy. He didn't, if it came to it, look particularly married either, in
the way that William looked married, arranged and ordered by somebody else. Luis Gómez Moreno looked very independent, almost
detached. Perhaps that was what happened to you when you had
chosen your own shirts and socks for fifteen years; you stopped
looking as if somebody else had a hand in you, you stopped looking
owned. That excellent haircut—curlier hair than his son's—that well-
laundered shirt, that collection of maps and objects in the glove
pockets and on the dashboard of the car, the efficient-looking car
telephone, were all his choices just as her blue skirt and the things in
her suitcase and the fact that her toenails weren't varnished were
hers. That's the single life, Frances thought, married or not; you
decide everything for yourself, all the time, and sometimes that's
exciting, and sometimes it makes you very tired.

"What are you thinking of?" Luis said.

They were bowling along a stretch of open road, with only a few
garages and half-finished buildings between them and the shining
sea. Frances turned to look at it.

"I'm afraid," she said primly, "that I don't know you well enough
to say."

He laughed again. Frances caught the glimmer of a gold tooth-
filling.

"Do you think, by the end of the week, we shall tell each other
everything?"

"I've never told anyone everything in my life, not even my twin sister."

"A twin? You have a twin sister? Are you very alike? Can I be sure I have the right one here?"

"Quite sure," Frances said. "My sister has a wedding ring and four children."

He gave her a quick look.

"Don't envy her the wedding ring."

"I don't. She has one kind of life and I have another."

"This is interesting. Differences are always interesting. The difference between the Spanish and the English is interesting. If I met you in the middle of the Sahara Desert, I should know you were English."

"And if I met you," Frances said, slightly nettled, "I should think you were any old Mediterranean or Latin American, just one of millions of olive-skinned, dark-haired men with brown eyes."

"Black," he said, grinning, hugely enjoying himself.

"Nobody has black eyes. Not really black."

"Mine are. And yours are blue."

"Blue-grey."

"Like English sky."

"Luis, I can't bear that kind of talk."

He smiled broadly, took one hand off the wheel, and lightly touched Frances's forearm.

"Nor me," he said. "Just testing."

They drove for two hours. The road went along stretches of flat coastal plain, through scruffy, concrete ribbon developments and the odd anonymous resort with signs to "*La Playa*" nailed to every tree and building, and then, in a vast, delta-like area filled with the torn and flapping remains of abandoned plastic greenhouses—"The melon madness," Luis said. "The courgette craziness. It was like a gold rush"—there appeared a great fork in the road, the coastal arm running on towards Almería, the other swinging left into some low, advancing hills.

"The mountains now," Luis said. "The lovely mountains."

Frances turned regretfully to look at the sea.

"Can we see the sea, from Mojas?"

"Far away. A small sparkle. I have put in a pool, a little blue pool, and around it there is a jasmine hedge."

"Do you know about gardening?"

"No," he said. "Certainly not." He waited a moment and then said teasingly, "In Spain, gardening is for women."

Frances ignored the implication of this remark. "Then how come the jasmine?"

"Because I am a very rare Spaniard."

"I see."

"You don't see," he said. "But you will. When you see the Mojas *posada*. Look at that, look at the view."

The road was running up rapidly into drama. Behind them lay the shore, the nondescript little towns, the failed market gardens, but ahead the hills were beginning to heave and fold themselves into mountains—brown, russet, rose-red and saffron—splashed with the new green growth of spring and backed by the steady blue sky.

"I love it here," Luis said. "The land is so big and so ancient, and tourism hasn't found it yet. The seashore towards Almería isn't so friendly for the sunbathers and these"—he waved an arm at the slopes beyond the road—"are not good for golf. You cannot make a playground from a country like this."

She murmured, "Your English is so good—"

"Twenty-five years I have it now. Are you tired?"

"Only a little."

"It is not much farther, not so much as an hour. Shall I stop for you to walk a little?"

"No, thank you," Frances said, "I want to get there."

"Come," he said. He twisted slightly in his seat, and with his right hand turned something behind Frances. The back of her own seat sank backwards. "There now. Relax a little."

Through the raised glass of the sunshine roof, the sky shone like a blessing. Frances watched it idly, contentedly, reminding herself of Davy, as a baby, in his pram, watching the moving apple-tree leaves above him with the same lazy satisfaction.

"Europe thinks we Spanish are all Castilians, very formal and stately, always deep in thought," Luis said. "But we are all different, region to region, even village to village. There is the story of the mayor of a tiny place near Madrid who declared war on Napoleon personally, himself. You will find Mojas like that, with its own personality, very local. Everybody thinks of Andalusians as gypsies, as flamboyant, and these people are so, in their way, but they are also, most of all, just the people of Mojas, just—" He glanced sideways. Frances was asleep.

He slackened speed at once, to avoid having to brake abruptly and wake her. How extraordinary, how confident of her to go to sleep so suddenly and completely, her hands folded in her lap, her face turned up to the square of sky visible through the sunshine roof. He drove even more slowly so that he could have a good look at her, at her thick, heavy hair, at her peculiarly English skin with the suggestion, on its surface, of all the components underneath that went to make it up—never visible on a darker skin—at the pronounced lines of her eyebrows and eyelashes. It was not, he decided, a beautiful face but it was an arresting one. He liked looking at it. Asleep, it was calm and strong, awake, it was full of movement. He glanced at the rest of her. Why dress, he wondered, to say nothing? Why choose clothes that could be anybody's, any age? José had reported her as being good-looking but not at all sexy. Letting his eyes linger on the blurred lines of Frances under the white cotton and blue linen, Luis was inclined to agree with the former assessment but not with the second. Yet why should she be sexy? She was almost gawky; her hands and feet were far too big and she—

"Don't stare," Frances said calmly, waking up but not moving.

"I am so sorry."

"Are we almost there?"

"A few more kilometres. There." Luis pointed. "On that hillside. That is Mojas."

Frances sat up. Across the valley a village lay scattered across the ribs of the hillside like a handful of white sugar cubes.

"The green in the middle is the *posada*, the *posada* garden."

"Aren't you tired, driving so fast for so long?"

"This isn't long," he said.

The road zigzagged down into the valley, crossed a swampy bottom filled with whispering bamboo and a few dried-up, unharvested clumps of Indian corn, and began to climb again. The slopes either side were terraced in graceful curves along the contours of the hill, the terraces held up with low walls of grey-and-ochre stone. They passed a boy in a baseball cap with a herd of piebald goats, jingling softly with bells, and then a man with a tiny donkey almost obscured under a giant bundle of firewood.

Frances said, without meaning to, "It's hard to remember that I'm here on business, somehow—"

"We think too much of business. We think too much of purpose."

"Do you think so?"

"Miss Shore—"

"Frances."

"Thank you. Frances, we will have a philosophical conversation later, but now I am the guide and you are the tourist. There you see to the right an almond orchard."

Trees as gnarled and twisted as those in an illustration to a fairy-tale stood in rough russet earth, stony and harsh.

"And now we are here," Luis said, "close your eyes. We are going in."

"But you said no cars—"

"No cars but my car and a few others."

The road twisted sharply to the left to continue climbing the hill-side. To the right, there was a wall, a high white wall with an opening in it, a narrow, dark opening that looked hardly wide enough for a bicycle.

"We can't—"

"Shut your eyes," Luis said. "Usually with guests, we tell them to leave their cars out here by the orchard, and the hotel staff will guide them in."

The car slid through the opening with centimetres only to spare. Having shut her eyes obediently, Frances found that this was more nerve-racking than opening them, so opened them and stared about her. White lanes, white alleys, whitened steps, cobbles, cascades of something brilliant—could it be bougainvillaea?—pots of gerani-ums, shutters tightly fastened, gates closed, vines across terraces, flashes of view, of sky, of cats, of kitchen chairs outside doorways, all steep and slanting and crooked and impossible; then a tiny, angled square with acacia trees and two old men on a bench.

"Here," Luis said.

"Where?"

"There," he said, braking and sliding the car into a black square of shade. "In the corner."

In the corner was a miniature cul-de-sac, and at the end of it a saffron-washed building, windowless with a big wooden door in a white frame, and beside it, a brass plate.

"The *Posada* of Mojas," Luis said.

They led her to a room on the first floor. The way to the room was through a series of irregular interior courtyards, balconied and full of lemon trees in pots and blue trails of plumbago. The courtyards were painted white and the balconies were painted deep russet and on the floor were tiles the colour of the ribbed roofs of the village, apricot and terracotta, earthy and soft.

"You will be comfortable here," Luis said, in the same tone of pride with which he had announced the temperature. "From this room you can see the garden and all the valley."

It was a long room. In one wall there was both a conventional window and a casement window that reached to the floor and with a balustrade across it to waist height. Both halves of this window stood open and the sunshine fell in across the floor, and the breeze blew the curtains in soft billows, new cotton curtains striped in yellow and white and blue, their hems whispering on the tiles. There was a carved bed and high white pillows and a dark chest like a small altar. On the floor there were cotton rugs, and on the walls, washed so pale a blue they were almost white, hung two old wooden panel paintings, one of a lily and one of an angel's head, curly and haloed.

Frances took off her shoes, stepping from the cool shadowed spaces of the floor on to the warm sunlit ones.

"I will be in the garden," Luis said. "We will have tortillas in the garden when you are ready. There is no hurry, there is never a hurry here."

She crossed the room and held the sun-warmed wood of the balustrade. Below her lay the garden, fashioned, like the fields outside the village, from several tiny terraces, their edges and the several sets of steps punctuated with amphorae, jars and pots in earthenware, cascading flowers and variegated leaves. There were trees, too, another acacia, several eucalyptuses waving their greeny-grey branches in swooping arcs across the sky, and in their shade were garden chairs, made of white wrought iron. Below the garden, the tilting roofs of the village fell headlong down the slope towards the valley, the rush only halted here and there by the occasional level roof terrace across which strings of washing blew, bright and orderly.

It was almost silent. From faraway down the valley came the faintest sound of bells—those goats?—and from the hotel kitchen, sleepy in mid-afternoon peace, came the distant clatter of a tortilla pan. Frances closed her eyes. Sometimes in life, just sometimes, she thought, there comes a moment of happiness that is close to rapture because it is so innocent, so natural, so right, a moment when you feel that everything's in tune, when . . .

"Frances?"

She opened her eyes again and looked down. Luis was standing on the middle terrace below her.

"Everything is all right for you?"

"Yes, oh yes—"

"Then come and eat," he said. "I am waiting for you."

Suellen Wedmore

(1943–   )

Spain has long been a destination for American students in year-abroad pro-
grams. Their parents often follow, piggybacking a trip to Europe and a visit with
their child. But they do not find the son or daughter who left the States only
months before, but a new person—one who has negotiated the streets of foreign cities, become bilingual, and calls strangers "my family." Suellen Wedmore's poem, "Visiting My Daughter, An Exchange Student in Spain" (1995),
resonates with parents who have made that journey.

Born in Chicago, Wedmore is the poet laureate emeritus for the seaside town
of Rockport, Massachusetts, where she has made her home for the last thirty
years. Her poetry has been featured in *Green Mountains Review*, *College English*, *Phoebe*, and other publications. After twenty-four years as a speech and
language therapist, she retired to enter the Master of Fine Arts Program in
poetry at New England College. Wedmore graduated in July 2004. Her daughter, the exchange student, is now a medical doctor and a mother herself.

VISITING MY DAUGHTER,
AN EXCHANGE STUDENT IN SPAIN

Of course, I believe that in this land,
where storks nesting in chimneys
guarantee a family good luck,
she will be unchanged:

eighteen, still with skinny wrists,
blond hair that won't take a curl,
and all her dreams,
bundled as they are with mine,

still in her pale-lashed eyes.
We meet her new family,
smile a conversation we don't understand,
and on the second day head west

in a rented Ford, toward Pizarro's tomb—Trujillo,
where garlic simmers
behind blanketed doorways
cacti scrabble up hillsides,

and in the town square,
when I toss a coin into the fountain,
I watch my daughter's face reflected there,
dissolve into clefts and ripples.

An old woman, billowed in black,
leads us to a saffron-hued church
at the top of the hill,
and when the sun slants across the tile floor,

she speaks to my daughter
in syllables filled with Gypsy music,
the sweetness of oranges,
My daughter laughs,

brushes the woman's shoulder,
and with my awkward American tongue,
I slip into shadow.

Edith Wharton

(1862–1937)

Edith Jones Wharton's passion for travel started when she was very small and her parents took her to Europe. Many biographers write that Wharton's father wanted his only daughter to be exposed to classical culture at a very early age, but Wharton wrote that "the depreciation of the American currency at the close of the Civil War had so much reduced my father's income that, in common with many of his friends, and relations, he had gone to Europe to economize." The Jones family spent the first winter in Italy and from there—despite being advised against traveling in such a rugged country with a small child—George Jones took his family to Spain. Although Edith was only four, she had vivid impressions. "I recall only the incessant jingle of *diligence* bells, the cracking of whips, the yells of gaunt muleteers hurling stones at their gaunter mules to urge them up interminable and almost unscaleable hills." Her father had been reading Washington Irving's *The Alhambra*, and young Edith was caught up in its romance.

Wharton recalled in her memoir that her early trip to Spain gave her "an incurable passion for the road." At five she tackled Irving's *Alhambra* with a fervor that equaled her father's. She remembered being immersed in its thick black type, pretending to read it and making up stories as she paced the floor. The Jones family went between New York and Europe for much of Edith's youth. In the early years of her marriage to Teddy Wharton, the couple continued the bifurcated life, crossing the Atlantic at least once a year. Many of Wharton's novels, including *The Reef* (1912) and *The Age of Innocence* (1920), deal with the clash between American values and European sensibilities.

The Whartons finally emigrated to Paris in 1906 but continued their restless travels, often by automobile. In 1912 Teddy and Edith went to Madrid for Easter. It was one of their last trips together, and they separated shortly thereafter. After her divorce Edith made at least four more trips to Spain, the last in 1930. There is an unpublished manuscript with her papers at the Yale University Library called *A Motor-flight to Spain*, which suggests that she might have intended to write a companion to her enormously popular travel book *A Motor-flight Through France* (1908).

From A BACKWARD GLANCE

My Roman impressions are followed by others, improbably picturesque, of a journey to Spain. It must have taken place just before or
after the Roman year; I remember that the Spanish tour was still considered an arduous adventure, and to attempt it with a young child
the merest folly. But my father had been reading Prescott and Washington Irving; the Alhambra was more of a novelty than the Colosseum; and as the offspring of born travellers I was expected, even in
infancy, to know how to travel. I suppose I acquitted myself better
than the unhappy Freddy; for from that wild early pilgrimage I
brought back an incurable passion for the road. What a journey it
must have been! Presumably there was already a railway from the
frontier to Madrid; but I recall only the incessant jingle of *diligence*
bells, the cracking of whips, the yells of gaunt muleteers hurling
stones at their gaunter mules to urge them up interminable and
almost unscaleable hills. It is all a jumble of excited impressions:
breaking down on wind-swept sierras; arriving late and hungry at
squalid *posadas*; flea-hunting, chocolate-drinking (I believe there was
nothing but chocolate and olives to feed me on), being pursued
wherever we went by touts, guides, deformed beggars, and all sorts
of jabbering and confusing people; and, through the chaos and
fatigue, a fantastic vision of the columns of Cordova, the tower of
the Giralda, the pools and fountains of the Alhambra, the orange
groves of Seville, the awful icy penumbra of the Escorial, and everywhere shadowy aisles undulating with incense and processions . . .
Perhaps, after all, it is not a bad thing to begin one's travels at four.

William Wordsworth

(1770–1850)

In 1808 Bonaparte named his brother Joseph the king of Spain and moved a large contingent of the French army to the Iberian Peninsula to enforce his choice. A small group of Spaniards called *afrancesados* welcomed the French and their model of government, but the majority revolted and resisted French occupation. The brutality that erupted was captured by Goya (see Billy Collins's poem "Candle Hat") and has seldom been equaled in European history. The people of Zaragoza held out against the well-equipped French forces for more than a year. An army of Valencians recaptured Madrid. The War of Independence (1808–1814) was an epic struggle on Spanish soil only rivaled by the Spanish Civil War more than a century later.

Poet William Wordsworth captured the irony of a "high-minded Spaniard" who is forced to endure the ruination of his land at the hands of Napoleon—all in the name of the "benefit" to the occupied country. The sonnet "Indignation of a High-Minded Spaniard" (1810) is reproduced here. Wordsworth was an unlikely champion of the Spanish cause. He was the seminal poet of the Romantic Age (along with his friend Samuel Taylor Coleridge). Wordsworth once wrote that poetry should be "the spontaneous overflow of powerful feelings from emotions recollected in tranquility." His most famous poems, "Tintern Abbey" and "I Wandered Lonely as a Cloud," were memorized by generations of schoolchildren. Although Wordsworth traveled widely for a man of his day—taking long trips to the Continent and to Scotland—there is no evidence that he ever went to Spain. When Ralph Waldo Emerson met the elderly and revered poet laureate in Rome, he asked him to name his favorite poem. Emerson noted in his diary that Wordsworth replied, "the sonnet, Feelings of High-Minded Spaniard."

INDIGNATION OF A HIGH-MINDED SPANIARD

We can endure that He should waste our lands,
Despoil our temples, and by sword and flame
Return us to the dust from which we came;
Such food a Tyrant's appetite demands:
And we can brook the thought that by his hands
Spain may be overpowered, and he possess,
For his delight, a solemn wilderness
Where all the brave lie dead. But, when of bands
Which he will break for us he dares to speak,
Of benefits, and of a future day
When our enlightened minds shall bless his sway;
Then, the strained heart of fortitude proves weak;
Our groans, our blushes, our pale cheeks declare
That he has power to inflict what we lack strength to bear.

Richard Wright

(1908–1960)

Like many black writers, Richard Wright moved to Europe after World War II. It was a long way from his birthplace, a plantation near Natchez, Mississippi, where his father was a sharecropper. When Wright was six his father left; his mother and the children moved in with his maternal grandmother, a devout Seventh-Day Adventist. During the Depression Wright worked for the post office, started writing in his spare time, and studied the works of H. L. Mencken, Theodore Dreiser, and Sinclair Lewis. He also joined the Communist Party and contributed articles to the *Daily Worker* and *New Masses*. His two best-known works, a novel, *Native Son* (1940), and an autobiography, *Black Boy* (1945), were published in the 1940s. Although he eventually broke with the party after World War II, Wright's disillusionment with America led him to emigrate. He became a French citizen in 1947.

In Paris, Wright became friends with Albert Camus, Jean-Paul Sartre, and Gertrude Stein. Stein advised him to go to Spain because "you'll see what the Western world is made of." *Pagan Spain* (1957, from which this is excerpted) is the result of three trips to Spain in 1954 and 1955. Wright did not intend to write a guidebook, but rather an examination of Spanish culture. Surprisingly, he found no racial discrimination. "Spanish youth was cut off from the multitude of tiny influences of the modern Western World," he wrote. "They had no racial consciousness whatsoever." The original manuscript of *Pagan Spain* was over five hundred pages, but publisher Harper and Row required that it be cut severely. In this excerpt Wright goes to a cave that houses a "Gypsy town" to see a primal exhibition of flamenco.

Richard Wright died in 1960 in France.

From PAGAN SPAIN

That evening I took a taxi and invaded the precincts of gypsy town. Blocks before I arrived I could hear the stomping of heels on tile floors, the thumping of guitars, the clicking of castanets, and the high-pitched and quavering bellows of flamenco. The night was warm, the sky filled with fiery stars. We climbed a steep mountain and the taxi stopped amid a throng of gypsies.

Gypsy town was situated upon a mountainside and I passed rows of caves dug out of hard rock. In these spacious cavities scores of gypsy families had made their homes. Legend had it that these gypsies were the most favored of all the gypsies in Spain, for it was reputed that their ancestors had aided Ferdinand and Isabel to drive out the Moors. They earned their living by giving singing and dancing exhibitions, among other things, for tourists. The front rooms of their cave homes had been converted into small dancehalls where a gypsy family or clan would, for a price, assemble and entertain you an hour.

For the sake of prudence, I chose a cave having a number of European clientele and went in. An exhibition was being organized, that is, a levy was being collected from those who had entered. When the traffic had been taken for all it would bear, an old, evil-looking woman began clapping her hands, the diamonds on her withered fingers flashing. As the audience, which sat in chairs along the wall, grew quiet, the old woman assembled her brood.

Back of the woman and along the whitewashed walls were photographs of gypsy ancestors and a few prints of Jesus preaching to multitudes. I was informed later that they practiced a kind of ancestor-worship religion, that they could not marry out of the tribe, and that you had better keep your hand firmly upon your pocketbook while listening to or looking at their "culture." These were tribal people living under urban conditions; their religion had made them reject the people around them and those people had, in turn, rejected them. They had thus been reduced to beggary, singing and dancing in order to eat and have a cave roof over their heads. If ever there had been anything romantic about these gypsies, it had long since been swallowed up in commercialism.

Three young men entered in tight-fitting black trousers, black hats, high-heeled shoes, with guitars slung under their arms. About twenty-five females, ranging in ages from eight to fifty, stationed themselves about the floor. Pink carnations were tucked into their jet-black hair; from their ears dangled gold loops; and they wore cheap cotton dresses that had loud, splashing patterns of color. Red-lipped, rouged, their faces were tired and damp in the night's heat; now and then one of them yawned.

The old witch clapped her hands; the guitars strummed; and the girls plunged into wild whirlings, their arms lifted and their castanets clacking, their cotton dresses rising and floating out at the level of their hips, their black hair flying about their faces, and the cave was suddenly filled with the scent of unwashed bodies and cheap perfume. Abruptly the dancers broke and crowded along the walls, leaving one lone girl in the center of the floor. A young man laid aside his guitar and joined her. Their dance was a wild sexuality lifted to the plane of orgiastic intensity. The man approached and then veered from the spinning girl, evading her while the girl, red lips pursed, her eyes half closed, her arms flung above her head, stood still in the center of the floor and stomped her heels madly, wringing and twisting her buttocks as though she were in the grip of reflex muscular movements only. Then she gritted her teeth in a grimace, clutched the hem of her dress with both hands, and put her fists upon her hips, disclosing her thighs and legs. She advanced across the room, stomping and writhing to the beat of the music, her face carrying an expression of one about to fall in a swoon. She then threw back her head, placed her palms upon her trembling buttocks and stomped back across the room to the pound of the music. The man approached the girl and they danced around each other, their heads tilted backward, their eyes looking into each other's.

The Germans, Swiss, Americans, Englishmen gazed open-mouthed at an exhibition of sexual animality their world had taught them to repress.

With sweat streaming off their faces, the girl and the man concluded and a child who looked to be about eight years old came into the center of the room, her castanets clicking. She had a thin, haunting face and her long, straight black hair fell down to her waist. The music and clapping blared forth and the little tot whirled, twisted her tiny hips, and rolled her eyes sensually. She too induced on her lips that expression of savage sexuality; she must have been copying it, for I was sure that she could not really feel what she was portraying. She had a charm, a grace, and freshness that the older women lacked, yet there was something pathetic about a child expressing sexual emotion far beyond its capacity to experience.

The pale white faces that looked on were shocked, but entranced.

PERMISSIONS ACKNOWLEDGMENTS

John Affleck: "Hemingway in Pamplona" by John Affleck (*Literary Traveler*). Reprinted by permission of the *Literary Traveler*.

W. H. Auden: "Spain 1937" from *Collected Poems* by W. H. Auden, copyright © 1940, copyright renewed 1968 by W. H. Auden. Reprinted by permission of Random House, Inc.

Gerald Brenan: "The Village Calendar" from *South from Granada* by Gerald Brenan, copyright © 1957 by Gerald Brenan (Penguin Books, 1963). All rights reserved. Reprinted by permission of the Estate of Gerald Brenan, administered by Margaret Hanbury Literary Agency, London, and Penguin Books Ltd., London.

Billy Collins: "Candle Hat" from *Questions About Angels* by Billy Collins, copyright © 1991 by Billy Collins (University of Pittsburgh Press, 1999). Reprinted by permission of the University of Pittsburgh Press and Billy Collins.

E. E. Cummings: "Picasso" from *Complete Poems: 1904–1962* by E. E. Cummings, edited by George J. Firmage, copyright © 1925, 1953, 1991 by the Trustees for the E. E. Cummings Trust, copyright © 1976 by George James Firmage. Reprinted by permission of Liveright Publishing Corporation.

John Doe Passos: Poems I–IV from "Winter in Castile" from *Pusgcart at the Curb* by John Does Passos, copyright © 1922 by George H. Doran